Ornamental Graces

A Novel

by Carolyn Astfalk

This book is a work of fiction. Characters and incidents are products of the author's imagination. Real events and characters are used fictitiously.

Ornamental Graces
copyright 2016 by Carolyn Astfalk

Multa Verba Publishing

ISBN: 978-0-9979718-0-4

Cover design: Carolyn Astfalk
Christmas background: Max Protsenko (Shutterstock)
Young couple silhouette: Eaniton (dreamstime)

To my mother,
Marcella,
renowned for her chocolate chip cookies

"Charm is deceitful, and beauty is vain; but a woman who fears the Lord is to be praised."
Proverbs 31:30

"In him we have redemption through his blood, the forgiveness of trespasses, according to the riches of his grace which he lavished upon us."
Ephesians 1:7-8

"She [Wisdom] will place on your head a fair garland [an ornament of grace]; she will bestow on you a beautiful crown."
Proverbs 4:9

1

Sortir du froid

(Come in from the cold)

It had come to this. Daniel Malone sold instruments of torture just to keep food on his crappy Formica table for one. Of course, that probably wasn't how others saw it.

They were bringing home a piece of the outdoors, a symbol of the season, a reminder of Christ's nativity and resurrection, the eternal—evergreen—promises of God. Dan had seen things that way too before the past year took everything he had and shredded it with a mulcher. Mustering his remaining whit of self-respect, he'd succumbed to desperation and now sat in a drafty shack waiting for the next giddy Christmas revelers to select a fresh-scented, needle-dropping nightmare.

Okay, so maybe the trees weren't exactly torturous, but he'd had enough of rough bark, sticky sap, and sharp needles to last a lifetime. After this, he'd be an artificial tree enthusiast—if he bothered to put up a tree at all.

Inside his small, weather-beaten shack, the one he'd assembled mostly from leftover wooden pallets, Dan couldn't smell the fresh, evergreen scent, the only trait of Christmas trees he still enjoyed. Instead, the odor of burnt coffee lingered though he hadn't made a pot in days. He never cared for the taste, burnt or not, but he had needed something to keep him awake during the long, boring hours when no customers visited his lot.

The space heater at his feet gave a death rattle, and its electrical hum ceased. He kicked it with the tip of his boot. Nothing.

Great.

Dan folded his large frame under the wooden table that served as his desk and jiggled the wire where it entered the cheap heater. It knocked against the laminate floor remnants and hummed to life. A blast of warm air hit his face and then penetrated his boots. As he sat upright, he glanced out one of the two square windows and spotted a young couple beneath the lights in the rear of the lot.

The man had lifted a Douglas fir from where it leaned against the rope Dan strung across the lot. He stamped its trunk on the frozen, dry ground a couple times and then twirled it around so the woman could see every side. It was a woman, wasn't it? No telltale pink gloves or hand-knit, sparkly scarf. No expensive boots designed for gawking rather than walking. Just a puffy, navy jacket and white tennis shoes. It could be a skinny dude.

The person spent less than three seconds observing it before planting hands on hips and signaling disapproval with a shake of the head. Yeah, definitely a woman.

Dan rolled his eyes. Another one. If nothing else, this job had given him an unforgettable real-life lesson in male-female dynamics—a lesson that would've been helpful a couple of years ago. The man would ferret out the best-looking tree, well-shaped and full, and the woman would turn up her nose, forcing them to cycle through four to seven more trees before one met her approval—sometimes the same tree the man had first shown her.

Poor sap. He had at least three more trees to go.

Dan grabbed his gloves from the table, pulled the lined hood of his jacket over his knit cap, and made for the door. He knew from experience that if he wasn't standing at the ready the moment the woman found *the one*, he risked losing a sale.

Dan glanced down to kick aside the rags that kept the cold air from creeping beneath the entrance. He twisted the knob and used his hip to shove open the door. The wind nipped at his bare neck, so he zipped his jacket over his beard and past his chin. He strolled toward the couple, expecting to see them examining another tree. Instead, he witnessed a scene that could serve as a death knell for any romantic relationship.

The man leaned toward her, gesturing wildly with one hand while the other clasped the tree trunk. When his hand dropped to his side, the woman yelled something Dan couldn't quite make out and kicked the guy in the shin. He hunched to rub his injured leg, and she swatted his back with her gloved hand. The tree careened forward, hit the ground, and sent out a small spray of dust and gravel.

The man regained his footing, gave the woman a light shove, and stomped down the row, out of Dan's line of sight.

The shove hadn't been forceful, but Dan decided he should probably check to see that she wasn't hurt. And that his tree hadn't been damaged.

A small, white puff of breath billowed in front of the woman and then dissipated. Unaware of Dan's approach, she crouched down and seemed to search for the best place to get a hold of the trunk. She muttered something to herself, the words unintelligible.

Dan stood beneath one of the overhead lamps, casting a shadow on the tree.

She rocked back onto her heels. "I'm sorry."

Light brown eyes with amber flecks peered out from under long lashes and a worn, gray knit hat. He expected a huffy, controlling glare, not that doe-eyed innocent look that reminded him of his oldest sister, especially with the twin rosy patches blooming on her fair, winter cheeks. She wore no trace of makeup, but by his estimation, she didn't need any.

She moved to grab hold of the tree.

"I got it," Dan said. From the kick and the whap she'd given her companion, Dan knew she didn't need his help, but the scrap of chivalry he maintained required him to at least offer.

"I didn't think he'd drop the tree. I make one little suggestion, and . . ." She growled. "I should've kicked both his shins, the big jerk."

3

Dan raised his brows. No way would he interfere in their lovers' spat. He'd right his tree and head back to his shack. She could stay out here and fume about her boyfriend or husband or whomever he was as long as she liked. He set the tree against the line and brushed the needles from his gloves.

"Did you see which way he went?" She stood and squinted towards the parking lot.

"Uh—" He jerked a thumb in the opposite direction. "Walked off that way."

Her gaze followed the path he'd indicated. Beyond the tops of the Christmas trees, a neon sign glowed in the narrow window of an aluminum-sided building. The front door swung open and shut as a couple of rotund men in flannel jerseys exited and thumped down the five wooden steps to the sidewalk. The unlit sign affixed to the second floor read: *The Watering Hole*. Beneath it, a smaller, vinyl sign read: *Voted Pittsburgh's Favorite Hometown Hangout*.

The woman huffed again. "I should've known. He only told me three times I was keeping him from relaxing with a beer."

Dan knew it was none of his business, but in an effort to wrap up the uncomfortable conversation and retreat to the relative warmth of his shack, he asked, "You going to join him?"

She let out a scoffing laugh. "I'd sooner army crawl naked over broken glass and a swarm of scorpions than sit in that stinky rat hole with him. I'll wait."

Dan suppressed a smile and shrugged. "Suit yourself."

He retreated to the shack, closing the door behind him, and toed the rags back toward the base. He dropped onto a folding chair and rubbed his gloved hands together. Not feeling any warmth coming from the heater, he nudged it with his boot until warm air circulated at his feet.

He gazed out the window, expecting the young woman to have gone back to her vehicle, but instead she stood beneath the light where thick snowflakes landed on her hat and jacket.

She rubbed her hands together and jumped up and down, presumably trying to warm herself. Maybe the guy had taken the car keys with him.

The snow came down harder, sticking to the cold ground. The wind gusted, blowing the flakes against the side of the shack. The woman clapped and did some kind of awkward hip-wriggling, bouncing jig to keep warm.

He didn't want company, especially female company, but his heart would have to be colder than his toes to let her stay out there when he had four walls and a roof, paltry though they were. He cracked the door and called to her.

"You can wait in here if you want."

She jogged toward him, her heel sliding on a patch of black ice partially covered with snow. Her arms flailed as if she were making a snow angel in mid-air before she caught her balance and stumbled forward, her cheeks redder than before.

He pushed the door open wider, and she slipped in. A blast of cold air followed.

"Thank you." Her teeth chattered, and she hugged her arms close to her body.

"You want some hot cider?" He motioned to a miniature slow cooker on the battered table in the corner. The pot and its contents came courtesy of his sister Colleen. The strangely odorless, brown liquid didn't tempt him, but maybe it would help warm her.

"I'd love some, thank you."

He stirred the cider, ladled it into two mugs, and handed one to her. *Now* the spicy, warm scent of cinnamon wafted through the cool air.

She slipped off her gloves and wrapped her hands around the steaming mug. After blowing on the hot liquid a couple of times, she raised it to her lips. "Mmmm. That helps."

Dan opened a metal folding chair and dusted the cushioned seat with his glove. He set it on the side of the table opposite him. "You can sit."

"Thank you." Her pink lips turned up in a small smile. She sipped her cider, draining the mug in no time. It must have worked in warming her because she unzipped her jacket and slipped the hat from her head.

Luxurious auburn-brown tresses spilled onto her shoulders, dark and luminous. His gaze traveled her back as her hair cascaded down. How could he have mistaken her for a man?

Her magnificent hair mesmerized him, but otherwise her features were pretty but not glamorous or beautiful like—

No. He would not allow her to invade his thoughts.

He turned his attention back to the cider and took a sip. Not bad. "I'll, uh, keep an eye out for your . . . your boyfriend? Husband?"

She sputtered and covered her mouth with the back of her hand.

"You okay?" He didn't need some stranger choking in his ramshackle workplace.

She nodded and cleared her throat. "He's not my husband or boyfriend. Robert is my stupid, know-it-all brother."

"Oh." Dan lifted his chin in acknowledgment. "Whoever he is, I'll keep a lookout." It explained their unnecessary roughness. He had four older sisters, and he'd admit to having shoved them a time or two. Not that he'd treat another woman that way.

"My name's Emily." She extended her right hand. "Thanks for letting me come in out of the cold."

"You're welcome." He took her small hand in his and gave it a firm shake. "Dan Malone."

She withdrew her hand and laid it inside her jacket, over her heart, her expression pinched.

"Are you okay?"

"Uh, yeah. Just . . . that was weird."

He had no clue what she was talking about, nor did he want to know. She wouldn't be hanging around much longer.

6

He hoped. He'd give the guy another five, ten minutes before he went over there and dragged him out himself. Apparently they were no longer in the market for a tree. Another lost sale, and only one day left before Christmas Eve.

"I don't know how Elizabeth puts up with him."

Dan raised his brows. Should he have known who Elizabeth was?

"His wife. He can be such a blockhead. Insists it's ridiculous for me to get a real tree when I'll hardly be at my apartment for Christmas. But he can't let it go at that. He's got to lay into all the old spinster jokes."

"Spinster?" Dan peered at her through squinted eyes. She couldn't be more than twenty-three.

"I know, right? I'm not even twenty-five." She flung her hair back and pouted.

Dan shrugged. "I'm twenty-eight. Guess that makes me an old bachelor."

She smiled, and it lit her face. It was a reserved smile intended to be polite and nothing more, but it made him wonder. When would a woman smile for him again? Not *at* him, at something funny he said or did, but because the joy he brought her couldn't be contained.

He hoped never.

Dan switched on the radio, wanting to fill the dead air with something other than silence, and dialed through four stations before he found one that wasn't playing Christmas songs.

The woman's eyes, *Emily's eyes*, glimmered, and her lips turned up as if she were suppressing a laugh.

"What?" It was his shack; he could listen to whatever he pleased.

She shrugged. "For someone selling Christmas trees, you seem intent on avoiding the sounds of the season. I understand passing over 'Santa Baby,' and 'Grandma Got Run Over By a Reindeer,' but 'Greensleeves' and 'O Tannenbaum'?"

"It's not Christmas yet. When it's Christmas, I'll listen to Christmas carols."

She opened her mouth to say something, but Dan pointed toward the window to cut her off. "Your brother?"

Robert stood in the center aisle of the lot, snow swirling around him. He called Emily's name as he turned in each direction.

"I should make him sweat," Emily said, her eyes narrowed at her brother. She stood, zipped her jacket, tugged on her gloves, and grabbed her hat. "Thank you for the heat and the cider."

Dan nodded.

"Oh, and I'll take the tree. The one we were looking at."

Dan rubbed his hand over his beard. Her brother may be a know-it-all, but she was one headstrong lady.

2

L'un est le nombre solitaire
(One is the loneliest number)

Emily rubbed her boot over the blue ice-melting pellets on the sidewalk, crushing the beads beneath her toes. She scanned the end unit apartment building with its nondescript red brick, darkened windows, and green shutters. With her arms folded over her chest, she huffed and waited as her brother untied the twine holding the tree to the roof rack of his minivan. He'd spent the first ten minutes of their ride badgering her about her stubborn streak and her foolishness for—how did he put it?—"getting cozy in some love shack" with a strange man.

"All I'm saying, Emily," he said as he stepped off the van's running board, "is you can't be too careful. You went behind a closed door with a guy you don't know. He's bigger, and he's stronger. He's got that Grizzly Adams thing goin' on with the beard. Who would've heard you if you screamed?"

"Certainly not you, since your butt was glued to a bar stool in that dive." Emily clenched her fists at her side. Robert had been smothering her with his overprotectiveness since their parents died seven years ago. If she didn't know his concern was born of love, she may well have strangled him by now. "If you hadn't stomped off to the bar, leaving me stranded in a blizzard, I wouldn't have been forced to sit in that rickety shanty with Scrooge, the tree salesman." A closed-off Scrooge, who obviously didn't want her there.

A twinge of guilt stung her conscience. Maybe she wasn't being fair to Dan. He had been kind enough to welcome her in out of the cold, but even a wallflower like her could tell his invitation was grudging. Sitting uncomfortably in his folding chair, he'd only contributed curt responses to the conversation. He was a man well-practiced in avoidance.

Had Dan not told her his age, she would have guessed older—maybe late thirties? With a hat pulled low over his forehead and a scruffy beard and mustache bristling the lower half of his face, the only clues to his age had been his eyes. Those hazel irises guarded more pain and weariness than a man in his twenties should harbor.

"Earth to Emily. You gonna get the door for me?" Robert stood at the edge of her walk, the tree hoisted over his shoulder.

"Oh. Sorry." Emily jogged to the door of the three-story building and opened it.

Robert stomped the snow from his boots, dragged the tree inside, and balanced it against the wall.

Emily, fiddling with her keys, rushed past him to get to her apartment door. Jostling the key in the lock, she turned it and held open the door.

Robert trudged by with the tree, trailing green and brown needles. "Where do you want it?"

"In front of the sliding glass door." Emily walked to the far side of her living area, which extended via the doors to a concrete slab patio outside.

The small apartment, nondescript in its pale walls and beige carpet, had been home for almost four years. Robert and her sister-in-law Elizabeth had protested when she announced she'd be moving out of their house, but she suspected they were secretly relieved. At the time, there had been three adults and three children under the roof of their 1,600-square-foot house. Since she'd moved out, they'd added two more children. While Emily appreciated their generosity, it had been well past time to strike out on her own. She'd moved less than two miles away, but it managed to give her and them some much-needed privacy.

"Okay," Robert said as he adjusted the tree in the stand. "Hold on and let me tighten it."

Emily steadied the tree as Robert lowered himself to the floor and slid beneath the lowest limbs. In several minutes, he secured the tree.

"Thanks, Robert. You'd better get home." Emily glanced at the wall clock. If he didn't leave soon, Elizabeth would be drowning in bedtime madness getting all the kids bathed and ready for sleep.

Robert groaned. "Yeah, don't want to miss an opportunity to chase a wet, naked toddler down the hall, strain a turd from the tub, or read *How Do Dinosaurs Say Goodnight?* for the thousandth time."

Emily smiled. She knew from experience that his kids were exhausting, but his small home nearly burst with love and life. *Will I ever have that kind of life, or am I doomed to always be alone?*

She ushered Robert to the door with a kiss to the cheek despite his infuriating behavior at the tree lot. Before she bolted the door behind him, she remembered she hadn't gotten the mail and padded out to the group of mailboxes in the entryway.

Robert called from the open door beneath the exit sign. "You're coming for dinner on Christmas Eve, right?"

"Yep. And we're still doing that seven o'clock children's Mass, aren't we?"

"Yeah. Hopefully they all fall asleep on the way home." The door swung shut behind him.

Emily hugged an arm across her midsection to fend off the cold air and gathered her mail from the metal box with her free hand. As she shuffled back to her apartment, she sifted through the mixture of catalogs, bills, and junk mail, finding two Christmas cards.

She closed and locked the door behind her, then plopped onto the couch. Sliding a finger under the seal of the first card, she pried it open. The photo card showed the smiling faces of her cousin, his wife, and their children in matching red and green scarves, relaxing in front of a fireplace. Twice she turned the envelope of the second card over in her hands, looking for a return address. Nothing. The postmark only said "Pittsburgh."

Emily opened the envelope and pulled out a card decorated with glittering poinsettias. A three-by-five-inch photo slipped out and landed in her lap. A blond-haired, blue-eyed, fair-skinned man in his late twenties stared up at her. The most handsome face she'd ever laid eyes on. The face of the only boy she'd ever loved. His arm wrapped snugly around an olive-skinned woman whose exotic dark hair, dark eyes, and flawless skin made her a natural candidate for Miss Universe. She possessed the kind of looks that made men—and women—stop in the street and take another look.

A text banner at the bottom read, "We're Engaged! Save the Date: August 3." Emily scooped up the card and photo along with the other mail and flung them onto her end table. She kicked off her boots and shuffled to the kitchen. Her stomach rumbled, and she realized she hadn't planned anything for dinner. Scanning the refrigerator, she found only yogurt, fruit, and lettuce. Nothing appealed to her. Celebrating Bryce's engagement to Miss Universe required carbs, specifically sugar and chocolate. She yanked open the freezer door. Pushing aside a bag of frozen baby peas and a container of leftover soup, she reached for the quart of Moose Tracks ice cream in the back.

Retail therapy befitted the rich or perpetually in-debt. Ice cream therapy? Now, *that* even an average-looking girl overlooked by men and boys of every age and race could afford to indulge.

"So, you've decided to take the plunge, eh, Bryce?" She lifted her spoon and gazed up, as if he stood before her. "You could've had the plain but virtuous Emily Kowalski, beloved by small children and dowagers. I see instead you've chosen beauty, which I'm sorry to say is shallow and fleeting." She jabbed the spoon into the ice cream, digging for a hunk of chocolate. "So, boo for you." She slid a heaping spoonful of ice cream over her tongue, slowly scraping the metal spoon between her teeth. Tears welled in her eyes, and she sniffed. "In your defense, Bryce, I don't think you knew I could make pierogies from scratch."

As her spoon hit the bottom of the paperboard container, Emily's stomach revolted. When would she learn? She pressed her hand to her belly and moaned. This wasn't the first time she'd drowned her disappointment and envy in empty calories.

After tossing the nearly-empty carton into the trash and the spoon into the sink, Emily plodded to the bathroom, uncertain whether or not her chocolaty meal was going to stay down. She stared in the mirror at her plain, ordinary face. Brownish hair, brown eyes. But her nose was cute, right? She bared her teeth. Perfectly straight (after thousands of dollars of orthodontic work). She wasn't ugly. She wasn't!

With a hard swallow to force back the rising tide of Moose Tracks, she breathed deeply and resolved to change. *Lord, I'm tired of waiting for life to happen to me. You have a plan for my life, and I'm fairly certain it's not written at the bottom of an ice cream container.*

The nausea settled. She filled a Dixie cup with water and held it up. "Here's to the new Emily." She sipped and tossed back her long, thick hair, easily her best feature. She lifted her chin and, for good measure, added, "Amen."

3

Une recontre fortuite

(A chance meeting)

Dan zipped his jacket as he shuffled toward the double doors at the rear of the meeting room. There went an hour and a half of his life he'd never get back. He'd attended the March township business association meeting because he thought it'd be a good networking opportunity. Instead, he'd suffered through a less-than-scintillating, in-depth discussion of the Pets on Parade event slated for summer.

People funneled out the exit at a snail's pace. What was the holdup? He'd had enough of the dry heat and stale air. He wanted out. He leaned to the side, trying to peer around the crowd in front of him.

As he took the three steps out the door into the night, he inhaled the cold, crisp air, but had to cough his way through a cloud of second-hand smoke.

A few people peeled off to the parking areas on the right and left, but a steady stream proceeded down the walk and across the street to Stanley's Stop N' Eat. A sign in the window advertised "Stush's Famous Fish Sandwich."

Maybe that's where the networking happened. He'd come straight from work. A fish sandwich and a beer sounded pretty good.

He stomped the cinders from his shoes before he entered. To his right, a small, brightly-lit dining room held square tables for two and four. In front of him and to the left sat a long, dimly-lit bar. He spotted an empty stool and took a seat.

The guy next to him, a husky man with wavy, reddish-brown hair and grease-stained hands, shrugged off his coat and swung it around the back of the stool. "Hey, didn't I see you across the street?" He nodded toward the township building. "At the meeting?"

"Yeah. You too?" Dan unzipped his jacket and tossed it on the back of the stool.

The guy motioned for the bartender and grabbed a menu from between the ketchup and malt vinegar bottles. "It was all I could do to keep my eyes open."

Dan laughed. "I know what you mean. Is it always like that? So dull?"

The guy turned the menu over and scanned the options. He set it down and swiveled toward Dan. "Yup. But the time I don't show will be the time they make me an officer or something."

The guy looked familiar somehow, but Dan couldn't place him. He scrolled through the possibilities of where they might have met. He wasn't a customer. He didn't recognize him from church.

Dan settled onto the stool and grabbed a menu even though he'd already decided on the fish sandwich. He scanned the beers on tap and slipped the menu back into place. "My name's Dan Malone. Can I buy you a beer?"

"Robert Kowalski. And I never turn down a free beer."

The bartender, a guy about his age with sleeve tattoos on both arms, stopped in front of them. "What can I get you?"

Robert studied the menu again.

Kowalski. Dan turned the name over in his mind. Polish last names were plentiful in this neighborhood. Why did this one stand out?

"And you?" The bartender had turned his attention to Dan. Must be his turn to order.

"Uh, give me an Iron City and the fish sandwich with fries and coleslaw."

With their orders in hand, the bartender headed to the other end of the bar. Dan grabbed a handful of peanuts from the bowl in front of him and surveyed the room. At least half the bar crowd had come from across the street. Someone dropped coins into the jukebox, and George Ezra's bass boomed over the speakers.

"Y'know, drafts are only a dollar down at The Watering Hole. You ever been there?"

Dan nodded. "A couple times." He'd stopped in once or twice after he'd closed the Christmas tree lot for the night.

That was it. The tree lot.

"You look familiar. Did you happen to buy a Christmas tree at the lot on West Main, across from the Gulf station?"

Robert chuckled. "Sorta. I took my sister down there a couple nights before Christmas."

Dan's eyes widened. His sister? He snuck another glance at Robert, trying not to look like he was checking him out. Same light brown eyes. Yep, it was him. Of all the people to run into, it'd have to be the guy whose sister had bedeviled him.

Robert leaned back in the stool and gave Dan a second look. "You sold us the tree, right?"

"Yeah." Dan's hands began to sweat. He'd sold the tree, all right. And sipped warm cider with his sister in the process.

The bartender slid the beers in front of them, and Robert took a swig. "You let my sister warm up in your shack while she waited for me." One side of his lips tilted up, as if he were trying to suppress a grin.

Nothing remarkable happened during that chance meeting with Emily before Christmas, so Dan had been surprised that his thoughts had turned to her multiple times over the next months. Thoughts of that gorgeous mane of hair and that pretty, pink-lipped smile, but mainly her spirit and determination.

"That was like a turning point for her."

Dan wrinkled his brow then gulped from the pint glass. "What do you mean?"

"My little sister's a piece of work. She's always been kind of shy and quiet, but something got into her that night. After I chewed her out for going in that shack with you, she fired right back at me." He took another drink and shrugged. "She hadn't done that since she'd moved out. Since Christmas she's been . . . different."

"She lived with you?" How many questions could he ask before it looked like he was interested? Cuz he wasn't. Was he?

"Used to. She moved out a few years ago, saying she was in our way and stuff, but to tell you the truth, she saved my butt with my wife and kids more times than I could count." He scooped some peanuts from the bowl and tossed them into his mouth. "I didn't like the idea of her living alone—our parents died when she was still a teenager. I thought she'd get herself in some kind of trouble, as innocent and naïve as she is, but she's done okay."

The conversation flowed easily over the sandwiches and beers as they talked about sisters, their businesses, and, inevitably, whether the Penguins would make the Stanley Cup finals this year. An hour later, Dan felt like he'd known Robert a lifetime, almost as if he were a brother.

He realized with sadness that he'd let nearly all his friendships fall away as he'd become progressively more consumed by Kristen. In hindsight, it was clear that's what it had been—he'd been more obsessed than in love. Enough so that it blinded him to her machinations.

Robert pushed his empty platter forward and glanced at his watch. "Shoot. I told my wife I'd be home a half hour ago." He dug a business card from his shirt pocket and laid it on the bar in front of Dan. "Hey, it was great talking to you. Whaddya say we have you over for dinner some time? You could meet Elizabeth and the kids."

"Uh . . ." His palms were sweating again. Robert had said Emily didn't live with them anymore, but they were close. What if she were around when he came for dinner?

"My wife's a really good cook." Robert patted his belly, which protruded over his belt.

When was the last time he'd had a home-cooked meal? Christmas? Dan's knee bounced at a rapid clip, and he stilled it with his hand.

"The kids'll be on their best behavior." Robert smiled. "I hope."

"I don't mind kids." He didn't. He'd missed out on most of his nieces and nephews growing up. So what *did* he mind? An image of that long, wavy auburn hair flashed in his mind.

Robert slid the card back along the bar and picked it up. "If you'd rather not—"

Dan shook his head. "No. I'd, uh . . ." He needed a friend. Needed to start living a normal life again, seeing people closer to his age and not just his grandma. "I'd love to come." He slipped one of his own cards from his back pocket and traded with Robert.

Robert stood and shrugged into his jacket. He clapped a hand over Dan's shoulder. "Awesome. I'll talk to Elizabeth and give you a call."

Dan lifted his chin. "Sounds good." It did, didn't it? Then why did his stomach knot up at the thought of sitting around a table with Emily's family?

***

Emily leaned over the arm of the couch and reached for the remote control that had fallen to the floor. Grabbing the controller, she spied tree needles between the couch leg and the baseboard. She huffed a sigh. "More? Seriously. It's April."

It chafed that Robert had been right about that tree. She'd spent nearly all of her time between Christmas and New Year's at his place. She'd enjoyed the tree at home for all of one evening. Not to mention she'd underestimated the amount of water a live tree needed. She'd let the reservoir in the tree stand dry up more than once. As a result, when she'd dragged the tree to the curb, she'd been left with a heavy trail of brown needles. She'd vacuumed the rug more than half a dozen times since then and *still* needles remained.

As she reached for the needles, she spied a quarter poking out from beneath the couch's fabric skirt. She plucked the needles and the coin from the carpet and strolled to the kitchen.

Opening the trash can with the foot pedal, she dropped in the needles then turned to the counter and the pretzel canister that served as her vacation savings bank. She'd glued a French flag to the outside.

She dropped the quarter in with a clink and shook it gently.

Pathetic.

Almost two years of saving and the container was only a third full. And most of the coins were pennies. At this rate, she'd be an old lady by the time she saw the French countryside.

She pulled open the junk drawer in front of her and thumbed through a France tourism brochure, gazing at the lush French meadow. What was the point? It's not like she had anyone to go with anyway.

She'd agreed to a blind date with a co-worker's cousin a month ago. Peter was fresh out of the Army, having just returned from Afghanistan. He wasn't the greatest looking guy; his face had a sort of pug dog look, but his appearance was less important than his personality. He'd seemed nice enough, but a little goofy maybe with his cornball jokes. Still, she had planned to accept another date and an opportunity to get to know him better. He said he'd call. He didn't. Maybe he—

"We're Off to See the Wizard," her cell phone ringtone, ripped through the air, shattering the silence.

She jumped. *Wow, what timing.* Could it be Peter? After all this time?

Emily cleared her throat. "Hello?"

A loud clatter sounded, as if the phone on the other end had been dropped. She waited a couple seconds. "Hello?"

"Auntie Em, it's me."

She grinned at the sound of her nephew's voice. "Maximillian. What's up, buddy?"

"You coming to dinner on Sunday?"

"Uh, who's issuing the invitation? You or your mom?"

"Me."

"Are you cooking dinner?"

The little boy giggled. "Nooooo. I can only make toast and cereal. Would you like that?"

"Uh, no thanks, bud. Does your mom know you're on the phone?" She folded the brochure, slid it back into the drawer, and pushed it shut with her hip.

"Momma's hands are all gooey with dough. She's baking a pie for dessert. She told me to call you."

"Okay. Then, I'll come, but tell your mom just for dessert. I've got some work to finish up." *And I really don't need all the calories from your mom's cooking.*

"Momma, she'll come for dessert!"

Emily pulled the phone away a second too late. Max's bellow made her ear crackle.

There was a pause, then Max spoke in his normal voice. "She says wear something nice."

Emily furrowed her brow. "Okay. She say why?"

"No, but she's really strict about that stuff. She says Clara can't wear her princess stuff at the table. And yesterday, she said told Baby Ben, 'no diaper, no dinner.'"

Emily laughed. "Alrighty, then. I'll be sure to dress for the occasion."

Lord only knew what her sister-in-law meant. She'd probably get there Sunday and find out Elizabeth didn't say 'to wear something nice' but to 'bring a bag of ice.'

4

Recontre la famille

(Meet the family)

Dan bit back a moan as he shoveled the last forkful of lemon meringue pie into his mouth. He pushed his chair out from the empty dinner table as the flaky pie crust melted in his mouth. The finishing touch on a meal of juicy meatloaf, creamy mashed potatoes, and tender broccoli. He hadn't had a meal this good since—well, since last time Robert had invited him to dine with his family.

The kitchen and dining rooms were connected by an open floor plan. From his seat, Dan studied the outdated kitchen cabinetry, countertops, and floors in shades of brown. Robert had said the brick, Cape Cod house, built in the 1970s, was ripe for an overhaul. He'd been tackling each room's redo as time and money allowed. With a bunch of kids and one income, it was a slow process.

"Elizabeth, everything was delicious." Dan leaned back and stretched the waistband of his jeans. "You're going to have to roll me away from the table."

"I can arrange for that," Elizabeth said on a laugh as she gathered stray silverware from the table. A clatter and a whiny protest in the next room caught her attention for a moment. "I think Max and Gianna could give you a little nudge."

"On second thought, I think I can manage." The rambunctious seven-year-old boy and his wiry, six-year-old sister had nearly toppled him when he came in the door a couple of hours earlier.

The doorbell rang.

Dan tensed. When he'd invited Dan to dinner, Robert had mentioned his sister might swing by. He hadn't mentioned it again, and there hadn't been a place set for her at the table.

Robert loped to the door. It clicked open. A shriek followed, then a giggle.

A few seconds later, Robert leaned against the dining room entryway. "Max and Gianna. Playing with the doorbell again." He sighed and headed down the hall in the direction of the bathroom.

Elizabeth dipped her hands into a sink filled with sudsy water. The back door slammed. Max ran in from the living room, Gianna on his heels, screeching as he skirted around the table and behind a chair.

Robert's wife exuded relative calm amid the chaos of her life as a mother of five children under eight. She said she made do by paring her duties back to the essential, but neither her cooking nor her appearance suffered. Her long, wavy black hair hung in a perky ponytail. The dark hair set off her light blue eyes and fair skin. Had his friends' moms looked that good when he was a kid? He didn't think so.

The doorbell rang for the second time that evening, and again Dan's nerves jangled. *Take it easy.* He knew this moment would come since the second time he and Robert had gone out for a beer. Eventually, he'd run into Emily.

"Hon, can you get the door?" Robert called from the bedroom where he had taken the baby and the toddler for diaper changes.

Elizabeth lifted her gaze from the sink. "Dan, would you mind? My hands are soaked."

"Oh. Sure. No problem." He probably worried for nothing. It probably wasn't even Emily.

A knot of dread tightened in Dan's stomach, causing instant indigestion. He wiped a sweaty palm on his jeans and pulled open the door. Dan swallowed a gasp and jerked back. He worked at keeping his eyes from bulging.

Emily stood before him. But she didn't look the same.

That beautiful mane of auburn tresses that he'd marveled at—gone, replaced by a pixie cut that highlighted her heart-shaped face.

"Hi," he managed as he stepped back to allow her entrance.

"Hello. Uh . . ." She scrunched up her nose. "Who are you?" She slipped into the living room, a breezy, floral skirt swirling about her knees.

He shut the door behind her. *She didn't remember him.* Why did that create an ache of disappointment in his chest?

"I'm Dan. We've, uh . . ." He searched for something to do with his hands. Finding nothing, he shoved them into his pockets. "We've actually met before. Dan Malone." He extended his right hand to her.

She took it. Her palm was as soft as he remembered, but warmer.

After a couple of seconds, he released her hand, and she pulled it immediately to her chest. Her face paled, and her brow creased. *Was she sick?*

"Are you okay?"

She nodded. "That's the second time that's happened. My heart does this little flippy thingy. I guess I'll have to get it checked out. I'm fine now."

He bit his lower lip, relieved, but still anxious.

"Help me out here," she said as they both moved toward the kitchen, where the kids had gathered with paper and watercolor paints. "You say we've met, but I can't place your face."

"I sold you a Christmas tree."

She stopped, turned her light brown eyes on him, and studied his face. Then she touched her thumb and forefinger to her chin. "You had a beard, right?"

He nodded and rubbed his hand over his jaw. "Oh, yeah. I was trying it out. I shaved it off a couple months ago." His cheeks heated. He'd forgotten. When they met, his face had been mostly hidden.

She nodded in recognition. "Of course, I remember you. You saved me from hypothermia and frostbite."

He smiled. "You, uh . . ." He half-gestured, half-pointed to the side of his head. "You cut your hair."

"Oh, yeah. I did the Locks of Love thing. They use the hair to make hairpieces for children that lose their hair during chemotherapy. Gianna and I did it together." She winked at the little girl with the short bob, who crashed into her, hugging her legs.

He'd never had reason to be envious of cancer patients. Until now.

"Hey, sweet pea," Emily said, and then bent to brush the little girl's head with her lips.

"You were supposed to come for 'sert, Auntie Em."

"I know, but I had papers to grade first." She gave Gianna a forlorn look. "Did you save me any?"

So, she was a teacher. Dan added that to the short list of things he'd learned about her. When Robert had said Emily had changed, was he referring to Emily's hair or something else?

Emily peered up at him from where she'd crouched to hug her other niece, Clara, who he thought was four years old. "So, did you?"

He realized his mind had wandered. "Did I what?"

"Save me any dessert. Gianna says you had two pieces of pie." Her eyes twinkled.

He smiled. "I think Elizabeth set some aside."

They stepped into the kitchen where Elizabeth dried her hands with a tea towel. "There's a piece for you on the buffet, Emily."

"Thanks. Your pies are the best." She snatched the pie, pulled out a chair and sat, immediately scooping a forkful of meringue into her mouth.

"Hey, you're late." Robert sauntered into the room, holding the baby on his hip. "What gives?"

"Sorry," Emily said. "I was grading essays and lost track of time."

Essays. She must teach older kids.

"So," Emily said, swiping a napkin over her mouth. "I didn't notice a friendship being forged while you two strapped that tree on the van. What did I miss?"

Dan looked to Robert to answer. The two-year-old, Tessa they called her, latched onto her dad's leg and squealed. Robert wrinkled his nose and glared at her. "Tessa, did you poop?"

The little girl giggled.

"I just changed you, little poopstress. For cripe's sake. Elizabeth?"

"Take your pick, load in the dishwasher or load in the diaper."

Robert sighed. "Diaper. C'mon, Tessa."

Emily looked to Dan, still waiting for someone to answer her question.

Dan pulled out a chair and sat catty-corner from Emily. "Well, Robert and I ran into each other at a township business association meeting. We had a beer together afterward, talked about some of the events they have planned, and shot the breeze."

"Fast friends," Elizabeth interjected. "They seemed to hit it off. And, Emily knows we're always looking for backup babysitters." She winked.

Emily's brows shot up. "Wow. They're considering putting you on diaper duty. You've really been welcomed into the fold."

"Ohhh no." He glanced at Elizabeth. "Don't go getting any ideas."

"So," Emily pushed away her plate and fork. "You can't sell Christmas trees year round. What else do you do?"

Dan cleared his throat and straightened in his chair. Why was making a good impression on this woman so important to him? He folded his hands on the table in front of him. "I have a hardscaping business."

Clara reached for Emily, and she welcomed the little girl onto her lap. "I don't know what that is."

"I install patios and walls and stuff like that."

She raised an eyebrow. "I didn't know there was a word for that."

Robert returned with a fresh-smelling Tessa, still holding the baby on his hip. "Speaking of patios, Elizabeth and I have been talking about doing something out back. Maybe you can give us some ideas and a quote on a little flagstone patio where we can put a picnic table and the grill. We need more outdoor living space."

"Sure. I can do that. I'll give you a call this week, and we can go over it."

The conversation stalled. A cacophony of children's squeals and laughter created constant background noise. It didn't bother Dan. Much. It reminded him of chasing his sisters through the house when he was a kid.

Elizabeth glanced at the clock above the buffet, and Dan figured bath and bedtime threatened. He should excuse himself, but Emily had settled into her seat, letting Clara play with a long silver chain hanging over her white shirt. He wanted nothing to do with dating—maybe ever again—but Emily intrigued him.

"So, Dan, do you—" An ear-piercing screech caused Emily to wince and wait. "Do you do landscaping too? Add plants and flowerbeds around the walls and patio?"

"A little. I'm learning. It's not exactly one of my talents."

"It's one of Emily's talents." Elizabeth pulled out a chair and sat across from Emily.

Robert handed off the baby, whose name Dan still couldn't remember. Joseph? John?

"Emily planted the bushes and flowers in the front, around our bay window and the porch," Elizabeth said. "They're all native plants."

26

Dan had noticed them. Green shoots poked out of the ground and the woody stems were putting out new leaves. "Really? Maybe you can give me some tips. I have a customer who wants me to work in some native plants and fieldstone around his dry-stack wall. In fact, I'm visiting a farm and a construction site Saturday morning to find some rock."

"Maybe Emily could go with you. To help." Elizabeth let her suggestion hang in the air between them.

There was no reason for Emily to go with him unless . . . this whole evening had been a bid to set them up, and Elizabeth had just attempted to further the cause. Emily cocked her head at her sister-in-law. "I'm sure Dan doesn't need my help." She gave Elizabeth, a strange, wide-eyed look, as if communicating nonverbally.

"Well, actually, if you know about the native plants . . ." Where was he going with this? He didn't need her tagging along.

"It sounds interesting." Emily smiled and gave him a shy sort of look. "I mean choosing the plants and stuff." Her gaze snapped to Elizabeth. "It's his business. Why would he want me along?"

"I wouldn't mind the company. The work gets kind of dull."

Emily shot him a glance. "Well, okay, I guess. What time?"

They squared away the details, and Elizabeth started rounding up the kids for baths.

"I'd better be going," Dan said. "Thanks for dinner. Everything was wonderful." He turned to Emily and tried to keep the dopey smile from his face. "Nice meeting you again, Emily. I'll call Thursday to confirm about the rock hunting."

"Sure." She smiled but shot an accusatory look at Elizabeth before giving Dan her phone number.

The kids, their faces still smeared with dinner and pie, bounded over with high fives and sloppy kisses, and he made his way out the door. He admired Emily's landscaping as he jogged down the steps and headed for his truck. He'd been set up, and he couldn't muster any outrage. A creeping sensation wove its way around his heart. It felt a lot like hope.

5

Brouiller les cartes

(Muddying the waters)

Emily carried her plate and fork to the sink, and then leaned against the counter. She blew out a breath and stretched her neck, tilting her head from side to side, letting her muscles relax. "Why did you have to go and do that?"

"What?" Elizabeth set the baby in his ExerSaucer and handed him a sippy cup.

"You totally set us up. Now I'm spending Saturday tromping around a muddy field with a guy who probably doesn't even want me around. Plus, he thinks I'm some kind of gardening guru, which I'm not."

"You sure he doesn't want you along? You gave him an easy out, and he didn't take it." She bumped Emily with an elbow as she grabbed a dishcloth from the sink. "He practically begged you to go with him."

Emily rolled her eyes. "Being married to my brother for so long has dulled your intuition. Dan was cornered."

Elizabeth wiped crumbs from the table and shook the cloth into the trash. "Maybe he's the one. We all need a little nudge sometimes."

"More like a shove," Emily muttered. "I appreciate your concern, but I'm done pining over guys and worrying about meeting 'the one.'" She made quotation marks with her fingers. "If it's meant to be, it'll happen. If not . . ." She shrugged.

"Do you like him?"

Tessa army-crawled in from the living room, rolled over, and kicked her feet against the floor.

"How should I know?" Emily pushed off the counter and stooped to help Tessa take off her shoes. "We've only spoken a couple times—and that's being generous." She quelled her rising irritation—or was it nervousness?—and recalled the fuss her nieces and nephews made when Dan had left. He seemed like a decent guy. Her voice softened. "He's kind of tight-lipped, isn't he?"

"Maybe at first, but once you get to know him, I don't think so."

"Well, whatever. I don't have enough to go on yet." She stood and folded her arms across her chest.

"But you think he's cute, right?" Elizabeth bit her lip, but couldn't hide her grin.

Um, yeah. She couldn't deny that. The strong jaw with a hint of stubble had its appeal. Losing the facial hair was definitely an improvement. He'd seemed scruffy and older the first time they'd met. "Maybe too cute."

"No such thing."

Emily shook her head. "Makes 'em cocky. He probably thinks he can have any girl he wants." She shrugged. "Maybe he can. Does Robert know what you're up to?"

"What *I'm* up to? Me?" Elizabeth opened her eyes wide and put a hand to her chest with dramatic flair. "I'm not up to anything. Just giving two single people an opportunity to get acquainted."

Emily shook her head. "My brother's new best bud and his sister? I don't know. He might not like it."

***

Emily slid from the passenger seat of Dan's truck into the knee-high, sallow grass. At least getting out was easier than getting in. She had feared she'd need a boost or a stepping stool to get into the thing.

Her boots hit the ground and sank. The farm field muck pulled at her heels as she tried to drag one foot in front of the other. She tightened her denim jacket around her waist and closed several of the snaps. The sun warmed her shoulders, but the air chilled her neck and chest.

Dan, wearing leather work boots, faded jeans, and a maroon hooded sweatshirt, rounded the front of the vehicle and waited for her. He tucked his hands in the sweatshirt's front pouch. "You ready?"

"Sure." Lifting her feet required more effort than she expected, but she trudged ahead, not wanting to be labeled a sissy.

"The farmer said to look along the fence line." He pointed across the meadow to a white farm fence with peeling paint standing sentinel in front of the tree line.

Emily nodded. "Okay. Let's do it."

They crossed half the field in silence. She dug her hands into her pockets, waiting for him to say something. Anything to move along this quasi-date. *Might as well get on with it.* "Have you always lived in Pittsburgh?"

Dan glanced at her and slowed his pace, allowing her to keep up. "Yep."

"And your family, they're still here?"

"No. My dad passed away when I was fourteen. Shortly after, Mom and my four sisters moved to Baltimore to be near her family."

She cast a sideways glance. "Why did you stay?"

"My grandma. Dad's mom." He blinked against a strong breeze, but his short-cropped brown hair remained unaffected. "She was all alone and not getting any younger."

The loyal grandson. Sweet. She turned to gaze at the line of tall oak trees in the distance, hoping he wouldn't notice her smile. "Do you get to spend much time with her these days?"

Dan pulled at the tall grass, running a blade between his fingers and letting the seed fall to the ground. "Not as much as I'd like, but more than I used to. Most of the time, I'm running her to doctors' appointments or the grocery store. Actually, groceries are our standing Saturday afternoon date." He tossed the stripped blade to the ground. "What about you? You're from here, right?"

"Yep. Born and raised from good Polish Catholic stock. My parents grew up in Polish Hill." She smiled and glanced up to see his reaction. He smiled but didn't get in a dig like she'd expected. His name bespoke an Irish heritage. Likely, he'd been raised Catholic too. "My parents are deceased. Seven years now."

"Robert told me." Dan stopped moving and waited until she made eye contact. "I'm sorry for your loss."

"Thank you." Her eyes teared up. All this time, and still the mention of their deaths could bring tears. Emily swallowed the lump in her throat. This quasi-date already had her on edge. She didn't need to add grief to the mix. She glanced behind them, to where the truck receded into the background as the fence inched closer.

"I'm, uh, sorry about the setup. Elizabeth only mentioned Robert had invited a friend for dinner."

Dan shook his head. "It's okay. My sisters pull the same stuff. Can't stand me being alone. They don't understand I want it that way, at least since . . . just that I'd rather be alone." He stopped and waited for her to meet his eyes again. "For the record, I'm not looking for a girlfriend."

Emily's cheeks heated. Message received. "Good. Because I'm done looking for a guy. At this point, I figure I'm scraping the bottom of the barrel anyway. Only the losers are left."

She'd said it to get a rise out of him, but he merely narrowed his eyes and nodded in agreement.

"Well, here we are." Dan stopped and examined the large tan and gray stones jutting out of the meadow. He bent and pried one up with his hands.

Emily walked up and down the fence line in both directions. She spotted a triangular rock with rough edges. Crouching low, she pulled on it once, twice, three times until she fell backward. Dampness soaked the seat of her jeans.

"You okay?" Dan plunked his rock down in a relatively dry patch.

"Peachy." She pushed herself up with her palms and tried again, this time lifting the entire rock out. She set it by the one Dan had already selected. They chose three more apiece before gray-blue stratus clouds blanketed the sky. A soft mist dampened the air.

Dan glanced up. "Let's get these back to the truck."

Emily shot a look at the big, burgundy Dodge Ram. Why hadn't they brought a wheelbarrow? Probably because of the mud. What about a shovel, gloves, or any other useful tools?

She wrestled a rock up into her arms while Dan lugged one he'd found. Twenty minutes later, halfway across the field but moving in opposite directions, they exchanged a glance. He gave an appreciative nod and went to grab another rock. She carried hers the rest of the way to the truck. In four trips apiece, they managed to get all but one of the rocks back to the truck. The last rock was more akin to a boulder, and it would require both of them to get it to the truck bed.

The rough edges of the rock dug into her palms, and the dirty underside shifted and slid beneath her cold fingers. A cool, steady drizzle fell as Emily started walking, backwards, to the truck. Dan continued to face forward, bearing the heavier end of the rock as they crossed the dozen or so final yards.

With Emily's next step, the heel of her boot caught.

It skidded.

Despite leaning forward and attempting to regain her footing, she fell backwards. Sky and field jiggled in her vision.

The rock slipped from her grasp.

Her butt hit the ground hard, and pain shot through her tailbone. "Ouch!"

The opposite end of the rock slipped from Dan's hands, and he grasped at air as it hit the ground. He stumbled forward, landing on his hands and knees.

"You okay?" Dan's brow creased and his tone exuded worry.

"Yeah, fine. Luckily, I have some padding." She leaned to the side and stretched.

He scrambled to his feet, and his eyes widened.

Emily glanced around. She sat in the middle of at least four inches of muck. Here and there a tuft of grass dotted the yard-wide puddle. It was big. Hadn't he seen it coming?

The corner of his lips twitched.

Emily sat forward and turned to each side, surveying the situation. She glared at Dan. "Don't even . . ."

He held up his hands in a gesture of surrender. "I wouldn't dream of it."

She struggled to get to her feet, flailing, failing, and flicking the mud from her hands, inadvertently spraying her face.

"Think of it as a spa facial. Only it's free." By that smile on his face, he'd apparently given up on hiding his amusement.

"A facial?" Clearly this man hung with a different breed of woman. "Hey, don't knock it until you try it." She shook her hand, flinging mud at him. "You ever had one of those fancy facials?"

He jerked back, laughing. A scoffing snort.

"Give me a hand up?" She stretched her arm out, palm up.

"Sure." Dan reached down and gripped her hand.

Her muddy fingers began to slip through his, and she squeezed tighter. Her heart did that flippy thing again for a half second before she yanked for all she was worth. She twisted to the side, and Dan toppled into the muck alongside her. Smearing both of her hands in the mud, she laid one palm on each of his cheeks and swiped from temple to chin.

"There. First one's on me." She swallowed the laughter bubbling in her throat.

Dan's jaw tensed and before she knew what happened, he had her back to the ground, her legs trapped between his knees. He ran a hand over his face, scooping as much mud as he could, then smooshed it in her hair, rubbing back and forth.

She tried three times to twist away with no success. She jerked her knee up, close enough to his groin that he finally rolled off her and let her get up. He offered a hand to steady her.

Emily pretended she didn't see it.

Filth caked the back of her body from head to toe. Splatters covered the front of her, including her face.

Mud encrusted Dan's face, reminding her of his beard. Drips and drabs covered his front down to his knees. Below, the denim and leather were no longer visible.

Emily stifled a giggle with the back of her hand.

Dan scowled, but laughter shone in his eyes.

In silence, they picked up the boulder and resumed their journey. Once they loaded it onto the truck bed, Dan fished an old, tattered quilt from behind the driver's seat and laid it over the upholstery. It didn't extend the entire length of the front seats, forcing Emily to sit in the middle.

She wrinkled her nose. "You smell."

He glanced at her and smiled, his eyes crinkling at the corners. They didn't look as weary as the first time they'd met. "So do you."

She broke into a grin, although she wasn't sure why.

Forty-five minutes later, the truck pulled up to Robert and Elizabeth's house, where Emily had left her car. The mud had begun to dry. It pulled at her skin, stiffened her hair, and cemented her clothes to her body.

Dan opened the door for her and offered a hand. She took it, grinning at how ridiculous they both looked.

He didn't step back as she landed on the sidewalk. Instead, he drew her toward him with a hand to her elbow. The teasing left his eyes as he gazed at her mud-streaked face, then he lowered his lids until his focus moved to her lips.

Her inexperience made her doubtful, but was he going to kiss her? Her mouth grew as dry as her mud-caked palms. She licked her lips and immediately puckered them as she tasted the earthy, gritty residue.

He laughed.

Laughed. The nerve.

Her cheeks heated, and she was grateful the mud covered her blush. She wanted to put him in his place, but not a single word came to mind.

His hand dropped, and he slammed the truck door shut. "You have something to put down in your car?"

She stomped her feet, loosening some of the mud on her boot soles. "No. I'll bum a drop cloth off of Robert."

He nodded. "Okay. I'm sorry about all the mud." His gaze drifted from her face to her filthy clothes. "But thanks for your help." A slow smile spread across his face, and he extended his hand to her.

She took his hand in hers, and her heart somersaulted.

It's him. I don't have a heart problem. Dan Malone causes my arrhythmia.

His smile broke into a grin. "If we can call it help."

Anger swelled inside her like a geyser, ready to blow. She lifted her chin and strode to the door without looking back. As she crested the steps, she called, "My pleasure, Dan. That's a good look for you. Oh, and I'll let Elizabeth know her efforts failed."

He'd never even asked about the stupid plants. Why had he even agreed to this disaster of an outing in the first place?

6

Les eaux peu profondes: pas de plongée (Shallow waters: no diving)

Dan jerked his truck into park and wiped the sweat from his brow. The air conditioning couldn't have picked a worse time to fail—in the middle of ninety-eight degree heat with humidity to match. He cut the engine and stared out the window at Robert's house. He'd been avoiding his friend for the better part of two months, all because of Emily.

Robert had offered the use of his swimming pool before he left for his weeklong beach vacation. Dan had no intention of taking advantage of the offer, but changed his mind after he'd spent nine hours shoveling out a patio in the heat. He couldn't wait to strip off his clothes and jump into the cool water. Naked would be best, but he'd grabbed his trunks and a towel from home in case the pool didn't offer complete privacy.

He slammed the door on his Dodge. He'd have to take the truck over to Robert's repair shop next week and get the air conditioning fixed. He jogged up the steps and walked around back, averting his gaze from Emily's native wildflowers. He couldn't help notice the white hydrangeas and a pink azalea in full bloom.

Pulling up on the gate lock, he caught sight of the water glistening in the sunlight. The in-ground pool measured about twelve by twenty-four and ran maybe six feet deep. An orange raft and a Dora the Explorer beach ball floated in the deep end. Green and yellow pool noodles lay along the edge.

Dan tossed his swim trunks and towel on a chair and yanked his sweaty tee shirt over his head. He unbuttoned the fly of his jeans and stopped. Turning slowly in a circle, he surveyed the neighbors' homes, gauging whether anyone could see the pool from their second-story windows. With the tree foliage it was unlikely, but better not to chance it.

He could change in Robert's shed. He reached for his trunks and—

A high-decibel scream like something out of a horror flick pierced the air.

He jerked back and spun around, searching for the source.

Emily.

Feet shoulder-width apart, eyes wide, she stood as if bolted to the walk. Her hair had grown out into a bob style a couple inches short of her shoulders, and either the sun or chemicals had added golden streaks. The style suited her spunk, and the color highlighted her wholesome looks. She wore a long tee shirt revealing shapely legs. A multi-colored towel and a teal terry-cloth cover-up lay in a heap on the ground next to her.

Her hand went to her throat and her shoulders relaxed as recognition reached her eyes. "Dan. You scared me to death. What're you doing here? They're on vacation."

Holding his trunks in front of him, he zipped his jeans, hoping she wouldn't notice, and edged closer to her. "Sorry. I didn't know you were here." He motioned to the water. Cool and clear, it rippled in the sunlight, begging him to plunge in. "Robert invited me to use the pool while they were gone. I didn't intend to, but—"

"It's so freakin' hot," she finished for him. She scooped up her towel and cover-up then shifted her weight to her hip.

He wanted nothing more at that moment than to cool off in the pool, but she had beaten him to it. He wouldn't intrude on her evening. "Yeah. But I can go. A cold shower and some air conditioning should do the trick."

She bit her lip, staring first at him, then at the pool.

He'd make it easy for her. He pulled his shirt on, picked up his towel, and jerked his thumb toward the gate. "I'm gonna head out. Enjoy your swim, Emily. Good to see you again."

Too good. He'd been trying to put her out of his mind for weeks. Ever since he'd almost kissed her. What had he been thinking?

He'd always gone for girls like Emily—Kristen being the notable exception. She was the sweet, girl-next-door type, but possessed smarts and spirit in spades. He could easily fall for her.

He'd done a good job of avoiding her since the disastrous mud fest. Best that he skedaddle on home to shower and cool off in his air-conditioned bedroom. If the unit held out.

Emily deserved better than he had to offer.

He lifted the gate latch and shoved the gate open with his arm. Sweat trickled down his back.

"Dan, wait."

He turned.

She'd crossed the lawn and stood only a few yards from him. "Don't be silly. I know I'm not your favorite person, but there's no reason we can't share the pool. You worked in the heat all day, and you've probably been looking forward to this."

True. He'd nearly salivated when he saw the water. "I'll stay on one condition."

"What's that?"

He propped his arm on the fence gate. "You tell me why you think I don't like you."

Emily shifted the towel and cover-up to her other arm, and the action revealed a simple, black, one-piece swimsuit, that while not immodest, showed more of her skin than he'd ever seen. The V-neck dipped low enough to show a little cleavage.

He ordered his eyes up to her face.

"Well, let's see. First, you tell me you're flat-out not interested in me. Second, you smear me with mud. And third, you've been avoiding any chance meeting between us by virtually ignoring my brother." She ticked each point off on her fingers, a hint of a smile curling her lips. "Yeah, he's noticed."

Dan let out a breath and glanced at his feet. "You got two out of three. I didn't say I wasn't interested in you, just that I wasn't looking for a girlfriend."

Emily shrugged. "Same difference. The point is, you don't have to go. We can share."

He hesitated, dreading the awkwardness that was sure to follow. His gaze drifted to the pool, the water lapping at the side in the warm breeze. "Okay. I'll stay."

She smiled, sashayed to a poolside chair, and draped her things over the back.

He pulled his shirt over his head and tossed it on another chair. "You came through the house, right? Can I go in and change?" He glanced at his sweaty shirt sleeve and spotted dirt streaks on his arm. "Maybe wash up first?"

"Sure." She tugged her suit down at her legs and strolled to the pool's edge. "You know where the bathroom is."

He nodded and let himself in the house. When he returned, Emily was already in the pool, treading water in the deep end. He jumped in alongside her, creating a huge splash. The cool water slapped his hot skin, refreshing him instantly.

When he surfaced, Emily stood a few feet away, wiping water from her eyes. "Don't make me regret my decision to share." Her smile revealed she hadn't minded the splash.

Muscles aching from a long day's work, Dan leaned against the pool's side and stretched his arms along the concrete rim.

Emily swam the length of the pool using a breaststroke, then a sidestroke. She glided underwater, a black strip shimmying close enough to send a chlorinated wave against his chest. Once she'd completed her laps, she shot to the surface opposite him, sending water spraying his direction.

"You hungry?" She dipped her head in the water, smoothing her hair.

40

"Starved." He envisioned stopping for a humongous Primanti Brothers sandwich on his way home. His mouth watered thinking about the sandwich topped with fries and coleslaw.

"Me too." Her eyes glimmered, and she lunged for the aluminum ladder. "Let's raid their kitchen." She climbed the ladder and snatched her towel.

He grinned. Emily was spontaneous without being foolhardy. Fun without being flighty. And feminine without being prissy. Rivulets of water ran down her bare back and legs. Definitely feminine.

She rubbed the towel over her hair a final time and shot him a look. "You coming?"

"You bet." He smiled then swam beneath the surface to the opposite side of the pool. He climbed the ladder, water rolling off his shoulders and dripping from his sopping trunks. While he toweled himself off, she threw on her cover-up and padded to the door.

She led him through the back door and toward the kitchen. The house was warm but not stifling. Robert had probably turned the thermostat up before he'd left.

Emily opened the refrigerator and stooped to look in the deli drawer. "Five kids. There are bound to be hot dogs here." Sure enough, she produced a pack of beef franks, waving them in the air.

"Check in the cabinet down there." She pointed to the low cabinet next to the oven. "See if you can find any baked beans."

Dan shuffled the cans of tomatoes and condensed soups until he found a can of Bush's beans.

"You any good with a grill?" She raised her brows and gave him a lopsided grin.

"I can manage hot dogs."

"Good. I'll take care of things in here. See the garden out there?"

Dan peered out the window where a row of staked tomatoes towered over smaller greens, probably bell pepper plants. At the far end, a tangled mess of vines spilled onto the grass.

"Find us a couple of zucchinis, and I'll slice and season them for us. You can grill those too."

"Sounds good." Dan stepped outside. After a few minutes in the house, warm as it was, the blazing heat hit him anew. Within seconds of searching beneath the leafy greens and orange flowers, he broke a sweat. Once he'd snapped off several small zucchinis, he returned to the house.

Emily had filled a platter with the hot dogs. Baked beans simmered in a small pot on the stove. A tray held plates, napkins, silverware, and a bottle of ketchup.

The door shut behind him, and she spun around. "Well?"

He held up his harvest for her to see. "How'd I do?"

"Perfect." She took the vegetables and ran them under cold water at the sink. After patting them dry with a paper towel, she sliced them on the cutting board and added them to the platter, opposite the wieners.

He realized he'd been staring and not helping. "Anything I can do?"

She opened the drawer on the island and removed a lighter. "Here, light the grill."

His hand twisted the door knob as she called, "Hey, look what I scored."

From somewhere below the island, she produced a bottle of Pinot Grigio. "Any wine enthusiast would tell you it's a perfect pairing with hot dogs."

Dan laughed. "Then by all means, pour me a glass."

He had a hard time pulling his gaze from the easy smile she gave him, barefoot in the kitchen preparing a meal for him. Hot dogs and beans. But still.

This feels too much like a date. Having a meal and a glass of wine with the woman whose image lined the underside of his eyelids in bed each night couldn't be construed as keeping his distance. In their bathing suits no less.

Ah, well. A man's gotta eat.

He fired up the grill, and Emily brought him the dogs and zucchini strips. In no time, both were grilled to perfection, their savory smell wafting beneath his nose. His stomach rumbled as he proudly deposited the hot dogs and zucchini on their plates.

Emily strolled through the lawn, carrying the food to the picnic table.

The table sat unevenly on the grass, reminding him he needed to stop by when Robert and Elizabeth got home and get some specs for the patio project.

He swung a leg over the wooden bench and sat. A breeze blew, and he pinned a paper napkin under his plate while moving his wine glass closer.

Emily, sitting with her hands in her lap, cleared her throat. "Uh, I pray before meals."

Dan smiled. "I kind of figured." She really was a nice girl. If only he were the guy he used to be. "Go ahead."

She cleared her throat. "Thank you, Father, for this meal. Bless this food that Robert and Elizabeth so generously provided." She glanced at him and giggled. "And thank you for the pleasant company." She gave him a shy smile then bowed her head. "Through Christ, Our Lord. Amen."

Dan made the Sign of the Cross and picked up his fork to cut the tender squash.

"So, you blessed yourself." She squirted a blob of ketchup on her plate and using her fingers, dragged her hotdog through the red sauce. "And with a name like Daniel Malone, I'm guessing you're Catholic."

He put a piece of zucchini in his mouth, chewed, and swallowed before he answered. "Yes, ma'am. Twelve years of Catholic school, rosary in my back pocket, crucifix hanging over my bed."

She studied him a moment, then averted her eyes.

He wasn't sure, but he thought his answer pleased her. He didn't need to tell her that a year-and-a-half ago she'd have been more likely to find him lying in bed on Sunday morning nursing a hangover than kneeling behind a pew in church.

"So," she stared, chewing, and then said, "what's your confirmation name?"

Twenty minutes later, Dan poured the last of the wine into their glasses. By the time they'd finished their supper, they'd discussed their confirmation names, favorite ways to prepare zucchini, the efficacy of swim diapers, and their favorite old television shows.

She twirled the stem of the wine glass between her fingers. "Mine was *Little House on the Prairie*. I wanted to be Laura Ingalls."

The more wine entered her system, the easier Emily smiled. Her hearty laughter relaxed him as much as the wine, and soon he'd nearly forgotten his convoluted reasons for keeping his distance from a woman he thought he could talk to all night.

"The wine's made me hot again." She pushed aside her glass. "How about one more dip?"

Something made him hot too, but it wasn't the wine. He glanced up. The traces of pink had faded from the western sky. The poolside lights flashed on, giving the water a cool, turquoise appearance. "Okay. A quick dip, and then I should go."

She jumped up, grabbed his hand, and yanked him from his seat.

He'd rarely swam at night. The water, the lights, and the sunset beguiled him. Not to mention his swimming companion. It wouldn't hurt to stay a little longer.

Emily tugged him along behind her and stopped alongside the pool. She pressed her hand to his bicep to steady herself while she dipped her toes in the water. Giving the pool a wary look, she blinked several times.

44

"You okay?"

"Yeah, just having second thoughts. The air temperature cooled—"

Dan gave a sneaky grin and then scooped her up like a baby.

She squealed in protest and pushed against his chest.

He swung her back and forth a couple times over the water, and on the third swing, he tossed her in.

Her yelp ended with a smack of flesh against water and a fine spray over his face and chest.

He plunged in beside her, the water cooling him as he submerged.

She surfaced, smoothing back her hair. Her eyes narrowed and glimmered with mischief. "You do know a bonehead move like that requires retaliation, don't you?"

He jerked his head back, his eyes wide and his tone incredulous. "Bonehead?"

She giggled then looped an arm around his collarbone and tried to force him back into the water.

He let her struggle for a minute before he grabbed her hands and twisted around to face her.

She giggled again, and he dunked her.

Emily grabbed his knees, pulling a leg out from under him, and he went under. He shot up and captured her by the shoulders.

Her long lashes batted, dark and thick with water, and her laughter ceased. Her pink lips parted.

All the air left Dan's lungs.

He closed his eyes for a moment. *Lord, she's your precious daughter. I don't want to hurt her.*

She bobbed in the water in front of him, eyes wide and expectation on her face.

He stood frozen in place, the water lapping against his chest, afraid to move.

Laying her hands on his waist, she rose on tiptoes and lifted her chin. Her eyes, a sultry mocha in the dim light, fixed on his face.

He couldn't muster an objection to what he knew was about to happen. His lids lowered.

Her lips touched his.

He didn't move save for his fingers digging into the soft flesh of her arms.

Her grip tightened on his waist, and she kissed him again.

Still he couldn't move. His lips burned for hers, but he couldn't get himself to reciprocate. His jaw clenched.

Emily released him and bounced back in the water, staring. She touched her fingers to her lips, and batted her eyes.

A casual observer might think the wetness on her face came from their horseplay, but he knew better. They were tears. Tears caused by his rejection. The sight of them singed his heart.

Emily ducked under the water and wriggled like a mermaid to the side of the pool. She raised herself out with only the strength of her arms. Hurrying to the chair, her wet soles slapped on the concrete. She snatched her towel and ran it over her hair and body.

"I'd leave, but I need to clean up." Her statement ended in a squeak, and her voice cracked.

"Emily." How could he explain? Even if she bought an explanation that totally contradicted his actions, it would only encourage her, and he couldn't afford that. Better to leave things as they were. "Let me help you."

With her gaze fixed to the ground, she shook her head. "No, I've got it. Please . . . please go, Dan."

His heart deflated. He hadn't had this much fun in years, and a little wine and relaxation had caused him to let down his guard. And Emily had paid the price.

He nodded and hoisted himself out of the pool.

Once she seemed convinced he was preparing to leave, she turned and strode toward the house. With her hand on the door knob, she turned. "I'm sorry. Please don't be a stranger to my brother. Don't let this ruin your friendship. It won't happen again."

The screen door slammed shut.

He wished the resounding smack was caused by a hand to his face, not metal on a door jamb.

7

La pitié . . . ou quelque chose d'autre?
(Pity . . . or something else?)

Emily headed for the kitchen sink, swiping the dirty dishes off the counter as she went. How could she have been such a fool? *The wine.* The stupid wine for which she'd owe her brother and sister-in-law twelve bucks.

She filled the sink with warm water, squirted some green detergent in, and swished it with her hand. She breathed deeply of the soapy green apple scent, hoping to head off the tears.

Fail. Her chin quivered, and her shoulders shook. She'd never been so embarrassed in her life. He'd said—more than once—he didn't want a girlfriend. She'd been stupid. Stupid, stupid, stupid. She clapped a wet, soapy hand over her mouth as she hiccupped.

A knock sounded on the door. It could only be Dan. She glanced at the cabinet beneath the sink and wondered if she could fit inside. It could serve as her proverbial hole: a place to curl up and die.

She'd ignore the knock and let him take the hint. She dunked the dirty dishes into the water, sniffling as she scrubbed them with the soapy dishcloth.

Another knock.

Go home, Dan.

She continued washing, rinsing, and placing the clean dishes and utensils in the drying rack, one by one.

A third knock.

Emily smacked the wet cloth against the counter, spattering her face with water, and stomped to the door. She wiped her wet hand over her cheeks, hoping to eliminate any traces of tears and suds. Gritting her teeth, she swung open the door.

Dan stood before her, his hair spiky and still damp. He shifted from one foot to the other, his right hand tapping against his thigh.

"I, uh, I think I left my keys inside." He gestured toward the hall. "I set them by the bathroom sink when I put on my trunks."

He hadn't knocked because he wanted to apologize or reassure her. He simply wanted his keys.

She stepped away from the door and waved him in.

"Sorry," he mumbled as he squeezed past her and headed for the bathroom.

She closed her eyes and waited. Only a minute more, and she could close the door behind him. For good. With a little luck and a lot of determination, she could make sure they never laid eyes on one another again.

The soft creak of the wooden floors told her Dan was drawing near. Then the footsteps stopped. In front of her.

She opened her eyes.

Dan dangled his car keys in front of her. "Got them."

"Yippee for you. Good night." She shouldn't be so mean. Until a few minutes ago, they had enjoyed a fun evening. She was the one at fault. She had kissed him. Had forced herself on him. She cringed inwardly and glanced at the kitchen, longing for that space beneath the sink.

Dan pocketed his keys but didn't move. "Emily, I'm sorry. I like you. It's just—"

She bit back tears and an angry retort. Holding up a palm, she shook her head. "No explanation necessary. Totally my fault." *Now please leave so I can maintain some shred of dignity.*

"It's not you, Emily; it's me."

She snorted. "You can't come up with something more original than that?'

"It's the truth. I'm not good for you. Can't we forget about this? Can't we just be—"

"Friends, Dan?" She chuckled sarcastically. "You want to throw any other tired clichés in there? You're not interested in me. I get it. Again, no explanation necessary." She flung an arm in the direction of the door. "Good night."

He stood there staring, not moving.

She averted her gaze.

He stepped toward her, invading her personal space. His palms encased her face on either side.

She had no choice but to look at him.

"Just so you understand, Emily. It's not you." His voice was barely more than a whisper, and he spoke slowly, punctuating each of the last three words with silence.

She twisted to pull her head from his grip, but he kept her face framed with his hands. Not able to bear his scrutiny any longer, she shut her eyes.

A second later, his lips brushed hers. Gentle, affectionate.

He released her but didn't move to leave. His eyes searched her face. For what, she didn't know.

A tear trickled down her cheek. "I don't need your pity kisses, Dan Malone."

His eyes reflected her own hurt. "I don't do pity kisses. That's not what that was."

She shoved his chest with her palm, pushing him out the door, then stepped back and closed it behind him. Her brain felt numb as she bolted the door and headed back to the sink.

Dan Malone sure sends an awful lot of contradictory signals.

***

While she waited for the light to change, Emily glanced at the fifth urgent text message from her sister-in-law.

"We owe you. Big time."

She smiled. Auntie Em to the rescue again. Robert and Elizabeth had dinner reservations, and the babysitter was a no-show. Emily was happy to help. It kept her mind off Dan, where it had drifted with great frequency over the last month since she'd made a colossal fool of herself. She'd kept her visits with Robert's family to a minimum in order to avoid running into Dan. A frisson of worry spread through her now, but she dismissed it. Dan had no reason to come by while Robert was out.

Robert and Elizabeth needed a night out. Something was up between them. She'd overheard more short-tempered remarks and seen more cold stares between them in the last month than she had in the previous couple of years combined.

She parked her car in front of the house and tapped a quick reply to Elizabeth. "Lucky for you I take payment in chocolate and kid kisses." Smiling, she tucked her phone in her purse and exited the car. As she rounded the front, she caught sight of the business name painted on the gray panel truck parked in front of her along the curb: Daniel Malone Hardscaping.

Her hand clenched in a fist, and she swallowed over the golf-ball-sized lump in her throat. If Elizabeth had set this up, she would kill her. With her bare hands. In front of her children.

Emily climbed the steps, rapped on the door, and entered. For once, no children's stampede greeted her.

"Hello?"

She stepped into the kitchen where four little bodies stood side by side, practically motionless and with palms pressed to the sliding glass door. Something in the backyard held their attention. Baby Ben sat at their feet, tugging at his socks.

Emily edged closer to them, peering to get a glimpse. "What's so interesting outside?"

Oh. Dan was what was so interesting outside, squatting as he pulled rocks and a hunk of sod from the area where the picnic table usually sat.

"Auntie Em, Uncle Dan's building us at paddy-o," Clara said.

"Dig, dig, dig." Tessa flattened her nose and lips against the glass.

Dan dug his spade into a patch of grass, scooped out soil, and piled it behind him. He wore a baseball cap but no shirt. Even from yards away, behind a glass door and a passel of children, she could see the beaded sweat running down his back. Faded, filthy jeans rounded out the grungy, yet somehow sexy, ensemble.

"*Uncle* Dan?"

"Not literally, Em. I won't be arranging your marriage." Robert strode into the kitchen, buttoning his cuffs. "The kids like him. He's a good friend."

"Yeah. He's good at 'just friends.'"

Robert smirked. What had Dan told him?

He rubbed her shoulder and leaned toward her, speaking softly so the kids wouldn't overhear. "His last relationship ended badly. I don't know details, but not only did it make him wary about women, it changed him. And not in a good way. I think he's still working through it."

And that gave him the right to toy with her? Flirting and playing, then refusing her kiss? Only to kiss her himself ten minutes later?

Emily slipped her hands into the rear pockets of her khaki shorts. "Will he be done soon? I want to help you guys out, but I'm not comfortable with him being here." Like the kids, she couldn't tear her gaze away from the action outside.

"Aw, come on, Em. He's working. Flagstone patio." Robert stooped to adjust his necktie in the five-by-seven-inch mirror stuck to the side of the refrigerator.

"Tell him to put on a shirt." Loose and long-sleeve would be good. Did they make man-burkas?

"I bet you didn't ask him to put on a shirt when you had your private pool party." He turned and cocked a grin.

"We were swimming. That was different." *That was also before I'd both fallen for him and fallen flat on my face, figuratively speaking.*

"You like him, don't you?"

Her cheeks grew warm. If her feelings were that obvious, he really did need to leave. Like, ten minutes ago.

"You want me to talk to him?"

"Yeah, maybe if this were middle school. Could you arrange a boy-girl party too with Spin the Bottle and Seven Minutes in Heaven?" Dan hadn't even given her seven seconds in heaven.

Robert smirked. "'Cause I'd be glad to put in a good word. Reassure him you're not totally psycho or anything, except for a few days a month."

She shot him a glare and punched his arm. "No. Heck, no. Don't you *dare* say a word to him about me." Where had Robert's sudden interest in playing matchmaker come from, anyway? "Has he talked about me?"

Robert shrugged. "He's sorry you're hurt. Says that's the last thing he wanted."

"Yeah, well, maybe he should've thought of that before he sipped wine and cavorted in the pool with me."

Robert lifted Baby Ben off the floor and play-nibbled at his chubby neck until the baby belly laughed. "That's pretty much what he said. Says he should've turned around and left as soon as he saw you."

Emily nodded. At least they agreed about that. "You know, this is an odd conversation to be having with the man who's single-handedly responsible for driving off every boy who ever showed an interest in me."

"You're exactly right. They were boys. After one thing, which they were not going to get from my little sister. Not on my watch." Robert slipped Baby Ben into his highchair, strapped him in, and offered him a plate of banana chunks. "We're talking about a man here. A trustworthy, hardworking, loyal, church-going man. Yeah, he's got a history, but he's bustin' his you-know-what trying to overcome it."

Emily grabbed a hand-sewn bib covered with jungle animals from the table and fastened it around Baby Ben's neck as he shoveled banana into his mouth with both fists. She turned to the backyard.

Dan squatted at the edge of the large square area he'd dug and laid a carpenter's level along the ground.

"Well, good for him, but I'm not comfortable with him here. Please tell him to finish and leave."

Robert let out a weary sigh. "Fine." He slid open the door and walked toward Dan.

Dan stood and smiled. Proud of his shallow, square hole, probably. Emily hadn't seen his finished work. Sure didn't look like much yet.

A couple remarks passed between them, and the smile left Dan's face. He stared at his boots and then his gaze shifted to the house. Somehow, through the reflections and the frenetic kid activity that had started up around her, he caught her gaze. He nodded, and grabbing a towel hanging from his back pocket, wiped the sweat from his brow and chest. He snatched his tee shirt from the ground, pulled it over his head, and tugged it down to his waist.

"Let's play Battleship, Auntie Em." Max carried the board game to the dining room table.

She smiled at her nephew and tousled Clara's hair as she cruised by on a pink push car several sizes too small. Emily glanced outside one last time to see Dan gathering his tools. *Good.*

Elizabeth rushed into the room, hopping on one foot as she stretched a sandal strap over her heel. "Chicken macaroni casserole's warming in the oven. If they're good, they can have ice cream for dessert. If you run out of wipes, there are more in the basement."

"Gotcha. Have a good time."

Elizabeth planted a kiss on each child's head and then followed Robert out the door.

"Can we watch a movie?" Gianna folded her hands in front of herself and repeated her request with a touch more whine.

Baby Ben screamed as he squeezed the remainder of the banana in his fists and smeared it on the tray.

"Please?" Gianna begged.

"I got it set up, Auntie Em. Your turn." Max bounced in his seat in front of the Battleship game board.

"Auntie Em!" Clara skidded into the room, breathless. "I think Kit Kat yakked in the bathroom. It's all like, orange and hairy." She shivered.

Great. Cat barf. This is why she didn't have a pet.

Emily unrolled a fistful of paper towels and strode toward the bathroom and the offending cat sputum.

Tessa screeched then cried in pain.

Emily stopped and spun to face her.

Tessa lay under the dining room table, clutching her right arm. Tears flowed down her cheeks as she howled.

"What happened, sweetie?"

Between gasps, she choked out, "Ana pull me."

She meant Gianna, who had suddenly disappeared from the room.

Max and Clara made up a little ditty about cat barf, Baby Ben screeched, Tessa howled, and the cat barf beckoned from the other room.

Tears welled in Emily's eyes. Where should she turn first? Tessa. Poor Tessa was in pain. She stooped until she could see Tessa, then carefully slid her out by her non-injured arm. She cradled her arm against her chest, but the little girl's sobs didn't ease. Should she take her to the emergency room? How could she do that with four other kids? And Robert and Elizabeth had taken the van with all the car seats. A tear rolled down Emily's cheek.

Above the cacophony, something rapped against the glass doors.

8

Une mission de sauvetage
(Rescue mission)

Emily repositioned Tessa on her hip, wiped a tear, and stepped over Clara's abandoned push car. Something stunk. Like rotten eggs. More like rotten diaper. She sniffed Tessa. Not her. Must be Baby Ben.

She slid open the door and came face-to-face with Dan. The only person less welcome would be wearing a child protective services badge.

Maybe he'd breeched an underground gas line, and he came to warn her about the imminent explosion. Dan would be to blame, and it would minimize her calamities.

Dan adjusted his Pittsburgh Pirates ball cap. He looked like a teenager and cute as all get out. And he didn't want anything to do with her. Except for whatever urgent business had brought him to the door.

"Hey. I wanted to let you know I'm leaving." He pointed to the patch of dirt he'd dug up. "If you can, keep the kids away from there. I strung some twine on stakes to mark the boundaries. They could trip on it."

Like something else could go wrong. Emily nodded and bit her lip. *Don't cry.*

Tessa howled again, and Max called from the kitchen. "Kit Kat puked on the bath mat!"

Emily tried to stifle a sob and failed.

Dan, his eyes creased with concern, looked at Tessa then Emily. "I heard the screams. I know you wanted me gone, but do you need a hand?"

Absolutely, from anyone but you, Dan. Scram!

She opened her mouth to say, "No," but Tessa squirmed and whimpered in her arms. The children's welfare trumped her pride.

"Yes." She stepped aside and let him in. "Thank you."

Dan glanced at the kids and chaos. "What do you need me to do?"

"Uh . . ." She sniffed and rubbed her wrist against her nose. "Gianna pulled on Tessa's arm, and she won't stop crying. Baby Ben wants out of the high chair, and I think he needs his diaper changed. And the cat puked in the bathroom."

"Those are my choices?" Dan wrinkled his nose. "Injury, feces, and cat puke?"

Emily shrugged. "There's also a game of Battleship in progress and a request for a movie."

Dan peered at Tessa's tear-streaked face. He gently touched her injured arm. "Where's it hurt, honey?"

Tessa responded with another howl that morphed into a screech.

"Can she move it?"

"I think so." Emily rubbed circles on Tessa's back. "But she's cradling it."

He slid his fingers gently along Tessa's forearm. "It doesn't seem swollen or red or anything."

Emily shook her head. "No."

"May I?" Dan extended his arms.

She handed Tessa over, and Dan carried her to the living room. He sat on the couch and set her on her feet in front of him.

Emily grabbed a damp cloth from the kitchen counter, wiped Ben's face and hands, and unbuckled the highchair's safety belt.

Dan held out his hand. "Can I shake your hand, sweetie?"

Tessa stared at him, sucking on her lower lip.

Dan placed one hand on her elbow and held her hand as if shaking it. He twisted her lower arm back and forth, raised and lowered it a couple times and released her.

Tessa had stared, wide-eyed, while he rotated her arm, but then she whimpered and stooped to pick up her ratty stuffed bunny from the floor.

Dan sat back and shot Emily a smile. "I think I fixed it."

Emily looked from the now-content Tessa, who used her bad arm to hold her toy, to Dan. "What was that?"

"A ligament thing." He stood and surveyed Clara scooting backwards now on the push car. "I think I got it popped back into place."

"Where'd you learn that?" Emily deposited Ben on the floor and, using a damp paper towel, wiped the banana bits from the floor.

Dan grinned sheepishly. "I, uh, may have yanked my sister Maureen's arm too hard three—or five—times. Pediatrician taught Mom how to fix it. She taught me."

Emily sighed. "Well. Okay. Thanks."

The opening of Pixar's *Incredibles* boomed from the other room. "I'll take the cat barf," Dan shouted over it. He grabbed the wadded paper towels from the table and headed for the bathroom.

No one had been granted permission to watch a movie. Apparently Max had taken advantage of the descent into madness around him.

"Max!"

Transfixed by the screen, the boy ignored her. Fine. They could watch so long as they behaved. She scooped up Ben and trotted him to the nursery for a diaper change.

In less than ten minutes, all five kids were gathered in the living room watching the movie. Emily pulled the casserole from the oven and set it on a trivet to cool. She set out silverware and juice boxes for each of the kids.

Dan returned from the bathroom holding the wadded towels as far away from him as his arm would allow.

Emily popped open the trash lid, and he dropped in the offending mess. She cinched the bag shut and marched it out to the garbage can.

When she came back, Dan was returning cleaning products to the top of the pantry. He washed his hands then scoured the sink with the cleanser that sat on the counter.

"I hate cats," he mumbled.

Emily laughed.

He turned toward her and smiled. "What?"

She shook her head. "Nothing. I'm more of a dog person myself, but they're known to throw up too."

Dan dried his hands and turned his back to the sink. "Looks like you've got it under control. I'll get out of your way."

"Dan—" She reached out a hand to lay on his arm then thought better of it. "I was ready to take Tessa to the emergency room." Emily chuckled. "I don't know how, considering I don't have car seats."

Max and Clara stared intently at the movie. Tessa played quietly with her bunny, and Gianna and Ben pushed wooden trains along the carpet and through a cardboard tube tunnel. Somehow, peace had been restored. "Thank you so much."

"You're welcome. Glad I hadn't already left." He winked at her.

Her cheeks heated with shame. "Yeah. About that. I'm sorry. You seem to be a fixture around here, *Uncle* Dan. I guess I need to get used to it."

"It's okay." He pulled his keys from his pocket. "I really did hope we could be friends."

She couldn't commit to that. His rejection and her embarrassment still rankled her. "Why don't you stay for dinner? There's plenty." She jutted her chin toward the casserole. "I can make us a salad to go with it."

Dan stared, shifting his keys to the opposite hand. "Okay. If you're sure."

"Sure, I'm sure. You saved my neck."

Seeing Dan sitting at the head of the table across from her with five children between them was surreal. She resisted the crazy thought that it was a premonition of sorts.

Without being asked, Dan stayed through bedtime and tried to maintain order while Emily wrestled little limbs into pajamas and brushed mouthfuls of white baby teeth. When Clara brought him her Pinkalicious book and asked him to read it, he didn't balk. Instead, he sat on the edge of her bed and read. He'd gone above and beyond for them. Why?

Emily gathered the kids in Max's room for prayers, and Dan prayed with them, his bass a perfect contrast to the children's soprano voices.

Hoping to forestall any tears, Emily squeezed her eyes shut. *It's just babysitting, Emily. You're not having a moment.*

Emily curled up alongside Tessa in her toddler bed. In minutes, Tessa's breaths came soft and even. Emily kissed her forehead and rolled onto the floor. She tiptoed out of the room, avoiding the creaky floorboards as best she could and blowing silent kisses to Clara and Gianna, asleep in their beds.

She returned to the living room, where Dan chucked dozens of brightly-colored Mega Bloks into a canvas container.

"Max is asleep?" Emily asked.

Dan continued to toss the blocks as if he were aiming a basketball at a hoop. "Yep. Out like a light."

"Baby Ben?"

"Haven't heard a peep."

Emily exhaled. "Good." She surveyed the disaster area that passed as the living room. "How did this even happen?"

Dan smiled. "Gremlins."

Emily got on her hands and knees and gathered up plastic cars, toy cell phones, Little People, teething rings, and cardboard sewing cards, depositing them each in their proper homes.

"Shouldn't we have had the kids clean up?" Dan slid the full basket of blocks onto a shelf and began tossing naked baby dolls into a wooden cradle.

"Yeah, but when I realized what time it was and how much effort I'd have to expend coercing them, I decided to let it go. Sometimes it's easier for me to do it myself."

Dan smiled. "So you're going to be the lax parent, huh?"

Satisfied that the floor was cleared of most of its detritus, Emily scooted back and leaned against the couch. "Eh. I think if it were my kids, it would be different."

Dan tossed a wad of baby doll clothes in the cradle and sat alongside Emily. He rested his arm behind her on the couch cushions.

She noticed his arms were no longer dirt-streaked, and he didn't smell of sweat. He must've washed up while she put the girls to bed.

"So, how many kids do you want to have, Emily?"

She rubbed a finger under each eye, trying to wipe away the smeared mascara she knew was there this time of day. "I try not to put a number on it. I don't know what the future holds. How about you?"

He crossed his legs at the ankle, revealing a hole in the heel of his sock. "Your brother and sister-in-law have a nice size family. There were five of us growing up."

She arched her brows. "So, you could do this every day?" Her exhaustion level made her doubt she could manage one kid all day, every day, let alone five.

Dan lifted a shoulder. "They usually come one at a time. You build up to it. We could do it."

Wait a second. He didn't want to kiss her and now he was talking about having a family together? "We?"

He grinned. "Me and my wife."

Her cheeks heated. Apparently her embarrassment knew no bounds with this man. "Ah. Well, good luck with that, especially since you're not in the market for a girlfriend." She shouldn't have said that. She should let it go. He'd been her savior tonight, and they'd gotten along well. Really well.

Dan chuckled. "Couldn't resist, could you?" His arm shifted from the couch to her shoulder.

Not again. Her heart did its little flippy thing. She wished it would get the message from her brain—this relationship was a friendship, at best.

"You okay? You got real quiet." His face was so close, close enough for a kiss. She noticed a brown freckle in the hazel iris of his right eye.

"Hmmm? I'm fine." *I hope.*

"Anyway, about not being in the market. I don't expect that to be a permanent situation. My last girlfriend . . . let's just say she left my life in a shambles. I'm not blaming her—not completely—I made a lot of bad decisions." He shifted and lifted his arm from around her, laying it in his lap.

She missed his warmth and closeness.

"But, I think I'm on the right track now, and lately I've been thinking if the right woman came along . . ." He shrugged.

"How would you know she's the right woman? I mean, I doubt there's going to be a neon sign over her head pointing out that she's the one."

"That would be helpful, but I think it will feel . . . right. Like friends, but with—"

"Benefits?" Dan was a church-going, praying kind of guy, but how deep did his faith go?

Dan jerked his head away from her. "No. Not benefits. I was going to say with a deeper connection." He tugged at his sock, trying to close the hole. "I can't explain it."

"Well, when you figure it out, let me know. Our friendship can be the control pairing. You can test the variables against it." She fought to keep any resentment out of her voice.

He bumped her shoulder. "So, you're good with us being friends now?"

God help her, she was an idiot. "Yeah, I think I am."

Did friends hold hands? Because that might make this moment perfect.

Did friends lose track of the conversation because they were distracted by thoughts of kissing? Because that was definitely happening.

Did friends go all ga-ga over reading bedtime stories, blowing raspberries, and rocking babies? Because that little display was ten times sexier than the shirtless shoveling.

"Emily?"

"Huh?"

"I asked if you want to play a game."

"Oh, uh . . ." She pointed to the abandoned game. "Battleship?"

Dan glanced at the game board, still on the table. "I don't think I can move that far. Those kids were more exhausting than eight hours of manual labor. It's like my legs are stuck to the floor. How about Two Truths and a Lie?"

She grinned. What was this, junior high? "How's it work?"

He slid his arm around her again. "I'll tell you three things about myself. You have to guess which one is a lie. I'll go first."

"Okay." Her shoulder warmed where he rubbed up and down. *Friends, just friends.*

"All right. Hmmm. One: I'm an Eagle Scout. Two: My first pet was a three-legged dog named Gomer." He paused for a couple of seconds. "Three: I've never been out of the country."

Emily pulled her legs up toward her chest. "Let's see. The dog is specific. I'm guessing that's true." She turned her head and gave him a once over. "You strike me as a homebody, so I'm guessing the last one is true. I think the first one is a lie. You seem like more of a jock than a scout."

He pinched her shoulder. "Wrong. Gomer was the love of my life. God rest his doggy soul." He laid a hand over his heart. "And, I'm kind of flattered you think I'm athletic, but I'm an Eagle Scout. The lie was not leaving the country. I've been to the Canadian side of Niagara Falls. Your turn."

Emily crossed her legs beneath her while she thought. His hand fell away from her shoulder. *Drat.* "All right. This is tricky. I got one."

She pushed a strand of hair behind her ear. With her short hair it wasn't necessary, but it had become a nervous habit over the years.

"When I was four, I hated my hair so much I chopped it off with blunt play scissors. I was a total book nerd in high school. My belly button is an outie."

"Well, the first one should be a crime. Your hair is beautiful." He let a section of her hair slide between his thumb and forefinger. "But lots of kids do that. And I can totally see you being a book nerd. So, the lie must be . . . easily verifiable." He lunged for the hem of her tee shirt.

She twisted away, laughing and holding down her shirt. "You win. I'm an innie."

"Prove it." His eyes flashed with life despite how beat she knew he was.

Emily didn't move. "My word should be good enough."

"Yeah, well, I don't have a good track record with women being good for their word. Prove it."

Who was the mystery woman in his past, and what had she done? He'd said more tonight about his sordid past than ever before.

He reached for the hem of her shirt again. "Just a peek. I'm not going to expose you."

Emily held up a hand. "Fine. In an effort to restore your faith in the female of the species, I'll show you." She knelt in front of him and grasped the bottom of her shirt. "Get ready. This is going to be quick."

He nodded. His eyes shone with a playful look, and he gave her a flirty smile.

Emily pulled the top of her shorts down a half inch with one hand and lifted her shirt with the other. It took all of two seconds. "Satisfied?"

"Yes. Thank you. It may be possible that not every woman is a conniving liar."

"Man, you must have been burned bad." Emily waited for him to respond, but he didn't. She turned around and sat next to him in front of the couch. "Your turn."

Dan scooted so that they sat face-to-face. He cleared his throat. "One: I wish I met you years ago."

His voice softened. "Two: Being just your friend is easy."

He leaned toward her. "Three: I want to kiss you again, and it has nothing to do with pity."

Emily's throat constricted. "Uh, the third one's the lie?"

He whispered a hair's breadth from her lips. "No. You lose."

Emily's heart pounded. "I don't feel like a loser."

Dan's lips brushed hers for less than a second before the door creaked and keys jangled, signaling Robert and Elizabeth's arrival.

Dan pulled back a few inches, a soft and tender smile on his lips. "Bad timing."

Emily nodded and pressed the back of her hand to her lips, not wanting to wipe away the kiss, but to seal it.

Robert's voice came from the foyer. The volume and the smack of his dress shoes on the wooden floor matched his progress. "Hey, Em, why's Dan's truck still—"

"Hey, Robert." Dan rose and brushed off his jeans. "I offered to stay and help out."

Robert raised his brows. "You did?" He turned to Emily, clearly not understanding why she'd accepted his offer after she'd told Robert to order Dan out.

Dan stretched a hand down to Emily and pulled her to her feet.

Her cheeks warmed. She worried Robert could tell what had happened. That she and Dan had sorta kissed. Not that they'd done anything wrong. It was just awkward.

Elizabeth strolled in and set her purse on the end table. "Everything go okay?"

Dan piped up before Emily had a chance to answer. "Great. Emily's awesome with the kids. Your cat coughed up a nasty hairball though."

"Eww," Elizabeth said. "Sorry about that. I appreciate you guys babysitting."

"Glad to do it," Emily said. "And it's good practice for Dan. He wants to have five kids." She shot Dan a grin and realized he'd been staring at her. Her cheeks heated again, and she turned back to Elizabeth. "You have a good time?"

"Um, sure." She smiled, but it seemed fake. "It's always nice to have an uninterrupted conversation."

Robert stepped toward Dan. "Hey, it turns out I'm going on a little camping trip next weekend. Me and the three oldest kids. You want to come along? I could use some adult company."

"You need help corralling your kids in the wild?" Dan asked.

"That too. You in?"

"Sure. Sounds like fun. I haven't been camping since, geez, I guess since college?"

Baby Ben's cry came over the baby monitor.

"Here we go," Elizabeth said, kicking off her shoes. "Thanks again, Emily. And Dan."

"You're back on Monday with the patio, right?" Robert asked.

"Yeah," Dan said. "I'm going to start with the large fill and then the fine stuff."

Emily mentally scrolled through next week's schedule. Could she find an excuse to visit? She and Dan had agreed on being friends. And then they'd barely kissed. He had her phone number. Would he use it?

"Emily?" Dan's voice brought her to attention. "Walk me to the door?"

"Uh, sure." She didn't miss the curious look Robert gave her.

Dan waited for her in the entranceway.

She stopped a foot or so away from him and smiled.

He punched her upper arm as if they were teammates, and she'd scored a goal. "Friends, right?"

What was that? She smiled and hid the pain that simple question caused. Didn't his lips brush hers? "Friends. I'll be friends with you. You be friends with me."

"Great. This'll work. Good night."

"Good night, Dan."

He descended the steps and climbed into his panel truck.

Emily slammed the door shut and turned her back to it. Never in her life had she met such a confounding man.

"So," Robert said, sauntering in from the living room. "You two seemed kind of cozy."

"Yeah, cozy like cellmates maybe."

Robert tilted his head. "I'm not condoning it, but some cellmates—"

"Shut. Up. And I wouldn't put 'our friend',"—she did the air quotes thing—"in charge of the campfire next weekend. He runs hot and cold. You never know which you're going to get."

9

Les confessions du feu de camp
(Campfire confessions)

A swarm of gnats buzzed around Dan's ear, and he swatted them away with his hand. A pair of cabbage white butterflies danced in front of him before fluttering over the grass and into bright midday sunshine. He pounded the final stake into the ground with the rubber mallet. Tent assembly completed.

"Hey," Robert yelled. "Stop running around those tents before you trip and—"

Gianna let out a bloodcurdling scream. She picked herself off the ground, hugging her right leg. "Ow! I'm bleeding!"

"What did I just tell you?" Robert's harsh tone matched the force he used to toss down the sleeping gear he'd been carrying. He stomped over to Gianna, pushed up her Capri-length purple leggings, and examined her knee.

"No blood. Just a nasty brush burn." He stooped to kiss the knee, and then helped her to her feet. "That's why I said no running."

He stood and craned his neck, searching for the other kids. "Max, Clara? Come look." He waited as they ran from the hollow stump they'd been poking with sticks. "Do you see all those ropes Uncle Dan pounded into the ground?"

"Yeah." Max jutted his stick left and right, wielding it as if it were a lightsaber.

Clara nodded as she scrubbed her shoe back and forth over a fat pine cone, breaking it into pieces.

"They're going to keep the fly on the tent and the tent in the ground. But if you go running around the tents, you're going to trip and get hurt. If you want to run, go over there."

Robert pointed to a grassy area between their tents and the neighboring campsite. "Got it?"

"Uh-huh." Clara whirled in a circle, looking at the sky.

"It happens again, and we're packing up and going home." He stomped back to the gear he'd thrown down, mumbling something about being outnumbered. He'd been on edge all morning, snapping at the kids and grumbling about the trip.

Dan took a seat at the picnic table and waited for Robert to cool down. He had to wait for Robert's instructions anyway. He didn't know what type of gear he had or where he wanted it. The last time Dan had been camping it had been more an opportunity for underage drinking and carousing than enjoying the outdoors.

He stretched his legs and crossed them at the ankle, taking in his surroundings. The park campsite sat in a level valley. Beyond the campsites and sparse trees, a small lake glistened in the sunlight. Several fishing boats and two bright-yellow kayaks dotted the water.

The nature center sat to the right. The air-conditioned building filled with local natural history might be a good retreat when the late afternoon sun made doing much else uncomfortable.

The point of the overnight with Robert's kids eluded him. The trip had only been in the works for a week. Robert made it sound like a dreaded obligation instead of a fun, family trip. And if he needed another adult along to wrangle the kids, why not Elizabeth or Emily?

"Dan, can you give me a hand here?" Robert crouched alongside the gear, tugging a sleeping bag from its stuff sack.

"Yeah. Sure."

Robert tossed him a couple of rolled sleeping mats and bags to place in the tents.

"So, what's the plan for the day?"

"To exhaust my kids so thoroughly that they go to bed early and sleep soundly."

"Ooo-kay." Didn't seem like an opportunity for making treasured family memories. Maybe Robert would clue him in on the impetus for the trip later. "How about a circuit hike, then? There's a fairly easy one on the park map. It'll take us around the lake."

"Perfect."

***

The last glimmer of the spectacular orange and pink sunset had drifted below the distant hillside. Little brown bats chattered and darted through the sky, swooping and dashing this way and that.

Dan stretched his legs, letting his boots rest on a log alongside the fire pit. The flames warmed his feet in seconds, and he loosened the bootlaces.

The hike, a visit to the nature center, and a dinner of hot dogs, beans, and roasted marshmallows had done the trick. At Robert's prodding, the kids, splotched with dirt and grass stains, had dragged themselves into their tent.

As he leaned his head back on the canvas chair and gazed at the brilliant stars, Dan's thoughts turned to Emily. What the heck was he doing with her? Friends? More than friends? He needed to pick one and stick with it. Otherwise his vacillation would strangle their relationship.

Friends.

Did a guy wonder how it would feel to run his fingers through his friend's hair?

Did a guy imagine what it would be like to feel his friend's head resting on his bare chest?

Did a guy fantasize about every possible way he could make love to his friend?

He sighed and sat straight in his chair. Grabbing the long stick Max had found for tending the fire, he poked and pushed the glowing logs so that the orange flames engulfed every piece of wood. Clara had dropped a charred marshmallow into the fire, and he shoved it further in to watch it melt.

Even if he were Emily's *boyfriend*, he shouldn't be thinking about her like that. Unbridled lust. More fallout from his toxic relationship with Kristen.

The zipper on the vinyl tent opened and Robert emerged. He plodded toward the campfire and slumped in the only other adult-sized camp chair, letting out a long sigh.

"Everyone asleep?"

"Yeah. Including me. Lying down with them kills me every time." Robert scrubbed his shoes in the dirt, shoving away some rocks. "Oh, hey. I brought us a couple of beers."

Dan's eyebrows raised. "I didn't think alcohol was allowed in the park."

"Shh. I won't tell if you don't."

Dan shrugged. A beer sounded good, but his days of rule breaking were done. Even if the rule was dumb.

"Actually, I think the ban is only on glass-bottled alcohol." Robert pulled two large cans from the cooler and handed one to Dan.

"Thanks." He popped the lid and took a sip. Holding the can in the firelight, he examined the writing on the side. "Eighteen percent alcohol by volume? What are you trying to do, Robert, get us drunk?"

Robert grunted. "Sounds like a plan."

In the past, Dan had a ready short list of reasons to drink himself stupid, but Robert had a near-perfect life as far as he could tell. Why would he want to escape?

Dan sipped his beer, enjoying the peace. An owl hooted in the distance, the fire crackled and popped, and the sound of bike tires over gravel and children's laughter drifted from the road. "You want to tell me what's up with this trip?"

Robert groaned. "I knew you'd ask eventually."

"I'm enjoying it and all. But I get the sense you don't really want to be here."

Robert grabbed a long stick and poked at the fire. "Elizabeth and I are having a disagreement. It escalated to an argument on the way back from dinner last week. She suggested we needed a little space to think—whatever the heck that means."

Dan nodded. "You want to tell me what it's about? You don't have to, but if you want someone to listen . . ."

"She thinks we're ready for another baby."

Maybe he shouldn't have asked. Having a baby was about as personal an issue as you could get, and Dan didn't want to take sides. "I take it you don't agree."

"We're maxed out as it is—time, energy, money, space. You've seen our house." He threw up his hands. "Where do we go with another kid?"

"Dresser drawer?"

Robert shot him a look and took another swig of his beer.

"I'm just sayin', people used to have much bigger families in much smaller homes." Dan took another drink.

"Did Elizabeth prep you for this or something?"

Dan laughed. "No. Whatever you decide is between the two of you. And God. But you do make awfully cute kids."

"Elizabeth's a better person than me. There's no doubt about that. She shrugs and says, 'God will take care of us.' Yeah, He'll take care of us, but He's charged me with feeding, clothing, and educating these little midgets. I don't think she gets that responsibility."

"I don't know. I'm not a dad, but I think it's a guy thing."

"The business hasn't grown the way I thought it would when I hired another mechanic, but the bills keep coming."

"I know all about bills." Dan enumerated the ones he'd incurred in starting his own business. Bills for supplies, tools, materials. And the ones Kristen had suckered and scammed him into owing. Credit card bills for thousand-dollar purses, shoes that cost him more than a week's income, and spa services he didn't even understand. What the hell were a bean polish and a fondue wrap? It sounded more like lunch than some kind of frou-frou pampering, but apparently Kristen needed both. On a monthly basis. When he told her he'd give her a hot rock massage by nuking some stones in the microwave, she laughed then used his credit card to have a professional do it to the tune of one-hundred-sixty dollars.

"Having your own business is definitely its own kind of stress. No sick days. No backup." Dan stood and grabbed the last pine log from the bundle they'd bought at the camp store and tossed it onto the fire. "So, how's this trip supposed to change your mind? Or is it a creative way of keeping you out of her bed?"

Robert shook his head. "She doesn't withhold sex. We agreed on that from day one." He stomped on some embers that fell at his feet. "Maybe she thinks that being away with them, sorta one-on-one, will make me realize how great they are. And make me want another."

Huh. Kristen had held sex over Dan's head at every opportunity. Manipulated him with it on a near daily basis. Her being on the pill was supposed to give them freedom. Instead, it stole every bit of love and life from their love life to the point that it became nothing more than a physical compulsion—one she doled out however she saw fit in order to get her way.

The silence lingered, and Dan's eyelids grew as heavy as the can in his hand. He closed his eyes. He hated that Kristen still had the power to sway his mood. If it weren't for the beer mellowing him, he'd be so angry he could take the camp axe and chop them another whole cord of firewood.

"My sister likes you."

Dan's eyes popped open. The thought of Emily brought a smile to his face. "I like your sister." His eyes closed again, and not conscious of whether he was speaking out loud or to himself, he mumbled, "Emily makes me want things I didn't think I could have. Things I don't deserve."

"Why don't you deserve them?" Robert's voice sounded slurred and distant.

The myriad ways Kristen had screwed him over and the destructive choices he'd made as a result weren't something he wanted to share. Even with Robert. Especially with Robert.

"Dan, if you'd get it together and stop acting so schizophrenic with her, I would be cool with you and her, y'know, dating. She's a good girl. She'd be good for you."

Dan didn't doubt it. The question was: Would he be good for her?

10

Balancer dans l'action
(Swinging into action)

As the daytime temperature dropped, a cool breeze brought dozens of kids and parents to the playground in the early evening. Older kids climbed the rock wall and slid down the firefighters' pole. Younger kids scampered between the slide supports, chasing one another up stairs and through plastic tunnels.

Emily pushed the baby swing higher, eliciting a giggle from Tessa. In the swing beside her, Baby Ben grunted and kicked his legs, communicating his desire for another push. She obliged.

Elizabeth, claiming loneliness while Robert and her older children camped, had invited Emily to join her at the park. Emily had been reluctant at first, intent on staying in with a bag of corn chips and a movie, but Elizabeth persuaded her to come along.

What am I doing here? Most women her age were out with their peers on a Saturday night at bars, clubs, movie theaters, and mini golf courses, doing date-night stuff and socializing. If women were hanging out with babies, they were their own.

She gave her niece and nephew another push. All around her children screeched and laughed as they raced one another up ladders and down slides. They swung, they scooped mulch in their chubby hands, they cried. Surrounded by all that life, how did Emily manage to feel so alone? She looked on as if she were merely observing, not living. Same as always.

A lump formed in her throat, followed by a bitter surge of envy.

Most days she could pretend that it was enough. That teaching fifth graders and hanging out with her brother's family were satisfying. That she was whole. She had started the year with renewed purpose, determined not to pine away over whatever guy caught her eye. A guy that would likely never know or care that she existed.

She'd done that. And still, there was a void. She'd given up longing and wondering, but it had been replaced by a subtler ache. Or maybe it had become obvious now that she'd eschewed indulging her adolescent crushes.

Life thrived around her.

She circled to the front of the swings, and it stared her in the face in the form of precious Ben and Tessa. Deep inside she had always held something back, always kept a little piece of herself tucked away. Why?

No pity parties, Emily.

"I'm back." Elizabeth wiped her hands on her shorts. "Not bad for a park bathroom, but remind me next time to go before we leave the house."

Emily smiled. "Or maybe not to guzzle an entire bottle of water on the five-minute walk over here."

Elizabeth resumed swing duty. "Did you miss me, cutie patooties?" With a hand on each swing, she pushed them back. As they swung forward, she grabbed at their sandaled feet. Tessa and Ben squealed.

The scent of melted marshmallows and chocolate wafted on the breeze. Two children and their parents were making S'mores over the rusted-out charcoal grill. She hoped her nieces and nephew had a nice big fire going to make theirs. "Have you heard anything from Robert?"

Robert was a reluctant camper. He took his family into the woods because as a cheap vacation, it couldn't be beat. Not because the great outdoors beckoned to him.

The smile left Elizabeth's face. "Nope. Not a peep. But then I didn't expect to."

Curious. "Why not?"

"Not much to say. We're at an impasse."

"About?"

Elizabeth lifted Tessa, then Ben out of the swings and guided them to the pirate ship playground equipment for toddlers. Tessa dashed up the ramp. Elizabeth sat Ben on his blanket in a patch of grass and dropped a chain of plastic rings in front of him. "Can we keep this between us?"

Sounded serious. She knew Robert and Elizabeth were at odds about something, but she figured it was an ordinary disagreement. The kind couples had multiple times a week. "Of course."

Elizabeth sighed. "I'm ready for another baby, and Robert's not. He *laughed* when I suggested it. Said I must be crazy, and there was no way either of us could handle another child. Not now, maybe never again." Tears welled in her eyes. She sunk onto the metal bench partly-shaded by a small locust tree.

Emily sat beside her. "I'm sorry. Whether he disagreed with you or not, it sounds like he handled it poorly."

Elizabeth laughed. "Yeah. You could say that."

"Maybe he needs some time to get used to the idea. You've been thinking about it, but maybe he hasn't."

Elizabeth nodded. "You're probably right. I can't shake this feeling that someone's still missing from our family." She brushed a couple pebbles from Ben's blanket. "Maybe he'll reconsider this weekend. The big kids are a good reminder that they don't stay little forever. The early years are tough, but they're short."

Emily nodded. All the years looked pretty tough from her vantage point. She recalled the disastrous evening last week when she and Dan struggled to manage their kids for only a few hours.

"Have you heard from Dan?"

"No." Emily pushed a fallen leaf through the grating on the bench. "Why would I?"

Elizabeth grinned and nudged her with her elbow. "Oh, come on. I know we walked in on something last week. Even Robert could tell."

Emily's cheeks heated. If she closed her eyes, she could still feel his breath against her face and the barest brush of his lips.

"It's obvious there's something going on between you two. Don't try to deny it."

"Something, but I don't know what. He sends mixed signals. He's all 'we're just friends,' and then—"

Tessa howled like a wolf as she came down the slide. Then she hopped to her feet, darted for the ladder, and tripped. Elizabeth jumped off the bench and helped her up. "And then?"

"And then he sort of went to kiss me." She grabbed a stick from the ground and traced a heart in the sandy dirt then immediately scribbled over it.

Elizabeth repositioned Ben on his blanket and pried a rock from his little fist. "Sort of?"

"Well, that's when you came home."

"Oh." Elizabeth grimaced. "Sorry."

Emily shrugged. "If he wanted, he could've kissed me at the door, but by then he had retreated to friend mode. Maybe it's better that he stays there."

"I hate to say it, because I really like Dan." She laid her hand on Emily's leg. "But you may be right. All that back and forth sounds like a recipe for a broken heart."

***

Dan dropped his car keys and mail on the kitchen counter and grabbed a glass from the cupboard. He filled it at the sink and drank it in two gulps.

His gaze skittered around his small apartment. A pile of invoices, bills, and landscape product specs still sat on the table. Grandma's broken Hummel figurine that he'd promised to repair lay on the counter. It's not like he'd missed much while he was gone. After a sweaty night in the sleeping bag and a morning packing gear, he couldn't wait to jump into the shower.

He scattered the glossy mailers and dull envelopes on the counter and surveyed each item. Two clothing catalogs, a local advertiser, three direct mail pieces, a credit card offer, and two bills—electric and credit card.

Using his index finger, he pried open the credit card bill. Only eight hundred dollars left on the balance. These were his best months of the year, financially. He'd have it all paid off next month.

Maybe then he could finally put all his memories of Kristen to rest. All the crap he'd funded on her secret shopping trips would be paid in full. What a relief to be rid of every last trace of her. Maybe he needed to cut this last tie to finally be free again, both from her and from his mistakes.

Maybe he'd been talking himself out of dating Emily for nothing. He knew at first he'd been guilty of acting like she was Kristen, which was ridiculous. Not every woman was like that—thank God. Emily was different.

Emily thought of others whereas Kristen thought only of herself. The endless stream of selfies Kristen took were evidence of that.

He trusted Emily. Heck, he'd even trust her with his credit card. Could he trust her with his heart?

He smiled as he stripped off his shirt and headed for the shower. He'd call her this week and make a date.

11

Une révélation malencontreuse
(Untimely revelation)

Pappy's Chaps Saloon sported a row of mounted deer heads on one wall and a row of framed platinum records on another. The interior consisted of wooden paneling with various farm implements affixed to the ceiling and walls in strategic places. High-backed booths and long tables surrounded the empty dance floor.

Dan rubbed his sweaty palms down the front of his jeans—the new, dark blue crisp ones he'd bought the night before. Country music, a Dierks Bentley tune he remembered from senior year of high school, thumped from the speakers above him. Maybe he should've chosen another booth. He and Emily might not be able to hear each other.

He twisted around and peeked over the back of the booth, checking for the third time to see if she'd arrived. Five women in tight jeans, button-down blouses, and cowboy boots blocked the entranceway. As he spun around, his gaze landed on a person no more than two feet away, and he jerked back in shock.

A thin man his age with blondish-brown, receding hair had taken a seat across the table from him. "Dan Malone. Where have you been hiding yourself, man?"

Matt Riley. His only remaining friend from the Kristen era. Maybe *frenemy* better befit their relationship. A grin spread across Matt's face, like he'd discovered a long lost relative. A filthy rich one on death's door.

Dan *had* been hiding, and Matt knew why, but that didn't make it any easier to admit. Like a beaten puppy, Dan had gone off to lick his wounds, burying himself in work, bad habits, and debt—even if the debt wasn't his doing. Matt had been the only one of the guys he hung with who had stuck around.

They hadn't parted on the best of terms. Despite the fact that Dan hadn't answered the phone or the door, Matt had come over and let himself in. He sauntered to the nearest window and snapped open the room-darkening shade, allowing sunlight to flood the dingy room, highlighting the pile of unfolded laundry, dirty socks, stacks of magazines, unopened mail, and other papers.

Dan winced at the light but didn't budge from the couch.

"It's sunny and sixty-five degrees out there. It's almost noon. You're wasting the day." He waved away the smoke in front of his face. "Or maybe you're just wasted."

He remembered Matt pitching an empty Doritos bag from the end table onto the couch, scattering cheesy crumbs across Dan's undershirt and the couch cushion. Then he toppled two empty beer bottles, snatched the remote control, and flicked off the TV. "It's lookin' like Kristen made the best decision of her life."

If his emotions hadn't been dulled, Dan would've been angry enough to pound him. As it was, he called him the crudest, nastiest name he could think of and ordered him out.

Dan cleared his throat, returning his attention to the present. He hadn't given Matt another thought until now. And this was not an ideal time for a reunion.

"I've been keepin' busy." Dan peered over the booth again, searching for Emily. Still no sign of her. He met Matt's gaze again and tried to hide his agitation. "Working. Paying the bills."

Matt leaned forward and studied Dan's appearance. "You've lost weight. How much? Twenty-five pounds?"

"Uh, thirty-five." Dan bounced his knee under the table. How could he get rid of Matt before Emily arrived? He didn't mind catching up, but this would be his first real date with Emily.

"Good for you. Things are looking up, then?"

Dan focused on Matt's question and realized with satisfaction that things *were* looking up. He could afford to relax a little. To show Matt a little appreciation. "Things are good now. Thanks. How about with you?"

"Never better, man. Still selling insurance with my dad. Been dating here and there. No one special." His eyes drifted from Dan to somewhere beyond the booth. "That's sure a pretty little thing coming this way. You waitin' on a woman, Dan?"

A shadow came across the table. Dan looked up into Emily's eyes, and his heart nearly stopped. "Pretty little thing" didn't do her justice.

Emily stood there, wearing a long Kelly green dress that seemed to have been made for her. Her hair, shorter but a bit fuller, framed her face and drew attention to her eyes. Her eyes—warm, soulful—focused on him. He'd never seen her with makeup. And shimmery pink lip gloss.

Dan jumped to his feet. "Emily, y-you're here." *Stunning observation, Captain Obvious.*

She gave him a nervous smile and glanced at Matt. "Sorry I'm late. I, uh, had trouble choosing what to wear." She fingered her dress then let the skirt fall. "And then . . . traffic."

"No problem. You look great." He touched her elbow, leaned in, and kissed her cheek.

A smile blossomed on her face, and her cheeks grew pink.

Matt cleared his throat.

Dan rubbed his finger along his forehead, grasping for ways to dispatch Matt in a hurry. "Uh, Emily, this is Matt Riley, an old friend of mine."

Matt stepped out of the booth and shook her hand. He soaked her up with his gaze.

Dan twitched. The look in Matt's eyes reminded him of the look Kristen got leaning over a jewelry counter. "Matt, my, uh, friend Emily Kowalski."

"It's nice to meet you, Matt." She glanced at the booth. "Are you joining us?"

Dan's gaze darted to Matt. No way. They'd exchanged pleasantries, Matt could move on.

Matt smiled and shrugged. "I'd rather be staring at you than a row of whiskey bottles at the bar."

No, no, no.

"Great." The disappointment in her tone was unmistakable. Of course she'd be disappointed. Dan had been precise when he'd called and asked her out.

He'd started to leave a message on her voice mail when she answered.

"Sorry, Dan, I just came in."

"No problem." He paced the length of his apartment, swallowing hard over the dry lump in his throat. "I was wondering if, maybe, you'd like to have dinner with me on Thursday?"

She'd hesitated.

He'd worried. Maybe he'd already alienated her by waffling back and forth. His heart thudded in time with each passing second.

Her voice was soft but confident. "Is this friends hanging out and eating or is this a—"

"A date. An, uh, appointment to meet at a certain time and place for the purpose of us getting to know each other better."

More silence. Then, "Yes. I'd like to go on a date with you, Dan."

They'd worked out the details, and she'd obviously understood correctly. She'd taken extra time with her clothes and appearance. The results made his mouth run dry. He'd smack Matt upside the head if he didn't get the heck out. Now.

Dan moved to let her into the booth.

She laid a hand on his forearm. "I'm going to run to the ladies' room. I'll be right back." She gave Dan a big smile, a smaller one to Matt, then headed across the dance floor.

Good. Now he could get rid of Matt.

Matt flopped on the seat, releasing an embarrassing-sounding blast of air, and grabbed a menu from behind the ketchup bottle.

Dan had to nip this in the bud. "Matt, it was great seeing you, but—"

His phone vibrated in his pocket. A text message. Maybe it was one of his sisters. His mom hadn't mastered texting.

Matt settled himself in the booth and perused the menu.

Dan sighed. "Excuse me." He pulled the phone from his pocket and glanced at the number.

His chest tightened, and he stopped breathing.

No way. No *freakin'* way.

He stared at the sender's name. Kristen. Couldn't be.

He'd called and texted her every day for a month after she'd broken up with him and nothing. Not one word. Almost a year and a half later, and she texts him *now*? He hadn't been out alone with a woman other than her, his mom, or his sisters since he turned twenty, and now on his first date, *this*?

He stared blankly at the phone, not knowing how to respond.

The table bumped into his gut as Matt pushed out of the booth. He jerked his thumb in the direction Emily had headed. "I'm going to use the restroom too. Be right back."

Dan nodded and reread the message: *We need to talk.*

He steadied his fingers over the phone then tapped back: *Nothing to talk about.*

After a half a minute, the phone vibrated in his hand: *Plenty. You owe me.*

He owed *her*? This was insane. She racked up so much debt on his credit card he'd had to dissolve his business and start over. And she had the nerve to say he owed her. His hand shook with anger and the knowledge that any minute Emily would return. He typed: *I don't owe you a thing.*

He waited for a response, drumming his fingers on the table as he watched the phone. The overhead music blared to life as someone dropped coins in the jukebox. A gaggle of teenage girls in cowboy hats drifted by the table leaving the noxious scent of bubble gum mixed with hairspray in their wake.

He bit his lower lip and craned his neck toward the restrooms. No Emily.

Finally, the phone shook and shimmied over the tabletop. He grabbed hold of it and read: *You owe me. Bigtime. And your daughter.*

12

Des indices sur un passé
(Clues to a past)

Emily waved her soapy hands under the faucet. Up, down, back and forth. What did she have to do to trigger the motion sensor? Finally, she thrust her hands forward and a spray of ice-cold water splashed her hands and the sink basin.

She dried her hands on a paper towel, tossed it in the trashcan, and checked her appearance in the mirror. For once, her hair had turned out the way she wanted. She missed her long hair, which she could easily style in a variety of ways. Her short cut had been simple to care for, but always left her feeling bare.

She grabbed another paper towel and blotted her lips. The thought of returning to Dan stirred the butterflies in her belly. She'd been looking forward to tonight all week.

The butterflies plummeted. Why had he invited a friend? What was his name? Matt? Maybe Dan hadn't invited him. Maybe they'd run into each other. She hoped so. If Dan retreated to friend mode once more, she was done with him. For good.

She pushed open the door, stepped out, and a man exiting the men's room pushed the door open so wide it nearly forced the ladies' room door shut on her.

She stumbled to the side then pushed back.

"Oh, sorry, Emily." Matt grabbed her door's handle and opened it wide, allowing her to pass. "Guess I don't know my own strength." He grinned and flexed his bicep muscle.

She resisted the urge to roll her eyes. "It's okay. No harm done."

He kept pace with her her as she headed for their booth. "So, how long have you known Dan?"

"Uh . . ." Should she count from the time they'd first met in the Christmas tree lot? Probably not. "A few months. He's friends with my brother."

"Friends? Glad to hear he made some new ones. He'd driven everyone but me away after . . ." He cleared his throat. "Well, he became a bit of a loner there for a while."

"Oh." Great. More about Dan's shadowy past that no one would actually speak about. Was this a bad breakup or was Dan part of the Irish Mafia or something?

Matt slid into his side of the booth.

Dan stared intently at his phone, not moving.

"I'm back." She thought she could get his attention without asking him to move.

He didn't budge, didn't look up.

She touched his shoulder. Her heart beat faster. Was something wrong? Had something happened to his grandmother? "Dan?"

He blinked a couple times as if he were coming out of a trance then looked up and gave her a weak smile. "Emily . . . Sorry."

He stood to let her in, his face ashen, his brow creased. All the light had left his eyes.

Emily sat and pulled a menu from the end of the table. Should she ask or act like everything was okay and wait for him to tell her? "So, um, what's good here?"

"The mushroom burger is awesome." Matt slid his menu to the side.

"Dan?" She glanced at him as he shoved his phone in his pocket. "What do you recommend?"

"Huh? Oh. Uh. I usually get the fish sandwich," Dan said, his voice dull and his gaze unfocused.

Emily sighed and scanned the selection of sandwiches. Dan had seemed eager to see her when she'd arrived, and now he'd totally withdrawn. What had happened while she was in the restroom?

After a moment of uncomfortable silence, Dan reached into his pocket and pulled out his wallet, jostling her. He laid a couple of bills on the table.

"I'm sorry, Emily. Matt. I can't stay. I'm not . . ." He shook his head. "I won't be good company tonight." He slid out of the booth, never meeting her eyes.

"Did something happen? Is your grandmother okay?" Emily inched closer to where he stood at the end of the booth.

"She's fine. Nothing like that." He pulled his truck keys from his pocket. "Just something I have to deal with."

"Business?" Matt spun his spoon in a circle on the table, not looking the least bit concerned.

Dan shook his head. "Personal." His gaze settled on Emily. "I'm so, so sorry." His lids closed over eyes glistening with unshed tears.

Before she could say anything, he turned and left.

"What was that about?" Matt said exactly what she'd been thinking.

She leaned back in the booth and sighed. "I have no idea. Dan Malone is the most mystifying man I've ever met. Has he always been this way?"

"No." Matt hesitated. "He used to be the kind of guy that knew what he wanted and went after it. Self-assured but not cocky. I mean, how many guys have their own business when they're like, twenty-four? Of course, then he mellowed out."

"Mellowed out?"

Matt pinched together his thumb and forefinger, raised them to his lips, and inhaled.

Her eyes widened and her brows arched. "Dan smokes *pot*?"

Matt grinned. "Used to. More than a little."

"Dan?" He seemed squeaky clean. And Robert and Elizabeth would never let some pot head hang out with their kids.

Matt shrugged. "I barely recognized him when I spotted him here."

Okay. So, Dan hadn't invited Matt. "What do you mean?"

"I mean, last time I saw Dan Malone, he was an unshaven, dope-smoking slob whose business tanked." He motioned for the waitress. "If you'd told me he lived in a van down by the river, I wouldn't have been surprised."

Emily laid her elbows on the table, leaned forward and squinted. "Are we talking about the same man?"

Matt laughed. "I don't know. You tell me. That guy who just left, he was more like the guy I first met—solid, competent, salt of the earth, decent kind of guy." He lifted a shoulder. "The look in his eyes before he left? I recognize that too—defeated, despondent, ready to cash it all in."

Emily bit her lower lip and recalled the teary look in Dan's eyes as he'd apologized for cutting out on her. Dan hadn't shared his past, and she certainly couldn't account for his behavior tonight, but one thing became crystal clear: Dan Malone was troubled. He needed a friend, not a girlfriend.

She was glad he had Robert. In fact, she'd call Robert and clue him in. But any notion she had about a romance with Dan—that had just been cut off at the knees. She'd pray for Dan, but she didn't want any part of his drama, even if her heart said otherwise. God gave her a brain as well as a heart, and she'd use it to write off Dan Malone. At least as a potential mate.

She breathed deeply and focused on the man across the table from her. Something about him irked her, but maybe she hadn't given him a fair chance. He wasn't bad looking. Short hair, brown eyes, strong jaw, nice features. He seemed easy going, friendly, and decidedly less complicated than the man with whom she'd expected to spend the evening.

"Enough about Dan, tell me about you, Matt."

His smiled broadened, and he leaned against the padded back of the booth. "How far back do you want me to go?"

13

Découragés

(Browbeaten)

Dan swore and beat the steering wheel with his fist. It didn't hurt enough, so he pounded it again, harder.

A kid? She had to be lying. She had to be lying!

He started the truck engine and peeled out of Pappy's Chaps parking lot, cutting off a black Mazda. The Mazda's horn blared, and Dan resisted the urge to flip off the driver. He pushed the pedal to the floor, only slowing when the traffic light in the distance changed to yellow and then red.

He had no memory of the rest of the ride home. Every thought, every feeling was buried beneath hurt and anger so deep. Why did he bother? Why did he bother paying down debts he hadn't incurred? Or getting up every morning and busting his butt all day to rebuild his business? Why bother caring about anyone or anything?

He took the steps to his apartment in twos, slammed and bolted the door behind him, and pulled every window shade down. He stalked to the kitchen and yanked a metal chair toward the counter with a clatter. Stepping on the chair's seat, he reached for the small cabinet above the refrigerator. Shoving aside half-empty, dusty bottles, he found the jar he sought. Moonshine.

Gripping the jar in his hand, he stepped down and kicked the chair back toward the table. His hand trembled as he poured the liquid fire into a rocks glass, spilling some onto the countertop.

I wish I had a joint.

Did he really want to go back to that way of life? Self-pity, self-destruction, and self-loathing? Indulging every whim he could—save one—as an escape. Sex was the only indulgence he wouldn't allow. He'd never toy with a woman's emotions, leaving her feeling as degraded and used as he did with Kristen. He'd satisfied his appetites with food, alcohol, and weed.

He may be a little girl's daddy. One drink, and then he'd get a grip on himself. He had to. He drained the moonshine in one gulp and trudged to his computer.

He double-clicked the search engine and typed "due date calculator" into the search engine.

The last time he'd been with Kristen was Valentine's Day of last year, hours before he'd asked her to marry him. They never had sex in the middle of the day. Kristen didn't want to muss her hair, wrinkle her clothes, or smudge her makeup. When she hadn't brushed off his advances that day, it helped him summon the courage he needed to propose.

Why was it so clear now, how she controlled and manipulated him, but so unrecognizable at the time? His sisters had always disliked Kristen, and he hadn't understood why. What a clod he'd been.

He stared at the due date widget on the screen. First day of last menstrual cycle? How the hell should he know? He typed February 14 into the calculator, the last possible date of conception. It returned a mid-November due date. The baby—a girl she'd said—would be seven or eight months old by now. He thought of Baby Ben, who was about ten months. He couldn't even change the kid's diaper. What did he know about being a dad?

Calm down. Breathe. This is Kristen. It could be a lie.

What if it were another manipulation? If it were true, why hadn't she told him sooner? If she wanted money, why wait this long to collect? He glanced at the credit card statement lying on the desk, crumpled it, and whipped it at the trashcan. And who the hell informs someone they fathered a child out of the blue with a text message?

Dan grabbed a paper and pen from the desktop and jotted down his questions. What was the baby's name and date of birth? Had she named him as the father on the birth certificate? He would demand a paternity test. His brother-in-law, Maureen's husband, was an attorney. He'd helped him with some business stuff. He'd have to trust him with this too.

He picked up his cell, ready to call Kristen and get some answers.

It buzzed in his hand.

Robert. What did he want? Had he spoken to Emily? Would he chew him out for standing her up?

"This is Dan." He blinked and rubbed his temple. The moonshine hit him, and he thought for a second he might topple out of the chair.

"Hey, you okay? Emily said you walked out on your date and left her with some chump. Said you didn't look so good. Something personal?"

"I'm okay." He shut off the computer monitor and stood.

"You sure? You don't sound okay."

Dan sighed. He desperately wanted to tell someone, to tell Robert, to vent and let it all out. But how could he? If Robert knew him even a year ago, he would've tossed him to the curb like a sack of used diapers. "Just something I have to deal with."

"This has to do with your old girlfriend, doesn't it? Did she call?"

Dan bit his lip. "She texted. She's claiming . . ." Should he tell him? What if Robert told Emily, and it turned out to be a lie? "I don't know. I was about to call her. I . . . she may be lying . . . and after money."

"Hey, don't sweat it. She's in the past."

But she *wasn't* in the past, because she refused to stay there. Dan had convinced himself he'd moved on, started over, and then another bill had shown up in his mailbox. Now this.

He ended his call with Robert and punched in Kristen's number. He blessed himself while he waited for her to pick up and realized he should have stopped and prayed before he'd called, but, as usual, he'd plowed ahead, letting his emotions rule his actions.

It rolled to voicemail.

"Kristen. You dropped a bomb in my lap, and I need some answers. Call me. Whatever the time."

He left the same message at the top of the hour for the next four hours. No response.

At midnight, he climbed into bed, laying his cell phone next to his pillow. How many of Kristen's lies had he bought, hook, line, and sinker? One likely candidate came to mind.

They'd been dating for a little over a year. That's when Kristen had begun pressuring him to have sex. Before they'd started dating, he'd been committed to waiting until he married. Although his convictions hadn't changed, over time he'd become less scrupulous, engaging in more and more behavior that pushed them dangerously close to crossing the line.

Kristen told him her doctor put her on the pill to regulate her cycle. He hadn't cared since they weren't having sex. Yet.

Kristen amped up her persuasion tactics, emphasizing that they wouldn't have to worry about a pregnancy. She plied him with vodka martinis and literally begged him. What man his age could resist that? A better man than him. Kristen had a fantastic body and a beautiful face. He thought they were in love. He was drunk. Naïve. He thought if they did it once, she'd lay off. But once wasn't enough, for either of them. Not only had he given her a part of himself he'd previously sworn to give only to his wife, but he surrendered all control in their relationship to her.

He hadn't thought to doubt or question it at the time, but later he wondered if she had really been prescribed the pill for medical reasons. She'd never complained of any problems with her cycle.

She *was* on the pill though. He'd seen her take them. So, how could she have gotten pregnant? He'd heard about it happening, a girl getting pregnant while on the pill, especially if she forgot to take it sometimes. Is that what happened with Kristen? Is that how he'd become a father? *Had* he become a father?

14

La vérité vous libèrera?

(The truth will set you free?)

The antique cuckoo clock ticked in time to the throbbing of Dan's headache. At the top of the hour, it chimed and the colorful bird emerged from the walnut door. Its intricate oak leaf design blended with the orange and brown kitchen wallpaper—also antique.

Seated at the undersized telephone table in Grandma's living room, Dan scrubbed his palm over his face and stared at her checkbook ledger. The aroma of fresh-baked chocolate chip cookies lingered in the air causing his stomach to rumble. He tapped through each entry with a pencil point, mentally reducing her balance as he went. He'd been through it three times now, and he still couldn't find the problem.

"One last time—" He smacked a palm to the table. "There. Found it."

"What was it?" Grandma flattened the newspaper in her lap, circling a death notice with a red Sharpie.

Dan erased two-digits and swapped them. "Transposed number." He recalculated the balance. "That's it. All reconciled, Grandma."

"About time. That one had you stumped." Grandma set her newspaper on the end table and leaned forward in her recliner rocker. "Do we still have time for groceries?"

He glanced at the cuckoo clock. "We sure do. You have your list?"

She used the strength of both arms to hoist herself out of the chair then shuffled to the foyer for her purse and cane. Once a strong and active woman, Grandma had slowed considerably in the past year. Her posture stooped, and she was less steady on her feet. Her mind remained sharp, despite a tendency to confuse words and names.

After forty-five minutes in the store, he'd helped her locate every item on her list then loaded the groceries into the trunk of the car she no longer drove herself. Dan used it to drive her to her appointments and errands.

"The cashier was pretty, wasn't she? And I didn't see a ring on her finger." She pressed her right foot into the passenger side floor as they approached a red light.

He tried to recall the cashier and came up with nothing.

"She had the prettiest eyes."

Now, he remembered. He couldn't recall her eyes, only her raccoon-like eye makeup. "She must be at least ten or twelve years older than me."

Grandma shrugged and gazed out her window. "She looked young to me."

Well, relative to eighty-five, seventy was young.

"How old are you now, Daniel? Twenty-five?"

"Twenty-eight." He glanced between her and the road.

"Almost thirty. You should be filling your wife's belly with babies, not chauffeuring some old lady around town." She repositioned the cane at her feet.

Not gonna touch that. Dread pitted in his stomach at the thought of telling his devout grandmother that he'd fathered a child out of wedlock.

He patted her leg. "You're not some old lady, Grandma. I love you. I'm happy to take you where you need to go."

She smiled, wrinkling her fair but freckled face even further. "There's no one special? I would think a good-looking, hard-working young man like yourself would be beating off the girls with a stick."

He laughed. "Not exactly." His thoughts turned to Emily. Special but unattainable. He'd seen to that when he'd left her at the restaurant with Matt.

It had been nine days, and still no word from Kristen. He'd swung by her old apartment only to learn she'd moved a year ago. She had one more day before he contacted a private investigator. With each passing day, he became more confident that her message was a ploy to get money out of him. If she really needed the money for the baby, she would have returned the call immediately.

He carried Grandma's groceries into her house and helped her put them away.

"I'm going to head out. You need anything else before I go?" He leaned in and kissed her cheek.

"Just a minute." She hobbled to the freezer, removed several small baggies, and placed them in an empty grocery bag. "Take some cookies with you. And banana nut bread."

"You know I never refuse your baking." He slipped the bag handles over his wrist.

Fifteen minutes later, he pushed open the door of his apartment, kicked off his tennis shoes, and set his goodies on the counter. He checked his phone, which he'd turned off while he was with Grandma. One voicemail message. His gut tightened, and he clenched his fists. Could it finally be Kristen calling back? He played the message back.

"Dan, my attorney came up with a total for you."

Kristen. His neck heated, anger rising.

"So, you can write a check, and I'm, uh, in the process of moving, so I'll give you the post office box you can send it to. Call me."

Convinced more than ever it was a con job, he punched in her number and tapped his foot frantically on the floor, waiting for her to pick up.

"Hello."

A burning sensation crept up his chest into his throat. "It's Dan." He was tempted to let loose on her. Why hadn't she told him? Where was his daughter? Instead, he stuck to business. He had a better chance of ferreting out the truth if he kept calm. "Listen, before I write a check, there're a few things I need to know."

Silence came from the other end of the phone.

"I want to know my daughter's name and date of birth. I'd also like to have a paternity test done before we set up child support and visitation."

Silence. What? She didn't expect any of that? Did she take him for a fool? Stupid question. He had been a fool. She expected him to hand over his wallet, no questions asked.

"Like I said, I'm moving. It would be simplest if you sent a check now, and then once I'm settled, I'll be in touch about the other stuff." Her voice was strained and squeaky.

Dan clenched his jaw and gripped the phone tighter. She was lying. "What's her name, Kristen? What's she look like?"

"Her name's B-Bella, and she looks just like you. Same hair and eyes. Really, you don't need the paternity test."

"Bella, huh?" Was he a dad after all? "I'd like the test all the same."

"Uh, okay. Yeah. We can do that, but, I mean, we've got to schedule it and all. I need the money right away. Formula's like, crazy expensive."

Dan winced. She wouldn't let the baby go hungry, would she? *His* baby? The responsibility gnawed at him, tearing at his gut. "I never priced it."

"Yeah, well, you didn't need to. I did." She let out a scoffing laugh—condescending but with a trace of unease. "So, let me give you the box number."

"Uh, box number," he repeated mindlessly. His question came back to mind, and he blurted it out. "So, when's her birthday?"

"Uh, December eighth."

Dan switched the phone to his other ear. "Huh." He caught her. It was almost too easy. "I guess we don't need that paternity test after all. Cuz there's no way Bella's my baby. The last time we were, uh, together was Valentine's Day. Even if that's when you got pregnant, and she was crazy late, she would've been born in November."

Kristen's breathing came quick and shallow on the other end of the line.

The tension left Dan's body, and a grin spread across his face. It was over. "Kristen, if you needed money, you could've asked." *I would've said no, but you could've asked.*

"Dan, just a couple grand." Pleading sounded in her voice. "I have a new job, I just need to put a down payment on—"

"Goodbye, Kristen. Don't contact me again." He ended the call and slid the phone across the counter.

Dan flopped on the couch. In an instant, all the energy drained from his body the way a coin rolled around a wide funnel in ever smaller concentric circles until it disappeared altogether.

The thought that he had missed the first months of his baby's life rattled him. But the prospect of being tied to Kristen for the rest of his life? That sapped every bit of hope he held for ever stuffing that part of his life firmly behind him and moving forward with a clean slate.

Despite his relief, a surprising twinge of disappointment surfaced. Proof he'd been spending too much time with Robert's family. Sure, he wanted kids of his own, but not until he'd found a woman to marry. He'd thought maybe it would be Emily, but now he'd never have the opportunity to find out.

The initial relief wore off, and realizing he was hungry, Dan pushed off the couch and checked the refrigerator. He rubbed his stomach, trying to suppress the hunger pangs. He could dig into Grandma's cookies or eat some real food. Only no real food existed in his refrigerator. Why hadn't he picked up something when he was at the grocery store?

He'd have to go out. A celebration was in order anyway. Too bad he had no one to celebrate with—a consequence of keeping the whole thing a secret.

In a half hour, he sat at the bar at Pappy's Chaps, still craving the fish sandwich he'd missed out on the week before. He sipped root beer from a bottle and stared at the Pittsburgh Pirates game on the screen hanging above the bar.

The bar and tables filled as the evening wore on. Dan's humongous fish sandwich and fries were gone, his bottle empty. He had no reason to stick around except that he wanted the company of other people.

At the end of the bar, a redhead with pale skin and freckles smiled as she sipped her drink. Dan nodded his head and averted his glance. He wasn't interested in starting a new relationship at a bar. His gaze drifted to the dance floor. He lifted his arm to drain the last drops of root beer from his bottle when recognition stilled his arm. The bottle hit the bar with a thud.

Matt swayed in a dark corner of the dance floor, his arms wrapped around Emily's waist. She wore a black skirt that twirled around her knees as she moved and a flowered blouse that brought out the beautiful auburn of her hair.

Dan's jaw clenched. He had no right to be irritated or jealous. After all, he'd essentially set them up on a first date last week.

Matt spun Emily around, and she threw back her head and laughed. The song was all about "settin' you free" and "fallin' in love." Matt's hand roved over her shoulders and back. One date, and he'd managed to engender more familiarity with Emily than Dan had over months.

Dan's leg bounced on the barstool. Should he slink out the door like the defeated coward he was or march over and say hello?

Matt leaned in and tried to kiss Emily's neck. She pulled back and gave him a look. A 'what-the-heck-are-you-doing' look. He said something, she smiled, and they resumed dancing. The fact that Emily had leaned into *his* almost-kiss and not pulled away like she had with Matt gave him the nudge he needed.

He settled the bill with the bartender and sauntered across the room.

Matt led Emily towards a booth at the edge of the dance floor, the same booth they'd sat at last week.

Dan swallowed hard, lunged forward, and tapped Emily's arm.

She stopped, pulling Matt with her.

"Dan the Man, didn't expect to see you here." Matt, looking like a weasel who'd just acquired access to the local Chick-Fil-A, slapped Dan on the shoulder. "Everything good? You didn't look so good when you cut out on us last week. Not that I'm complaining." His smile and his gaze shifted to Emily, and he slipped an arm around her waist, pulling her closer.

Her feet shuffled toward Matt, but once she had her footing, she took a small step away. Her chin lifted, and her lips quirked in a sort of frown.

"Everything's great. Thanks for asking." He turned his gaze to Emily. "I apologize for having to leave like that." He wanted to say more, to explain there were few things that could have pulled him away from her that night. The text from Kristen happened to be one of them. But he wouldn't say more in front of Matt, and he wasn't ready to have that conversation with Emily.

She dipped her chin in response, but her eyes showed no sign of forgiveness. He could be content with remaining her friend but not with her being angry with him.

"Matt, I'm sure you won't mind if I steal Emily for one dance."

Matt's mouth opened then shut, and the left side of his lips rose in a sly grin. Oh, he minded all right, but he probably didn't want to look like a possessive, jealous jerk.

"Not at all." He released Emily's hand and smiled at her.

Emily stood there staring, not moving.

"Emily?" Dan motioned toward the center of the dance floor. "One dance? Please?"

She hesitated then let out a breath and stepped toward him.

Grateful for a chance to make things right, Dan took her hand and led her back to the dance floor. A slow George Strait number started. Perfect.

He found a spot away from the speaker where she would be able to hear him. He stopped and held out his hands as she turned to face him.

Her gaze flitted from one open hand to the other. She took a half step toward him and placed her left hand in his right.

Dan made up the space between them and rested his free hand on her back.

She turned her head away from his, limiting her view to the restroom entrance and a stack of crusty high chairs and booster seats.

"Emily."

She faced him. "Dan."

He shook his head. "Is this so awful? Dancing with me?"

"No, but I don't get *why* we're dancing. Did you want to talk to me, tell me what happened last week?"

Dan's stomach knotted. This dance was a mistake. So, she was miffed with him. He should've let it alone. "Like I said, I'm sorry. I'd been looking forward to our date all week. I couldn't wait for you to get here. And you looked . . ."

She batted her eyes and her feet slowed, throwing off their rhythm.

"You looked so pretty. You do tonight too, by the way."

Her eyes glistened. "But?"

His throat tightened. Now wasn't the time for details. "I got a message I couldn't ignore. I had to resolve it."

"It took all week to resolve? Because I didn't get any messages from you this week. No text message, no voicemail. Robert didn't say anything." Her gaze dropped to their feet. "I was worried about you, okay?"

The tightness in his throat and chest eased. "Actually, I just got it resolved this afternoon." He nodded toward the bar. "This was me, celebrating."

Emily lifted an eyebrow. "By yourself, at the bar?"

Dan shrugged.

She averted her gaze. "You could've had company." Her tone bordered on snide. "The red-head was eyeing you up."

One side of Dan's mouth lifted in a grin. "You were watching me."

Emily's cheeks reddened, and she glanced back toward her booth with Matt. "You're distracting me from the point. Why so vague and secretive? Don't you owe me some reason, some explanation for leaving so abruptly?"

Dan rubbed circles on her back with his hand. The smooth fabric of her top was cool against his calloused hand. This felt so good, having her close like this. "Trust me, Emily. If there was any way I could've stayed, I would have."

Her hand tensed in his. "Trust you? When clearly you don't trust me?"

Dan's feet stopped and irritation crept into his voice. "What's that supposed to mean?"

"You don't trust me with the truth. Unless you're the mild-mannered cover for some superhero, I think the problem is fairly obvious—you're hiding something from your past. How little do you think of me that you can't tell me? You don't think I've made mistakes? Made poor decisions? Am I such a self-righteous, holier-than-thou little b—?"

"No. That's not it. Why would you think that?"

"You haven't told me anything to the contrary. I have to assume—"

"You assume wrong." He dropped his hand from her back, the other holding hers between them. "It had nothing to do with you."

"And neither do you, Dan." She wrenched her hand away from his. "You're a coward and a liar. And you care more about your pride than you do about me." Her eyes welled with tears. "Goodbye."

She spun around and bolted to her table, to Matt.

A couple bumped into him from behind and muttered their apologies. Dan blinked, then forced his feet off the floor, one after the other. Emily's accusations stung, mostly because they were true.

15

Une mission de miséricorde
(Mission of mercy)

Emily crossed the freshly-mowed yard, clumps of bright-green grass sticking to the soles of her sandals, probably staining her toes. She inhaled deeply, enjoying the scent of grass mixed with wood smoke and food grilling. A screech followed by a bawling howl came from behind Robert and Elizabeth's house. Sounded like Clara and Tessa. Or maybe Gianna.

As she rounded the house toward the backyard, Emily admired the new patio. The flagstones blended seamlessly with large stepping stones and dry-stacked walls of fieldstone. Small copper-topped lights bordered raised beds filled with grasses, shrubs, and flowering perennials. A couple of small river birches were bordered by spotlights that would make the area come alive at night. Dan had done a fantastic job.

Half a dozen plastic dinosaurs lay sprawled beneath large green leaves along the fence. They looked as if they were in their natural habitat. Emily grinned. Elizabeth had said the kids enjoyed the yard more now that there was something to hold their interest and spark their imaginations.

The gate clicked shut behind her, and Clara, Tessa, and Max ran toward her—or the plastic container of pumpkin Snickerdoodles she held.

"Auntie Em, can I have one? Can I, can I?" Max licked his lips, his gaze never leaving the container.

"Me too. Tessa hun'gwy." Tessa hopped up and down, pretending to grab at the cookies.

"Sorry gang, they're for after dinner." Elizabeth reached over her kids' heads and took the container from Emily.

"It smells wonderful. Are you grilling portabellas?" Emily followed the delicious aroma to the grill.

"You got it." Robert sauntered from the house with a platter of hot dogs and fixings and set it alongside the grill. He pulled his iPhone from his pocket and fiddled with it until the sounds of blues music filled the air. Robert could never get enough of Stevie Ray Vaughn.

Emily turned her head from side-to-side, scouring the yard for the source of the music. Nothing. "Where's the speaker?"

Robert smiled and pointed behind her. "Right there."

Emily spun around, her gaze scanning the huge bunches of daisies, some ivy-like ground cover, and a couple of big rocks. She recognized a distinctly square-shaped stone with browns and gold throughout that she and Dan had hauled from the farmer's field. It jogged the memory of her tumble in the mud that day. And then of Dan, his jeans and his face streaked with mud. She shook the memory away. "Uh, *where's* the speaker?"

Robert laughed. "Right there." He pointed again.

"Right where?"

He stepped around her and walked into the flowerbed, tapping the largest of the mini-boulders.

Emily noticed the circle of small holes on the side facing the patio. "That's a speaker? It blends in perfectly."

"I know. Cool, isn't it?" He grinned as he plunked the hot dogs onto the grill grate.

"Yeah. I would never have spotted it." Dan excelled at what he did. No doubt about it.

When Elizabeth had texted the invitation for the impromptu cookout this afternoon, Emily had called to ask if Dan would be there. After an exasperated sigh, Elizabeth confirmed he wasn't coming. So, why then did she miss him?

"So, where's Dan tonight?" Did he have other plans? A date?

Elizabeth shot her a look. Busted. Then she proceeded to set out paper plates and plastic ware around the picnic table.

"Not sure why you'd care," Elizabeth said through a grin, "since you take great pains to avoid him, but he's sick."

"Sick? In the middle of summer?" Emily grabbed a pile of paper napkins and began folding them. "What's wrong with him?"

Elizabeth shrugged. "Robert, what's wrong with Dan?" she called toward the grill.

"Sounded awful when I called him. I don't know how he worked all day. Said he's got a fever, chills, sore throat, a headache. Summer cold or something, I guess."

Emily bit the inside of her cheek trying to quash the maternal instinct cropping up in her. Why did she suddenly want to take him a pot of chicken noodle soup and lay a cool cloth across his forehead? A grown man could take care of himself.

"Ouch! Dammit!" Robert kicked away Tessa's push car, which had careened across the patio and into his leg. He rubbed the scraped skin on his leg and examined his toe, the front of which appeared to be bleeding. "Elizabeth, can you get me a Band-Aid?"

Who was she kidding? Her brother, her father, her nephew—they wanted to be babied when they were sick or injured.

Elizabeth ran into and out of the house in a flash and offered Robert a bandage for his toe. She turned and rolled her eyes at Emily, mouthing the word "helpless."

Emily gave her a half-grin and joined her at the table as she set out the napkins, salt, and ketchup. "Do you think Dan's okay?"

"You two are going to drive me crazy." Elizabeth shook her head. "I wish you'd make up your minds and either be together or not." She huffed a breath. "I'm sure he's not in danger of death."

Emily set plastic cups with water in front of each of the kids' places. "Do you think if I . . . if I took him soup or something, he would take it the wrong way?"

"I don't even know what 'the wrong way' is, Emily." She stroked Clara's silky hair. Twisting under her mom's touch, the little girl gripped Elizabeth's waist and rubbed her nose against her mom's shorts. "It's a kind gesture. It shows you care, but depending on the day of the week or some other whim, I don't know if you want him to think you care or not."

Baby Ben cried from his swing, where he'd come to a complete stop. He thrashed his legs, trying to gain some momentum. Emily strolled over and gave the swing a push. Ben giggled with glee and kicked his legs.

Elizabeth came over, grabbing Ben's bare feet as he swung forward. Ben belly laughed.

Emily leaned against the slide ladder. The hot dogs plumped on the grill, their juices probably oozing from the little holes Robert's fork had left behind. Her belly panged with hunger.

"I don't know what it is with you two, but if you want to check in on him, do it." Elizabeth unbuckled Ben and lifted him from the swing. "I'm sure he'd appreciate it."

Emily stilled the empty swing. "I don't want him to think it's some kind of romantic gesture. We're not going down that road, but obviously we're still connected, cuz of all of you."

"Sure, blame us." Elizabeth's tone was teasing as she slid Ben into his high chair. "If he's as sick as Dan says, I doubt he's thinking about anything romantic anyway."

***

Emily stood on Dan's stoop holding a plastic grocery bag. She knocked for the third time, her foot tapping against the concrete. Maybe he was asleep. Maybe if she called him he'd hear the—

The door swung open. Dan leaned against its edge, as if he needed it to hold him up. His hair stood on end, the dark brown a contrast to his pasty complexion. His eyes were dull and tired, and a five o'clock shadow bristled his cheeks. He wore a black, faded Lynyrd Skynyrd tee shirt with a small hole on the side and a pair of navy basketball shorts.

"Emily? What're you doing here?" His voice was raspy.

She lifted the plastic bag in her hand. "I heard you were sick. Thought maybe you could use some soup. It's not homemade, but . . ." She shrugged a shoulder.

"Thanks." He held out his hand as if to take it from her then glanced over his shoulder. "I'd invite you in, but I don't want you to catch this."

Emily pushed past him, and he backed up to let her pass.

He didn't look to be in any condition to prepare a meal. She'd warm it for him on the stove. "Don't worry about me. I have a strong immune system. I'll just heat this up for you."

"Thanks," he mumbled as he closed the door and plodded toward the couch. He dragged a frayed, tan afghan off the back then, despite the heat, bundled himself.

Dan's small, nondescript kitchen featured a tiny, basic model gas stove. The entire space was bare and dim, lit only by a single recessed light. The beige countertop, which matched the beige walls, was littered with empty cups and a smattering of crumbs that trailed from a stainless steel toaster. She lit a burner and began opening cabinets in search of a saucepan. Finding one, she set it on the burner and poured in the quart of chicken noodle soup she'd bought at the grocery store.

Wrapped in his afghan, Dan shuffled to his Formica table and sat on a cushioned chair with a large piece of gray duct tape across the back. It looked like a vintage set you'd find in an antique shop. Or a dump.

The lid clattered as she fitted it on the saucepan. Then she turned to Dan and laid her palm across his forehead. "You're hot."

Dan gave her a weak smile. "That's what the women tell me."

She rolled her eyes. "I mean, you've got a fever. Have you taken any medicine?"

"Nah. It'll burn itself out." He pulled the blanket tighter.

"Did you take your temperature? That's not a low-grade fever." She grabbed a wooden spoon from a tin container on the counter and stirred the soup. "Where's your thermometer?"

"I don't have one."

"For goodness sake, Dan, this can't be the first time you've ever been sick." She plunked the spoon down on the stovetop.

"I don't need a thermometer to tell me I've got a fever."

Dan loosened his afghan and let it fall over the back of the chair and onto the floor. "Emily, why are you here?"

Her pulse kicked up a notch. Why was she here? "Random act of kindness."

She turned and began opening cupboards and drawers in search of a bowl and a spoon.

"On your right. First shelf."

"Thank you." She placed the bowl on the counter and stirred the soup. The warm, hearty aroma filled the kitchen.

"I don't think it qualifies as random if we know each other."

He was right, so she ignored his comment. She turned off the burner, ladled soup into the bowl, and slid it in front of him.

"Thank you." His eyes closed as he breathed deeply. Steam wafted from the bowl into his face. Then he bowed his head for a few seconds before he dipped his spoon into the broth and lifted it to his mouth.

Uncomfortable watching him eat, Emily surveyed the room for something to do. The living area consisted of an overstuffed couch that had seen better days, a wingback chair, a large cathode ray TV, wooden coffee table, and a bookcase filled to capacity. A dark hallway sat at the opposite end of the room, presumably the way to his bathroom and bedroom. The kitchen didn't look lived in save for a scraggly spider plant on the windowsill and a small pile of dirty dishes in the sink. Once he finished his soup, she'd wash those along with the pot and bowl. Her gaze travelled the rest of the room to the refrigerator. A crayon-colored stick figure on construction paper hung by a magnet. Probably something one of her nieces or nephews made. In the upper corner was a snapshot of—her and Dan?

She'd never seen the picture, but she remembered when it was taken.

The night they'd babysat together, Max made it his mission to take an "epic selfie." She and Dan both admitted to being horrible at taking selfies, but Dan offered to try in order to show Max how to do it. He must've had a print made. Why?

"Emily?"

She hadn't realized how far her attention had drifted. "Yeah?"

"I don't think I can eat anymore. It hit the spot though. Felt good on my throat."

"Good." To ensure he wouldn't get the wrong idea from her visit, she gathered up his dishes and took them to the counter with the efficiency of a busy waitress.

He glanced at her through heavy-lidded eyes and gave the hint of a smile.

She riffled through a deep drawer until she found a Tupperware container for the leftovers and filled it with the soup. Hot water rose in the sink as she added a squirt of detergent.

He stood, grabbed his blanket, and pushed in his chair, leaning on it for support. "What are you doing, Em?"

Em? He was giving her a nickname? Her heart did its little flippy thing. And she was worried about *him* getting the wrong idea? "I'm doing your dishes." She sunk her hands into the warm soapy water.

"You don't have to do that."

"No big deal. There's only a few." She rinsed a small plate and set it in the drying rack. "You should rest."

He trudged to the living room, reclined on the couch, and bundled in his afghan. His eyes closed.

She finished the dishes and dried her hands with a paper towel. In the living room, she spotted a laundry basket filled with towels alongside his chair. In minutes, she'd folded all his bath towels, hand towels, and washcloths.

Dan groaned, but didn't open his eyes. Sweat beaded along his brow.

She grabbed a washcloth from the basket, ran it under cold water, and wrung it out. As she laid it over his forehead, a warm feeling stirred inside her. This was exactly what she'd imagined doing when she'd learned he was sick.

"Mmmm. Thank you," he murmured. He seemed barely conscious.

"You okay here tonight?"

"Huh? Yeah. I'll be all right."

He couldn't even open his eyes to answer, and she was expected to believe he'd be fine and dandy here? She supposed he would be. All he'd likely do was sleep.

"I'll call you in the morning to check on you, okay? You need anything, call me."

He shook his head. "Won't be here. Gotta take Grandma shopping."

Emily laughed. "You are in no condition to take anyone anywhere. *Especially* not your grandmother. You don't want to get her sick too, do you?"

Dan's eyelids half-opened. "She needs groceries. And it's her routine. We shop on Saturdays."

"Oh, for goodness sake. I'll take her shopping." She fluffed a dingy, stained throw pillow on the opposite end of the couch and repositioned it. "I'm not having you go over there and give the poor old woman pneumonia. Give me her phone number." She braced for a protest, but none came.

Dan repeated the phone number, and Emily put it into her phone.

"You sure you're okay?"

"Yep. Nothing that sleep and lots of fluids won't cure." He moved to open his blanket and get off the couch.

She held up a hand. "Stay put. This place is the size of a matchbox." *And about as inviting.* "I can find my way to the door."

He grinned and leaned back on the couch. "Thank you. You're an angel."

"You're welcome. And you're delirious with fever." She resisted the urge to run her hand over his hair and kiss his head. "Rest."

"Yes, ma'am."

***

Emily closed the cupboard on the last of Grandma's groceries. She scooped up the plastic bags scattered over the kitchen floor, balled them up, and shoved them into another bag. "There. I think we're done, Grandma."

Emily had called her to introduce herself and make plans after she left Dan's. At first his grandma had been confused, but Emily explained twice she was a friend of Dan's, and he was sick. The elderly woman had asked Emily right off to call her "Grandma."

Shopping had gone smoothly, despite the fact Emily had to learn what brand of products Grandma wanted and where to find them in the grocery store.

"Good, now we can have a treat and get to know each other." Grandma opened the freezer and pushed aside a half-dozen Zip-loc bags in search of something.

"Oh. Okay." The cuckoo clock chimed noon. She had plenty of time to go home and clean her apartment. Grandma probably looked forward to Dan's company on Saturday more than anything else. She could stay and chat.

Grandma shuffled to the counter and stacked large chocolate chip cookies onto a plate. She carried them to the table, hobbling as she went. "Can I get you something to drink? Milk or tea or a glass of wine?"

A glass of wine? It was barely after noon. Grandma was a firecracker. "Milk always goes well with cookies." Emily sat at the square, wooden table for two. "These look delicious. They're homemade?"

"Oh, yes." Grandma lowered herself onto her chair, the seat of which she'd raised with a square throw pillow. "I make chocolate chips two or three times a week."

"That's a lot of cookies. What do you do with all them?"

"I like to keep them on hand to take to people. Grieving families, new moms. I deliver little packages to the girls in the doctor's office, the hairdresser, the mailman. Dan eats his share." She smiled as if they shared a special secret concerning Dan. "So, how did you two meet?"

Emily recounted their initial meeting at the tree lot and then how Dan and Robert had become friends. She dunked a cookie into her milk and took a bite. Sweet, rich comfort food baked with love. Couldn't be beat.

"I imagine you and Dan will have very beautiful babies." Grandma smiled around a mouthful of cookie.

Emily swallowed her mouthful. The delicious morsel dropped like lead to the pit of her stomach. A walnut lodged in her throat. She coughed, scrambled for her cup, and took another sip of milk. "I'm sorry if you misunderstood, but Dan and I are just friends. We aren't even dating."

Grandma waved a hand as if she were swatting a pesky flea. "Oh, goodness. I don't believe that for a minute. There was none of this 'just friends' nonsense when I was young."

"Well, tell that to your grandson." Emily took another cookie and bit into it. Hard.

"I will." Grandma dabbed her mouth with a paper napkin. "I'm surprised he hasn't mentioned you."

It stung a little that he hadn't, but then why should he? They hadn't had a real date.

"Oh, wait now." Grandma tapped a rhythm on the table, as if it would help her recall. "Are you the young lady he got all mud-covered with?"

Emily grinned at the memory. "We found some fieldstone, and, yes, we, uh, got a little dirty."

"A little? He came over here caked in mud. I had him strip down to his shorts, and I washed everything with a double shot of Oxyclean."

With reluctance, Emily dismissed the mental picture of Dan in his underwear.

"And now I'm certain that friends bit is nonsense. He talked all about you and your pretty hair and how much spunk you have."

Emily's cheeks reddened. Dan liked her hair? He thought she was spunky?

"That boy had better get a move on. I want to be at his wedding, and I'm not getting any younger." She blessed herself. "Thank God things ended with that b-i-t-c-h."

Emily jerked back in her seat then hid a grin. Grandma didn't mince words.

"I know he took it hard, but it was the best thing that ever happened to him. Marrying that woman would have been a disaster. Dan deserves a woman that cares about him and not what she can wring out of him."

Emily's brows rose. Grandma had dropped more information about Dan's shady history than she'd ever heard. She was tempted to ask for more detail, but she stifled the thought. It wasn't any of her business. If Dan wanted her to know, he'd tell her.

"Dan has never spoken about her." Emily glanced down and brushed the crumbs from her blouse. "I don't think he cares to share anything that personal with me."

Grandma sighed. "He's embarrassed is all." She shook her head. "Boy's got more pride than he's got sense. Lucky for him, he's got a handsome mug."

Emily smiled. That, he did.

16

Pressés encore ensemble
(Thrust together again)

Dan held the screwdriver loosely between his thumb and forefinger as he lowered the cover on the bathroom fan. He backed down the stepladder, shook the desiccated bugs from the cover into the trash, then rinsed it clean.

The walls of Grandma's Pepto-Bismol pink bathroom hemmed in on him and the scent of baby powder filled his nostrils—a combination that made him queasy.

"Did you know Emily dreamed of being a French expert?" Grandma's gaze met his in the bathroom mirror as she sat on top of the commode, supervising his work. The simple bulb replacement was likely the highlight of her day.

"No, I didn't. Can she speak French?"

"Four years in high school and a college minor." Grandma used a piece of toilet paper to wipe clean the dust gathering on the toilet tank.

"So, why didn't she do that or teach French or something?" Dan tapped the cover against the sink and wiped it dry with a rag.

"When her parents died, money was tight. Robert couldn't afford to send her to France to study." She crumpled the dusty wad of toilet paper in her fist. "At that point, she wanted to stick close to home anyway."

It was bad enough he had a hard time keeping his mind from wandering to Emily in his idle moments. Now every visit to Grandma included an Emily update. He had learned more about Emily from Grandma over the last month than he had in speaking to Emily over the course of six months.

Somehow she had ferreted out all kinds of trivia, all of which Dan turned over in his heart and committed to memory. He'd learned Emily had an allergy to amoxicillin, she'd bought her first bra when she was thirteen, she despised rap music, and she'd competed on her school swim team.

Emily and Grandma had hit it off so well, that Emily had begun taking her to the library on Wednesday evenings and visited her most Sunday afternoons.

Dan climbed the ladder, removed the blackened bulb, and screwed in the new one.

"Emily is taking me to Mass on Wednesday." Grandma reached a hand around the shower stall to steady his ladder.

"I take you to Mass, Grandma. And why Wednesday?"

"You take me on Sunday, but there's a Mass for Grand Pap on Wednesday morning. You have work, so I asked Emily since she's done with summer school. And she said she'd take me."

"Okay." Dan was being replaced. Emily was stealing his grandma. "She's really generous with her time."

"Well, she has plenty. No boyfriend." The ladder wobbled, and her bony hand whitened as she gripped it tighter. "Just that friend of yours, Mark. She goes out with him sometimes."

"His name's Matt." She was still seeing him? He jammed the bulb into the socket and wrenched it into place.

"Whatever his name is, I don't think she cares much for him."

He wouldn't touch that one. Whether she cared or not was none of his business, even if the thought did cause his heart to race. He held the light cover in place and pushed the first screw into the hole.

Grandma released the ladder and sunk back onto the commode. "Emily's a virgin, you know."

The screwdriver clattered down the metal ladder and hit the porcelain tub. The cover fell onto the top of the ladder, and he slapped a hand over it. "You didn't *ask* her that, did you?"

"Of course not," she said, folding her hands in her lap. "She's never had a boyfriend, and except for this Mark—"

"Matt."

"Matt, she's never dated a man more than a month. She's a sweet Catholic girl, not out bonking guys she meets in bars."

Dan climbed down and retrieved the screwdriver. "Bonking?"

"Is there another term you'd rather I use?"

"No, I just . . . don't you think that's kind of personal?" He climbed the ladder and pushed the cover into place. "I don't know if she wants you talking about all this with me."

She sighed. "I didn't think there were any nice girls left. All I see on the TV is you young people rolling around in bed together."

"Hey, I know I made a lot of mistakes with Kristen, that being the biggest . . ." He tightened one screw and then the other. "But I've barely kissed a woman in the past year and a half."

"'Barely kissed?' What's that? You either kissed her or you didn't."

Technically their lips had touched—on several occasions. He fixed his gaze on the light fixture, willing himself not to conjure up the soft feel of Emily's lips and the sweetness of her breath. "We kissed."

"Who?"

Dan grinned. "Uh-uh. I love you, but that's none of your business."

She pushed off the toilet and shuffled to the doorway. "Of course it's not. Emily's so open with me. I guess I forgot how stingy you are with information." She stepped into the hallway, not looking back. "I can ask Emily. Maybe she knows who you kissed."

***

Dan flicked through the cable menu. Nothing. Nothing live, nothing on demand, nothing on Netflix that interested him that he hadn't already seen. He tossed the remote on the end table and grabbed the newspaper instead. Lots of back-to-school articles and ads—backpacks, pencils, a gross of glue sticks. Nothing about that pertained to him. How was Emily's school year going? He hadn't run into her since he'd been sick a couple months ago. He'd texted her a thank you for the soup, and she'd responded with only a smiley emoji.

The phone rang, and he picked it up without looking at the caller ID.

"Dan, it's Robert. Hey, man. I need a big favor." His voice sounded strained, panicky.

"Sure." He folded the newspaper and slid it to the end of the table. "What's up?"

"I've got to take Elizabeth to the hospital, and we need someone to stay with the kids. They're all asleep. You just have to be here in the house with them. I tried calling Emily, but she's not picking up."

Dan grabbed his tennis shoes and slipped them onto his bare feet. "I'll be right there. Is Elizabeth okay?"

Robert sighed. "She's pregnant. Seven weeks." His voice was low. "We think she's losing the baby. Something's not right."

"O-okay. I'll be there in fifteen minutes." He had assumed their disagreement about having another baby had been resolved, and apparently it had, but not the way he'd thought.

Dan shoved his cell phone in his pocket, laced his shoes, and grabbed his keys.

Ten minutes later, he pulled his truck in front of Robert and Elizabeth's house and took the steps two at a time.

Robert stood at the door, waiting. "You won't need to stay long. Emily called me back. She'll be in here in fifteen minutes. Elizabeth's in the van." He nodded toward the street. "We're gonna go now."

"Go. I've got this. And Robert—?"

"Yeah?" He turned, halfway down the steps.

"Tell Elizabeth I'm praying."

"Got it. Thanks."

After the minivan pulled away from the curb, he stepped inside the house. It was eerily quiet, and only a floor lamp in the corner lit the living room. The floor was cleared and uncluttered, the toys all in their places. He'd never been there this time of night when some order had been restored. The light on the baby monitor flickered, signaling it was on, but no sound came from it. He walked from Max's room to the girls' room and then the nursery, checking on the sleeping children. Eleven o'clock and all was well. At least at home. The story at the hospital might be different. He prayed Elizabeth and the baby would be okay.

He sat on the couch and rested his hands on his legs, staring at the photos of the kids on the mantle across the room. Their Auntie Em would be here soon. His muscles twitched, and his nerves twanged. *Friends, friends, friends.* He repeated the mantra.

A key turned in the lock, and the door clicked open.

Emily. Three brown plastic clips held her damp hair up in various places. She wore glasses, an oversized pink tee shirt, and Pink Panther sleep pants. Her feet were bare. She looked both a wreck and more beautiful than he'd ever seen her.

He stood and walked toward the door. It wasn't objectively possible that she grew prettier each time he saw her, especially not in her current state. Yet he'd never found her more attractive than tonight.

She pulled the door closed behind her. "I'm sorry you had to rush over. I didn't hear the phone the first time Robert called." Her voice had a nasal tone to it, as if she had a cold.

"You okay? You sound all stuffed up."

"I am. I caught something."

"Can't blame me. We're well past the incubation period." He recalled her laying a cool cloth across his warm head. Better than Florence Nightingale.

She sniffed, fished a tissue from her pocket and wiped her nose. "I sent three kids home with it this week. This is day three. I'm actually much better. I'm down to scratchy throat and head congestion."

"What happened to that all-powerful immune system of yours?" Seeing her tissue was near to disintegrating, he grabbed another from a box on the edge of the counter and handed it to her.

"Thank you." She blew her nose then pulled a small bottle of hand sanitizer from her pocket. "Why don't you go home?" It was more an offer than a demand. She kneaded her hands, and the scent of rubbing alcohol filled the air.

"I can stay."

"They're my family. I got it."

"I've got my grandma too, but that doesn't keep you away." He smiled to let her know he was teasing.

She grinned then sniffed. "Your grandma's the best. You're blessed."

He smiled. "I know it. She's great."

Emily went to the kitchen, opened the cupboard and fished a cough drop from somewhere in its recesses.

"Do you usually wear contact lenses?"

Emily touched her glasses. "Yeah. Since seventh grade." She settled on the couch then pulled her legs underneath her.

Dan sat next to her. "I didn't know that. And more surprising, apparently Grandma doesn't know because she hasn't shared it with me."

Emily laughed then coughed. "There's a lot you don't know about me. And plenty I don't tell your grandma."

He raised a brow. She had secrets?

In seconds, her expression slid from happy to concerned and then sad.

"Hey, what's wrong?"

She dabbed at her eyes under her glasses. "I'm worried about the baby. They were so excited. I know Robert was a little reluctant about adding a sixth kid to the mix, but he was thrilled about the baby. He always is."

Dan wanted to hold her and comfort her. Stroke her hair and tell her it would be all right. But he didn't have a right to act so familiar with her despite how he felt when they were together like this. He settled for rubbing her back for a few seconds. "Do you want to pray for them? A Rosary?"

She wiped her eyes again and uncurled her legs. "Yeah, I don't have my beads though." Emily eyed him carefully, as if trying to gauge whether his question was serious. "I left my purse at home."

He leaned and pulled his rosary beads from a back pocket. "I've got mine." He let the simple black beads slide through his fingertips. "How about you rest your voice and let me lead?"

A small, slow smile curled her lips. "Sounds good."

In twenty minutes, they'd completed the Sorrowful Mysteries. Emily's head rested against his shoulder. She hadn't moved for the last five minutes.

"Em, you still with me?"

"Hmmm? I'm awake." Sure didn't sound like it. "Tell me about your Eagle project."

"My Eagle Scout project?" He rubbed his palm on his thigh. "Hmmm. Promise not to laugh?"

Her head shook gently against his shoulder. "No. If it's funny, I'll laugh."

He grinned. "Fair enough. Our church bought this expensive outdoor nativity display for Christmas—Mary and Joseph, baby Jesus, angel, shepherds, the whole gang. But they had no manger or stable. So I designed and built one."

Emily leaned into him and tucked her legs beside her on the couch. "Why would I laugh at that?"

"Because I didn't account for snow and ice weight on the roof. We had a real wet snowfall on Christmas Eve and on Christmas morning the roof collapsed. And decapitated Joseph."

Emily giggled. "Oh my. Did they revoke your rank?"

"No. I did a rebuild with a reinforced roof the day after Christmas. They still use the stable."

She looped her arm around his and burrowed into his side. Warmth spread straight through to his heart. He may not want to leave this couch. Like, ever.

"I like a happy ending."

Her words seared his heart. He wanted to give her a happy ending, maybe more than anything he'd wanted in his life. But how could he? She deserved better.

He shifted back, making himself comfortable against the cushions. Her head settled against his chest, and he put his arm around her shoulder. "You want to play Two Truths and a Lie?"

She giggled. "Think I'll let something good slip when I'm half asleep?"

He grinned and pulled her tighter. "Something like that. You first."

"Give me a second." She was quiet for a whole minute, and he thought she'd fallen asleep.

"Ready? . . . I can't stand Matt . . . I'm in love with Matt . . . I want to live in France." With each successive statement her voice grew weaker, and she leaned into him more heavily.

Dan tensed. Half-asleep or not, she had said two things that had the potential to break his heart and one that made him hopeful. Based on what Grandma had told him about her interest in France, he guessed the last one was one of the truths. The other two were contradictory, so . . .

He rubbed her arm.

She didn't move.

He whispered into her hair. "The lie is that you're in love with Matt."

No response.

She was asleep.

He kissed the top of her head. "Okay. My turn," he murmured. "I could easily fall in love with you. . . You're the most beautiful woman I've ever seen. . . I'm not afraid to say either of those things when you're fully awake." He closed his eyes and concentrated on the feel of her lying against him.

It seemed like only moments later when the sound of the door woke him.

Robert ushered Elizabeth into the house, nodded at him on the couch, and took her straight to their bedroom.

Dan feared moving would wake Emily, so he remained still.

Robert returned minutes later, rubbing a hand over his face. Dark circles hung beneath his red-rimmed eyes.

Dan was suddenly conscious Robert might not be pleased to see him curled up on the couch with his sister. The girl Dan had emphatically denied dating.

Robert acted as if he didn't even see Emily there. "She's miscarrying."

Dan's chest tightened. He couldn't imagine what it felt like to know his baby was dead or dying and be unable to do anything to stop it. "I'm so sorry. They just sent you home?"

"Yeah. She'd rather be here anyway." He ran a hand through his already-tousled hair. "I don't know what to do with the kids in the morning. We're not going to sleep—"

"It's Saturday. I can come back."

Robert glanced at Emily. "How sick is she?"

"Congested, but she didn't seem too bad. Tired."

Robert nodded. "She'll probably want to take them to the park or something."

"Okay." He shifted Emily to the side and eased out from underneath her. She curled inward toward the back of the couch, and he pulled the blanket from the cushions and tucked it around her.

"You can let yourself out, right? I want to check on Elizabeth."

"Sure. Tell her how sorry I am. I'll be praying."

"Thanks." Robert gave him a grim smile and strode down the hallway.

Dan leaned down and pressed a kiss to Emily's head. "Feel better, Em."

17

Un calamité d'un caméra des bisous
(Kiss cam calamity)

Emily pried her feet from the sticky floor and leaned back in the stadium-style seat of the movie theater. She surveyed the four small heads beside her. Tessa, Clara, Gianna, and Max rocked in the large red chairs, their faces lit by flashes from the big screen. Max sucked lazily on his straw while the girls stuffed their mouths with buttery popcorn. Emily shook a few Raisinets from her box, offered a couple to Ben on her lap then popped the rest into her mouth.

A man and a little boy settled into the seats behind them, and the light but woodsy scent of cologne permeated the air, much like the scent that clung to her pajama top this morning when she'd awoken. Dan's cologne. Her sleeping arrangements had left her with a crook in her neck, but otherwise she felt better. She coughed now and then, but the congestion was gone.

What exactly had happened last night? She sifted through her fuzzy memories. She remembered laying her head against Dan after they'd prayed. If she hadn't been so exhausted, she'd never have had the nerve to do it. Did he mind? If he did, he didn't let on. They'd talked about his Eagle Scout project, and they were going to play Two Truths and a Lie, but she couldn't recall them actually playing. She had woken feeling loved, content, and secure.

Until she saw Elizabeth.

Her heart ached even now, picturing Elizabeth's pale, tear-streaked face. She wore a baggy tee shirt and yoga pants, her hair pulled up in a messy ponytail. Her gait was awkward as she crossed the living room to the couch then collapsed into Emily's open arms.

Elizabeth had acted as a sister, mother, and friend to Emily after Emily's parents had died, offering advice about boys, warnings about mean girls, and plenty of ice cream and chocolate when warranted. In return, Emily had tried her best to meet the expectations she and Robert set and served as their mother's helper and babysitter for the kids. The relationship was lopsided when it came to emotional support. Until last night.

Emily held Elizabeth and rocked her while she cried.

"I can already hear what people will say." Elizabeth wiped tears from beneath her eyes, highlighting the dark circles. "They'll say, 'you're so blessed to have five healthy children already.' And I am, but—"

"Shhh. It doesn't matter how many babies you've had." Emily squeezed Elizabeth's hands. "You grieve this one however much you need to."

The movie screen dimmed, and Emily glimpsed a piece of popcorn being lobbed at the people in front of them. A tow-headed boy popped his head over the seat. "Hey!"

Emily leaned forward and glanced down the row, trying to determine who the culprit was.

Clara clapped a hand over her mouth and giggled.

"Clara, no, no." She kept her voice determined but not louder than a whisper.

Emily touched the shoulder of the woman in front of her. "I'm sorry. Did that hit anyone?"

"*Non, c'est* . . . it is okay." Emily's ears perked at the French words and the obvious accent. With her short, blonde hair, light eyes, and big hoop earrings, she appeared younger than Emily, way too young to be the mother of the boy and two girls beside her.

Ninety minutes later, the movie ended, and Emily hoisted a sleeping Ben over her shoulder while motioning the other children out of their seats.

"Do you need help?" The young woman in front of her had her charges already lined up according to height at the end of the aisle.

"Thanks, but I think I got them." Emily stepped out of the row and let the older children pass. "Your accent . . . are you French?"

The young woman smiled, revealing a row of straight, ultra-white teeth. "Oui. I'm here for six months as an au pair."

"I'm jealous. Sounds like such an adventure." Here was someone doing the thing Emily often dreamed of but didn't dare—taking a chance and immersing herself in a different culture, a whole new world.

The children filed out, talking to one another about the movie, while Emily chatted with the young woman about France and her summer job. They introduced themselves then parted in the parking lot, herding the kids into their respective vehicles.

As she drove Robert and Elizabeth's kids through the quiet side streets toward home, Emily's thoughts turned to the somber scene that morning. Robert had been uncharacteristically quiet. Once he'd fed and dressed the kids, Emily offered to take them for the day. Their agenda included the park, McDonald's, and the movie. Would Elizabeth be up to fixing dinner and readying the kids for bed?

She parked the minivan in front of their house, unstrapped the little ones from their car seats, and carried Ben to the door.

Elizabeth and Robert had showered and dressed. Her eyes were still red-rimmed, but Elizabeth smiled with what looked like minimal effort as she hugged each of her children.

Robert nudged Emily's elbow. "We got this tonight. Thanks for taking them."

Emily's gaze searched Robert's face. Were things really okay? "You sure? I can stay."

He shook his head. "Listen, I have two tickets to the Penguins game tonight. Dan and I were going to go." He glanced at Elizabeth sitting on the couch surrounded by kids. "But I can't leave Elizabeth. And I'm not up for it anyway." He strode toward the kitchen, lifted a magnet from the refrigerator, and grabbed an envelope beneath it. "Dan's either forgotten or figures it's off, under the circumstances. It'd be a crime to waste these though." He offered the envelope to Emily. "Why don't you go with him?"

Emily's mouth opened but nothing came out. Go with Dan? Her heart pounded. No, it sounded too much like a date.

Robert pushed the envelope into her palm. "I know, I know. You two aren't a couple, and this seems like a date. You keep saying it, but I come home last night, and you're sleeping on top of him." The corner of his mouth lifted in a grin.

Tension crept into her neck. "I was not. I felt like crap last—"

Robert raised his hands. "I don't care, Emily. Really. We owe you both for coming over. Take the tickets and have a good, fun-but-not-dating time."

Emily peeked in the envelope. Good seats. And she hadn't been to a Penguins game in years. "I don't know."

"If you don't take them, they'll go to waste."

She sighed. "Okay. Thank you."

Robert glanced at the clock. "You're going to have to hustle to get there on time. Go home and get changed. I'll call Dan."

"Okay." She stood on tiptoes and kissed Robert's cheek. "Hang in there. And take care of Elizabeth."

"Got it. Now go."

***

It felt like a date. There was no way around it.

Dan had shown up at her door in jeans and an old Mario Lemieux jersey with a black baseball cap. Nothing special about what he wore, but it was how he wore it that got her. In

129

a good way. Everything about him was so masculine. *Well, duh, Emily. He's a guy.*

She didn't have any Penguins gear, so she wore a long-sleeve black tee shirt and faded jeans. Her hair wasn't quite at the point she could pull it into a ponytail, so it hung around her face as usual.

He opened doors for her, led her with a hand pressed to her back, and chitchatted about the weather, Robert's kids, and hockey.

As they climbed the steps toward their seats, she became conscious of her butt at his eye level. *Friends wouldn't worry about such things.*

The game noise limited conversation to the essentials, like: "You want to split a soft pretzel?", "Who scored that?", and "Is the ref blind?"

Tied at two late in the second period, the Penguins scored a short-handed goal, prompting Emily to squeeze Dan's knee and applaud.

Dan grinned at her as if he were pleased.

Her cheeks heated. "I'm sorry. Inappropriate touching. I was excited."

Dan shook his head and smiled. "I don't mind."

Emily averted her gaze and tucked her hands between her knees. Why was she being so scrupulous? She hadn't apologized for falling asleep on him the night before. Her gaze flicked to his chest. She'd felt so relaxed, so secure with her head resting against his sturdy body.

The horn blared, signaling the end of the second period.

"You okay? Want to take a walk or hit the restroom?" Dan shifted in his seat and lifted his phone from his pocket.

"I'm good."

He tilted the phone in her direction. "You mind if I check some stuff?"

"Nope. Go ahead." Emily sat back and stared blankly at the jumbotron. She glanced to her left as Dan's arm curled around her shoulder, resting on the back of her seat. Maybe she should just relax and enjoy the evening. Maybe he considered it a date. A good one to make up for their first failed attempt.

She could deny it to Robert and even Elizabeth, but not to herself. She was long past ready for a steady relationship, and she wanted to date Dan. But was he ready? Or was something in his past still holding him back?

As the players warmed up for the third period, the words on the big screen changed: scores from around the league, stats from the first two periods, winner of a ticket giveaway. Suddenly, the messages on the jumbotron dispersed and the Kiss Cam appeared. "Are You Gonna Kiss Me Or Not?" pumped over the loudspeakers.

She smiled, anticipating the fun segment. The camera focused on a young couple in matching Sidney Crosby jerseys, who gave each other a quick kiss. A portly middle-aged couple stretched their arms around one another, and he pecked her on the cheek. A man scooped up his preschool daughter and let her give him a messy kiss on the cheek. A thirtysomething couple kissed liked he was a sailor returned from months at sea. A guy in a Mario Lemieux jersey . . .

Oh. My. Gosh. It's us.

Dan stared at his iPhone, not paying a lick of attention to the screen.

The cheers amplified as the camera focused on Dan, distracted by his device, and Emily, caught like a deer in the headlights.

Her nerves jangled as she elbowed him in the side. "Dan."

"Yeah?" He didn't look up.

Rhythmic clapping combined with the cheers.

"Uh. We're on the scoreboard."

"What?" He glanced.

His face paled.

The cheers and whistles reached a crescendo as the crowd anticipated the kiss.

Dan's arm disappeared from behind her, and he rested his elbows on his knees, his gaze traveling to his shoes.

The cheers turned to boos.

"Dan?" Could he hear the desperation in her voice? Thousands of people were waiting. All he had to do was plant a little kiss on her cheek. She'd seen him do it to her nieces plenty of times.

He didn't answer.

The booing swelled.

Emily's cheeks heated and tears welled in her eyes. Tightness grew in her chest until she thought it might explode. She wrenched herself out of the seat and stepped over Dan, nearly tripping on his big shoes. Racing up the steps as fast as her legs would go, she didn't stop until she reached the restroom. She peeked for feet under the stalls. Finding an empty one, she stepped in, locked the door, and cried.

***

A meaty paw smacked Dan's shoulder. He jerked his head up at the screen in time to see Emily's retreating feet on the steps behind him.

He hadn't heard boos so loud since the goalie knocked in the puck during a shootout last season. Thankfully the camera moved on to another couple, who promptly kissed and earned the crowd's favor.

Dan sat back in his seat and let out a breath. All the life drained out of him while stinky jalapeno-breath filled his nostrils. He wrinkled his nose.

"If you don't wanna kiss her," a voice from behind grumbled, "there's a couple thousand guys here that'd take your place."

Dan lifted his shoulder and inched away from the intruding voice and offensive breath.

"You're in the doghouse. Maybe for the rest of your life. Better go after her."

Dan turned and narrowed his eyes at the busybody nacho-eater. "I'm not her boyfriend, and this wasn't a date."

"Well, you're something to her because she ran out of here crying."

Crying? He sucked in a breath and held it. Where'd she go?

Dan jogged up the steps and into the concourse. He turned his head from side to side, hoping to spot her. Nothing. He scrubbed his sweaty palms against his jeans and paced the lobby for five minutes. She was nowhere in sight. He pulled out his phone and texted her. *Where are you?*

People straggled by, returning to their seats after using the restroom. A short line snaked around the side of the concession stand. Still no sign of her.

His phone buzzed, and he glanced down.

Why do you care? Shoot. He'd upset her, all right.

I'm your ride, remember?

The phone buzzed almost immediately. *I'll Uber home.*

All this over a stupid Kiss Cam? His irritation made hitting the precise keys difficult. *The hell you will. Meet me at the truck. Five minutes.*

He waited several minutes. Nothing. He typed again. *Emily?*

It buzzed.

Fine.

Five minutes later, he approached his truck. Emily leant against the passenger side. Her faded jeans tucked into leather boots and the silky hair blowing around her face grabbed his attention. But he couldn't dismiss her arms folded across her chest and how she looked away when she saw him coming. He didn't like her being out there alone at night, and his irritation grew. "You couldn't wait in the concourse to talk—?"

"Open the door, please." Her tone was sharp, angry.

A night he'd filled with all sorts of dreams dissolved into a disaster before his eyes. Using his remote, he unlocked the truck.

She climbed in and slammed the door shut before he'd even gotten his side open.

Obviously the whole Kiss Cam incident bothered her a lot more than it did him. "Emily, I didn't—"

"I don't wanna hear it."

He glanced at her.

"I mean it." Her eyes, a smoldering brown, shot daggers at him.

He shook his head. What happened to the mellow girl who'd snuggled up against him last night?

She turned toward her window and crossed her arms over her chest. She couldn't get any further away from him and still be inside the truck.

Neither of them spoke for the remainder of the ride. Her body language remained icy even as he pulled up in front of her apartment. The second he killed the engine, before he could get out and open the door for her, she bolted from the vehicle.

Dan slammed his door and jogged to catch up with her. He grabbed onto her elbow and spun her around to face him. "If I'd known it was such a big deal, I would've—"

"What? Given me another pity kiss?" Her eyes, still angry, grew watery. "It's *not* a big deal. In fact, it's not a deal at all." Her jaw clenched—from fury or in an effort to stop the tears, he couldn't tell.

He tried grabbing hold of her hand, but she pulled away. "Emily, there were twenty thousand pairs of eyes on us, I just—"

"That's *exactly* it, Dan. There were twenty thousand pairs of eyes on us. And what do you think they saw?"

Dan shrugged. "Two friends at a game. Just because someone points a camera at us doesn't mean—"

"I'll tell you what they saw." She stepped closer to him, toe-to-toe. "A guy who was more interested in his phone and his . . ." She looked at his beat-up Reeboks with disdain. ". . . his ratty shoes than the woman he was with." Her voice cracked as a sob choked her. "They saw a girl so plain, apparently so repulsive, that you couldn't stand to kiss her."

Plain? Repulsive? What was she talking about? How had she taken this so personally? He wanted to kiss her. He thought about it all the time, and he planned on doing it tonight. "Emily—"

She held up a hand. "You know, you didn't have to jam your tongue down my throat or anything. A simple peck on the cheek would've been enough. Heck, you could've kissed my forehead or my hand, and it would've been over in a flash. I'd even offer you some hand sanitizer to make sure you got all my cooties off."

Damn. He had drastically underestimated the importance of this Kiss Cam thing. He hadn't even considered kissing her cheek. When he thought of Emily and kissing, he thought of those pretty pink lips. Couldn't she understand he wanted their first real kiss to be private, special? He wanted to talk to her first, to make sure there was nothing between her and Matt and come clean about his past with Kristen.

"I'm sorry. What else can I say? Can I do it now?" He leaned in to kiss her cheek.

She backed away like he had a deadly communicable disease. "Don't you *dare*." She nearly shouted. He half expected her to spit venom.

"Please. Give me a chance."

"What's her name, Dan? This faceless, nameless—" She clamped her lips together as if she were biting back a nasty word. "This woman who screwed you over?'

His heart ached. It always came back to Kristen. He'd never be free. "Not like this, Emily. Let me come in—"

She shook her head. Tears spilled from her eyes onto her cheeks. "Have a nice life, Dan." She spun on her heels and ran toward the front door.

Dan sunk his hands into his pockets and gazed up at the night sky. He'd really messed up this time. Damaged their relationship beyond repair. A few stars dotted the blackness, all out of reach, forever beyond the grasp of a man weighed down by a past that hung like a millstone around his neck.

Make it a clean break, Lord. No updates from Grandma, no more shared babysitting duties. *I think you've slammed enough doors shut with this woman. I get it. I'm done with her.*

He hopped into the truck, cranked the key, and jerked the vehicle into reverse. Giving his anger free rein, he stomped the gas pedal then the brake before he shifted. Time to leave Emily and the stupid Kiss Cam behind for good. Then he floored it, his tires screeching as he pulled away.

18

La poussière retombant
(Settling dust)

Dan drove behind a navy Cadillac that was—of course—doing the speed limit. He tapped the steering wheel. "C'mon. Move." His gaze darted to the dashboard clock. He was late, and Grandma would call him on it. They'd be at church in plenty of time for Mass, but she liked to be early—a solid twenty minutes before the opening hymn.

He smothered a yawn with his hand. He'd barely slept the night before as he replayed the embarrassing scene at the hockey game over and over in his head. He should've kissed Emily like she said. A simple kiss on the cheek. Even friends did that. Heck, strangers did that in some countries. Probably France. All he'd focused on was the kind of kiss he *wanted* to give her—later, after they'd talked, in private.

He whipped his Dodge Ram into the driveway, pulling alongside Grandma's car, then slammed on the brakes and shifted into park. He rubbed his hands over his tired eyes then pushed open the truck door.

Grandma stood, cane in one hand, purse in the other, where the sidewalk from her front door met the driveway. The bottom of her mauve, floral-patterned dress and white support hose poked out beneath her long, wool coat. Sensible, boxy, bone-colored flat shoes rounded out her attire.

"Grandma, why are you waiting outside?" He rushed over and steadied her arm as she teetered toward her car—the one only he drove.

"You're ten minutes late, Daniel. I like to be early."

"Sorry. I didn't sleep well last night." He opened the passenger-side door for her. "We'll still get there in time."

She grumbled but let him help her into the car.

From his seat behind the wheel, he helped her buckle in and started the car. "How're you feeling?"

"Oh, same old aches and pains. Reminds me I'm still here."

He smiled. This was what he needed, to go out and be around other people and put last night out of his mind. He'd just soak up the comfort of his grandma's loving presence and the peace of a Sunday morning.

"Were you out late last night?" Grandma laid a hand on the dashboard as he swung the car into the church parking lot.

"No, not really." The kiss-cam fail cut the evening short, getting him home long before his normal bedtime. He turned off the engine and pushed open the car door.

"Colleen says you're on the ViewTube." Halfway out the door, Dan stopped and turned back. "You mean, uh, YouTube?"

Grandma chuckled. "That's it."

"When did she call? This morning?" His sister usually slept late on weekends.

"Yep. She said there were seventeen-thousand views before eight this morning."

"Views of what?" His heart pounded against his ribcage.

"Her girlfriend was at the hockey game and spotted you on the big screen. One of those crazy kiss cameras." She grabbed hold of her cane, readying herself to exit the car. "She said you refused to kiss your date."

Dan raked a hand threw his hair and swore. "Sorry. It wasn't a date. And I didn't think it'd be on YouTube."

"So, it *was* you?" She pinned him with a stern look through her bifocals.

"Yeah, it was me."

"Who were you with? Colleen said she was pretty. She liked her better than Kristen, just to look at her."

Dan stood and leaned his head back into the car. "Emily. I was with Emily."

He slammed the door and darted around the car before Grandma could react. She'd have to wait until after Mass to ream him out. And he'd have to wait to watch the video.

"Daniel," Grandma said as she slid from the seat and transferred her weight to her cane, "I know in my heart that you like that young lady a lot more than you let on. You took her on a date—"

"It wasn't a date." He closed the door behind her.

"When a non-related man and woman go out alone on a Saturday evening for dinner or recreation, it's a date." Grandma shuffled toward the handicap entrance. "Any fool knows that."

"This fool didn't." Dan gritted his teeth, determined not to give it a thought until after church. But as the Mass progressed, that was all he could think about. He'd swear he caught a couple of teens and a woman about his age all staring, snickering.

Once Mass ended and Grandma had time to chat with her friend Alice, he helped her back to the car. He started the engine, and then pulled up the video on his phone.

With his index finger hovering over the play button, he scanned the clip's statistics and groaned.

"What?" Grandma peeped over the gearshift.

"Twenty-four thousand hits."

"Hits?"

He glanced at her, and the frown she wore knotted his stomach. "That's how many times the video's been watched."

"Hmmm. You're famous."

His free hand tightened into a fist, but he held the phone out to her. She peered over the rims of her glasses and read aloud, "'Man Refuses to Kiss Date at Hockey Game.' See, even the ViewTube man knows it was a date."

His head flopped back against the headrest. "It's YouTube." He pressed play and straightened so he could watch with her. He bit his lower lip as he and Emily appeared on the screen—her staring at the scoreboard, him intent on his phone.

Grandma watched in silence until the end, when Emily dashed up the steps. She gasped. "Daniel, how could you?" She pressed her hand to the front of her beige cable-knit sweater. "You broke that poor dear's heart."

His chest ached. "I didn't mean to. I *wanted* to kiss her. You don't know how much. But I didn't want to do it in front of twenty-thousand strangers." He closed the app and dropped the phone into the cup holder between them. "I needed to talk to her about a few things first."

Grandma shook her head.

They rode home in silence, but without the easygoing mood of their earlier ride. When they arrived at her house, Dan helped her inside.

"Come in for a minute." She set her purse on the chair in the foyer. "I have something I want to give you."

Dan sat at her dining room table where a small bag of cookies rested, waiting for him. He chose the biggest one, broke it in half, and popped a piece in his mouth.

She sat across from him and surveyed the growing pile of crumbs on the table before him. Reaching across, she swept them into a tidy pile, then adopting a serious look, held out a white envelope.

Dan took it from her. "What's this?"

"My rings and all my wishes for my funeral."

A chunk of cookie lodged in his throat, and he coughed. He pushed the envelope back at her. "I don't want this." She'd just seen her family doctor. Everything was fine—or so she'd said. "You've got lots of years left in you."

She shrugged. "Maybe I do, maybe I don't. That's up to the good Lord." She forced the envelope back at him.

"I wrote down where I want to be laid out and what I want to wear. The hymns for Mass and the type of headstone." She tapped the lumpy envelope. "And my wedding rings are in there for you."

Dan sighed. He didn't like to think of Grandma dying, but at her age you never knew. If it brought her comfort to be prepared, then he'd go along with it. "Okay. I'm going to put this stuff in my safe and pray I don't have to look at it for a very long time."

She patted his hand. "Good. You take those cookies, and I've got two more bags for you."

***

Emily lay sprawled across her bed. She opened her laptop and searched "French countryside," sighing at the bucolic images of rustic cottages, mountains, and flowery meadows.

"I'm adrift," she said to no one.

Pushing herself into a sitting position, she leaned against the headboard. *What am I doing, Lord? Where am I going? Where do you want me?*

Too impatient to wait on an answer, she pulled the laptop closer. Her fingers hovered over the keys. She shouldn't, but she had to check. Again.

"Fifty-four thousand hits?" She clicked on the little triangle, and the most humiliating moments of her life played back. She tapped the keyboard's volume so that the booing grew louder. Did Dan even know it was on YouTube? How many times had he watched it? Did he even feel bad about it? Or was she blowing the whole thing out of proportion?

She watched herself leap from her seat and bound up the metal steps. Nope. It was not too much to ask that a friend—a friend whom she'd prayed with and fallen asleep on the night before—give her a little peck on the cheek. He'd given her that pity kiss of his own volition. And the other almost-kiss at Robert and Elizabeth's house. Of course, thousands of people weren't watching. Maybe that was it. Maybe having the world see him kiss her—plain, boring Emily—was too humiliating.

The worst part was that as long as Dan and Robert remained friends—and she had no right to ask that they didn't—at some point, she'd have to deal with Dan again.

141

She opened Facebook and scrolled through her friends list. An idea had been percolating in the back of her brain since she'd closed the door on Dan and his pathetic apology. She clicked on the page of the young nanny she'd met at the movie theater—Chantal Durand.

A glimmer of excitement sparked inside her. She clicked on the message box and typed, "Bonjour, Chantal! Quick question for you. What's the name of the placement agency you used?"

Then she opened the search engine and typed "international au pair opportunities."

19

Recommencer
(Do over)

Dan dunked a chocolate chip cookie in a glass of milk, soggy crumbs gathering on Grandma's table. "I'm glad my disastrous evening at least gave you a laugh."

Grandma chuckled as she eased into her chair and opened the church bulletin in front of her. "Serves you right for setting the date in the first place."

Tired of being as bored and lonely as he'd been since his fifteen minutes of YouTube infamy, Dan had decided after three weeks of hiding that he needed to get out.

He rubbed his eyes with his thumb and forefinger. He should have stayed home and watched TV or worked on his business's website. Anything but go on a blind date set up by Matt.

Matt, fresh off Emily letting him down easy, had made a date with some woman he'd met at Pappy's Chaps. He needed another guy to come along for her friend. Dan, a little too eager to help redirect Matt's affection away from Emily, said he'd think about it.

He hated blind dates, and he only tolerated Matt, but after considering the invitation a dozen times, he decided he had nothing left to lose.

He was wrong. He still had a shred of self-respect.

Marlena, a petite, fiery ginger-haired girl, managed to talk faster than Dan could hear. She spent the evening chattering to her friend while he and Matt sipped their beers and watched Thursday night football on the multiple screens hung around the restaurant. When Dan had remarked about the offense showing blitz, Marlena had slapped him—a hard crack to the face like he'd seen in movies.

It stung. And for the life of him he couldn't understand why she'd done it. Best he could make out, she thought the remark meant something dirty.

Dan had spent the remainder of the evening coming up with ideas for ending the evening early: starting a grease fire in the kitchen, feigning appendicitis, or claiming he had to run home and give his nonexistent dog an insulin injection.

Grandma nudged another bag of cookies in his direction. "You have no business going out with strange, slap-happy women when your heart belongs to someone else."

Emily. She'd visited Grandma several times when there was no possibility of running into him. As the days turned into weeks, he worried that without even realizing it, he'd lost his heart to her.

"She's restless, Daniel. You've hurt her, and she's disillusioned." Grandma flipped the bulletin over and folded it in half. "If you don't make things right, I'm afraid you're going to miss out on your chance for happiness with her."

Dan sighed. He'd thought it through a thousand times. If he had something to offer Emily, if he were a better man, nothing would stop him. He'd follow her to the ends of the earth and beg her to forgive him. As it was, he'd just drag her down.

"She cares about you, you know."

He shrugged a shoulder. "She cares about everyone. She's a good person."

Grandma's lips twisted into a frown. "I don't mean that. I mean her eyes light up when I mention you. And if I don't mention you, she finds what she thinks is a subtle way to ask. At least until the kissing camera ViewTube thing." Grandma waved her hand dismissively.

YouTube. Dan finished his cookie, letting it settle like a brick in his gut. Hearing that Emily cared only gave him false hope. Even if she'd accept his apology, it didn't change the fact that he had nothing good to bring to her life.

Grandma pressed her hand firmly atop his. "Daniel. Look at me and hear this."

He pushed away his empty milk glass and focused on the gray-green eyes that had seen so many loves lost over the decades.

"You are not the sum of your sins and imperfections."

He averted his gaze. His throat thickened and his chest tightened.

"Daniel, pay attention to your old grandma."

He forced himself to look her in the eye.

"You are a good, God-fearing man. You will not taint or corrupt Emily. Take her down off the pedestal. She's got her own sins and flaws. She doesn't need you to be perfect. She needs you to love her."

***

Dan sat at the drafting table in the corner of his bedroom. With a pencil, he sketched a multi-tiered waterfall and retaining wall for a client he'd met a couple days ago. Tapping the pencil against the table, he tried to recall the type of brick the man said he liked. He spun the pencil in his hand then rubbed gently to erase a ragged edge on the bottom of the waterfall. He brushed aside the eraser crumbs and glanced out the window.

The leaves on the maple tree had turned a deep red. A breeze blew and a dozen or so fell from the tree, swirling to the ground. In no time, it would be Christmas. He needed to make a decision about doing the tree lot again. Last year, it was a measure of financial desperation. This year, his financial position had improved, and the debts would soon be paid off. Still, it gave him something to do during the slow months and provided much-needed income, not for debt repayment, but for living.

Had it been almost a year since he'd first met Emily? What had changed since then? Had he made any progress? His heart had opened to the possibility of someone else, that someone else being Emily, but every attempt to move forward had been thwarted by the remnants of Hurricane Kristen.

Was Grandma right? Was he good enough for Emily? Had he raised her to some kind of unrealistic level that precluded him being part of her life? Maybe there was something he could offer her. What did Emily need or want? Maybe it was time he asked her.

He grabbed his cell phone from the corner of the table and selected Robert's name from the contacts. They'd barely spoken since what Robert had called the Kiss Cam Calamity. He joked, but Dan sensed some irritation as well.

Dan picked up the pencil and doodled Emily's name on the corner of his page. "Hey, Robert, you got a minute?"

A child screeched in the background. "I got a few. What's up?"

"I wondered if you could help me with something. Can you get a pair of those Penguins tickets again for next weekend? Same seats as before?"

"Maybe. The brother of my guy at the shop has season tickets but can't always make it."

"I'll take the set." Dan drummed the pencil against the desk. "Whatever he's asking for them. And I'll split a seat with you."

"Split a seat? How?"

Dan explained his idea, which was met with silence. "Robert, you still there?"

"I'm here. I was thinking about how in high school, my buddies and I swore we'd never let a girl come between us. That's proven to be good policy, but this girl is my sister."

Dan licked his lips and swallowed. He valued his friendship with Robert and didn't want that to change no matter what happened with Emily.

More silence. "One day I come home to you playing house with her, the next day you're rejecting her in front of thousands of people. And all over the Internet. If it were any other guy, I would've kicked his ass on both counts."

A child's soft voice murmured in the background. Robert's response was muffled. "Give me a minute, Max; I'll be right there. Sorry, Dan." He sighed. "Before I agree to this, I want to know that you're serious."

"I am." Dan gripped the pencil so tight his knuckles whitened. "Never more serious."

"Emily's always done what she's supposed to. What our parents wanted, what she thought would please me and Elizabeth. I'm not sure she recognizes what she wants or needs or that she's even allowed to chase her own dreams. And part of that's probably my fault, scaring off guys and using her as our babysitter on-demand." His voice was urgent, as if Emily's welfare depended on him getting this right. "She won't say it, but I'm pretty sure she thinks she's missing out. That she should have her own life with her own family and her own adventures. And she should. And I think she'd happily include you in all that, make you the center of it, if you'd open up to her." He paused a moment, then spoke softly. "Just let her in."

What had Grandma said? *She needs you to love her.* Dan breathed in and out, choosing his words carefully. "I know I could love Emily, if I don't already. I promise to be straight with her from here on out."

"Okay." More kids' voices filled the background. "I'll take care of the tickets and Emily and touch base with you before the weekend."

"Thanks, Robert." A smile spread over Dan's face. "I won't make the same mistake twice."

20

Trop peu, trop tard
(Too little, too late)

Emily's thighs burned as she climbed the steps to their row. She stepped in, placed her Pepsi on the floor, and shrugged out of her jacket. Vendors hawked their beer and peanuts while players from the opposing team warmed up on the ice below. Hard rock music blared from the speakers. Emily's gaze landed on the jumbotron, and her eyes welled with tears.

Robert placed his coat over the seatback and sat. "Good seats," Robert said, sipping his beer.

"Yeah. Great view of center ice." This would *not* be a repeat of last time. If the Kiss Cam landed on them, her brother knew enough to give her a fraternal kiss on the cheek, not pretend she was the invisible woman.

The natural silence between them put Emily at ease, and as long as she kept her eyes off that stupid scoreboard, she enjoyed the game.

Near the close of the second intermission, she stood and stretched. Her arm bumped the knee of the guy behind them. "Sorry," she said over her shoulder.

"You're back," he said. "With a different dude, I see. Hope you have better luck this time."

She turned to the barrel-chested, balding man behind her. Robert stifled some kind of snort, whether a sneeze or a laugh, she wasn't sure.

"The last one was an idiot." The guy gave her a seedy smile. "That Kiss Cam lands on you again, you lean back here and Byron'll take good care of you."

She studied Byron's stringy beard, smelled his nacho breath, and suppressed a gag. "Yeah, thanks. We're good." She shot Robert a look.

He shrugged, meeting her gaze. "I'm gonna run to the men's room." He grabbed his coat, slid out of the row, and climbed the steps.

"You're taking your coat to the restroom?" she almost said. But he'd always been a paranoid goofball, afraid someone might steal his stuff.

The players from both teams returned to the ice, skating in circles. The chorus of Thompson Square's "Are You Gonna Kiss Me or Not" blasted over the sound system.

Emily sat and slid down in her seat. An invisibility cloak would be good. She glanced at Robert's empty seat. That should be enough to keep the camera off of her.

The jumbotron showed a couple of little kids, probably brother and sister, then a couple in their twenties, already practically sitting in each other's laps.

Her heart pounded.

The seat next to her opened and she caught Robert's jeans in her peripheral vision. She wouldn't take her eyes from the board until—

Robert hadn't worn jeans.

He had on green work pants. Great, she had to shoo a stranger.

The bright yellow of the Lemieux jersey caught her attention before his face. She hadn't had the nerve to face him since the last time they were here.

"What . . . What's going on? What're you doing here?" She drilled him with a searing look, her pulse kicking up a notch.

His eyes sparkled with a playful glint, and a hint of stubble bristled his strong jaw line. It had only been weeks, but somehow he appeared more handsome than she remembered, even though he was dressed the same as last time they were there.

He twisted his ball cap around so that the bill pointed backward. His gaze rose to the jumbotron, and he pointed, the hint of a smile on his face. "It's called a do-over, Emily.

You told me to have a nice life, but I'm not." He draped his arm over the back of her seat, and his gaze settled on her. "You wanna know why?" He glanced at the jumbotron.

"Not especially." She scooted forward, away from his arm. "It was a flippant remark said in anger." Her heart pumped wildly in her chest, and her mind was a jumble. Where had Robert gone? What if the camera landed on them again? And why did Dan's nearness fluster her like this?

His hazel eyes hypnotized her. She tore her gaze from his and glanced at the jumbotron.

It was them.

She sucked in a breath. She couldn't do this again.

Her chest ached, and every muscle in her body tensed.

As some of the people in the crowd recognized them, a round of cheers started.

Not again. She pressed her hands on the arm rests and twisted toward him, ready to push out of the seat and bolt.

Dan's one hand brushed her side; the other touched her cheek, gently turning her attention to him. "Em, it's not nice because you're not in it."

She stared, her eyes wide, her heart galloping at a frantic pace. She had to get out. *Now.*

His eyes slid to half-mast, and he leaned forward. With his lips millimeters from hers, he stopped. Gripping her loose sweatshirt sleeve with his fist, he closed the short distance between them.

The crowd roared and cheered.

Emily's hands groped for the front of his jersey, where she clung to him as he kissed her with a determination that made her insides turn to jelly. This was no peck on the lips meant to satisfy the invasive camera and boisterous spectators, although she was relieved it would do that too. Like a blanket on a cold night, this kiss warmed her to the core, soothing her worries with comfort and peace.

Emily could count on one hand the number of times she'd been kissed. They'd been over-eager, fumbling lip-locks with boys more interested in kissing than in kissing her. Dan's kiss was neither awkward nor puerile. It was the practiced kiss of a man who cared about her, whose passions may be guarded, but ran deep.

For the first time, she felt capable of returning affection and devotion that held back nothing but gave, gave, and gave some more.

The cheers and whistles came to a crescendo for several glorious seconds.

What she had considered Dan's lame excuse suddenly made sense. No wonder he had wanted their kiss to be private. It was an intimate expression, a baring of his soul.

Dan pulled away. A grin spread across his wet lips. His chest rose and fell in quick rhythm. He was satisfied with himself.

God help her, if he could kiss like that, he should be.

She hoped the camera had moved on because she must look like a dumbstruck, love-struck fool. She sensed he wanted her to say something, but her nerve endings registered nothing but that kiss. Nothing else crossed the synapses.

"Have I redeemed myself?" He reached for her hand and held it, rubbing his thumb over the back.

She nodded. He hadn't just made up for the last time they'd been here, he'd made up for it all. Every time she'd felt overlooked, ignored, and passed over by any boy or man. "You surprised me."

He laughed. "That was the plan."

"Robert was in on it?"

He nodded. "Robert, the staff here. It was a coordinated effort."

She scanned the sea of people clad in black and gold. Their attention rested fully on the game. A rush of euphoria rolled over her as dread pitted in her stomach. Dan had finally let go of whatever held him back. And the timing couldn't be worse.

He touched her arm.

She faced him.

"Do you want to watch the rest of the game? Because I thought we could go somewhere private and talk." His eyes sparkled. She'd never seen such joy on Dan's face.

Her chest ached, but she nodded.

One side of his mouth quirked in a grin. "Yes, you want to watch the game, or, yes you'd like to go talk?"

"Talk. We need to talk." Her voice shook.

His eyes narrowed, and his brow wrinkled. "You okay? Did I—?"

"The kiss was perfect. Wonderful." A tear trickled from her eye, and she wiped it away. "We need to talk."

He smiled but looked less assured than a moment before.

They climbed the steps to the exit. As she reached the top, Dan came up alongside her, resting his hand on her lower back. She kept walking until they reached a dark, empty spot away from the food and the restrooms. She turned to him, but hid her face behind her hands.

"Em, what's the matter?" He pried her hands free. She dropped her arms to her side, and he gently rubbed them, as if he were trying to warm her.

"We should go to my place or yours."

He slipped his hands into his pockets. His eyes were serious, his manner, pensive. "I can, uh, take you home."

Emily nodded. She already missed that joyful look she'd seen on his face.

They walked to the parking lot in silence, and Dan opened his truck for her. After she'd climbed up and slipped inside, he leaned in and gave her a quick kiss.

Given what she'd have to tell him, she wondered if it would've been better if tonight—glorious as it was—wouldn't have happened.

"So, I decided to do the tree lot again," Dan said. He rambled, obviously trying to get a conversation going. "I thought I'd add some other stuff this year. Wreaths with bows, miniature decorated trees. That sort of thing. What do you think?"

I think my heart is going to break in two. "Sounds like a good idea." She tried to sound upbeat, but her time in Pittsburgh had an expiration date, and Christmas was well past it.

Dan walked her to her apartment and waited as she unlocked the deadbolt. He'd never seen her place before. In a few seconds, he'd see it and more. Enough to realize that soul-stirring kiss they'd shared may have been one of a kind.

She stepped into the dark entranceway and turned on the floor lamp at the edge of the living room. The room lit, revealing bare walls and an entire side of the room lined with cardboard boxes.

Dan's gaze shot to the boxes, each labeled with its contents: books, kitchen stuff, photos and memories, small appliances. "Did you find a new apartment?"

Emily glanced from Dan to her packaged possessions. "No." She stepped closer to him. "I'm . . ." She bit her lower lip. "I'm moving."

Dan's mouth set in a grim line. "To?"

"To France."

He staggered back. "France? As in Paris, the Eiffel Tower? In Europe?"

She nodded. "The Arc de Triomphe, the Louvre, Notre Dame."

He paced the room, his hand touching the tops of the boxes as he glided by. "When did this happen?"

She stepped toward him, wanting to stop him, to tell him how sorry she was. "I've always wanted to go, but I started looking . . . I got serious after the last hockey game. It felt like the right time to go, to do something for me instead of waiting on . . ." She glanced down, unable to meet his gaze. ". . . I don't know what."

He stared out her sliding glass doors onto the bare lawn below. "What will you do there? Do you know anyone?"

A nervous laugh escaped her lips. "Not a soul. And I'm not fluent in the language. I'll be an au pair."

"A what?" He turned toward her, the moonlight casting a blue glow over his shoulders.

"A nanny. I'll be taking care of four boys. Living with their family." She reached into her purse for her cell phone. She found a picture of the children and passed it to him. "They're eight, six, three, and one."

He took the phone from her hand and glanced at the boys. "Lucky kids." He passed it back. "Robert and Elizabeth will miss you."

And you? Will you miss me, Dan? She set the phone on the counter. "I'll miss them too. And the kids."

"For how long?"

"Four to six months at least. But it could become permanent."

His gaze met hers. His brow creased and his lips turned down as he slowly nodded.

"I mean, not *forever* permanent. I don't want to spend my whole life there, but maybe a year or two? I think I could do that." She spoke faster, anxious for . . . for what? His approval?

Dan cleared his throat. He strode toward her and took both of her hands in his.

Her heart leapt. *Confounded organ, give it a rest already.*

"I-It sounds like a great opportunity." Dan turned away from her and rubbed the top of a box. "And I'm sure those boys will love you." He glanced over his shoulder then turned to face her, his smile flat. "And you'll get to immerse yourself in the culture." He wiped a hand over his mouth and neck, then took a breath as he stepped toward her. His gaze fixed on her eyes, and his lips parted, but the words came a second later. "I wish you all the best. I mean that."

Her eyes stung with tears, but she blinked them back. "Thank you." But that kiss. Their kiss replayed in her mind, a flash, the rush of warmth it caused . . . "Dan, about tonight—"

He shook his head and squeezed her hands. "No. Forget tonight ever happened."

She laughed and retracted a hand to wipe fresh tears from her face. "I couldn't if I wanted to. And I don't want to."

"Try to, okay? You've . . . wow, Em, you've got the whole world ahead of you." He dropped her hand, turned away, then back, tapping his folded hands to his mouth as if thinking. "There's so much I could say. So much I wanted to tell you, to explain, but now . . . the timing. I screwed up so many times, and I apologize."

"There's email, and phone calls, and Skype, and it's not forever."

"And I'll use every one of them to keep in touch with you. But, Em, there's long distance, and then there's long distance." He pinched a lock of her hair and slid his fingers down its length, framing her face. "An ocean will separate us."

"Would you . . . would you consider a visit?" *Please, say yes.*

"I have my own business, Em. I don't work, I don't eat. And the airfare—I couldn't afford it. I'm sorry."

She swiped at the tears on both cheeks. "Maybe it's just not . . . maybe we're not . . ."

He lifted her chin with his finger. "Meant to be?"

She nodded.

"God has a plan, Em."

"He has a plan, but what if we screw it up? Is there a Plan B? And what if I don't like Plan B as much as I like Plan A?"

"I think He'll always give us what we need. If we get out of His way." He settled his hands on her waist and pulled her closer. "I think I've been blocking the way for a long time. I'm sorry. There are reasons, but mainly I've been afraid. Grandma made me realize I need to trust a little more. To have a little faith. I'm only sorry . . ."

She closed her eyes and leaned into him so that their foreheads touched. His breath, the scent of his cologne, his nearness. Her senses kept tugging her back to that kiss.

"I'm sorry I realized too late."

Too late? Was it? Did it have to be? "Maybe it's not." But it was. She'd made a commitment to the family, bought her plane ticket, packed her belongings.

He rubbed his forehead gently against hers, and then straightened. "It is. You have my number. Once you're settled, let me know how I can reach you, okay?"

Settled? She didn't think she could be settled apart from Dan, which was crazy because a few hours ago she had been resigned to a life apart from him and everything she'd known and loved.

"Bon voyage, Emily." His lashes lowered and his gaze drifted to her lips. Hands to her forearms, he tugged her to himself.

Kiss me. Please. Like before. She feared if she had only one memory of his kiss, she would minimize it, rationalize it, or somehow forget what she already considered a treasured memory.

His lips grazed her forehead. They stood like that for a moment . . . two, and then he released her, turned, and walked to the door.

A blast of cool air came in with his exit. Disappointment rose like angry bile, scorching her heart. She hugged her arms around her chest and shivered.

21

Bon voyage

(Have a good trip)

"I might throw up." Emily held a hand over her stomach and scanned the airport's curbside dropoff from inside Elizabeth's minivan. A group of teenagers in matching jerseys huddled together, tapping on their phones. Businessmen in crisp suits whisked by, rolling their luggage behind them. A young woman clung to a tall, muscled man in Army fatigues.

Elizabeth grabbed Emily's shoulder and shook her gently. "You're fine. It's just nerves. Breathe in. Breathe out." She made little motions directing Emily to inhale and exhale.

"What if I'm making a huge mistake?"

"The planes fly in both directions."

Emily fiddled with the fringe of her scarf. "He kissed me, Elizabeth. It was the beginning of something."

Elizabeth laid her hand over Emily's, stilling her. "Did he ask you to stay?" Her eyes darted back and forth, as if searching Emily's face for an answer.

She sighed. "No. He said it was a good opportunity and bon voyage." She gave a frail wave.

Elizabeth raised her chin and squared her shoulders. "Then you need to honor your commitment and go."

Emily nodded, wishing she felt as resolute as her sister-in-law looked.

"I just wish you had told Robert about your plans before he helped set you up for the Kiss Cam redo."

"Me too." But then she would've missed out on that kiss. "I think. I don't know." She dug her finger into her forehead where a headache brewed. "I waited because I was afraid he'd try to talk me out of going."

Elizabeth snatched empty candy wrappers from between the seats and shoved them into a small trash receptacle then held a hand out to Emily.

Taking Elizabeth's hand, Emily let her head flop onto the headrest.

"Honey, I know you're confused and scared, but take a chance. Go. You don't know what's waiting for you on the other side of the Atlantic. Maybe you'll find love there. Maybe you won't. It's only a four- to six-month commitment. Dan will be here. He's not exactly a fast mover."

Emily giggled through a sudden burst of tears. She wiped them away with the back of her hand. "I guess not."

Elizabeth rubbed Emily's back like she did her kids' when they were upset. "And who knows? Time and distance have a way of clarifying and solidifying. The old, 'You don't know what you've got until it's gone.' Believe me, your brother never looks as good to me as when he's been gone, and I've been missing him."

Emily sniffed and nodded. "You're right. I'm going to do this. Dan said he'd keep in touch, so, there's that too."

The alarm on Emily's phone chirped.

"Time to go." Elizabeth smiled, and her eyes grew watery.

Emily scooped her purse from the floor and slung it over her shoulder. "Oh, no you don't. You are not allowed to cry." Her voice cracked on the last word. She threw her arms around her sister-in-law and squeezed her. "I'm going to miss you. And the kids. And maybe even Robert."

Elizabeth chuckled and squeezed her tighter. "Be safe and have fun. This is your dream, Emily. France."

Emily didn't have to force her smile. It *was* a dream come true. She only wished it didn't fly in direct opposition to her other dream. As she released Elizabeth and opened the door, she saw someone out of the corner of her eye. A man near the airport entrance. Dark hair, a little under six feet. Dan? She blinked and scanned the sidewalk. Whoever it was, he had gone.

She hugged and kissed Elizabeth. "This is it. Love you."
Then she grabbed her purse and carry-on bag and headed for
the entrance. She didn't look back.

***

Dan pointed the leaf blower toward the street. A
whirlwind of red, orange, and yellow skittered in front of him,
kicking up the cool, musty scents of autumn. He couldn't
begin work on the outdoor fireplace until he cleared the
leaves from his workspace. He blew the pile into the native
hibiscus the owner had pointed out. Dan had struggled to
focus on the remainder of the conversation, his thoughts
drifting to Emily and her knowledge of native plants.

How many days had Emily been gone? Four? Still no
word from her. He glanced at the sky. About ten in the
morning. That made it four in the afternoon in France.

Had he done the right thing by letting her go? He wanted
her to stay, wanted to tell her about Kristen, then date her for
real. But how could he stand in the way of her dream? He
couldn't. The do-over kiss had been too little, too late.

Satisfied that his work area was clear, he set aside the
blower. He'd check his email once before he got to work. He
skimmed through the new messages. Four spam messages for
male enhancement drugs, weight loss schemes, and
mortgages. And one from . . . Kowalski, Emily. He tapped it
repeatedly, willing it to open faster.

Bonjour, mon ami!

*I arrived safely. The village I'm staying in is beautiful,
and I can't wait to visit Paris.*

*The boys are high-energy and demanding but seem like
good kids. Mr. and Mrs. Lacroix are nice but very busy.
Especially Monique. I've hardly seen her.*

*My French is rusty, though I understand most of what is
being said. It's saying something back that is tricky.*

Two Truths and a Lie

1 I had to use the barf bag on the airplane.

2 I was groped by men twice at the Paris airport.

159

3 Our cottage has a beautiful garden, waterfall, and rustic patio. I thought of you.

Hope all is well in the 'Burgh. Please tell Grandma I'm okay. I will send her a postcard via snail mail.

Emily

Dan settled onto the edge of the retaining wall he'd completed the day before and sent a quick reply.

Dear Emily,

Glad to hear you arrived safely. I'm sure you'll be fluent in no time.

I'll see Grandma tomorrow and will let her know you are well. She said about five Rosaries for your safe arrival.

Number two had better be the lie, although I'm sorry to hear that you were sick. Here are my three:

1 Clara asked me to marry her.

2 I said yes.

3 You took the sunshine with you when you left. It's been dreary for days.

He typed "Love," then deleted it.

Dan

He checked his email eleven times before a reply came early the next morning.

Dear Dan,

You're wrong. The first one was the lie. I was a little motion sick and nervous, but thankfully I didn't puke on the plane. Now yours. I hope the second one is the lie. You're much too old for Clara. I also know she hogs the bed, eats ketchup from the bottle, and cheats at Candyland. You can do better.

Sending a little sunshine your way.

Emily

WYWH XOXO

Dan smiled, his heart swelling. The XOXO surprised him. He should've gone to the airport with her and given her one last kiss. He'd used work as an excuse for not being there, afraid he'd make a fool of himself by either clamming up or begging her to stay. What was WYWH? He opened his web browser and searched for it. In a second, he had his answer. It meant Wish You Were Here.

Me too.

How could he do this for four to six months? Or a year or two? One day at a time. That was all he could manage.

22

L'autre côté de la grande mare
(Across the pond)

Dan wrapped multi-colored bulbs around the light pole next to his shack. All the supports were in place. A cold breeze chilled his cheeks and ears. The temperature had been dropping all day, and the forecast showed flurries overnight.

Friday morning the first delivery of Christmas trees would arrive. That would give him four weekends to sell.

"I got the price sign staked," Robert called from the end of the aisle. He rubbed his gloved hands together. "Got anything else?"

"Nope. Gonna set out this rack for the wreaths and boughs, and that's it." His homemade rack had turned out better than he'd expected. "It's good to go."

"Great. I'm frozen." Robert folded his arms tightly around his chest, and his gaze skittered across the lot toward the flashing neon sign. "What do you say we go next door and have a beer?"

Dan stood back and evaluated his work. A few more colored lights would make it seem more festive. "Sure. Sounds good."

He and Robert tromped across the lot to The Watering Hole. The door swung open and the smell of stale beer and cigarettes wafted out. Dan decided on one quick beer and getting out. As it was, his clothes would reek of the place.

Robert climbed onto a barstool, and Dan sat next to him.

"What can I get you?" A rail-thin woman of undecipherable age approached. She wiped a dingy rag over the bar.

"I'll take a Yuengling lager." Robert scooped up a handful of peanuts from a bowl.

"Same." Dan slid the bowl closer and grabbed some peanuts for himself.

The bartender shuffled in the other direction and drew their beers from the tap. In a minute she returned, sliding the drafts in front of them. Her gaze dropped to Dan's hand where it rested on the bar. To his bare ring finger?

She winked before returning to work.

Dan curled his fingers, slid his hand onto his lap and sipped the beer.

"So, you and Emily keeping in touch?" Robert said around a mouthful of peanuts.

Dan swallowed and nodded. They'd traded a lot of messages over the past couple of weeks. "Yeah. We send emails back and forth every day."

Robert jerked back in his seat "Every day? We're lucky we get a few messages a week."

Dan's heart burned and swelled, but he kept his expression neutral. He'd assumed Emily kept in touch with her family at least as much as with him.

He missed Emily every waking minute, but they communicated better now that she lived an ocean away.

Robert drummed his fingers on the bar in time to the Tom Petty song coming from the speakers. "She say much about this Gilles guy she's working for?"

Dan rested his hands around the base of his beer and cocked his head toward Robert. "Not really. Why?"

Robert pulled his cell phone from his pocket. "Look at this." He swiped through his email until he found the message he wanted and opened the attachment. "She's there to watch this guy's kids. What the heck is this?"

In a poorly-done selfie, Emily stood in front of a guy who didn't look much older than her. His longish brown hair, high cheekbones, and the playful glint in his eyes gave him an artsy-fartsy dandy look. His square chin hovered above Emily's shoulder. Two blonde boys stood in front of her, the image cropping their faces below the eyes.

Dan tore his gaze from the picture. "That's him? How old is he?"

"Late thirties, I think?" Robert frowned. "I don't like him."

The picture rankled Dan a little too, but it was just a dumb picture. "What's she said about him?"

Robert took a swig of his beer. "Nothing to me. But she told Elizabeth she's got to watch the guy's hands."

Dan's hand tightened around his beer mug as a flicker of anger surged inside. "I don't like the sound of that. I remember her saying the mom was never around."

"Yeah, Monique is some kind of corporate bigwig." Robert rolled his eyes and grabbed his drink. "Kids never see her. And I don't like it either, but what can I do? She's an adult." He sipped his beer. "Elizabeth says it's nothing, and I shouldn't worry."

Dan's leg started bouncing on the barstool of its own accord. "Now I'm going to worry too."

"Sorry. I'm used to looking out for her. Maybe that's part of the reason she wanted to get away. Waiting until two weeks before to even tell me." He paused a moment. "She complained I was overprotective."

Dan laughed. "And here I thought she left because of me." He twisted on his stool and surveyed the room. The bar was filling up.

"Yeah, well you too, for sure." Robert gulped the rest of his beer and reached for his wallet.

Dan held up a hand. "I got this. Thanks for helping me get the lot set up." He pulled a few bills from his wallet and laid them on the bar. He glanced up to locate the bartender, but a blonde woman at the opposite end of the bar caught his attention. Long blonde hair falling loose around her shoulders, pert nose, a low-cut top. He had to look twice to be sure it wasn't Kristen.

She sat practically in the lap of the guy she was with. His hand ran idly up and down her back and over the curve of her denim-covered backside. She laughed at something. He leaned in and kissed her neck and her ear, then groped her breast. Granted her chest nearly toppled out of the tight tee she wore, but still. She turned into him, giggling, and he buried his face in her neck and hair.

Dan blinked a couple of times and tried to remember. Had he behaved that way with Kristen? No, not in public. He hoped. But everything about life with Kristen had been seductive. She had a way of getting what she wanted. She did want him. For a while anyway, right?

When they first started sleeping together, he had continued to attend Mass. Kristen had no interest in going with him, but he went. Pulling himself out of bed to go to church became more and more difficult each passing week. There was never any conscious decision, just a gradual, almost natural, sliding away. It started with sitting in the back of church. Then coming later and later and spending the entire time thinking of Kristen and when they'd be together next.

The more steeped in sin he became, the wider the gulf between him and God grew. At some point he realized he shouldn't receive communion, and he stopped. He began to resent the people who did go to communion, whose spiritual life wasn't being rent open by sin. In spite of the growing self-loathing, he couldn't let go. Couldn't—or wouldn't?—stop having sex with Kristen any more than he'd stop eating or breathing.

Church became more and more uncomfortable. He stayed home one week because he was sick. Staying home the next week didn't seem so foreign, and then he stopped all together. Out of habit, he continued to pray morning and night. Then as the mood struck. Soon that stopped too.

Little by little, his convictions took a back seat to her way of life. He lived that way for years until Kristen's rejection sent him to the pit of despair. Only then, finally, did he work his way out and back to a life of grace.

"You ready?" The stool rattled as Robert stood and shoved it back toward the bar. "I promised Max I'd play some video games with him before bed tonight."

"Uh, yeah." Dan blinked and rubbed at his eyes. "I'm ready. Do me a favor?"

Robert buttoned his jacket. "Another?" He lifted one side of his mouth in a grin.

"Yeah. Tell me if Emily mentions any problem with this Gilles again."

"Sure thing. You'll keep me in the loop if she says anything to you?"

"You got it." As they walked side by side back to the lot, Dan breathed deeply, inhaling the cool, fresh air. No trip to France would be worth the loss of Emily's innocence, the loss of her trusting nature, or alienation from her faith.

***

Dan sat at his kitchen table, staring at his phone. He glanced at the clock. Almost three in the morning. Midnight Mass had gone an hour and a half then Grandma had chatted with Alice. When he took Grandma home, she brought out the cookies, cheese and crackers, and tea. Tack on some travel time, and here he was, wondering how Emily was spending her Christmas morning.

They'd kept up a steady stream of email messages, most light-hearted and frivolous, but some venturing into deeper waters. Once or twice he let slip how much he missed her. Never more than tonight. Christmas and Emily would be forever entwined in his mind.

What did an international call cost? And did his plan cover it? He had no clue, but he needed to hear her voice. Emily kept mentioning Skype, but he hadn't signed up and installed the app.

He dialed Emily's number and sucked in a breath, his pulse racing.

"*Allo.*" She sounded breathless, as if she had run to grab the phone.

"Merry Christmas, Em." There was a pause.

"Dan? Oh, my gosh! Merry Christmas! What time is it there? Like three in the morning?" Her voice rang with excitement. Maybe she had been missing him too. He could hope.

"Yep."

"Why aren't you asleep?"

Dan pushed the chair away from the table, stretched his legs, and crossed them at the ankles. "I took Grandma to Midnight Mass, saw her home, and she fed me. I was getting ready to go to bed, and I thought of you." Was that too much? He wanted her to know he cared. "I wanted to wish you a Merry Christmas."

"How sweet. Thank you." A shuffling noise came from the other end and then what sounded like a door clicking shut. "Tell me, Dan. Are you on Santa's naughty or nice list?"

Was she flirting with him? *This may be the best present I get short of getting her back on this side of the Atlantic.* "I live like a monk and drive my elderly grandmother to the grocery store and church. If that doesn't qualify me for nice, I don't know what does."

"A monk, huh?" She giggled. "I thought maybe you were a Jedi in training or something."

He grinned. "Hey, you're gonna blow my cover. Can I show you my lightsaber some time?"

"Dan!" Her voice was incredulous, but she broke into a laugh. "You'd better watch. Santa still has time to move you to the naughty list."

His smile widened. "Emily Kowalski, get your mind out of the gutter. I'll have you know I own a Darth Vader replica lightsaber. It was a Christmas gift from my parents when I was nine."

"Want to know what I got when I was nine?"

"A Princess Leia slave girl costume? Cause I'd love to see that."

"Hey, when you wake up to a lump of coal in your stocking, don't come complaining to me. For your information, Santa brought me a Happy Holidays Barbie Doll."

His mind conjured visions of Emily as a little girl tearing open her Christmas presents. Softer, he said, "Tell me about your best Christmas ever, Em."

"That's easy. The last Christmas before my parents died. It wasn't anything special, really. We were all together, and it snowed. So picturesque. I can still hear the laughter, smell the gingerbread cookies, taste my mom's homemade chocolates." Her voice cracked. "I'm sorry. I didn't mean to get all nostalgic and weepy."

Dan stood and strolled to the window in his living room. Condensation covered the corners where the seal had broken on the old glass. He traced a letter E in the moisture then rubbed it away with his fist. "You okay?"

She sniffed. "Yeah. Just homesick."

"There's a cure for that, you know."

Silence. He considered retracting his implied invitation. He'd encouraged her to go because it was a great opportunity. Nothing about that had changed. The change was in him. He missed her more than he anticipated. More each day than the one before.

"I was at Robert and Elizabeth's last night. I think they pity the lonely Christmas bachelor."

"Yeah. Having a hard time feeling sorry here, since I'm usually the object of their pity. Being with the kids makes Christmas though. What are they all asking for?"

"I don't know exactly. Max wants some video game. Oh, and Clara asked Santa for her Auntie Em to come home."

"No. She didn't."

"She did, apparently."

"Ahh." Her voice came out strained. "My heart's going to break."

"In case Santa doesn't come through, she's asked me to come get you."

"Are you? . . . Coming to get me, I mean."

"Do you want me to?" His breath lodged in his lungs.

"You said you can't afford to visit." Evasive maneuvers. She still didn't quite trust him.

"I'd find a way." Quiet again. He let it drop. "I saw your baby pictures. Including the bare bottom ones."

She groaned. "I'm going to kill Elizabeth."

He laughed. "They weren't so bad. Tessa is your mini-me, you know."

"Yeah, I guess she does sort of look like me when I was little."

"Sort of? She's a dead ringer."

A knock sounded in the background.

"Hang on, okay?"

He waited through the sound of a muffled background conversation. He didn't know why she bothered to cover the phone. He didn't understand a lick of French.

"I'm back. Sorry about that."

He kicked off his shoes and drifted to his bedroom. "Any plans for the holidays?"

"Yes." Her voice filled with excitement again. "Gilles is taking us to the Riviera."

"Family vacation?"

"Uh, sort of." Did he detect a mite of discomfort in her voice? "Monique is visiting her family, so he's taking us for a little vacation."

Us? The guy was travelling to one of the most romantic spots in the world at Christmas with his au pair instead of his wife? Dan whipped his bedcovers back with more force than necessary. He tried to.quash the rising ire. It was Christmas, and Emily was a grown woman. A smart one at that. He wouldn't say anything now, but he'd be sure to mention it to Robert later.

23

Les catalyseurs
(Catalysts)

Raindrops pattered against her window, nearly lulling Emily back to sleep. She sprawled across her unmade bed and flung her arm across her eyes, trying to block out the overwhelming floral theme of the bedroom. She loved flowers as much as the next person, but the wallpaper with blood-red blooms the size of cabbages had caused disturbing dreams. Combined with the black frills and fringe that hung from every piece of fabric and furniture, she envisioned herself in a Tim Burton movie gone bad.

She glanced at her phone. Nothing yet. Emailing back and forth with Dan had become slow and inconvenient, and Emily longed for real-time conversation. Since Christmas, they'd been using a message app. They'd worked it out so that if he stayed up late and she woke early, they could get in an uninterrupted exchange. Dan promised to do better than an undershirt and sleep pants if they did video messaging, but Emily insisted if they were doing this at six in the morning her time, there would be no visuals.

The phone dinged, and she snatched it off the nightstand, snagging the edge of a black doily that fell to the floor. She rolled onto her belly and sunk her elbows into her pillows, staring at the small screen.

Good morning! Want to play?

Sure. You first. A smile stretched across her face. Who'd-a thought dark o'clock would become her favorite time of day? Since Christmas, everything between her and Dan had seemed more heartfelt. She longed for home—for Dan—more each day. Especially after last week in the Riviera.

A new message popped up.

I cooked a real meal this weekend. Meatloaf, baked potato, broccoli . . . I joined a gym, and I've been working out every day . . . I miss you like crazy.

Emily took a second to re-read them. Dan in a gym? Nah. She hoped the last one was true. *The second one.*

Nope. Wait until you see my rock-hard abs. The first one's the lie. It's still takeout or Ramen noodles around here. Your turn.

She thought for a few moments then typed her three. *I met a guy from Pittsburgh on the Eiffel Tower . . . I went topless on the beach last week . . . I miss Grandma (and her cookies).* She rolled over, pushed aside the comforter, and sat cross-legged.

The lie had better be the second one.

Emily grinned and bit her bottom lip. Was Dan jealous? Or overprotective like Robert? *You're correct. Made you squirm, huh? It's winter! Way too cold for the water. Besides, I'm saving that for my husband.*

Lucky man. Your husband.

Think so? She sucked in a breath and held it, waiting for his answer.

Know so. Hey, I need to be serious for a sec. Please pray for Grandma. Nothing specific is wrong. I just see a change in her these last couple of weeks. Forgetting things. Slowing down.

Emily envisioned Grandma bustling around her kitchen, an oven mitt in one hand and a spatula in the other. Her mind was sharp as a tack. *I pray for her every night, but I'll step it up a notch. I love your grandma.*

It's mutual.

"Ask me to come home, Dan," she murmured. She flopped back on the bed, twirling a few strands of hair around a finger. "For Grandma. For you. I'd be on the next plane."

She loved France and its historic charm. Loved strolling along the Seine and sampling pastries in village cafes. But it turned out a vacation would have filled her yearning for the lavender-covered countryside. It didn't require a move halfway around the globe. Maybe Gilles had caused France to lose some of its luster too.

When the kids had been napping and otherwise occupied at the resort, Gilles had presented her with a slinky blue nightgown. A present for her hard work, he'd said.

"Is this . . ." She pulled it from the gift bag, its lace trim and spaghetti straps puddling in her lap. A quick glance at the lascivious look in his eyes made her skin crawl. "Thank you." She stuffed it back in the bag and handed it to him. "I can't accept this. I'm sorry."

His face fell then his lips twitched. He snatched back the present with a huff and slipped out of the room. Then, on the train ride home, while they zipped past lavender fields and quaint cottages, he'd rested his hand on her knee.

She jerked her face from the window. "Gilles, I don't think that is—"

His hand slid up her thigh, inching under her skirt.

She slapped her hand over his and shoved it off her lap. "I'm here to care for your children. Nothing more." She gave him a sharp glance.

He cleared his throat and averted his gaze, but expressed no remorse. When they'd returned home, Monique arrived, and he'd kept his distance. Gilles didn't intimidate Emily, but being in his presence now made her feel foolish.

Robert had hinted in his messages that she should be wary of Gilles. Irritated with what she perceived as his overprotectiveness, she had dismissed his concerns. His instincts, though she loathed admitting it, had been dead on—even from thousands of miles away. The last thing she wanted was to go home with her tail between her legs and admit she'd been naïve.

Gotta go, Em. I can hardly keep my eyes open. Take care. Same time tomorrow?

Same bat-time, same bat-channel. And I want a picture of those six-pack abs. ;-)

***

"Tired, Robert?" Dan wrinkled his nose and shouldered past a couple of guys that reeked of—sewage? He glimpsed the fire-engine red logo on the backs of their jackets: a regal-looking toilet with the name "Theo's Port-a-Thrones" emblazoned above and below.

He hadn't thought it possible, but this township business association meeting had been more boring than the last. A dozen people filed out of the row ahead of him, drifting toward the scent of hot coffee in the rear of the room.

"I'm exhausted." Robert slipped his arms into his jacket and turned his back on the portly man with a greasy comb-over who had put nearly the whole room to sleep. He stretched his arms over his head. "I'd say we go out or you stop over, but a couple of the kids have this croupy cough. Elizabeth was up with them half the night, and I need to get home and give her a hand with bedtime."

"No, problem. Hope they're feeling better." Dan's thoughts skittered to Grandma. Maybe she'd been fighting some bug and it'd slowed her down, thrown her off. Taxed her immune system. He zipped his jacket as they sauntered toward the door. "Hey, I wanted to mention to you—about Emily?"

Robert grinned. "It's always about Emily with you, man. What's up?"

Dan rolled his eyes. "Did you know Gilles took her to the French Riviera with the kids? And not his wife?"

Robert wrinkled his brow. "That doesn't sound right."

Dan gave the port-a-potty guys wide berth as they crossed in front of him, heading toward the exit. "She didn't complain of any problems. Just seemed off to me. I didn't like it."

"Jealous, Dan?" Robert raised his brows at him.

Dan sunk his hands into his pockets and shrugged.

"Elizabeth says I have to start treating Emily like a grown up, so I'm trying to back off. I just wish she'd come home. All

I hear is, 'When's Auntie Em coming home?', 'I wanna go see her!', and 'Can we go to France?' I can't even afford to take them all to the circus, for cryin' out loud."

Dan laughed. "I hear ya."

***

Dan tapped the steering wheel with his gloved hands and sped down the tree-lined street. His breath came out in white puffs in front of him. Winter had been fairly mild through January, but February blew in with an arctic blast. He cranked the heat up as far as it would go.

Grandma had called last night suggesting a later Mass time. The weather forecasters were calling for a dusting of snow, and she wanted to avoid the potential for slick sidewalks. The last few years she'd been hyper-vigilant about weather conditions. At first Dan had tried to reassure her, but now he acquiesced. Better safe than sorry.

Dan's heart beat out of rhythm. Why hadn't Grandma answered the phone this morning? He'd called before he left his apartment to let her know he was on his way. She didn't answer. She'd probably been in the bathroom or otherwise unable to get to the phone, but at her age, it made him nervous.

What if she'd fallen in the tub last night and hit her head? Maybe her hearing aide had died. Either way, he was going to look into one of those alert necklace things for her in case she couldn't get to a phone in an emergency. Maybe his sisters could chip in to pay for it.

He pulled alongside the curb in front of her house then started her car in the driveway to warm it. He jogged to the door and knocked, hopping lightly from one foot to the other in an effort to stay warm.

Grandma didn't come to the door. She should've been ready and waiting.

He knocked again.

No answer.

Dan's throat constricted. He jogged back to his truck and popped open the glove compartment. Paper napkins, mini flashlights, insurance cards. Where the hell was the spare key? He tossed the contents onto the front seat, rummaging through them again. No key.

His teeth clenched, the panic threatening to overcome him. He ran back to the concrete slab by the front door and peeled up the grass-green, all-weather carpet. He lifted a paper envelope enclosed in a Ziploc baggie. "Key" was written on the front in big, black letters. He tore open the bag and ripped the key from the envelope.

Dan jammed the key in the lock, wriggled it, then twisted left, opening the door to Grandma's living room. The aroma of warm banana bread and the scent of Grandma's floral perfume wafted toward the open door.

He wiped his boots hurriedly on the welcome mat. "Grandma?"

No response.

His heart pounded in his chest. He yanked off his gloves and jammed them into his pockets.

"Grandma!" He walked through the empty kitchen. A chocolate chip banana bread lay on the cooling rack on the immaculate countertop.

He took the steps two at a time and stomped down the short hall toward Grandma's bedroom, peering into the empty bathroom as he passed.

He stopped short in the doorway.

Grandma lay on her already-made bed, eyes closed, dressed in her Sunday best for Mass. Her hands rested at her sides. Her purse sat next to her.

"Grandma?" He bolted forward and carefully touched her arm.

She didn't move.

A knot formed in the pit of his stomach.

"Grandma?" his voice cracked on the last syllable as he slid his hand down her arm and grasped her fingers.

They were unnaturally cold in her warm bedroom.

He turned her hand over and fumbled with finding a pulse on her bony, wrinkly wrist. He felt nothing, but doubted he could find his own pulse that way.

He leaned into her, the strong scent of her perfume nearly choking him. He brought his ear to her mouth, listening for a breath and hoping to feel a puff of air against his cheek.

Nothing.

With a hand on either of her slim arms encased in her favorite gray cardigan sweater, he shook her gently. "Grandma. It's Daniel. Wake up, Grandma."

As he said it, he knew she wouldn't be waking up.

A half-dozen memories flooded his mind. Grandma holding her chubby white poodle, Millie, nearly twenty years ago. Scooping heaping spoonfuls of her breakfast casserole onto his plate on Christmas morning. The All Souls Day Rosary procession at the cemetery when she hobbled along despite the painful phlebitis in her leg. The way she'd mouthed "Hallelujah" when he'd told her things were over with Kristen. Holding his sister Kerry's newborn boy in the hospital. The fierce hug she'd given him when he'd announced he'd stay in Pittsburgh when his mom and sisters moved. And those blasted cookies—golden brown with crispy edges and gooey chocolate centers, straight from the oven.

His beloved Grandma was gone. He clasped her cold hand in his, lay his head on the bed beside her, and choked back a sob.

24

Annoncer le nouvellle
(Breaking the news)

Baby Ben rammed into Dan's legs and grunted—his universal plea to be held. Dan pushed the chair back from the table and hoisted Ben into his lap. Ben giggled and smacked the wooden table with his hands.

Marginally aware of the kids' antics as they flitted in and out of Robert and Elizabeth's dining room, he stared blankly at the tabletop as Ben bounced in his lap.

Tessa climbed behind him, stood on the chair rung, and pulled on his shoulders. "Piggyback ride," she whined.

"Guys, now's not the time." Elizabeth set a cup of steaming coffee in front of Dan.

He didn't have the heart to remind her he didn't drink coffee.

"Give Uncle Dan some space." She shooed Tessa away from the table and plucked Ben from his lap.

Gianna slid through the kitchen in her tights, still dressed for church. "Can I have a snack?"

Robert came in from the hall, pulling the sleeves of his sweatshirt down. "Everyone out." His bellow drew the attention of every kid but Gianna, who continued to rummage through the refrigerator. "Max, take everyone downstairs and put a movie on."

The kids scampered from the room and tromped down the stairs, arguing about which movie to watch. Dan glimpsed Gianna's pigtails as she slammed the basement door behind her.

The distractions had been annoying, but Dan thought the unnatural silence might be worse.

Elizabeth slid into the seat next to him and squeezed his hand. "Are you hungry?"

Dan shook his head. "Thanks, though." He had no appetite for food or, surprisingly, anything else. For the first time in two years, stress didn't trigger his desire for a beer or a joint. He craved only one thing, only one person's presence.

He needed to hear Emily's soothing voice, feel her arms around him.

"So." Elizabeth's voice was gentle. "You found your grandmother?"

Dan nodded. "I went to pick her up for church, but I got there later than usual because of the weather." He turned the mug so the handle fit in his right hand. "She didn't answer the door, so I let myself in with the spare key." He cleared his throat and sipped the coffee, refusing to make a face at its bitter taste. "I found her lying on her bed, dressed for church, purse right next to her."

The wooden chair scraped over the floor as Robert took a seat across from him. "Had she been sick?"

Dan encircled the warm mug with his hands. "No. She was fine last night, although I'd noticed some subtle changes over the last month or so." Had he missed something critical? Something that could have saved her? "She was slipping a little."

The worst morning of his life replayed in his memory. Calling 9-1-1. The EMTs checking her for signs of life. Then the coroner's arrival. Dan had stood half-dazed as they took his grandmother's body. He'd stumbled out the door and sat in his idling truck where he'd called his mother, his sisters, then Grandma's friend from church, Alice. He'd had to look up her number. The news would spread quickly from there.

He'd pulled out of the driveway not knowing where to go or what to do. He couldn't make arrangements yet. An hour later, he found himself pulling into Robert and Elizabeth's driveway, only a few miles from Grandma's house.

"What can we do for you?" Elizabeth's eyes brimmed with maternal compassion as she gently rubbed his back.

A tear trickled from his right eye. He brushed it away. Her offer was sincere, but he didn't have a clue what needed to be done.

"I don't know." He sipped the coffee, not because he wanted it or enjoyed it but because he didn't know what else to do. "There is one thing. Could one of you call Emily?" He glanced at his watch. It was early evening in France. "She'd want to know. It doesn't seem right to tell her by message, but I can't . . ." He cleared his throat again and forced back the tears. "I don't think I can do it."

Why was that? He'd told his mom that her mother-in-law had died without a quaver in his voice. He'd told each of his four sisters and listened to them cry, never shedding a tear. He'd told a sweet old lady she'd lost her oldest, dearest friend and then repeated it three times so that she could hear. Not a single sob choked him. Maybe he'd used up his restraint and needed a good cry himself, but he knew the second he heard Emily's voice he'd dissolve into a helpless puddle of tears.

Robert stood and squeezed Dan's shoulder on the way to the coffee. "I'll call her in a little bit. There's nothing on arrangements or anything yet, right?" He filled a mug from the carafe on the counter. "She's going to ask."

Dan shook his head. "Not yet. She wrote down all her preferences though and gave it to me a while back. I didn't think I'd need it for a long time. I hoped, anyway."

He finished the cup of coffee and stifled a grimace at the aftertaste. "I think I'll go home for a while, check on that information Grandma gave me."

What was he going to do? There was nothing to do but endure this limbo where what needed done couldn't be done, and nothing else mattered. Go home and cry, that's what he'd do. After that, he wasn't sure.

"Will you come back for dinner?" Elizabeth stood and gathered the mugs from the table along with a couple of empty yogurt containers and wrappers the kids had left behind. "I'm making a giant pan of lasagna. You need to eat."

"Thanks. But I don't think so. Maybe some time alone would be good."

"You're welcome to—" Elizabeth started.

"Do whatever you need to do." Robert shot Elizabeth a sharp look. "I'll give Emily a call now."

Dan stood, set his mug alongside the sink, and grabbed his jacket from the coat rack. "Thanks. I did think of something else you could do."

He shrugged into his jacket and zipped it to his chin. "Pray for Grandma . . . And me."

***

Emily rinsed her hands in the sink and dried them on the black bath towel. At least it didn't show the dirt. What would she do with the rest of the evening? Head into the city? Most nights, she'd be putting the boys to bed, but tonight Monique was home and took care of it, giving Emily the evening off.

She'd heard of a little comedy theater in Paris that she wanted to check out. She could head there. It would be more fun if she had some company, but—

Her phone vibrated in her pocket, and she scurried from the bathroom to her bedroom, worry creeping in. Not many calls came this time of the day. She glanced at the phone.

Robert and Elizabeth's number. Since she'd been abroad, Robert had sent her a few messages inquiring how she was doing or asking about what to do with mail that had come for her, but otherwise, she'd spoken to Elizabeth. She shared all her adventures, disappointments, and funny language mix-ups with Elizabeth, assuming the essentials got back to Robert.

"Hey, Elizabeth, how's it goin'?"

"Emily, it's me, Robert." His voice was low and serious.

Her fingers tensed around the phone. Her brother didn't chitchat on the phone. Ever. If there was something important to say, he said it, getting on and off in a hurry. "Robert? Are the kids okay? Elizabeth?"

"They're fine. I have some bad news though." There was that grim tone again.

Bad news? About what or whom? She had spoken to Dan this morning, and he was fine. Had he been in an accident? "Okay. Give it to me."

A second of silence and then: "Dan's grandmother passed away."

Emily sunk onto the edge of her bed. "Oh, no. Grandma. What happened?"

"Not sure. Dan found her this morning when he went to pick her up for Mass."

She crossed her legs beneath her. "Dan found her? Is he okay?" Her heart ached at the thought. The love between Dan and his grandma was deep and constant.

"Dan's all right." His voice held a hint of uncertainty. "He found her lying on her bed. They don't know yet what happened. She didn't have any injuries. Appears to have gotten dressed for church, lied down, and died."

Emily hugged her knees. Not a bad way to go, and she'd had a long full life. She was right with God. But, oh, how she would be missed. Especially by Dan.

"What are the arrangements?" It only took her two seconds to decide. Regardless of how Robert answered, she was going home.

Without divulging the details of Gilles's inappropriate passes, Emily had given Monique notice that she wouldn't be staying on beyond the initial four-month period. This would merely step up the timetable.

"None yet, but probably viewing on Valentine's Day and funeral Wednesday? I'm just guessing."

Emily walked to the closet and slid the hangers to the side, assessing what she'd need to take with her on the plane and what she could ship back. "I'm coming home."

"What? No one expects you to come home, Emily. Not from Europe. Dan doesn't expect—"

"It's not just about Dan. I want to come for me. And because of Grandma." She laid several dresses on the bed, looking for a couple that might be appropriate for a funeral. "It's time, that's all."

He was silent for a couple seconds. "Everything okay? Cuz if that Gilles guy—"

"Everything's fine." She rolled her eyes as she pulled a black dress and a navy blue one from the pile. She'd tell Robert about Gilles, but not now.

"You're coming home for good then?" His voice was hopeful.

A surge of love for her brother rose within her. Robert had been there for her through it all—*très bon* and *très mal*. He looked out for her and loved her, even if his love had been stifling at times. "Yes, if you can put me up until I find a place of my own. I'll be jobless and homeless."

"You've always got a place with us. You can try out your European nanny skills on my kids as long as you want."

She smiled. "Thank you. I'll send a message when I have my flight details. I want to be home by Tuesday afternoon, at the latest."

"One of us will pick you up at the airport. Safe travels."

She sat on the bed next to the dresses. Would it be tipping her hand too much to ask about Dan? "Thanks. Hey, before you go, how's Dan handling it? For real."

He sighed. "I think he needs some time to process it. Elizabeth's trying to feed and comfort him, but I don't know. I don't think that's what he needs yet." The line went quiet for a moment. "I'm only saying this because you've already made up your mind to come home, but I'm glad for his sake you're coming. I don't know exactly what's going on between you, but it's obvious he cares an awful lot about you. He needs you here."

Emily bit her lower lip. Was Robert right? Did Dan really need her? Her pulse throbbed in her neck. "Thanks, Robert. See you soon."

She plucked an unsent postcard of the Arc de Triomphe from the dresser, flipped it over, and read the message she'd written to Grandma.

Missing you and your cookies.

She ran her finger over the place where she'd written and erased "and your grandson." Grandma's eyes wouldn't have detected it. She'd written the words on a bench outside of Notre Dame. She'd been lonesome and introspective.

We're all travelers abroad on a grand journey. It's the longing that makes the coming home so sweet. Homesick.

She wiped a tear from her eye and tucked the postcard in her drawer. *Guess it's time for both of us to go home, Grandma.*

25

Le retour

(Homecoming)

Dan stood inside the baggage claim, one hand clutching a bouquet of purple flowers, the other lodged in his jacket pocket. He rocked back and forth on his heels. He should be dead tired, but he was so wired that his sleep deprivation didn't even register. Any minute she'd be here.

A half dozen people came through the double doors, suitcases trundling behind them. From Emily's flight? He took a couple steps toward the door, his heart flip-flopping in his chest.

Emily.

She slung her purse onto her shoulder and started toward the exit.

Her hair had grown. It was almost as long as when he'd first met her. She wore a navy wool coat with a thick belt tied around her waist, something she must have bought in France. Old jeans and tennis shoes poked out from underneath the mid-thigh length coat. She pulled a large, green, rolling suitcase behind her.

He reminded himself to breathe. She'd been almost four thousand miles away, and he'd fallen in love with her. Was that even possible?

She stopped and looked in either direction.

He should wave or something, but he took a second to take her in, all her innocent beauty and generous spirit. He needed to bury his grandmother first, but then he'd talk to her, beg her to stay if that's what it came to.

She spotted him. Her eyes widened, and her mouth opened. She'd probably expected Robert or Elizabeth. A second passed, and she smiled.

He wanted to run to her, pick her up, and cover her face and hair with kisses. His feet flexed in his shoes. *Take it easy. Meet her halfway.*

Dan strode to her.

She moved toward him, the suitcase bumping along behind her. She stopped within a foot of him, let go of the suitcase, and her purse fell to the floor. Her eyes filled with sadness, compassion, and somehow peace. She flung her arms around his neck, pulling him to her.

Clutching the bouquet, Dan wrapped his arms around her. He thought he'd gotten the tears out of his system at home, alone, but a sob caught his chest, and the tears fell into her hair. Her silky, luxurious, auburn hair that smelled like citrus and sunshine.

"Dan, I'm so sorry." She cradled the back of his head and stroked his hair. "Shhh," she whispered into his ear. "It's okay."

Dan gripped the back of her coat. He didn't dare speak even her name until he got his emotions under control. He rocked her gently from side to side a couple of times, not wanting to let her go. It was an airport and Valentine's Day. He figured he could get away with it.

Valentine's Day. He wanted to buy her a dozen red roses, but given the uncertain state of their relationship and the reason for her return, he had chosen something different.

He sniffed, clearing his nose and taking one last whiff of her hair. He released her coat and stepped back.

Tears streaked her cheeks.

He yearned to wipe them away. Kiss them away maybe. Instead, he dug a clean tissue from his pocket and offered it to her.

"Thank you." She dabbed her eyes and smiled.

He held up the bouquet, lavender tied with a strip of thick beige fabric. "Happy Valentine's Day, Em."

She took the flowers and raised them to her nose. "It's lovely. Thank you."

"In case you miss the pretty purple countryside."

"Now that I'm here, the only thing I'm missing is Grandma." Her eyes watered again.

He rubbed her back. "I didn't expect you to come back. It's so far—"

She stilled him with perhaps the sweetest smile he'd ever seen. "I wanted to be here."

He wanted to ask her for how long but just nodded. He gestured toward her suitcase. "Can I get that for you?"

"Oh. Thanks." She handed over her luggage.

Shifting the handle to his other hand, he started toward the door. Her cold fingertips grasped his, squeezing them gently.

Emily was right. It was going to be okay.

***

Sunlight reflected off the snow outside, so when Emily stepped into the dim funeral parlor, it took a moment for her eyes to adjust. She secured one of the bobby pins holding her thick hair in a loose chignon and smoothed her navy dress.

Dan had taken her for a quick breakfast before the expected arrival of his mom and sisters. When she'd gotten to Robert and Elizabeth's place, only the three youngest children were at home, but they clustered around her, demanding hugs and games, even following her around the house as she attempted to get dressed for Grandma's viewing. Ironing her dress in Robert and Elizabeth's basement without burning a small child had proven to be a challenge.

Emily stood in the entranceway to the large parlor where Grandma lay in her coffin. Walls papered in muted shades of green and burgundy and soft, mellow music set a somber tone. More than a dozen baskets of flowers surrounded the open casket, their smell combining into a fragrance Emily associated exclusively with funeral homes.

Ten or fifteen people were scattered about the room in advance of the posted viewing hours. Emily had arrived about ten minutes early hoping to have a few moments with Dan before it got crowded, as it surely would. Grandma was a beloved fixture in her church and the community.

Women in black dresses and conservative heels stood gathered in front of a row of chairs, talking quietly. A couple yards away, Dan stood alone, his black suit jacket flared at the sides where his hands remained hidden in his pants pockets.

Emily approached, catching the attention of one of the women, a short brunette. She whispered to the woman next to her, a woman of about the same size with a gray-streaked bob-style haircut. The brunette turned to Dan and said something.

Dan swiveled around and spotted Emily, speaking loud enough for her to hear. "She's here for me."

He slipped his hands from his pockets and walked toward her. "Hey, Em."

"Hi." The moment she'd been dreading had finally arrived—viewing Grandma.

Dan grasped her hand and waited until she had moved alongside of him. Then they walked toward the casket, stopping short of his family.

Emily glimpsed Grandma's white hair arranged on the ivory satin pillow and her pink gown. She had never seen her in something so fancy. Narrow pleats, pearl-like buttons, and white lace trimmed the dress bodice. The fact that she was really and truly gone, never to return, hit Emily square in the chest. She pressed a hand to her mouth and turned into Dan, closing her eyes.

He held her against his shoulder and rubbed his hand up and down her back. "You okay?" His breath warmed her ear.

She nodded against the stiff fabric of his suit and straightened. "Yeah. It finally hit me. She's not coming back."

He gazed at her with tired eyes, red-rimmed but dry. "I know. I keep expecting her to call and ask me when I'm stopping by or to pick something up for her."

Emily laid a hand across her chest. "I hadn't known her all that long, but she felt like a grandmother to me too. I missed our visits when I was in France." More and more, Emily wondered if the whole trip hadn't been a huge mistake. She'd gone off and chased what she thought was her dream, never giving much thought to the consequences of leaving all the people she cared about.

Dan pushed a clean tissue into her hand, making her realize she'd started crying.

"Thank you." She wiped her eyes and sniffed.

"Come on." Dan tugged her hand. "Let's go see her."

She walked hand-in-hand with Dan toward the casket, conscious of the many pairs of eyes following them. Quiet conversation continued, occasionally marked by light laughter.

Grandma's face, natural and peaceful, looked more asleep than dead. Is that how she had looked when Dan found her? Her bony, wrinkled hands held a pearlescent rosary, the crucifix laid neatly on her gown.

Emily inched toward the *prie-dieu* and knelt, Dan sinking softly alongside her. She folded her hands in front of her and bowed her head.

Thank you, Lord, for allowing me to know this beautiful woman. She was generous with her kindness, her love, and her cookies, and I pray that she is with you now. Please comfort Dan and his family.

She recited an Our Father and a Hail Mary silently, then lifted her head.

Dan's head bent over his folded hands. She and Dan had shared many light-hearted moments, some tender ones, and a few angry ones too. Their grief added a new dimension to their shared experiences, to what she'd come to think of as their deepening relationship.

Dan's masculinity had always appealed to her, whether he wore jeans and a sweatshirt or his dirty work clothes. Clean-shaven and dressed in a crisp, tailored suit, every hair in place, he appealed to her in a new way. His demeanor, somber but not dejected, moved her. She found him so attractive that her heart began to ache in an entirely different way than what it had as she'd first knelt before Grandma.

A beautiful swag of red roses rested on the opened lid of the casket. The golden lettering on red ribbon said "Grandmother."

Dan shifted his weight beside her and stood. He extended his hand to her, helping her to her feet. His arm encircled her waist as they walked toward the side of the room.

She caught the stares of several women. Dan's sisters, she presumed. More people filtered into the parlor from the rear entrance.

Dan's arm fell away, and he faced her. "Would you like to meet my family?"

Emily nodded. "I'd love to." Using the tissue he'd given her, she wiped under her eyes. "Do I look okay?"

A smile spread across his face. "You look absolutely beautiful, Emily. I would never have asked you to come all this way, but it's so good to have you here. I . . . I can't put it into words." He lifted her hand and pressed a kiss to her fingertips.

A tingling sensation shot from her hand up her arm.

He clasped her hand and led her to his family, who quickly encircled them, apparently eager to be introduced.

"Emily, this is my mom, Jean, and my sisters, Colleen, Maureen, Kerry, and Trish." Dan gestured to each one of them in turn.

She didn't know who was the oldest or the youngest, but Colleen was the sister Dan mentioned most often.

"Everyone, this is . . ." He hesitated for a second, apparently unsure of how to characterize their relationship. "Friend" had become such a charged word between them, but after all these months, friendship best described their relationship. Instead of a dismissive "just friends" acquaintance, it was a relationship of deep and abiding affection, one that more and more filled her heart with intense warmth and tenderness that was both amiable and romantically-charged.

"This is Emily Kowalski," Dan continued. "She's . . ." He cleared his throat. "She's the light of my life."

Stunned by his admission, Emily turned to Dan.

He gazed down at her, his expression thoughtful and earnest. He meant it.

"Thank you," she whispered to him. Then, to everyone else, "It's nice to meet you. I wish it were under happier circumstances."

Dan touched her elbow. His gaze landed across the room where he'd apparently spotted someone he needed to greet. "I'll be right back," he whispered.

Emily nodded. She gave his family an anxious smile, not sure what to say. A tall man in a bowtie approached from the opposite side of the group, introducing himself, and Dan's mom and all but one of his sisters moved in that direction.

Colleen smiled warmly and guided Emily toward a small round table in the corner. They sat opposite each other in high-back chairs with plush upholstery. A small vase of light purple flowers stood between them reminding her of the lavender bouquet Dan had given her. Elizabeth had placed it in water on the kitchen island where it perfumed the air.

Colleen looked to be in her early thirties, about Emily's height. She had long brown hair, wavy like her brother's, brilliant green eyes, and freckles dotting the fair skin of her cheeks and nose. Based on her sophisticated dress, Emily guessed she had both good taste and disposable income. While those attributes would ordinarily intimidate Emily, they didn't, mainly due to Colleen's genuine smile. "I'm so happy to finally meet you. Dan mentioned you a few times, but I didn't know what to make of it. Until Grandma told me about you."

"Grandma mentioned me?" Emily swallowed back tears, again thinking of Grandma and the heart-to-heart conversations around her table.

"The last time I spoke to her. She said you could be the best thing that ever happened to Dan if he'd let go of the past. It seems like maybe he's finally done that."

Emily shrugged. "I'm honestly not sure. I've been away, out of town. Dan picked me up at the airport this morning."

"That's right. I think Grandma said you were in Italy?"

"France. Dan and I actually communicated better while I was gone than we had when I lived here." Emily touched the base of her neck and twisted her strand of faux pearls. "Our history is a little complicated. I guess I expected something he wasn't ready for, and then when he was ready, I had made plans to leave. We've kind of been at cross purposes."

"Until now," Colleen said, the hope evident in her voice.

Emily glanced at her folded hands. "I don't know. We haven't really had a chance to talk."

"I'm sorry. I'm being nosy. Dan will ream me out about it later, I'm sure." She held up a finger to someone across the room, indicating she'd be right there. "Of course you haven't had a chance to talk. You're here for a funeral. I just want you to know, Emily, and I think I can speak for my sisters and my mom, we're so happy that you're part of Dan's life. He's a special guy, and he has a lot of love to share with the right woman. Unfortunately, the only woman he's been with was—" She gritted her teeth, stopped, and smiled. "Anyway, I hope he can see now that her rejection of his proposal was all for the best."

Proposal? Emily nodded, not knowing what to say. She'd assumed Dan had broken up with this noxious woman, not that he'd proposed marriage and been refused. It sent her mind reeling.

"Excuse me, please." Colleen stood and strode across the room.

Emily scanned the room and spotted Dan talking to a couple of older gentleman. They shook hands, and the men moved forward to Dan's mother.

Dan glanced around and caught her gaze. He smiled and started toward her.

Emily stood. Finally, some of the reason for his fixation on this past relationship became clear. Despite the many negative comments she'd heard about this woman—some from Dan himself—he hadn't wanted it to end.

26

Les retrouvailles
(Reunion)

While the aroma of banana bread had long-since dissipated from Grandma's kitchen, the faint scent of her perfume lingered in her bedroom. Dan tossed aside a couple of pillows covered in white eyelet and sat, sinking into the deep mattress.

He spread a few snapshots with white, scalloped edges on the bedspread. Fingering the glossy paper, he stared at the black and white images. Two teenage girls in dirty dresses, their arms looped together, standing in front of a wooden-sided row house. A chubby middle-aged lady scattering feed to a couple of ducks. A young man in Navy dress blues, a huge smile on his face. On the back of each, someone had scratched a date in blotchy blue ink. Unfortunately, none of the photos were marked with the names of the people pictured. *Who were they to Grandma?*

He gathered them into a small pile and returned them to their shoebox. A small manila envelope in the box caught his eye. He opened the brittle flap and dumped the contents out. Spreading them across the bed, he fished through the papers trying to determine their importance when a knock sounded on the storm door.

Emily.

She had stood alongside him at the funeral parlor for two days, then at Mass and the cemetery service. Only after lunch had she said she needed to return to her brother's for a while. She had agreed to meet him at Grandma's once she'd taken a short nap and made some phone calls. He recalled her saying there was a problem with her luggage. He hadn't realized anything had been missing when he'd picked her up at the airport.

"Come on in, Em," he called. "I'm in the bedroom."

The door opened and shut, and the sound of high heels clicked across the hardwood floor then padded up the carpeted steps. Several seconds later, Emily stood next to him rubbing his shoulder. He'd finally had a chance to take off his suit coat and loosen his necktie, and the sensation of her hand over his cotton dress shirt both charmed and soothed him.

"What are you looking at?" Her gaze moved over Grandma's things. Emily had added a matching black knit sweater to the dress she'd worn for the funeral, its neckline a stark contrast to her creamy skin.

"Not sure. Lots of old pictures and papers." He shuffled through some loose photos. "Look at this one."

The photo pictured Grandma and Grand Pap outside their home. Grandma, dressed in a dark, pleated skirt that skimmed her knees, sat with her legs crossed on the hood of a 1946 Chevy Stylemaster. Pap stood next to her dressed in trousers, a light shirt and suspenders, his arm draped over her shoulder.

"Wow. That's so classic looking." She squeezed his shoulder. "Look how beautiful she was."

He smiled, pushed the items aside, and patted the bed next to him.

Emily sat, tugging on the hem of her sleek black dress.

"Speaking of beautiful, I feel like I'm not supposed to notice at a funeral, but you looked amazing." Something had changed in France. She had left as a pretty girl and come back as a beautiful woman.

Color bloomed on her cheeks. The beauty of her heart exceeded even her external beauty. She'd been his rock these past days, supportive and understanding, while she too grieved the loss of Grandma.

She'd styled her hair up again, in a tighter knot today than yesterday. The light from the hallway highlighted the contour of her graceful neck. Simple silver ball earrings dangled and bobbed from her ears. Despite their long days and her recent flight, she showed little sign of jet lag. Her makeup still drew his gaze to her sable eyes and her lush, glossy lips.

They should talk. He should tell her he'd fallen in love with her. That he wanted a future with her. He should beg her to stay. But this moment felt perfect. So perfect words seemed an intrusion. He'd let his heart speak, plain and unfiltered, for her to hear.

Dan slid his hand along her slender neck and wove his fingers behind her head and through her hair, drawing her to himself. Enough for her to lean forward so that their faces stilled within inches of each other.

Her eyes shimmered. She reached for him, resting her hand over his thundering heart.

They lingered like that for a moment, the house silent around them, sharing the same air, their souls mingling as much as their breath. He only trusted himself with one syllable, "Em."

He kissed her, tasting her minty lip gloss, her sheer essence, all that was Emily.

As she leaned further into him, a small pile of photos slid from the bed onto his foot and the floor. He didn't care.

She parted her lips, and he deepened the kiss, aware that Emily, by her own admission, was inexperienced. He moved slowly, gently. He wanted her to feel loved and cherished, not anxious or uncomfortable. If her response was any indication, he'd gotten it right.

Her lips were soft and insistent, and for the first time he hadn't a single doubt about their mutual attraction. She slid her hand around his back, pulling him closer.

"Em . . ." His lips slid from her, needing a breather. "Grandma wanted us to be together, and I've been dreaming of this . . ." He groaned. "Feels like forever. But I can't do this on her bed."

Emily pulled away, laughing. "Yeah. Not the best spot in the house for this."

He took her hand and stood. "Let's go downstairs." He led her to the living room and sat on Grandma's couch, her treasured floral-print antique with oak-tipped legs and armrests. In third grade, sick with the chicken pox, he'd laid across it reading a Hardy Boys book never dreaming some day it would be his.

Emily dropped onto the cushion alongside him, her shoulder touching his. "So, what's going to happen to this place?"

"Well . . ." He smiled and squeezed her hand, holding it on his knee. "I thought Grandma would leave it to me and my sisters, and we'd sell it, but it turns out she left it to me."

"Oh, Dan, that's wonderful!" Her eyes sparkled with joy. "This is such a great little house. There's so much love and character. And it's, uh, way better than your current digs."

Dan chuckled. "Well, that's not saying much. A bed at the Y might be better than my place."

"It's not going to cause hard feelings with your sisters, is it?"

"Nah. They're great. Like you, they said it was a step in the right direction for me."

"So, nowhere for life to go but up, huh?" She gave him a flirty look that set his heart racing.

He shifted in his seat so he could face her. "You tell me, Miss Kowalski." He'd ignored the obvious question for as long as he could. The funeral was over, and there was no avoiding it now. "This feels good, what's going on between us. You agree?"

A smile lit her face. "That kiss didn't tell you everything you need to know?"

He turned her hand over so he could interlock his fingers with hers. "How long do we have? Before you go back."

Her smile grew. "Let's play, Dan. Two Truths and a Lie."

He nodded. It was hard not to be hopeful when she seemed so happy.

"One: Gilles is the best boss ever." She exaggerated "ever" for emphasis.

"Two: I'm jobless and homeless." She puffed out her lower lip and gave him a pitiful look.

"Three: I bought a one-way ticket home." She grinned and waited for his response.

His pulse kicked up. "Em, don't mess with me."

She shook her head. "I'm not messing with you."

His heart pounded. "One. One's the lie." *Please, Lord, let it be one.*

"You are . . ." She bit her lips together on a smile. "Correct! I couldn't wait to get out of that house." She giggled.

He wrapped his arms around her, squeezing her tightly. "Thank you, God. She's here to stay."

Emily laughed against his shoulder.

He released her, easing her back so he could see her better. "You can stay here, at Grandma's. It's perfect."

Her smile vanished. "But aren't you going to move in here?"

"Eventually. But you need a place to stay, it's furnished. I have a spare key." He winked at her. "I think it's perfect."

"Are you sure? What would your sisters or your mom think?"

He shrugged. "It's mine to do with what I want. They won't mind anyway. In fact, they'll probably throw you a housewarming party."

He hugged her again, tucking her head beneath his chin. "Tell me about Gilles."

She sighed and sank back in the couch. "I can't bear to tell Robert yet, because he suspected all along, but Gilles is a dirtbag. I got tired of fending off his passes."

"Em, did he—" Dan didn't care how many miles separated them, if that chichi little letch so much as touched her—

She held a hand up. "He didn't get near as far as you did on Grandma's bed." Her mouth tilted in a lopsided, satisfied grin. "He was just a pest. I got tired of slapping away his hands and enduring his leering glances."

Dan stifled his irritation, glanced at their hands, then back into her brown eyes shining with affection. How did he ever get so lucky? Time after time he'd screwed things up with Emily, and here she sat, essentially telling him she wanted to be his. "I feel like celebrating, and yet we buried Grandma this morning. How messed up is that?"

Emily squeezed his hand and planted a soft kiss on his lips. "Not messed up at all. You and I did almost everything we could to drive each other away. Who tried to bring us together at every turn, encouraging us, praying for us?"

Dan's eyes filled with tears. "Grandma."

She kissed him again. "Uh-huh. I don't think it's a coincidence that her death became the catalyst I needed to come home."

A third kiss landed on his lips, resting there longer than the other two. "Does this couch work better for you than the bedroom?" Her voice, a sultry whisper in his ear.

"Much." They were going to have to talk about some physical boundaries because he, for one, needed them. Tomorrow they could do that. Tonight he wanted to revel in the fact that he had somehow won the heart of the most amazing woman he'd ever met.

27

Des vrais aveux
(True confessions)

A sharp rap sounded on the door. Dan's gaze darted around the room. Dirty dishes in the sink. Old magazines in the recycling bin. He blew out a breath. There hadn't been time to buy a furniture cover at Walmart like his sister Trish had suggested.

A second knock sounded. He breathed in then exhaled slowly, squaring his shoulders. Time to face the music. He intended to force a smile as he opened the door, but once he saw Emily, the smile came naturally.

"Hey, come in." He touched her elbow and kissed her cheek, pink from the cold air.

As she strolled in and laid her purse on the floor next to his couch, he decided to step up the time table for getting her in Grandma's house. Their current options for staying in together were limited to Robert and Elizabeth's "Romper Room" madness or his hole in the wall that put the shabby in shabby chic. Minus the chic.

Emily shrugged out of her navy coat, revealing a dark green, long-sleeved knit top and faded jeans. "I think I've finally caught up on my sleep."

"Oh, here, let me take your . . ." He tugged her coat before she finished removing it, practically ripping it from one arm.

"Thanks." She gave him a comical look.

He nodded and backed away. "There's no closet, so . . ." He glanced around. Where should he go with her coat? He hung his on the hook behind the door. Would it hold another? He found a little loop inside the neckline of her coat and draped it over the hook and a couple of his jackets. It slid to the floor.

"Oh, um, sorry." He stooped for it, to the sound of her laughter. "I'll just put it on—"

"Just toss it on a chair." Her eyes shone, and her lips curled in a smirk.

"Yeah. Okay." He draped it over the back of the pea green wingback chair Grandma had salvaged from the parish rummage sale. "Uh, I slept good too. Better than I had since before . . . since before Grandma died."

He'd spent all day both anticipating and dreading this evening. He'd told Emily he wanted to tell her everything. Everything about his past that had held him back. That, if he was honest, still affected his reactions and his choices. She deserved the truth.

Emily hadn't resisted. She must have heard bits and snatches of his story from Matt, Robert, and for all he knew, Colleen, who had taken an immediate liking to Emily. Now she could consider it all and decide whether she still wanted to be in a relationship with him.

"I picked up a bottle of wine." He strolled to the kitchen counter and held up a bottle of Riesling. He'd bought it in hopes of bringing a smidge of class and refinement to their evening, but now he wanted a drink to settle his jangling nerves. "Would you like some?"

"Sure." Emily settled herself on the couch and rearranged the pillows, probably hoping they'd keep her from falling through. He couldn't wait to kick that thing to the curb.

He handed her a glass—his only wine glass—and sipped his wine from a water glass.

"Thank you." She tasted the wine then patted the cushion next to her. "You said we needed to talk. I'm all ears." Her smile exuded confidence, but he detected a bit of uneasiness in her eyes.

He wiped his mouth then took another swig of wine. He nodded and sat next to her. "This is kind of like lancing a wound, so bear with me here." He took her glass and set it on the end table with his.

"I'm not proud of anything I'm about to tell you." His palms grew sweaty, and he rubbed them on his jeans. "But I think you have a right to know, if . . . if things get serious." Which he hoped they would.

She nodded and folded her hands in her lap. "I'm ready. Got tissues in my pocket and everything."

He gave her a half-hearted smile. "Where to start . . ."

"How about the beginning?"

***

Emily kneaded her hands together, both eager and anxious. She wanted nothing but honesty and transparency in their relationship, and tonight would go a long way in getting them there. Still, some of what he had to say might be hard to hear.

Dan stood and paced, staring at his feet and the floor in front of him. "Okay. Here's the short version. I'll put it out there. You can ask me anything you want, and I'll answer it."

She nodded.

His gaze met hers. "Her name is Kristen."

Finally, a name. She'd expected something a little more sinister—Maleficent, Cruella, or Medusa. Kristen seemed so . . . innocuous.

"We were together about six years. It ended when I asked her to marry me, and she turned me down." He stopped moving, faced her, but stared beyond her toward the kitchen.

Her jaw clenched, and her hand tightened into a fist. He'd confirmed what Colleen had let slip. Ultimately, it wasn't his decision to end the relationship.

"Soon after the breakup, I discovered she'd racked up a lot of debt on my credit card. Thousands and thousands." He met her gaze. "The debt affected my name and my business. Even my ability to earn new business. That's where the Christmas tree lot came in—the need for cash."

Emily's heart did that little flippy thing it hadn't done in months. Huh. If Kristen hadn't robbed him blind, she and Dan may never have met.

"I may have been an altar boy, but I haven't always behaved like one. I handled the whole breakup poorly and made a lot of bad decisions for a while before I got my act together." He sat next to her. "As recently as this past fall, she tried to get more money out of me."

Emily stared through him, trying to organize the questions forming in her mind. The one that wounded her heart the most rose to the top. "When you say you were together . . ."

"We were a couple." Dan's gaze met hers.

"Did you live together?"

"No." His answer relieved her. There probably weren't any legal or other financial ties.

"Did you sleep together?"

Dan squirmed in his seat but maintained eye contact. "Yes."

Emily cleared her throat. His answer wasn't unexpected. "Was it a one-time thing or—"

"Once it started, which was like a year into it, it was every chance we got."

She winced. Maybe she shouldn't have asked. Maybe it was better not to know.

If Dan noticed her reaction, he didn't let on. "Later it was at her whim. Her doctor had put her on the pill to regulate her cycles, or so she said, so . . ."

So what? The pill gave him a free pass? No pregnancy, no consequences? She took a deep breath, and stifled her anger. Dan had said he wasn't proud of any of this. He was just being honest with her.

Emily had harbored a dislike for Kristen long before she'd known her name, but now she had a new reason to dislike her. Not only had she broken Dan's heart and stolen from him, but she and Dan had stolen from Emily too—taken something precious that, if things proceeded like she thought they might, would only have existed between her and Dan.

She stood and drifted toward the large, single-pane window. The several inches of snow on the ground had melted and refrozen, giving it an icy sheen. She stared blankly at it, absorbing the hurt.

Dan moved beside her and reached for her hand.

She recoiled instinctively, pulling her hand into her shirtsleeve the way a turtle retracts into its shell. She hugged herself and studied a lone tree, its bare branches bent in the breeze.

"Don't sugarcoat it for me, Dan." She meant to hurt him the way his revelations hurt her. Unfair, and she knew it.

Dan tried again to touch her, stroking her arm with a soothing, gentle motion. "I don't want to hurt you, Em. I could give you excuses, but in the end, I don't think they matter. There were no pregnancies. No diseases. We were both virgins."

That was sort of good news, right? Why didn't it feel good? A tear trickled from her eye. "I'm sorry."

Dan laughed. *"You're* sorry? What do you have to be sorry for?"

She turned to him. "My reaction. I didn't expect it to hurt like this. I mean, we didn't even know each other. I had no right to expect—"

Placing a hand on either arm, he leveled his gaze at her. "You have every right to expect a man to wait for you the same as you've done for him." He swallowed hard. "If you want to keep waiting for that man—"

She shook her head. "No." She didn't want there to be any misunderstanding on that point. "No, the past is the past. I'm only interested in it because some of it affects the present. And the future."

His hands dropped to his sides.

"We've both done things we regret, Dan. I need a little time to accept it, you know? I should have let go of my crazy notions a long time ago. I kind of figured the type of relationship you had. I mean, nobody waits." She glanced down. She had always been the odd one out as far as sex was concerned. From tenth grade on, she'd been laughed at when she'd confessed her intention to wait until marriage.

Dan tipped her chin up with his index finger. "No," he said gently, "some people do wait. I didn't, and I've regretted it ever since. But never more than now."

His honesty and contrition helped ease her disappointment, but she needed more answers. Later, she'd savor those words and what they might mean. She tried a small smile. "I have a couple more questions."

"Shoot."

"Do you use illegal drugs?"

His eyes bugged. "What?"

"Drugs? Do you use?" He wouldn't deny it, would he? Or had Matt lied?

Recognition dawned on his face, and he lifted his chin. "Ah. Matt, I guess. No, I do not use drugs."

"But you used to?"

"For a period of about six months I smoked pot. Often." He shoved his hands into his jeans pockets. His eyes darted around the room as if he were looking for a hidden escape hatch.

She hated having to ask him these questions. "When's the last time you used?"

"A year and a half ago."

"Okay. What about alcohol?"

"I binge drank during the same period I smoked pot. I haven't done it since, and I'm not an alcoholic." He pinched his eyes shut with his thumb and forefinger.

"I'm guessing those were the bad decisions you were referring to. Is there anything else?"

Dan breathed deeply. "I gained a lot of weight lying around feeling sorry for myself. I severed my relationship with God. It had already taken a hit during my time with

Kristen, and I'd stopped going to Mass. After the breakup, I even stopped praying."

She touched her hand to her lips, trying to control her emotions. "I'm so sorry." She whispered as tears rolled down her cheeks. How badly he must have been hurt. It was as if they were talking about a totally different person. Dan had never been drunk or high in her presence. He appeared fit as a fiddle. He carried a rosary in his pocket, prayed before meals, and didn't miss Mass on Sundays.

Dan wiped her tears with his thumbs. "Where are your tissues?'

"Oh." She dug one from her pocket and wiped her eyes then sniffed and stemmed the flow of tears. "One more thing."

"Go ahead."

"You said in the fall Kristen tried to get money from you. How?"

He raked a hand through his hair. "She claimed she had my baby, and I owed her. For the child support."

But how? He said he'd never gotten her pregnant.

"I caught her in the lie." He pressed the back of his hand to his mouth, then sucked in his lower lip. "Remember our first date? Our attempt at one?"

"Uh-huh." How could she forget?

"She texted me while you were in the restroom. That's why I had to leave. I was rattled. I couldn't believe—didn't want to believe—it was true, and I had to get to the bottom of it."

"Oh, Dan." Her heart hurt for him. "You must've been sick." If only he'd told her. She'd been so hard on him, writing him off again. "To think you had a baby."

"I hated walking out on you like that. Leaving you with Matt."

She let him pull her into a hug, nestled her face against his chest, and breathed in his scent. A light fragrance, crisp and smelling vaguely of cedar.

"I'm so sorry, Em. So ashamed." He pressed a kiss onto her hair.

She squeezed him, loving the feel of his heart beating beneath her cheek. He had it all wrong. All he saw were his weaknesses, mistakes, and sins. None of his strengths, virtues, and accomplishments. She pulled away just enough to make eye contact. "You know what?"

"Hmm?" His eyes dimmed with regret, but she detected something else too.

"I see a man whose character and work ethic are so strong that he's built his own business—twice. A man who has the integrity to admit his mistakes and make big changes. Ones that are hard to make. And a man, who in spite of all he's suffered, has the courage to try again."

Dan squeezed her tight then released her. With unmatched tenderness, he held her face in his hands, searching her eyes as if deciding whether or not she meant what she'd said.

His hazel eyes darkened, bordering on gray. "I love you, Emily."

He *loved* her? How long she'd waited to hear those words from a man. She'd recognized after Christmas that's what she felt for Dan, but she didn't dare hope he felt the same way.

"I don't use the word lightly. When I say it, I mean it, and all that goes with it." Lifting one hand from her cheek, he twisted a lock of her hair on his finger, then let it unfurl, watching it spring back into place. "Vows, Emily. Vows I will make and keep for the rest of my life."

She shivered and blinked. Was this real? Had he said what she thought he'd said? That he wanted to marry her? "I love you too, Dan. I've only lately realized how much."

He kissed her, first gently, then with such fervor that when his lips moved from her mouth to her cheek, then her ear and neck, she sighed in pleasure.

His hands tightened around her waist, and he leaned his forehead against hers. "We don't need to rush this, Em. We can do this in a way that honors God and respects you and me. I don't want you to sacrifice your dreams for me; I want to make them come true."

Tears crested her lids and rolled down her cheeks.

He smiled, a devilish gleam in his eyes. "We're going to need some boundaries, okay?"

She nodded. They'd moved into uncharted territory for her, but being that one kiss had made every cell in her body cry out in need for him, she concurred. Some self-imposed limits would be good.

With his fingertips, he stroked her hair, then her temple, and traced a line down her shoulder and arm. "I need them. I wish I didn't, but given my past . . ." He shrugged. "I remember what happens next. And what I felt before was lust masquerading as love. It looks like a bad case of puppy love compared to what I feel for you."

"I thought I was in love once." She let her arms slip from his waist to his lower back and hooked her thumbs in his rear pockets. "It was one-sided. I can't even compare that with this."

"Don't try. This is all ours."

***

Emily cracked open the door and stepped inside a dark, quiet house, so she tugged the door closed without making a sound. She slipped off her shoes and headed for the basement stairs. Light from the kitchen fell on her path. Peering around the corner, she spotted Elizabeth at the kitchen table, her drooping head propped on her palm. "Elizabeth? What are you still doing up?"

Elizabeth tilted her glass of red wine. "Unwinding after a long physically- and emotionally-taxing day." She sipped from her goblet. "Care to join me?"

Emily turned the corner and pulled out the chair across from Elizabeth. "Why not? Just a half glass."

Elizabeth grabbed another glass from the cupboard and poured from a nearly-full bottle. "I need some kid-free time at the end of the day no matter how late it is."

"Robert's in bed already?"

"He felt like he was coming down with something, so he went in right after the kids." Elizabeth pulled the elastic band from her ponytail and let her hair fall loosely over her shoulders.

Emily sipped her wine. Better tasting and probably more expensive than what Dan had offered her. Should she tell Elizabeth about her evening?

"So," Elizabeth said with a knowing smile, "you and Dan seemed awfully cozy yesterday. Were you with him tonight?"

Emily bit her lower lip, trying to hold back the smile. Her heart filled to near bursting. Yeah, she'd tell Elizabeth.

"We had a long heart-to-heart." She folded her arms in front of her on the table. "About his past. And our future."

Elizabeth lifted a brow. "Future, huh?"

Emily twirled the stem of her wine glass. "He told me he loves me. He didn't propose or anything, but he said he wants to marry me."

Elizabeth leaned back in her chair, her eyes wide. "Wow. He said you were in touch while you were in France, but I had no idea!

"And, I've got a place to stay, so you can have your basement back."

Elizabeth glanced toward the hallway then leaned forward, speaking in a low voice. "Dear God, Emily, if you tell me you're moving in together, your brother will skin you alive. You know that, right? Right after he beats the tar out of Dan. If he even suspects that you and Dan are—"

"We aren't." Emily chuckled. "His grandma left the house to him, and he said I can live there. He'll stay in his ratty apartment." She wrinkled her nose.

Elizabeth let out a breath. "Good. I mean, not that his apartment is ratty, but, you know."

"That we're not moving in together? You know me better than that, don't you?"

"I thought I did, but the way you worded that . . ." Elizabeth emptied her glass, rinsed it, and placed it on the kitchen counter.

"Anyway, it'll be perfect since I can be out of your hair and have somewhere to live rent-free for a little while."

Elizabeth leaned against the kitchen counter as she removed her earrings. "That reminds me. I was talking to Jenny Simspon's mom at the funeral home yesterday morning. Jenny is the French teacher at Bishop MacVeigh High School, and she's going on maternity leave soon. They're looking for a long-term sub."

Emily's eyes widened. "For real? Oh, my gosh. That would be perfect. I'll stop by there tomorrow with my resume."

Elizabeth flipped off the light above the sink. "So, marriage, huh?"

Emily smiled and swirled her wine glass. "Yeah. Maybe." She drained the last drops and carried the glass to the sink.

"And this mystery woman—"

"I got her name. Kristen." She narrowed her eyes as she said it.

"Ah. Kristen. She's completely out of his system and out of his life?"

"Yeah. Bad breakup, but he's worked through all of it. She was after him for money a few months back, but he put an end to that."

"Good. You and Dan are good together. I'm happy for you both."

"Thanks." She hugged Elizabeth, grateful that they'd talked uninterrupted and without little ears listening in. Elizabeth had been a supportive, constant presence in Emily's life for so long, she seemed less like a sister-in-law than a sister, best friend, or sometimes even a mother-figure. "A week ago, I could never have imagined I'd experience such sadness and such happiness in so short time."

"Yeah. You never know what's around the corner."

28

Au coin de la rue
(Around the corner)

Dan held a bag of Chinese take-out in one hand as he pushed open the door of his apartment and allowed his sister Colleen to enter. The scents of soy and spicy General Tso's chicken teased his nostrils and taste buds.

They had spent six hours sorting through Grandma's things. A few more hours and a thorough cleaning, and the house would be ready for Emily to move in.

"Where should I go with this box of knickknack stuff?" Colleen labored behind a large cardboard box with dirty artificial Easter lilies poking from the top.

"Over there against the wall." Dan directed her with a nod of his head as he laid the takeout bag on the table. He slipped off his jacket and hung it on the back of a chair.

Colleen grunted and lowered the box to the floor, then followed him to the kitchen.

"I don't know why you couldn't let me carry it." His sisters still treated him as if he were the baby brother, not a full-grown, capable man strong enough to throw any one of them over his shoulder. "The bag of food was a lot lighter."

Colleen shrugged. "I managed just fine." She removed white containers with wire handles from the takeout bag and arranged them on the counter.

Dan grabbed the desk chair from his bedroom and set it alongside the table. "Want something to drink?"

"Water's fine." Colleen sat and began scooping white rice onto her plate. "So, Emily's moving into Grandma's, huh?"

"Hmm?" He heard her fine, but admitting he was nothing short of ecstatic about having Emily so close, in his own house even, embarrassed him. "Yeah. As soon as I get it cleaned. She just got back from France, has no job, and no real place to stay but her brother's—which is already overcrowded—so this is perfect for her."

"For her?" She smiled. "What about for you?"

His cheeks warmed. "Why don't we pray?"

Saying grace didn't distract Colleen from her line of questioning. "So, what kind of work does she do?"

"She's a teacher," he said around a mouthful of savory chicken.

Colleen kept the questions coming—How old is she? Where'd she go to college? She likes kids, huh?

He took a long drink of water. "What? Isn't this Twenty Questions? You've got at least two more."

"Very funny." She wiped her mouth. "I like her. A lot. Better than—"

He held up a hand. "Don't even say it." He'd felt a hundred pounds lighter after his conversation with Emily, getting everything about him and Kristen out in the open and firmly in the past. He finally had hope for the future. He was a new man embarking on a new stage in his life. "I'm not even going there, but, yes, Emily's great. She's a good person, you know?" He scooped a forkful of chicken into his mouth. "Makes me want to be a better man."

She piled her crumpled napkin on top of the remaining grains of rice scattered on her plate. "Well, you've got my blessing."

"Not that I asked for it, but thanks." He held back a grin.

She dumped her napkin into the trashcan and set the dish in the sink. "I'm heading out."

Dan pushed away from the table and set his plate atop hers. "I'll walk you to your car." He helped Colleen into her brown corduroy jacket. "I forgot to bring in the mail anyway."

Shivering as the cold air penetrated his thin tee shirt, he followed her to her car. "Thanks, again. I wouldn't have known what to do with some of that stuff." He hugged Colleen then held her car door open. He'd been blessed with the best sisters—caring, considerate, and easy to get along with. He couldn't wait to bring Emily into the fold.

Colleen slid behind the steering wheel, started the engine, and cranked up the heat. "You're welcome. Going through her things was kind of fun. Sad, but interesting. And it gave us a chance to catch up too."

"Text me when you get home, okay?"

The taillights on her little Volkswagen faded from sight. Once she'd turned off of his street, he jogged to the mailbox alongside the curb. He yanked open the plastic door and withdrew a bundle of mail. Stretching the dirty rubber band, he popped it off the mixture of envelopes and catalogs and slid it onto his wrist.

Plodding up the walk to his apartment, he flipped through the stack of mail. Cycling catalog, grocery store circular, a couple of direct mail pieces from a car dealership and a consignment furniture store, charity solicitations from an order of nuns and a veterans organization, electric bill, and something from a bank with which he didn't do business. He slid his finger under the seal of the bank envelope.

Ouch. Paper cut. Blood seeped from the half-inch cut, pooling and dripping onto the envelope. He smeared it on the paper to keep it from staining his clothes then pulled out the contents with his other hand.

He scanned the page, expecting some kind of solicitation. Maybe a free appliance for switching his checking account to their bank. His feet ground to a halt, and he stumbled as his final footfall landed on uneven concrete.

Dan sucked in a breath, dread and confusion battling for supremacy. He gritted his teeth and bit out a curse. Letting his other mail fall to the ground, he held the letter in two hands, twisting it as if to tear it down the center.

He stopped, cursed again, gathered his damp mail from where it lay soaking in the slush, and stomped to the house. Without a glance, Dan tossed the mail in the direction of his end table and went for his phone. Scrolling through his contacts, he found his sister Maureen on speed dial and hit send.

While he waited for her to pick up, the sickening memory of Kristen's smiling face flashed in his mind. His stomach twisted, reliving the memory . . .

"Try this one." Kristen emerged from the kitchen holding out a margarita. Clad in a tight mini skirt and clingy top, she swayed her hips as she carried it to him. "It's a little stronger than the last one."

She sat beside him on the couch and raised the drink to his lips.

He smiled, his head buzzing. "I got it." He took the drink from her, spilling a little onto his tee shirt. "How many more of these do I need to try?"

She shrugged and using a long, polished fingernail, traced a blazing trail from his chin to his chest. "A couple? I want to make the perfect margarita for my mom's birthday party."

By the time he'd drained his fourth glass, she'd jammed a pen in his hand and thrust the loan papers in front of him.

"Hey, Dan." His sister's voice brought him back to the present. "What's up?" Maureen sounded as perky as ever.

He glanced at the letter in his grasp, his hand shaking in anger. "Hey, Maur. Is Steve around?"

"Uh, yeah. What's up?"

"I've got a legal issue."

"Oh." She sounded indifferent or annoyed.

Maybe he should've spent a few minutes making small talk, asking about her and how she was doing, but he couldn't focus on anything but the letter from the bank.

"I'll get him."

A minute passed before Steve took the phone. "Dan, what can I do for you?"

"I'm being sued."

29

Des adaptions
(Adjustments)

Dan waited on Robert and Elizabeth's porch, twisting his hands and cracking his knuckles.

"See you later, little punkins." Emily's voice carried from inside the house.

His heart leapt into his throat.

He'd planned on taking Emily to an upscale restaurant for dinner, but with what he had to tell her, he thought a nice walk at the West End Overlook might be better. No more secrets. This would be a true test of their fledgling relationship.

Emily opened the door. She wore her hair pulled up into a complicated twist with tendrils dangling on either side of her face, her cheeks luminous. How could he ever have thought her plain? The beauty started in her soul and seeped out her pores.

"I'm ready," she said, bouncing on her heels. She wrapped a rainbow-colored scarf around her neck and closed the door behind her.

Dan stepped closer and kissed her, inhaling the citrusy scent of her hair. "Good. Let's go."

His truck idled in front of the house, keeping the interior warm. She slid into the seat, and he jogged around to the driver's side.

"I'm sorry about changing our plans. Maybe we can do dinner Wednesday night?"

"No problem. Wednesday's good." She fiddled with the vent on the dash and pointed it at her mid-section. "Hey, I was thinking. Next week I move, so the following week, I'm going to make a big pierogi dinner for us and invite Robert and Elizabeth and their gang. I can't wait to have a real kitchen to cook in and room to have people over. I think I'll—"

"Maybe you should hold off on that." Dan gripped the wheel with white knuckles.

She scrunched her brow and tilted her head at him.

"Just, y'know, wait a little bit 'til, uh, things settle."

"What's to settle? It's not like I have a ton of stuff."

Dan unclenched his hand from the wheel and laid it on her leg. "Em, it's just . . ." He detested Kristen. *One thing.* He wanted to do one nice thing for Emily, provide something she needed, take care of her. And now he couldn't. Because of Kristen. "You're probably wondering why I suggested we skip dinner. I need to . . . Something happened."

Little wrinkles creased her face. "Is everything okay?"

He sighed. "Yeah. Mostly." Was she worried his feelings had changed? "I love you, Em. That'll never change. This is only a little setback."

He shifted the truck into gear and pulled onto the street. "I'll explain everything."

She nodded and gazed out the window. The happy mood drained from the cab, lingering amid the cold air behind them in a stinky blue cloud of exhaust.

Twenty minutes later, Dan pulled his truck into an empty parking space in front of the overlook.

Emily sat taller in her seat, peering over the hood of the truck and up the hillside gazing toward the city beyond. "Wow."

He cast a glance at her, smiling. "You've never been here before?"

"Uh, it's kind of known as a make-out spot. What would I have been doing here?"

"Looking at the view. I've been here plenty of times." As the words came out, it occurred to him how that sounded. "Uh, with my family," he blurted. "Never with a girl."

She squinted an eye at him. "Really? You've never brought a date here?"

He shook his head. "No. I didn't date much." He exited the truck and walked around to her door, offering a hand as she slid out of the seat. They walked toward the ornamental fence that ran the length of the hillside. Couples leaned against the fence either gazing at the view or each other. A few kids scrambled in the grassy area beside their parents.

"This is spectacular." Emily tugged his hand, pulling him toward the fence.

Yellow-white lights sparkled on every floor of the buildings dotting the skyline. In the forefront, a couple of barges floated on the Ohio River, passing the lit fountain at Point State Park. Off to the side sat the science center and the empty football stadium. No city could match the beauty of this one, despite its reputation for pollution that had dissipated decades ago.

Dan smiled. He'd respected Emily's desire to travel and visit France, but he never understood it. When his mother and sisters had left, he'd stayed in Pittsburgh for Grandma. She'd passed on, but the Steel City would always be in his blood.

He gazed at Emily, the lights reflecting in her eyes. She stood rapt, admiring the view.

"Let's walk." He took a couple of steps up the sloping concrete path. "There's something I've got to tell you."

She stopped and wrenched her hand from his. "You're breaking up with me, aren't you? Dan, my heart—"

He stopped and turned to her, placing a hand on each of her arms. "No." He shook his head. "I don't want to break up with you. Not now. Not ever."

She exhaled. "Then what is it?" Worry stole the softness from her eyes.

His hands dropped to his sides. "When I got the mail last night, I found a notice from a bank I don't normally deal with. They're suing me."

She stared, obviously anticipating further explanation.

Spit it out. Get it over with. "About three years ago, I cosigned a car loan for Kristen."

Her jaw tightened, and she tilted her head. "You didn't."

How pathetic he must seem to her. Stupid and pathetic. Why did she even want to be with him? "She plied me with alcohol." He glanced down and shook his head then met her gaze. "But that's no excuse. It was just plain dumb. I had completely forgotten about it until yesterday."

She moved her hands to her hips. "Let me guess. Kristen hasn't been making payments."

"Apparently not. So I'm obligated . . ."

"To pay it all back." She let out a deep sigh that ended in a groan.

"Yep."

"How much?"

He winced as he pictured the amount on the letter he'd received. "Eighteen grand."

She raised her hands in question. "Dan, where are you going to get . . . ?" The dawn of understanding lit her eyes. "Grandma's house."

"I'm so sorry, Em." He tried to keep the pleading tone from his voice. "I've turned it over in my mind a thousand different ways. I ran the numbers, and that's the only way I can think to do it. I won't sell it, but the rent money is the only way I can make the loan payment."

Emily's face fell. "So, I'm being evicted before I even move in, huh?"

This moment and the moment Kristen laughed at his marriage proposal vied for 'most emasculated moment of Dan Malone's life.'

Emily probably had second thoughts about him. The same thoughts he'd been having: *Will I ever be free of Kristen? Or will my mistakes and sins haunt me for the rest of my life?*

"I understand." Her voice was flat. She turned and strolled in the direction they'd been walking. "Guess I'll be at Robert and Elizabeth's for a while. I got a lead on a sub position, so, maybe I can find a place of my own soon."

He wanted to say something encouraging and reassuring, like how she'd be able to move into Grandma's in no time. But he couldn't. Even if he used the rental income to double up on the loan payments, it would take him years to pay it off. What did that mean for their relationship? He hadn't thought about that. He already had a small business loan, and he didn't want to drag more debt than that into a marriage. Emily probably had school loans of her own. At least they wouldn't have to worry about a mortgage since—

"Dan?"

"Hmmm?"

She looped her arm around his waist. "Where were you?"

"Just thinking. What were you saying?"

She stopped and leaned against the fence, grabbing his hands and pulling him close. "I said, the plane ride home from France was very long, and I had a lot of time to think."

"About?"

"Whatever the heck I've been chasing after. I spent years waiting for life to happen to me, like it would only begin when a guy finally noticed me. I got fed up with that and decided I'd let God lead me. Only I acted like a pet on a leash. 'Just point the way, God, and I'll follow,' which wasn't any better."

She threaded her arms through his until they wrapped around his waist. "In both cases, I was lazy and shirked responsibility for my life. But France wasn't a total bust, because something happened there."

Dan slid his palms over her scarf and behind her head, getting lost in eyes that could swallow him up, drown him in matching pools of melted caramel. "What happened?"

"I'd left everything behind, thinking God wanted me to go do this thing for myself, but it wasn't enough. It was like

219

He wasn't enough. God wasn't enough. But He has to be, right?"

Dan nodded. Where was she going with this?

She closed her eyes and breathed in and out before she opened them again. "We're not meant to be alone. We're supposed to live in communion with each other. With Him. Messy, sloppy, dirty—like humble, dirty communion that looks a lot like tolerating a brother's over-protectiveness, or babysitting nieces and nephews, teaching a bunch of kids long division . . ."

She tilted her chin, and her eyes sparkled. "Or accepting the mistakes of a good man, who not only notices me, but treats me like I matter—to him and to the whole world. I spent years living backstage, waiting for the spotlight to hit me when the whole time I was supposed to be part of the crew bringing the story to life." A lone tear rolled down her cheek. "I guess what I'm saying is, I don't care where I live, as long as I can live. As long as I can give. Maybe I'm a failed nanny and an out-of-work substitute teacher. I'm Auntie Em. Or I'm your Em."

His heart burned. She was his Em. Now and forever.

"As long as I can breathe, I can give. I can be right in the middle of the mixed-up mess of my life, not knowing exactly where I'm going but confident that's where God wants me. That His plans don't look like my plans. That perfect doesn't necessarily mean flawless, but more like completed. Fulfilled."

She clutched the front of his jacket and inched closer to him. Her eyes watered but remained focused on his. "What I'm saying is, it's okay. You don't have to keep apologizing for your mess. Your mess is mine."

Tears welled in his eyes, and he blinked twice to hold them back. Then he released her face and pulled her in against his chest, smoothing her hair and squeezing her tight. He'd confessed his sins years ago, and God had forgiven him. Forgiving himself had been an ongoing process. Every time he got close, Kristen's antics pulled the rug out from under him again. And here Emily had forgiven him, without his asking.

He tucked Emily's head under his chin and concentrated on the feel of her body next to his from her head to her feet. She fit him.

Why had he ever asked Kristen to marry him? Was it to lend legitimacy to the way they lived? To keep her from leaving? Because it was expected? By whom? Certainly not his mom or sisters.

Emily shifted in his arms, lifting her face toward his. "Am I a little disappointed I'll be bedding down where I might wake up with a diapered kid on my head? Yeah, but it's all good."

Her warmth soaked through his jacket and chest. A breeze rattled the few crisp brown leaves that clung to the tree branches above them, and the cold air licked his neck and ears.

Emily shivered.

"Let's go back to the truck."

She peered up at him, her eyes wide. "You're taking me home already?"

He released her then held his arm out for her.

She took it.

"Who said anything about going home? I brought you to a make-out spot. I think we ought to make our visit worthwhile." He flashed a grin.

"Oh. In that case, let's go." She broke into a run.

The wind kicked up again, and he matched her pace.

***

Based on when they'd left the pizza shop, Dan guessed it was close to two in the morning when they reached Robert and Elizabeth's house. Other than a dog barking in the distance, the silence of the moonless night matched its darkness.

Emily laid her arm across her belly and groaned as she took the last step onto the porch. "I should've stopped at one piece of pizza. It's not sitting well."

"It was pretty greasy." Dan rubbed her back.

"But it was so, so good."

He smiled. Getting up in the morning would be killer, but she was so worth every lost minute of sleep. He stepped closer and lowered his head to kiss her.

Brilliant yellow light burst from the lamp affixed to the porch. Even with his eyes nearly closed, it blinded Dan.

Emily pulled away from him, squinting at the door.

The storm door clicked and pushed open. Robert stood barefooted and bare-chested in a pair of flannel sleep pants dotted with Pittsburgh Steelers logos. "Yinz guys are preparing me for having teenagers in the house." He held the door open with his backside and motioned them in. "It's freezing out there."

Emily stepped in, refusing to smile at his use of Pittsburghese. "Only I'm not a teenager, and you're not Dad." She loosened her rainbow scarf, untwisting it from around her neck. "What are you even doing up?"

Robert shut the door behind them. "Gianna wet the bed. Sheet change." He nodded toward a stack of clean, pink sheets lying on the back of the couch. "I saw Dan's truck. Sorry to, uh, to interrupt."

"I'll bet you are," Emily mumbled.

Dan stifled a laugh. "What's up, Robert?"

Robert cleared his throat. "Yeah. I was going to call you in the morning. Had this guy in the shop yesterday to look at the catalytic converter on his panel truck. He does fencing, and he told me about this big job at the zoo. He said they're looking for landscapers, and they're redoing some retaining walls and patios. Thought you might want to call and find out about it."

"Yeah." Dan rubbed a hand over his chin, missing the extra warmth the beard had provided last winter. "I'll do that. Thanks."

His gaze shifted to Emily. They had spent a couple hours or more talking and kissing in his truck at the overlook, but he hadn't gotten a goodnight kiss, and he wasn't leaving without one. His gaze darted back to Robert.

Robert arched his brows.

"Mind if we, uh, say goodnight?"

Robert's cheeks pinked. He glanced at Emily, who stared at him, her lips twisted in annoyance. "Oh, go ahead. Sorry." He pointed a finger back and forth between them. "So, is this thing on again?"

Emily rolled her eyes.

"Oh, yeah. It's on." Dan grinned as Emily's cheeks reddened too. He didn't wait for Robert to excuse himself. He rested his hands on Emily's elbows, leaned in and kissed her. In under three seconds, Robert fake coughed.

"I love you," he whispered in her ear then shook Robert's hand. "Goodnight, man. Better get those sheets on the bed." He inclined his chin toward the bedding.

"Ah . . ." Robert cursed, grabbed the sheets, and trudged down the hall.

A childish whine came from the direction of the bedrooms. "Dad-dy!"

Emily giggled and patted Dan's chest. "I love you too. Call me."

Dan nodded and let himself out. On the porch, a blast of cold air seeped through his sweatshirt, and he zipped his jacket. Definitely getting colder. He jogged down the steps and toward his truck, a cloud of exhaust forming behind it. The night went better than he expected, thanks to Emily's understanding. He never wanted to go to her with something like that again.

30

L'amour sur la glace

(Love on ice)

Dan stooped and pulled the frayed laces of a rented hockey skate tight around his left ankle. He dropped his foot, the silver blade hitting the ground with a thud. He crossed his other ankle over his knee, spread the leather skate wide open, and shoved in his foot. "How did you ever talk me into this?"

Emily stood in front of him, laces tied, wobbling on white figure skates. Thick red socks and black fleece leggings poked out of the skate tops. She wore the navy pea coat she'd bought in France and her long, rainbow scarf wound loosely around her neck. Waves of auburn hair shone and spilled over her shoulders.

Visions of him, Emily, a cozy couch, and a roaring fire flashed in his mind. No one made him feel as contented as she did. All his best instincts rose to the surface when he held her in his arms, leaving him feeling protective, chivalrous, capable, and more like a man than ever.

She glanced at the skaters whirring around the outdoor rink then back at him. "Talk you into it? I guess I caught you in a weak moment." One side of her mouth lifted in a grin.

He recalled Sunday night in his truck at the overlook. Yeah, he may have been a little vulnerable to persuasion. Good thing she'd set her sights on ice skating and not bungee jumping or cliff diving. "I haven't skated in ten years." He lined his skates up in front of him, hoping for some kind of muscle memory associated with the sport.

Emily held out her hands, he grasped them, and she pulled him into a standing position.

"There. Just like riding a bike. You'll be fine." She tottered toward the ice on unsteady legs with Dan following.

The second she stepped on the ice, her feet glided with ease and agility.

He limited his movement to sporadic, shaking bursts in which he thrust one foot in front of the other.

She grabbed his elbow to steady him.

He jerked his arm away. "I got this."

Emily arched a brow. "Geez. Just like Grandma. She'd never let me help her either."

Dan's ire softened at the mention of Grandma. Not a day went by he didn't miss her calls, their conversations, or her nudging a bag of cookies across the table toward him. He sighed. "Let it be known the cycle of pig-headed independence stops here." He lifted his elbow, and she placed her hand on it.

With a few refresher lessons from Emily, Dan circled the rink with her at a modest speed without his legs flailing in opposite directions.

The wind picked up, stinging his cheeks as they skidded to the edge of the rink. Dan's skate tip caught the rim where ice met concrete, and they both stumbled forward, laughing. Their breaths created little white puffs in the frigid air. "How's hot chocolate sound?"

"Perfect."

He bought each of them a steaming cup of cocoa, and they sat on a bench alongside the rink.

Dan sipped his drink, gazing at the glass buildings that towered over them. Once the sun set, the windows glimmered, reflecting the colored lights aimed at them. He'd lived in this city his whole life and had never been to the downtown skating rink before.

"I have some news." Emily gripped her Styrofoam cup in her gloved hands and blew on it. "The Bishop MacVeigh sub position has already been filled, but I got an interview with one of the public high schools on the other side of town."

"You did? That's great, Em. Which school?"

"Monongahela High." Her bright expression shone with pride.

While not an inner city school, its location wasn't the best. It was only an interview though, and he didn't want to dampen her enthusiasm. "You're going to be an awesome French teacher. And the prettiest too." He leaned in for a quick kiss. "I have news too. That lead on the zoo job Robert gave me? It was good. There's some red tape I have to get through, but I think they're going to hire me. I'm probably going to spend fifty percent of my time this spring and summer at the zoo."

"Oh, Dan, that's fantastic!" She swung an arm around him, and he held out his cup of hot chocolate to steady it. She pressed her warm lips against his cold cheek.

He wished for the thousandth time that he'd been able to move her into Grandma's, no, *his* house like he'd planned. Would they ever be able to spend a quiet evening together indoors without the intrusion of her family? Maybe she could help him fix up his apartment to make it homier. How exactly did one make peeling paint and rodent damage appealing?

Dan took her gloved hand in his. He preferred the feel of her bare skin, but he'd take what he could get. He tried to block out the syrupy pop song coming from the speakers and concentrated on the happy squeals, laughter, and other ambient noise. Taking a final sip, he emptied his paperboard cup and set it on the ground beside him. As he leaned back in his seat, the cell phone in his pocket vibrated.

Emily's thigh jerked away from his. "I think your leg is buzzing."

He squeezed her closer. "You like that? Just hold still and—"

The phone vibrated again. She giggled and scooted away. "That's weird. Answer your phone."

He pulled her toward him. This was a date, and she deserved all his attention. "Nah. Whoever it is can leave a message." Probably someone eager to get a quote on a patio once the weather broke.

A minute or so passed with no buzz. A four-note chime sounded instead.

She tilted her hip to the side. "I think someone wants to communicate with you. Maybe you should check. It could be something urgent—your mom or one of your sisters."

He sighed and pulled the phone from his pocket. One swipe and the message materialized in front of him. His chest tightened, he cursed and sprung from the bench, teetering on the narrow blades.

Emily stood and rested her hand on his back. "Everything okay?"

It would never freakin' end. Never. And Emily would be privy to all of it. Every last bit. There was no way to hide it, not that he wanted to anymore. He just wanted it to stop.

He bit his lower lip and swung his gaze to Emily.

Her brown eyes reflected the shimmering lights strung in the trees surrounding them. Concern etched her features.

"It's Kristen."

"Kristen?" Her hand fell away from his back and the concern morphed into confusion. "What does she want?"

"What she always wants. Money." He glanced at the phone and read the message aloud. "Sorry I lied about the kid. Doesn't change that you owe me. I need a little cash to get me to the end of the month. If you ever cared, you'll help me."

Emily didn't respond. What could she say?

What could he say? He turned his back on her and took a few wobbly steps away from the rink, stabbing at the tiny keypad with his fingers. He re-read his message.

For the last time, I don't owe you. I'll call you tomorrow.

Apparently he hadn't been clear when he'd told her not to contact him again. She knew he'd assumed payments on her loan, didn't she? Steve had said he didn't have a case. He'd cosigned, and he'd have to pay. He'd tell her under no circumstance should she call him again. Too bad he couldn't change his cell number, but he used it for work and the number was printed on his business cards and advertisements. He powered the phone off and shoved it back in his pocket.

Emily circled in front of him. "What are you going to do?"

He pasted a smile on despite the fact Kristen's message left him wanting to pummel something. He glanced around as if he might find something suitable. Unfortunately, every inanimate object in sight looked rock hard.

"I'm going to take you for one more spin around the ice. That's what I'm going to do." He kissed the top of her head and grabbed her gloved hand. He toddled toward the ice, but she didn't follow.

"Dan?"

He sighed and let his head fall back. "I know, I know. I'll deal with her. But not tonight. She's already intruded on our evening enough. I'll call her tomorrow."

His answer seemed to satisfy her, and she shuffled toward the ice with him. He wanted to enjoy the rest of their evening, but his irritation compounded, sending a tight, burning-sensation through his chest. Tomorrow he would cut ties with Kristen, once and for all.

31

La fin de l'ignorance

(The end of the ignorance)

The phone lay on the counter in front of Dan. He stared at the time. After ten in the morning. If Kristen was still asleep, well, too freakin' bad. He punched in her number and waited.

Kristen slept late, long into the mornings. It irritated Dan then, but he'd overlooked it because . . . why? All of her other good qualities?

He'd blotted them out since their breakup, but there were good qualities. She'd been beautiful, of course. But vivacious too. She lived life to the full. But only after mid-morning. It had been the source of more than one argument when they'd made plans to go somewhere and he'd show up at her door only to find she hadn't gotten out of bed.

Next to the couch, he spied a basket of clean laundry, his folded bedding, and his mind drifted to the mornings he'd woken tangled in Kristen's sheets. Even having him next to her, his hands roving her body, desperate to repeat what they'd done the night before, she wouldn't sacrifice a minute of her precious sleep. Without fail, she'd slap his hands away, roll over, and pull the covers around her like a shroud. She even met his lone attempt at breakfast in bed with indifference. He ate her meal at the coffee table, half-listening to a Sunday newsmagazine show.

A knot formed in his chest as he relived his idiocy. Dan had reveled in the way Kristen soaked up every bit of his attention in the beginning. It only served to deepen his pain when she rejected that attention later. He rubbed a hand over his eyes and pushed the self-defeating thoughts away. Ancient history. His life was back on track, and he had a future to think about. One with a beautiful woman, who for some crazy reason, genuinely cared about him.

He pulled the phone away from his ear and glanced at the ticking seconds. Would Kristen ever answer?

"Dan." Her voice came through the speaker, and he scrambled to get the phone back to his ear. At least she sounded awake. "I was wondering if you'd call." Her smooth voice made his chest tense, his grip tighten on the phone.

"I said I would." *Some people don't lie with every breath that escapes their lips.*

"Yeah. Did I interrupt something last night?"

Emily was none of her business. He was none of her business. No way was he going to let her turn this into a fishing expedition.

Uncomfortable silence ensued.

"Okay, then. I'll get to the point." Her voice held a hint of amusement, rather than annoyance. "My roommate moved out, so I've got, like, double the rent, and my hours have been cut. I've got the car payment—"

"You don't have the car payment." She really didn't know the bank had sued him?

"I've got the car payment." Irritation rose in her voice.

"No, Kristen. I've got the car payment. I was your co-signer, remember?"

Silence.

"And since they've come after me, I don't think you've had the car payment in a long time."

"Like I said, Dan, my roommate left—"

"I don't need the sob story, Kristen. Here's the deal. I'm already paying for your friggin' luxury vehicle while I drive the same beat-up pickup truck I've had for ten years." He pushed off the counter and paced the length of his apartment, gesturing as he spoke. "I've also been paying off all the debt you racked up using my credit card for your pansy-ass pedicures, massages, and whatever else you felt like charging to my account. To top it off, I had to sink more money into rebuilding my business after you ruined my credit and my reputation."

He took a breath, half expecting her to jump in and refute him.

She didn't.

"So, as I see it, I don't know owe you a thing. Get this through your head, Kristen—it shouldn't be too hard since you're the one that laughed at my proposal and left. We. Are. Done. D-O-N-E. No more texts, no more phone calls and pleas for money. I don't even want to see snail mail with your name on it. Got it?" She couldn't misunderstand that. He'd be done with her for sure. Getting it all out felt better than he anticipated. He felt lighter, freer.

"So, Dan's got a girlfriend." She said the last word in a sing-song voice. "What's her name? Let's call her 'Kitty,' since she's obviously got you whipped."

Dan yanked the phone from his ear and jerked his arm back, ready to hurl the device across the room. Only that would be one more expense he couldn't afford.

"Still there, Dan-o?"

He gritted his teeth and put the phone to his ear. "I'm here. Just long enough for you to confirm what I've said. You are not to contact me again under any circumstances. Do you understand?"

"You still owe me."

Infuriating. If they had done this conversation in person, he may have strangled her by now. "I just recounted all the debt you've incurred in my name. How the frick do you figure I owe you?"

"You owe me." Her voice cracked with emotion. "For the abortion. Five-hundred fifty dollars."

Dan's mouth opened but no words came out. A sick feeling spread from his stomach causing an ache in his chest. Lies. More lies. "What abortion? You were never pregnant."

"And how would you know? As I recall, you were clueless. A month-long stomach bug? Really? I could hardly believe you bought that." Was she choking on laughter or tears?

Dan's mind ticked back over their time together. A series of canceled dates. Complaints of nausea. Her lying in bed longer and later than usual. She'd said it was a virus.

Pregnancy had crossed his mind. She'd been putting him off a lot, but one time was all it took. She'd insisted it was something she'd caught. And then she'd gotten better. He'd assumed whatever it was had run its course.

Another lie. But which was the lie—what she'd told him years ago or what she was saying now? He wished they *had* done this in person. He needed to see her eyes, to give her shoulders a firm shake, to get the truth from her at last.

"It was my body. I was the one who would be sick and fat and knocked up. Y'know, it's not all knitting booties and hanging teddy bear mobiles." She said it in a voice so saccharine he wanted to vomit. He pictured her flipping her hair and rolling her eyes the way she used to when she brushed him off. "I'm sending you a picture."

Dan's heart pounded. *Please, Lord, don't let it be true.*

His phone dinged, and a photo message came through. He flicked his fingers over the image to enlarge it.

Planned Parenthood.

Termination.

Twelve weeks with conscious sedation.

$550. Paid in full. Cash.

Her name and the date—a plausible one—appeared on the bottom.

The pain in his chest sharpened, but he could only stare. Then she yammered at him again, and he pulled the phone to his ear.

"I carried your baby for twelve and a half weeks wishing I'd miscarry, and it would be over. When it didn't happen, I took care of it." All the emotion left her voice, as if she'd driven light years of distance between her and the baby they'd conceived.

They'd conceived a baby. Dan's mouth fell, as did his stomach. He was a father. *Was* a father. His own flesh and blood had lived and died, and he'd never known. An empty blackness engulfed him to the point of nausea. Phone to his ear, he plodded to his bathroom. A darkness pervaded his spirit, but the mirror reflected an inverse image. His face turned ghostly white, save for his eyes, which appeared dull and gray.

"Swear to me," he growled into the phone. "Swear to me you are telling the truth." His tone softened, weakened. His faced sagged in the mirror. "Please, Kristen. If you are honest about one thing, let this be the one."

The line went quiet for a few seconds. Then, in a voice so soft, so meek he could barely hear it, she said, "I swear it."

Dan stumbled back. The blackness inside him rose, forcing bile into his throat. Hatred coursed through his veins. Maybe it was better over the phone. He couldn't be sure he wouldn't hurt her if she were with him. The black animus within him sought retribution for the scorching pain, and right now, Kristen was the target.

"How could you? Our *baby*, Kristen. You hate me that much? You let me in your bed. I thought I loved you. Why didn't you tell me? I would've done anything for you. For our baby." His voice quavered, soft and low. "If you didn't think we could raise that baby, we could've put it up for adoption. I would've," he said, choking back the thickness in his throat, "I would've raised the child myself."

She laughed.

The darkness spread to his leaden limbs. His eyes darted around the room searching, but he didn't know for what. An escape? A lifeline?

"You? Oh, yeah. You'd be a great dad. I stayed in touch with Matt, you know. I know what happened after we broke up. Smoking weed, getting drunk. Driving your business into the ground. Yeah, some father you'd make."

He ignored what she said, forestalling the blackness from swallowing him up. "You know how I feel about abortion. How *could* you?" For all he knew, his baby had been carved up, its parts sold for research. His lips trembled as he formed the words. "You aborted our son. Or our daughter. Do you even know which?"

"No. Of course not."

Of course not. Was she being dismissive? His own emotional state was so tangled, he couldn't discern hers.

"Hear this, Kristen. Do not contact me again." His voice had gone so low and gravelly he wondered if it was audible. "Do you understand me?"

"Don't you dare end this conversation, Dan Malone. Not until you promise me you'll send the money."

"Send you the money? Are you insane?" He shouted now. "Are you not hearing me? You think I'm going to reimburse you for the cost of ending our baby's life?" He laughed, and his voice was unrecognizable even to him. Joyless. Bitter. Hurt like he'd never known seeped from his bones. The dark months after their breakup paled in comparison.

"I know I share the guilt here. You didn't get pregnant by yourself. But not a penny of mine will ever be associated with what you did."

The other end of the line went quiet. Dan couldn't think of another thing to say. He slouched against the wall—weak, exhausted, sick, overcome. He willed the darkness to take him.

"God, have mercy on us both," he muttered before he dropped the phone and sank to the floor.

32

La culpabilité
(Guilt)

Dan didn't move from the bathroom floor. Didn't budge. Just stared at the cracked tiles, their intricate pattern of squares and rectangles hemmed in by blackened grout. A maze of succeeding dead ends. He couldn't think, couldn't feel. From a precipice, he stared into the gaping vacuum looming before him.

Slowly, gradually, unbidden thoughts broke through the numbness. He pictured Baby Ben lobbing handfuls of peas from his high chair. Would his little boy have done the same? Maybe it had been a little girl, dressed in a frilly gown, gazing at him with wide, innocent eyes, hanging on his every word. "How do I look, Daddy?"

The hard, unforgiving tile floor made his butt sore. He needed to move. He pressed his fingers into his eyes and rubbed, trying to focus. Where had his phone gone? He scanned the small room and found it near the back of the toilet. Crawling toward it, he reached behind the bowl. The sickly-sweet smell of urine seeped from the subfloor beneath the commode. Fitting odor for all his piss-poor decisions.

He grabbed the phone, checked the time, and sat back on his heels. An hour and a half he'd been here, doing what? Staring into nothingness?

Pray. The idea resonated in his heart. A nice, pious thought, but he couldn't do it. Not yet. He couldn't face himself, let alone God.

The phone's ringtone sounded, and he jerked back, opening his hand and letting the phone clatter to the floor. His thoughts turned to Grandma as they did every time his phone rang. She'd be so ashamed of him. At least he could be sure it wasn't her calling.

It rang again, and Dan picked it up. He swiped across the phone and held it to his ear. "Hello?" His voice still came out gravelly, barely recognizable.

"Dan? Is that you?"

Emily. He should've let it roll to voicemail.

He cleared his throat. "It's me."

"I was calling to see how it went with Kristen."

His emotions warred within him. He couldn't bear facing her with yet another consequence of his sins. She was generous and forgiving, but how much would one woman take before she'd decide enough was enough? And yet, he needed her. She was all light, purity, and innocence—his polar opposite. If he had any hope of climbing out of this pit of despair he'd sunk into, it was her.

"Dan? Are you there?"

He drew his knees up to his chest and breathed deeply. "I'm here."

"How'd it go?"

For once his pride didn't win. "Em, I need you." His voice caught on a sob.

Alarm laced with concern sounded in her voice. "Where are you?"

He dragged his sleeve over his face, wiping away tears. "My apartment. Can you . . . can you come?"

"I'll be there in fifteen."

"Oh. Okay. Just come in." He wasn't sure if she was still on the line.

He opened the web browser on his phone and found the due date widget he'd used when Kristen had claimed she'd had his baby. He plugged in a date from around the time he thought Kristen would've conceived. The app calculated a month and a day. Spring. The baby would've been born in late spring making him or her about three months short of two years old.

Dropping the phone, he buried his face in his hands. Images of chubby baby cheeks and pudgy fingers danced behind his closed eyes. Then images of Kristen. Images of what she'd done and endured, terrible, sickening, mournful images that played like a horror reel. He couldn't rid them from his mind.

"Dan? Where are you?" Emily's voice brought him out of his trance. She'd probably knocked first, but he hadn't heard it.

Two seconds later, she stood in the doorway. She wore a pale pink tee shirt and navy sweatpants and her hair clipped back on the sides.

She dropped to her knees. "What happened? Are you okay? Are you hurt?" Her brow creased with worry.

His heart was rent in two, but that's not what she meant. He forced himself to stare into her eyes. Beautiful brown eyes brimming with worry. Worry he'd put there. He shook his head. "I'm just messed up from talking to Kristen."

"What's going on?" She clasped his hands where they lay on the floor at his sides and squeezed his palms. "You can tell me."

He could tell her. She'd listen without judgment or demand. Without anger or any trace of negative emotion. That didn't mean it might not drive her away later.

He sighed. "I called Kristen. Told her to stop. Stop calling, stop texting, stop claiming I owed her anything."

"And?"

"And I told her I'm paying for her car. She acted like she didn't know." He shrugged a shoulder, still unsure if he bought that. "I recounted all the other debts I'd incurred because of her and demanded that she stop."

She nodded. This is how she would've expected the conversation to go.

"And then she demanded payment for something else."

Emily's hands slid out of his and onto her own lap. "For what?"

A shudder ran through him. He'd asked Emily to come. Now he had to tell her, to say it out loud. He didn't think he could bear to see the look in her eyes as she realized he'd helped bring a life into the world. A life that had been taken.

Emily leaned in, peering at him. "Dan, pay for what?"

He steeled his nerves and forced the answer out. "Her abortion."

Her eyes widened, and she blinked. "I don't understand. Is she pregnant? Why would she come to you with that?"

Dan fisted his hand and tapped it against his pursed lips. How should he say it? He shook his head. "It happened . . . it happened almost three years ago. She . . . she aborted our baby." He recalled the dates and the receipt. "Late in the first trimester."

Emily's hand covered her mouth, and tears welled in her eyes. "Oh, Dan. I'm so sorry."

He shook his head. "I didn't even know she was pregnant. I swear it. I wouldn't have let it happen. I'd have found a way to stop her."

She bit her lower lip. "Which is probably why she didn't tell you."

Of course it was. Why hadn't he thought of that?

Emily uncurled her legs from beneath her, leaned forward, and gathered him into her arms. She tucked his head beneath her chin and combed her fingers through his hair as if she were comforting one of her nieces or nephews.

"I didn't know, Em. I was with her, I was probably sleeping with her while my baby was growing inside her, and I never knew it. I did nothing to protect my own child."

She tensed for the briefest of moments, and he knew he'd hurt her. He hadn't meant to, but he had. How would he feel if he had to hear her go on about how she'd slept with another man? He doubted he'd bear it as gracefully as she.

A few tears trickled from his eyes, but nothing like the torrent he'd expected. He supposed even his grief had been swallowed by the black abyss.

She stroked the hair behind his ear, smoothing it against his head. "Why are you here, in the bathroom?"

For a second, he couldn't recall why. "I, uh, I felt sick."

She released him and stood. "Come, sit on the couch. I'll make us some tea." After wiping her eyes, she slipped out of the room, heading for the kitchen.

He staggered to the living area, where he collapsed onto the couch.

Emily stood at the sink, the ancient tea kettle rattling as she filled it with water. Grandma had given the old thing to him, another of her rummage sale finds.

Emily pivoted and turned to the stove, her hips swaying a bit. She set the kettle on the burner then reached into an overhead cupboard. Her tee shirt rode up, revealing a sliver of skin. She pulled down two mismatched mugs and the tea tin. His gaze followed her every movement, lingering on every soft curve.

He wanted her.

Not peeling her out of some fabulous gown or elegant lingerie on their wedding night. Now. In worn sweatpants and a tee on his battered couch. He needed her—not just her hugs and soothing words, but her touch, her tenderness, and her passion. He needed to fill that empty ache inside, to pretend, if only for an hour, that someone could love him after what he'd been party to, unknowingly or not. He needed to feel whole—a man, strong and capable of providing and protecting.

But he couldn't have that with Emily. Not all of it. Not yet anyway. Maybe not ever. He didn't deserve to breathe the same air as Emily, let alone do *that* with her.

His twisted desire disgusted him. After all, failure to keep his pants zipped was what created this mess in the first place. "Mess" was too kind a word. The stakes—a baby's life—were much higher.

The kettle chirped, then whistled, and Emily poured boiling water into the mugs. She dunked each tea bag several times, brought the mugs to the couch, and set them on the coffee table. The scent of chamomile filled the room.

"Thank you."

"You're welcome." Despite the steam that wafted from the mugs, she attempted a sip. "You should name the baby."

Was she crazy? "Name the baby? I can't."

"Why not?"

It would make it too real. It would hurt too much. "I don't know if it was a boy or a girl."

"Choose one. You have a 50/50 chance of being right. Or pick a name that would work for either."

How could he ever forget—ever put this behind him—if he attached a name to the hole in his heart? He shook his head. "I can't."

She sipped her tea, backing off a bit as the hot liquid touched her lips. "Robert and Elizabeth named the baby. The one they lost." She fanned the steam with her hand. "Elizabeth didn't tell me the name, but she said it helped. Kept it from being a nameless, faceless being." She touched his knee. "A baby needs a name, Dan. Even in heaven."

Heaven. A place he'd likely never see. "I know you're trying to help, Em, but, no."

"Think about it, okay?" She patted his leg. "And maybe you could talk to Robert. He'll understand."

Understand? Was she insane? Robert was a model dad with happy children nurtured by two loving parents. He and Robert had nothing in common. Even if Robert could be a sympathetic friend, he'd never accept Dan as a potential brother-in-law. Not now.

Emily stayed the afternoon, grilling cheese sandwiches and heating canned soup. She held him and murmured soft reassurances in his ear. She tried conversation, both small talk and the heavy stuff, and when neither worked, she sat in silence with him.

She shuffled through her purse and withdrew a rosary from a white vinyl pouch. Laying it in her lap, she untangled the beads. An image of Our Lady of Guadalupe completed the loop that linked the decade beads to the ones used for the opening prayers.

He stared at the medal.

She ran it lightly between her fingers. "Mary was pregnant in this depiction, but you can hardly tell."

What was her point?

"Do you want to pray?"

He shook his head.

"Do you mind if I do?"

"No. Of course not." He did, but he wasn't about to say so.

She sat beside him in silence and prayed an entire Rosary, her fingers moving over the beads as she did so.

He closed his eyes and settled on the edge of the abyss, not sure if he wanted to dive in or claw his way out. Emily was there, throwing him a lifeline—heck, she was even calling for backup—and he didn't know if he wanted it anymore. He wanted to be alone, to wallow in his own filth, the mess he'd made of his life. The mess that had cost his baby its life.

He opened his eyes, studying Emily as she prayed. Beautiful. With her eyes closed, her lips moved the tiniest bit. Her lips. In his truck, at the overlook, her soft, tender kisses so filled with love had driven him crazy. He wanted to drown himself in those kisses tonight, get lost in the feel of her skin beneath—

What was he thinking? There'd been little doubt before, but now he knew with certainty. Emily was better off without him. If she couldn't see it herself, he'd make her see it. He'd ensure she'd cut ties with him forever.

She blessed herself with the rosary's crucifix and returned the beads to her pouch.

"Em, I appreciate you coming. And staying."

She smiled weakly. "Where else would I be when you need me?"

Another fissure opened in his heart. "If you don't mind, I think what I need now is to be alone."

She blinked in surprise. "Oh. Well, whatever you want. I can go."

He nodded. "I think that would be best." He didn't trust himself alone with her like this. Not in the state he was in.

She'd been sitting next to him praying, for cripe's sake, and in the intermittent seconds when his grief ebbed, his impulsive need for her physical assuagement teetered dangerously close to overriding his convictions. As if his capacity for virtue were trapped in a necrotic eddy.

The obvious hurt on her face broke what was left of his heart.

She ambled to the entranceway and pulled on her coat. No rainbow scarf today.

He held the door open for her.

She laid a hand to his cheek, her fingers rubbing feather-light over his skin, scratching against the stubble. "Don't you give up. I know it's bad right now, but there's always hope. Your sins have already been forgiven."

He trembled. Maybe they were, but it sure didn't feel like it.

She shrugged. "Maybe you should've suspected, but she lied. You didn't know." Tears filled her eyes. "I'll call you in the morning. We can go to church together."

He nodded, not wanting to commit to anything. He needed to get out of this apartment. To forget, even if it were only for a few hours.

The door clicked shut behind her, and he strode to the bathroom. He showered and shaved, leaving a hint of beard. After splashing on aftershave and a clean shirt and jeans, he grabbed his keys off the counter, foregoing even a jacket.

He needed a drink. He wouldn't slip back into old, bad habits, but what could a beer—or two—hurt?

***

Dan swung a leg over a barstool at The Watering Hole. It wasn't exactly in his neighborhood, but he could be reasonably sure he wouldn't run into anyone he knew.

The bartender approached, a squeaky-clean-looking guy with a chipper grin.

Dan wanted to sock him.

"What can I get you?

"Shot and a beer, please." Dan's gaze skirted the room.

An olive-skinned woman about his age leaned against the bar. Long, dark hair hung so low on her back he couldn't see where it ended. A sun-shaped medallion rested on her tanned chest above ample cleavage. A little white tank top poked out beneath a plaid flannel shirt tied at her waist. She was cute. In a way. Her nose was a little long, and she had an overbite, but her eyes shone with obvious admiration for him.

She smiled flirtatiously.

He smiled back, liking the attention.

The bartender brought his drinks, and he threw back the shot then sipped the beer.

The woman slid from her bar stool and slinked between several couples, making her way to the empty stool beside him. "Mind if I join you?"

33

Le péché appelle le péché
(Sin begets sin)

Emily savored the yeasty aroma of Elizabeth's kitchen while she turned the handle on her great-grandmother's antique nut grinder. Bits of walnut pushed through the small, round holes and fell in clumps to the bowl beneath. She winced at the blare of sirens from the next room as the action sequence in the animated movie reached its crescendo. "Something's not right, I can feel it."

Elizabeth glanced up from the cutting board she'd dusted with flour. "I don't know what to tell you. I understand you don't want to break Dan's confidence, but without knowing what's got him so depressed, I don't know what to suggest." She took a ball of dough, sprinkled it with flour, and flattened it with a rolling pin.

Emily grabbed another handful of shelled walnuts and dropped them into the grinder. "It's not like he swore me to secrecy or anything. It's just personal. It's not something he'd want to share."

"What about with Robert?"

Emily rotated the handle a few times then stopped to shake out her arm. Her muscles ached from the continuous motion. "I encouraged him to talk to Robert, but he resisted."

"What exactly makes you think there's something wrong?" Elizabeth took Emily's bowl of nuts and poured it into a larger bowl where she combined it with sugar and milk.

"When I called this morning, he said he needed me. Not that he wanted me there, he needed me. And he did." She turned the grinder handle again, trying to decide how much to share about Dan. When she'd arrived, his sallow cheeks and drooping eyes alarmed her. His hair stood on end as if he'd tried to pull it out. "I held him. I sat with him. I prayed. And then he up and asked me to leave, saying he wanted to be alone." Tears stung her eyes, and she blinked them away.

"It does sound odd." Elizabeth counted the long loaf pans she'd arranged on the counter, ticking them off on her fingers. "Again, I don't know the nature of the problem, but you don't think he'd hurt himself, do you?"

The crushed nuts stopped moving through the grinder. He wouldn't, would he? "I-I don't think so, but if something happened . . . Do you mind if I take a break and try to convince Robert to go see him?"

Elizabeth motioned toward the living room. "Go ahead. He probably fell asleep in there anyway. Kids' movies put him out every time."

"Thanks." If Emily couldn't get through to him, maybe Robert could. "Maybe Dan needs to talk to another guy."

***

Dan shut his apartment door and fell against it. He exhaled a mixture of relief, shame, and defeat. The details were fuzzy, but when the woman from the bar pressed her body against him in the cab, tracing the line of his jaw with the back of her finger, he hadn't resisted.

Her fresh, linen-scented perfume teased him. "You shouldn't be alone. Not tonight." He agreed. He needed Emily. Wanted Emily. But he couldn't have her.

"I can stay." She slid her hand down his thigh. Her invitation was clear, even to his clouded mind.

He shoved every thought of Emily far from his head.

He'd steeled himself emotionally and numbed himself physically, but when the time came, he not only didn't want to, he couldn't. His body, quick to respond to the mere thought of Emily, let alone her touch, wouldn't cooperate.

Emily's face had flashed in his mind. Right after the first time she'd kissed him, in her brother's pool. The tears and the hurt on her face. He couldn't be responsible for that again.

He should be grateful that it hadn't gone too far tonight. He'd done nothing with—what was her name? Alaynna?—that he hadn't done with Emily. And that wasn't much. If he couldn't kiss the woman without feeling sick to his stomach, chances were nothing south of there was going to feel any better about it.

A knock sounded on the door, jerking him to attention and causing his heart to pound. He hoped the one and only time he'd picked up a woman in a bar he hadn't chosen a psycho stalker who would turn his life into a living hell. Not that he wasn't already well on his way.

He turned and twisted the knob then opened the door. His throat leapt into his chest.

"Who was that?" Robert's voice was gruff as he nodded in the direction in which Alaynna had left.

Busted. "No one."

"She doesn't have a name, or you didn't catch it?" Robert's gaze drilled him.

Dan's guilt metastasized. Either answer could condemn him.

Robert stepped into the apartment. He stared at Dan for a long minute. "Are you drunk?"

Dan shrugged. Robert's presence had a sobering effect. "Half way."

Robert shook his head and ran a hand over his hair. "What the hell are you doing?"

Dan winced. He deserved this, but it didn't make it any easier. "Nothing happened. I kissed her. That was it."

"Is that the truth?" Again with the piercing look.

"Yes. It's the truth. I had to get out of here and get my mind off . . . things. I had a couple of drinks and then we shared a cab ride. I mean, I guess I knew what she wanted." Of course he knew. He wasn't *that* drunk. "I invited her in, but I couldn't . . . " His stomach roiled. Was it from the alcohol or disgust?

"So, what did you intend?" He meandered into the room, surveying Dan's shabby digs. "To cheat on my sister by screwing some random woman you picked up?"

Hearing it out loud nauseated him. What was he thinking? Did he really want Emily to hate him as much as he hated himself?

"I'm pissed, Dan. If I didn't know what kinda day you had, you'd know exactly how much." Robert dropped onto the couch, his face red. If any second steam blew out his ears, Dan wouldn't be surprised. He breathed in and out. "Sit down."

Dan didn't ordinarily take orders from Robert, but in this case, he complied by flopping into the chair opposite Robert.

"I know the circumstances are different." Robert's tone was firm but fused with concern. Maybe sympathy. "Very different. But I think I have some idea what you're feeling."

What had Emily said? Did he know? What did it matter now anyway? He'd wanted to give Emily a reason to leave. Now she'd have it.

"Emily told me." He leaned forward, folding his hands. "About the abortion. I'm sorry."

Dan's throat tightened. He felt as if he were shrinking right before Robert's eyes. He hoped the alcohol hadn't diminished his ability to hold back tears.

"Don't be mad at her. She's worried about you."

Dan shook his head. "I'm not. And she shouldn't worry."

Robert huffed, making a frustrated sound. "Why not? She loves you. She worries. That's how it works."

Dan sat forward, rested his elbows on his knees, and dropped his gaze to his feet. "I'm not worth it."

"She disagrees. I disagree. Although what I'm seeing here tonight might make me reconsider." Was that the hint of a grin?

Neither spoke for a full minute. The whole thing resembled a nightmare. Or a cable-TV program profiling some angst-ridden idiot who creates all his own problems then feels sorry for himself.

"Last summer . . . when Elizabeth lost the baby . . . you can't fix it. That's the worst." Robert's voice was soft but sincere. "You can't stop it, you can't help it. You can't undo it. No matter how bad you want to, how hard you pray."

Dan's heart clenched.

Robert understood. His gaze remained on his hands folded and resting on his knees.

"The part that kept me up at night, that made my chest ache." Robert's voice cracked. "I wanted to hold my child in my arms. Just once. Look at those itty bitty fingers and toes. The wrinkly skin. Fuzzy hair. That newborn smell." He shook his head. "But there was nothing to hold. Nothing to bury."

Curse the alcohol. *Now*, Dan was going to cry. He tried with everything in him to hold back, but he couldn't. The sobs wracked his body, his shoulders shaking and snot running down his nose. He swiped at the tears with his fingertips.

Robert shoved a pack of tissues at him.

Dan took one, dried his eyes, and blew his nose.

Robert stood, cleared his throat, and strolled toward the door.

Too humiliated to even stand, Dan remained seated.

"You're not alone." Robert's hand rested on the doorknob. "Unless you want to be. You want to talk, man-to-man, I'm here. Always."

Robert held the door ajar. "Emily's my sister. You don't get a pass on what happened before I got here. She thinks she's going to Mass with you tomorrow. I suggest you tell her afterwards. If you don't, I will."

Dan caught Robert's gaze. It was promise, not a threat. Dan had put his friend in an awful position.

The door clicked shut.

The darkness engulfed Dan again.

34

La patiente a toujours raison
(The patient is always right)

Dan trudged up the steps to Robert and Elizabeth's porch and rang the doorbell, hoping Emily would answer and not one of her nieces or nephews. A sleepless night left him incapable of making small talk with the cute little ankle-biters he usually enjoyed. He'd tossed and turned, alternately excoriating himself for somehow not knowing about Kristen's pregnancy and the idiocy of his actions between Emily's and Robert's visits.

The door opened, and Emily stood before him, her navy pea coat over black pants. He exhaled. No sleepy-eyed cherubs toddled behind her. Robert didn't bellow at an errant child in the background.

"Good morning." She smiled, and love glimmered in her eyes.

Dan glanced away. Knowing what he had to tell her, the love that shone there nearly brought him to his knees.

"Yeah. Good morning." He dug his hands into his pants pockets. "Where's the gang?"

She stepped outside and pulled the door closed behind her. "Oh. They got an early start. They're visiting Elizabeth's parents today in Zelienople."

She stepped toward him, and he resisted the urge to back away. If she knew about last night, she wouldn't want to be anywhere near him. She didn't know—yet—so she encircled him with a hug.

"How are you today? You don't look like you slept much." The concern in her voice warmed him, and his shame grew.

"I didn't, but that little bit helped." It did. After a good cry, he'd foraged for and found a bag of Grandma's cookies in the back of his freezer. One by one, he'd dunked each cookie in a glass of cold milk until he'd consumed the whole bag of them. He'd fallen asleep with a prayer on his heart, even if it hadn't yet made it to his lips. The darkness still reigned, but unlike yesterday, today he could almost believe it wouldn't always be there. That maybe someday, somehow, the light would break through. If only he'd given himself a little time instead of succumbing to despair.

She nestled her head against his shoulder. "I hope you don't mind my telling Robert. I thought—"

"It's okay. I'm glad you did." He let his cheek fall against her hair. He wanted to memorize the fragrance so unique to her and the softness of the thick tresses caressing his jaw. If Emily's convictions were as strong as he thought, this might be his last opportunity to savor her as his own.

She continued to offer her quiet strength and support, not pushing him into banal conversation when she knew his heavy heart could focus only on his loss. She held his hand in the car and in church. Her brown eyes warmed him with the empathy they communicated. With her every kindness, a bitter stab born of his stupidity seared his chest.

In the silent moments at Mass, his wounds and his sins stung, keeping him in the pew while it seemed the entire church scrambled past him for the Communion line.

The pain of learning about the abortion had been sharp and sudden. Now, like a splinter lodged beneath his skin, it remained hidden but festering. He had to begin the journey, again, of bringing it all to the light. It would start with confessing to Emily after Mass, then sacramental confession. After that, it was slogging through each day, resisting the renewed self-doubt and despair that had been nipping at his heels for the better part of two years.

They stepped out of the church to a canvas of gray. Rain or snow was on the way, depending on the temperature.

"Em, I need to talk to you."

She stopped in front of him on the sidewalk, the wind whipping her hair around her face. "Sure. Want to go back inside?" She pointed to the big church doors. "Or we could go to your place or go back to Robert and Elizabeth's."

This might not be a quiet conversation conducive to sitting in the presence of God and Mass stragglers. If Emily wanted to shout and scream and throw something at him, she should be able to do it in privacy. The walls of his apartment already seemed as if they were closing in on him.

"Let's go to Robert and Elizabeth's." He tried to remain calm, but the nerve endings in his palms and soles quivered with anxiety. He considered taking the coward's way out and letting Robert tell her.

He held the truck door for Emily, and she slid into the seat. As he lifted the handle on the driver's side door, his phone vibrated in his pocket. Dan climbed in, closed the door, and checked his phone. He scrolled down a long message from an unidentified number, taking in its entirety. The last line caught his eye before the first.

She's in Mercy Hospital, and she's begging to see you.

He re-read from the top down.

This is Jim, Kristen's brother. Found her this morning almost unconscious. She overdosed on some pills. Won't talk to me. Won't let me call Mom or Dad.

He texted back, conscious of Emily's gaze on him.

If this is a ploy for cash, count me out.

He hated to be insensitive, but Kristen was prone to theatrics, never despair or depression. Besides, if one of them meant to end it all last night, he would've been the more likely candidate.

A reply appeared. *Come see for yourself. Not asking much considering she could be dead.*

Jim never did like Dan. Ten years Kristen's junior, Jim had been jealous of Dan from the beginning. A quiet, introverted kid, he always lurked in the margins of Kristen's life on summer and holiday breaks. As he grew older, he wasn't above putting in digs about Dan. In every minor quibble that had arisen between Dan and Kristen, Jim had sided with his sister.

Then when their dad left, taking his six-figure income and a young hottie with him, Jim and Kristen had both changed. Kristen had grown coarse and rapacious, and Jim had grown mistrustful and protective of her.

Dan snuck a peek at Emily as she played with the fringe on her scarf and stared out the truck window.

"Em." He sighed deeply, wishing this day would come to an end. He was ready for the roller coaster to pull into the station, but by the way this day was shaping up, the chains were still grinding on their first big ascent.

"Hmm?" She turned her attention to him, her eyes wide and curious. "Important text?"

"Maybe. I hate to drag you into this."

"What?"

"Kristen's brother texted me. I guess he got my number from her phone. He says Kristen overdosed last night. She's in the hospital, and she's asking for me."

Her brows pinched together. "You should go, Dan. I know after the bomb she dropped yesterday it'll be tough, but it sounds serious."

"That's sort of what I'm thinking. But why does her serious stuff have to involve me? She's the one that ended things." Palms raised, his outstretched arms tensed. "Why am I still expected to jump at every wag of her tail?"

"I'll go with you if you want. For moral support."

His chest ached. He didn't deserve her kindness, but he appreciated it. Having someone on his side, so to speak, boosted his confidence. Plus, he'd rather get to the hospital and get it over with, so he agreed.

In twenty minutes, they arrived at the hospital. Emily sat on a stiff chair in the family waiting room on Kristen's floor.

"Cup of coffee?" He stood at her side, reluctant to leave her alone. How could he do this to Emily? Drag her into this mess? He should've taken her straight home.

She smiled, her eyes bright with encouragement. "I'm good. Thanks."

He swallowed the growing lump in his throat, leaned down, and kissed her. "I'll make it quick."

A tall, lanky figure strode nearly past the opening to the room then stopped, backed up a few steps, and stared.

Jim.

His tattered tennis shoes squeaked on the floor as he stepped into the entranceway. He flicked his head, sending a wayward strand of blonde hair toward his temple. His glance shifted from Dan to Emily, his eyes raking her from head to toe.

Dan stepped between them. "Jim, where's Kristen's room?"

He peered around Dan to Emily then jerked his head toward the hall. "Follow me."

Emily smiled reassuringly. "I'll be here."

Dan followed Jim down the beige corridor. They passed metal carts loaded with slim computers and plastic-encased instruments, bulletin boards dotted with spring decorations, and a pervasive, chemically-clean scent that burned Dan's nostrils.

Jim stopped outside Room 310. He laid his hand on the door, half turned to Dan, and spoke in a harsh whisper. "I hold you responsible. All those years. Instead of manning up and marrying her, you up and leave. Now she's stuck. No income, no roommate. Then you come around cryin' about your own debts. You can stick it. If she knew about the county-fair princess you got sittin' out there waitin' on you, she wouldn't even bother with you, loser. Once she's better, I'm gonna tell her. When you leave this room," he said, jabbing a finger at Dan's chest, "I don't never want to see your ugly puss again." He shoved the door open and let Dan pass.

253

County-fair princess? Dan guessed it was a slap at Emily's wholesome beauty. And all the insults and threats? Tough speech from a kid who looked like he'd be blown away if he even stepped outside the hospital doors this morning. He'd made so many patently false statements Dan didn't know where to start with him. In the end though, they wanted the same thing—complete separation between him and Kristen, so he'd play along.

The door swung shut as a fresh round of antiseptic odor hit him.

Kristen sat upright in the bed tapping on her iPhone. No one would dispute her beauty—those brilliant eyes so blue they were often mistaken for contact lenses, her flawless fair skin, high cheekbones, and full, pink lips.

She glanced up as he entered. Not a trace of anxiety marked her face. In fact, her makeup was perfect, her hair bobbed in a perky ponytail, and her voice bordered on giddy. "Dan. That was fast."

Tension crept up his neck, and his pulse hammered in his head. He'd been had, used by her yet again. As if yesterday hadn't been bad enough. "I'm giving you five minutes. What am I here for, Kristen? Because you're obviously not in any distress."

"Shhh. Jim can hear you." She shushed Dan with her hand and beckoned him closer. "It won't take much time. I know there's another girl, Dan. It's all over your face." She rolled her eyes. "I really don't care."

There wouldn't be another girl for long, and Kristen's part in that irritated him more. "Get to the point."

"Well, as you know, I'm in a bit of a financial bind. When I texted you the other day, I didn't know the bank had gone after you for the car loan. Your responsibility since you signed and all." She shrugged as if the massive debt he'd incurred was inconsequential. "Anyway, you're maxed out. How you think you could afford a baby on top of that I don't understand."

His head throbbed harder, and he clenched a fist at his side. He sent up a silent prayer for patience and anything else the Holy Spirit wanted to throw at him. God knew he needed it.

"Anyway, I need you to back me up on the money stuff. For Jim and the doctor. He'll be here in a minute."

The doctor? Why would the doctor care about her debt? The hospital financial office maybe, but not the doctor.

The door swung open, and Jim entered followed by two men—one in dress pants and shirt and a tie, the other wearing a lab coat over the same attire. The one with the lab coat appeared young, in his mid-twenties Dan guessed. Good-looking in a preppy sort of way. Probably a student.

Kristen sat straighter. Her eyes lit up and zeroed in on the young doctor.

Dan imagined her as a cartoon character, dollar signs painted on her lids as she batted her eyes at the student physician. Didn't she know how much money those guys owed in loans?

"Right, Dan?" Kristen's question broke through his thoughts. Apparently they'd moved past greetings and introductions.

"I'm sorry, what?"

Kristen huffed. "I want you to confirm we had an emotional conversation yesterday, that I was worried about money, but that I was okay." Her eyes shot daggers at him. "I'm having a hard time convincing the good doctors that a psychological evaluation isn't necessary. I just made a mistake by combining a prescription med with an over-the-counter drug."

Dan didn't move, didn't speak. His stillness belied the frenzied action in his brain circuitry as he tried to decipher Kristen's game plan. If anyone needed a psychological evaluation, she did.

Kristen jumped in, determination in every word. "Dan knows I can formulate and execute a plan better than anyone.

If I had wanted to kill myself, there would have been no mistake." Her gaze shifted to Jim leaning against the wall in the far corner, his hands shoved in his jeans pockets. "My brother is being overprotective in this case." Her gaze swung back to Dan.

The pieces of the puzzle came together.

"Kristen goes after what she wants, and most of the time she accomplishes it. I can't argue with that." Dan had the empty checking account and broken heart to prove it.

The young doctor stared at Dan, then at Kristen. There was no mistaking the infatuation in his gaze. He cleared his throat and addressed the older doctor. "Kristen lives in the same building as I do. If we agree that a psych evaluation is unnecessary, I'd be happy to check in on her over the next several weeks. Make sure she's getting along okay." A smile curved his lips.

Kristen beamed. Her machinations succeeded.

Dan tuned out of the conversation as he laid it all out in his head. After they'd talked yesterday, Kristen realized Dan couldn't provide any more cash. The young doctor, whom she'd obviously already been acquainted with, was Plan B.

She'd concocted an accidental overdose story, maybe making herself a little sick in the process. Once Jim brought her to the hospital, she'd reassured the doctors she would be fine—with perhaps a little extra care from her neighbor.

Jim had become the fly in the ointment, somehow getting wind of Kristen's argument with Dan the day before and assuming Kristen despaired and attempted to end her own life.

Far-fetched and ridiculous? Yes. Would he put it past Kristen to try and pull it off? When a good-looking guy with potential for a hefty six-figure income was at stake? Nope.

Kristen had manipulated Jim into calling Dan to back up her story. Yes, they'd had a tough conversation, but she had been fine. He was the one who had been an absolute wreck, not that Kristen would notice or care. Her wounds, if she bore any, were well concealed.

The older doctor excused himself from the room while the young doctor sat on the edge of Kristen's bed. Dan stacked rocks and laid stone for a living, but it didn't seem very professional to him. Jim remained in the corner, his glare piercing Dan's gaze. Did the kid have any clue what a master manipulator his sister was?

Dan's mood grew lighter than it had been in a day. Not by much, considering he'd lost a child he didn't know he'd had and botched things with the woman he loved, but the possibility that things with Kristen might finally be over soothed his wounded soul. He stepped backwards toward the door.

Kristen didn't need him. She giggled as the doctor took her pulse, something Dan had ever only seen nurses do. Only Jim noticed Dan's movement, looking as if he were ready to push off the wall and give chase.

Dan took his chances and slipped out of the room and down the hall to the waiting room.

Emily sat holding her coffee, flipping through a magazine. She set the magazine aside as Dan dropped into the chair beside her. "How is she?"

He shook his head. "She's fine. It's all a ruse. One that her brother is taking too seriously."

Emily's brow wrinkled. "I don't get it."

He sighed. "It's complicated. Let's just say I'm hopeful that I've heard the last from Kristen."

Her eyebrows shot up, and her eyes widened. "Really?"

He shrugged. "I guess time will tell." Dread knotted in his stomach as he recalled the next item on their agenda. "Let me take you home."

"Sure." She sounded uncertain, probably as confused by the whole episode as he was. In the end, regardless of what Kristen had done, he'd made his own mistakes. He'd have to face the consequences.

The ride to Robert and Elizabeth's was short and quiet. Emily tried small talk a couple of times, a happy lilt in her voice, but Dan couldn't feign interest.

They entered the house, and Dan helped remove her coat and hung it on the rack behind the door. He laid his own jacket over a chair.

"Have you ever heard it so quiet here?" Emily glanced about the empty room where only a couple of toys littered the floor and a basket of folded laundry sat next to the couch.

"Only when the kids were asleep." He thought back to the couple of evenings he and Emily had spent here after the children were in bed. Both times he'd felt secure with her. Connected. All kinds of warm, happy, and loving.

She patted the couch. "Sit with me."

He sat beside her, falling into the seat like an old man. Like he'd aged several decades in the last twenty-four hours.

He rubbed his hand over his face, gathering his thoughts. How should he start?

Emily massaged his shoulder, squeezed his neck, and rubbed his back, making it more difficult for him to concentrate. She inched closer until her knee touched his.

Of all the times for her to be romantic.

She leaned toward him, pressing a hand into his chest. "You wanted to talk?"

Tension coiled in the pit of his stomach. "Yeah." He lifted her hand, kissed it, and set it back on her lap. "About last night."

35

C'est fini

(It is finished)

Emily angled herself so she could peer into Dan's eyes. If he'd look at her, that is. Despite the sweet kiss he'd given her hand, it had stung when he'd moved it from his chest to her lap.

Nothing good came from conversations that began with, "I need to talk to you." The use of "need" instead of "want," well, that said it all. Robert had used those words on the darkest day of her life, when he'd taken her out of physics class and, through teary eyes, informed her Dad was dead and Mom lay in a hospital burn unit 300 miles away.

This morning, while waiting for Dan at the hospital, Emily had wanted to appear calm and composed, but her mind whirred through a series of increasingly grim possibilities for his need to speak to her. Was he angry that she'd confided in Robert, despite what he'd said? Was he rethinking their relationship because of Kristen's abortion? Was there more to the story?

Dan cleared his throat, capturing her attention. He glanced at her, his eyes blinking rapidly. "Last night, after you left—"

"I would've stayed. All night if you wanted." She stretched her hand toward his then retracted it, fearful he'd break the connection between them again. "My heart ached for you, all alone in your apartment."

"Yeah. About that." He shifted positions, inching away from her, but finally meeting her gaze. "After you left, I went out."

He'd gone out? She couldn't imagine him wanting to be in a crowd considering the state he'd been in. "Where'd you go?"

"The Watering Hole."

She wrinkled her nose. "Ew. Why?" Calling that place a dive was generous. She'd seen the seedy characters that stumbled out its doors, the smell of stale smoke and cheap beer chasing them. "You told me you wanted to be alone."

He pinched his eyes closed with his thumb and forefinger. "I lied."

"Why?" she whispered, trying to hold the growing ache in her chest at bay. He lied? After their heartfelt conversations, he'd kept something from her?

His gaze flitted in every direction, landing somewhere beneath her chin. "I didn't trust myself with you. It was like . . . like someone churned my heart in a blender. My feelings were all mixed up, including my feelings for . . . well, uh, the way I'm attracted to you." His neck reddened, and he tugged at his collar. "And my apartment . . . I needed to get out."

The first time a guy admitted attraction to her, and she couldn't focus on it. Not until she understood. "Okay. So you went out for a couple beers."

He stood and paced the length of the room and back, rubbing his brow with his knuckle. "More than a couple, but that's not it. I—I met someone." He stopped and glanced at her. "A woman."

A sick feeling grew in her stomach. "Kristen?"

His answer came quick. "God, no. I hope I never see her again."

"Then who?"

He crouched in front of her, looking her in the eye without flinching. "I didn't know her before." He sighed. Then the words tumbled out. "Before she came home with me."

Emily grew lightheaded. "Y-you . . . you hooked up with a stranger?" Her voice cracked.

Dan closed his eyes and nodded his head. "Yes. I mean, no, not really. I took her there—"

This can't be happening. Not able to bear listening to another word, she sprang from the couch, nearly knocking him onto the floor.

He steadied himself and stood, a pained look in his eyes.

She'd been betrayed, plain and simple. "Yesterday you said you needed me. You said that you loved me."

He reached for her arms, but she backed away.

"I do. I do love you, Em. More than anything in the world."

She furrowed her brow, anger rising and tightening her chest and fists. "But you brought a woman back to your apartment for sex?"

His eyes widened, looking panicked. "Nothing happened."

She laughed, a cold and sarcastic cackle. "What? You got there and decided a rousing game of UNO would be more fun?"

"I couldn't do it. Do that." Desperation tinged his voice. He clutched her arm, his gaze steady and sincere. "All I could think of was you."

She ripped her arm from him and turned, kicking a pink and turquoise plastic pony from her path as she stomped away from him. "Why did you want to?" She faced him. "With someone else, I mean." Every hidden insecurity she'd tried so hard to stifle bubbled to the surface. "Am I so hideous? Or is it because you knew I'd say no? Which, by the way, was something I thought we agreed on."

He crossed the room in a few steps, coming to stand in front of her. "Hideous? You?" His brow crinkled, as if her were genuinely puzzled. "You're beautiful. More beautiful every time I see you. And we do agree. We did. I didn't want to make you sin."

"You just wanted to sin with someone else?" She shook her head, unable to discern his logic. "I don't understand. You were practically nonresponsive yesterday afternoon, yet you were so desperate that you sought out some stranger in a bar?"`

He shook his head, biting his lips together "No. I think I—I wanted that kind of comfort. To feel loved like that—by you—but that's not why—"

"I don't make you feel loved unless I have sex with you? I held you while you fell to pieces. That doesn't qualify as love?" She'd read him wrong. What happened to the decent, respectful, faith-filled man she'd fallen in love with? "Do you have any idea what it took for me to sit there and listen to you tell me you'd conceived a baby with another woman? When I thought that someday we'd . . ." She glanced at the door, and her throat constricted, tears rising in her eyes.

"I'm so sorry, Em. I can't explain it to you—"

"Why? Am I too naïve to understand what a man needs?" She drew the word 'needs' out in exaggerated fashion and made quotations in the air. She pushed past him, moving toward the entranceway.

He followed. "That's not what I meant. I'm not excusing it; I'm confessing it. And that's not why I did it anyway."

She turned on him, her hair whipping around her face. "Then why did you?"

He paused, his jaw tense and a determined look in his eyes. "Because I'm not good enough for you. I wanted to give you a reason to make a clean break, to get rid of me."

Tears coursed down her cheeks, her heart and stomach both aching. She shouted this time. "Well, congratulations! You succeeded." She lunged for the door, wrenched it open, and motioned him out with her arm. "Get. Out. I don't ever want to see your face again."

His brow creased, and he pursed his lips, looking confused, as if he hadn't seen that coming when he'd just said it was what he wanted.

A gust of cold wind blew, rattling the plastic Easter egg wreath on the front door. Emily shivered and hugged her arms to her chest.

He stared a moment then gathered his coat from the chair. His eyes wet with tears, he stepped past her then turned back, his voice thick with emotion. "I hope one day you can find it in your heart to forgive me. Not for my sake, but for yours." He brushed a tear from her cheek.

She flinched then scowled, eager for him to leave before sobs overcame her.

The wind gusted, but Dan didn't budge. He sniffed and his jaw flexed. "I love you. Always will."

She laughed, hiccoughed, and cried all at the same time. Then she caught her breath and whispered, filling her words with the poisonous rage and hurt that pervaded her spirit. "I pity you, Dan Malone. You wouldn't know love if it smacked you in the face."

He stumbled back, as if he'd been hit, but didn't turn to leave.

She slammed the door.

Something whacked the storm door and scraped against it. Probably the wreath hitting the ground.

She whirled around and bolted through the kitchen, sobs bubbling up in her chest. The basement steps creaked and groaned as she pounded down them then flung herself onto the bed. How could she have been so wrong about him?

36

Le changement et la guérison prennent du temps

(Both change and healing take time)

"So, when is the ad running?" Colleen stood on tiptoe atop Grandma's stepstool as she adjusted the living room curtains she'd hung. Dirt streaks marked the back of her white tee shirt and paint speckled a leg of her faded jeans.

"This weekend." Dan pushed another set of curtains over the rod. A few finishing touches, and the place would be ready to rent. For the past two weeks, he'd topped off his ten-hour workdays with four hours cleaning and prepping the house. It kept his hands and mind occupied, which he considered a blessing. Less time to dwell on the baby he'd never know and the woman he had once hoped would give him babies of their own.

"It looks great, Dan. You should be able to fill it fast." Colleen stepped backward onto the floor and rested her hands on her hips. "I'm sorry it's not Emily staying here though." She repositioned the stepstool in front of the other window and glanced at him. "You ready to talk about it?"

He'd told her about Kristen and the baby, but only that his past had ruined his relationship with Emily. He couldn't bear to tell her the truth of what else he'd done—or considered doing—and see the shame in her eyes. She'd never found his cagey explanation satisfying, so now at every turn she tried to pry the truth from him.

"No. Not yet." How many weeks could he put her off until she let it go?

She stepped up again, and he handed her the rod for the front window.

"No one will take away your man card if you see a counselor." She positioned the rod and slid the curtain into place. "I can refer you to one of my old classmates. She's good. She's experienced in post-abortion counseling. And she sees the whole picture. The spiritual stuff too."

Dan shook his head. "I don't think so." Why did everyone's solution involve him sharing the most humiliating moments of his life with more and more people?

"If you don't see her, will you at least make an appointment with your pastor?"

Really? Would she never let up? "Father Adamczak?" A good man. A great priest. But burning incense at the wrong altar. After seeing Dan at daily Mass for two consecutive weeks—and never with a serious girlfriend, Father had approached him.

"Glad to see you here bright and early every morning." Father Adamczak shook Dan's hand with a firm grasp.

"Yeah, well, I think I need the grace." Dan liked Father, but if the morning Mass thing was going to fly, he had to get in and out and get to work.

Father Adamczak didn't seem to be in a hurry. "Do you think God may be calling you?"

"Calling me?" Dan jerked his head back. "You mean . . . to be a priest? Uh, no. Definitely not my thing." And Colleen wanted Dan to go to him with all his baggage? Well, that would convince him Dan wasn't priest material.

Colleen teetered on the stool as she reached for the edge of the rod.

Dan steadied her with a hand to her back.

"Maybe Emily's forgiven you. Maybe she'll give you another chance."

It had only been a couple of weeks. They both needed time to heal. He hadn't thought of second chances. "I don't deserve another chance."

"No, you don't." She held the rod steady and looked him in the eye. "You won't say, but I have an idea what happened."

Not able to hold her gaze, his attention drifted to the floor. Its newly-refinished surface gleamed. How could she know? The only people that knew were Emily and Robert. Had he let something slip?

"That's what mercy's for, Dan. Ask, and you shall receive."

"I'm good with God. I went to confession. Emily shouldn't have to be merciful."

She elbowed him as she descended from the stepstool. "You'd deprive her of an opportunity to become more Christ-like?"

Dan rolled his eyes. "You're stretching it now, Colleen. I'm not saying never, I'm saying not now. I've got stuff to work through."

"Hmm?" She tapped her chin. "Who could help with that? Maybe a . . . counselor?" She smirked, the big know-it-all.

Dan growled. He grabbed the stool, folded it, and set it in the utility closet. "I'll think about the counseling, okay? Just lay off on Emily."

"Fine. But don't wait too long or you might lose her forever."

If I haven't already.

***

Six months later

Emily propped her fuzzy-slippers on the footrest. Making sure her long, fluffy robe concealed everything it should, she lifted her teacup from the end table and sipped. "Thanks for letting me share your birthday gift, Elizabeth."

The posh spa was a treat for both of them. They sat side-by-side on the shaded terrace in oversized armchairs while they nibbled fancy cookies and gazed at the late summer gardens in bloom below them.

Elizabeth reached over and patted her knee. "These things are more fun with a friend. And you are my very best one."

Emily smiled. She'd relied on her best friend a lot these past months. Elizabeth was always at the ready—well, after the kids had gone to bed, anyway—with some combination of wine, tissues, and chocolate.

For weeks she'd struggled to understand Dan's convoluted reasoning. Was their entire friendship a farce? What made him choose to seek comfort somewhere else? Why did he feel he wasn't good enough for her?

A soft breeze blew, carrying the scent of freshly-mowed grass and the aroma of pastries from the café downstairs. Emily breathed deeply. Only recently had she begun to make some peace with it and with him. The start of a new school year and a new job had given her some perspective. Dan had problems of his own that she couldn't fix. The best things she could do for him were to maintain her distance and to pray.

"How was the baby shower?" Elizabeth referred to the out-of-town party Emily had gone to the previous day. It was a four-hour drive each way, and Emily had stayed in a hotel the evening before, but it was worth it. Julianna was the first of her college friends to marry and now the first to have a baby.

"Good." As happy as she was for Julianna, the afternoon had been a keen reminder of what Emily was missing. She longed for a baby of her own. The prospects of that happening in the foreseeable future were dismal.

"With you gone . . ." Hesitancy marked Elizabeth's voice, and her gaze didn't meet Emily's. ". . . it seemed like a good time to have Dan over." She chanced a glance at Emily. "He brought some delicious dessert wine. Robert fell asleep right away. Of course. But Dan really opens up after a glass or two."

Emily's muscles tensed. Mention of Dan instantly undid all the good things a spa day was supposed to do. She remembered the horseplay and the conversation she and Dan had shared after they knocked off a bottle of Robert and Elizabeth's wine at their private swim party. "Yeah. I think I knew that."

"He told me what Kristen did." Her eyes shone with sadness. For her? For Dan? The baby? There was enough heartbreak to go around.

Emily bit her lower lip. Heaviness settled on her heart every time she thought of it. "How's he doing with all that?" A tear slipped from her eye, and she brushed it away.

"He's been seeing a counselor. For that, and I guess everything that had to do with her."

Emily nodded. "Good. I hope he finds peace."

Elizabeth rested a hand on Emily's arm, drawing her attention. "What he did . . . that hurt you so much . . ."

"You mean hooking up with some skank?" Okay. So maybe she hadn't quite found peace yet either.

"Yeah. Not bitter much, are you?" Elizabeth chuckled and patted her arm.

"Don't I have a right to be bitter?"

"Bitter?" Elizabeth shrugged. "I was wondering though . . . . was that the same day he found out . . . about the baby?"

"Yes." A tear trickled from her other eye. She let it go and focused on her coral-painted toenails sticking out from the ivory, chenille slippers.

"Don't you think maybe it affected his decision-making skills?"

"I don't know. I mean, I guess it did, sure. But it's still an excuse." Her teacup rattled in its saucer as she tried to steady her hand on it. She'd been over this in her mind a thousand times.

"It doesn't seem like the kind of thing Dan would do."

"No, it doesn't. I think that's why it hurt so much." Her gaze caught on a thriving bunch of Black-eyed Susans toppling over a short fieldstone wall.

Elizabeth faced her. "And the . . . the skank. He only kissed her?"

Emily narrowed her eyes. "Isn't that enough?"

"I'm not judging your decision." Elizabeth's words came out quickly in reassurance. "I'm trying to understand."

Emily rubbed the ache building in her brow. "Yes, he said all he did was kiss her. He couldn't do anything else because he couldn't . . . he couldn't stop thinking of me." By the time she'd reached the end of the sentence, her voice was barely audible.

A few minutes of silence passed between them. Emily leaned her head back on the cushioned chair, closed her eyes and tuned into the New Age music flowing through the overhead speakers. A woman opened the door behind them, and the relaxing scent of lavender oil drifted out, soothing Emily's frayed nerves.

Elizabeth's voice broke through her near-trance. "He's renovating his grandma's house."

A surge of tension forced her head up and her eyes open. "Good."

"And the Mass for your parents last week? I took the kids. Dan was there. On a Tuesday."

Emily let her head roll to the side, facing Elizabeth, and arched a brow.

"Turns out he goes to daily Mass now."

Emily breathed a sigh. "And he's kind to small children and stray animals too, right? I get it, Elizabeth."

Elizabeth touched her hand. "I know you still care about him, Emily. At first I only suspected, but then when I helped you set up your classroom last month, I noticed the picture you keep in the corner of your desk calendar."

Darn that picture. Dan had asked another skater to take their picture at the ice rink. She'd taken one with each of their phones. Emily had the photo printed. They both looked so happy and in love. The eyes. They said it all.

"I also know you've refused to meet three guys Robert offered to introduce you to."

Emily faced straight ahead. A pair of yellow goldfinches darted across the gardens below, alighting on a small dogwood tree. There was no point in denying it.

"All I'm saying is, don't seal off that wall around your heart, Emily. Leave a little room. Someone might want to tear it down."

***

Max thudded down the stairs in his Teenage Mutant Ninja Turtle pajamas and vaulted onto the edge of Emily's bed. "Hey, Auntie Em."

She folded her legs beneath her to give him some room. "Hey, Maximillian. What's up?"

Max fiddled with the hole in his sock. "Uncle Dan was here last night."

Emily tensed. The second time in two weeks. The mere mention of his name still caused her heart to spasm. "I know."

"Is that why you went to the movies by yourself?"

Sharp kid. She set aside the stack of vocabulary quizzes she'd been grading. "Uh-huh."

Max yanked at the hole, making it larger.

"Don't do that, Max."

He tugged at the toe of the other sock instead. "Do you hate him?"

"Hate him?" Is that what the kids thought? That she hated their Uncle Dan? "No, sweetie. I love him. But I'm angry with him. He hurt me."

Max's eyes widened. "Like, hit you?"

"No, no. He hurt my heart." She laid a hand over her chest.

"But you still love him?"

Kids were straightforward. It was a beautiful thing—when it was aimed in someone else's direction. "Yeah. I kind of can't help it. I thought God wanted us to be together, but . . ." She shook her head.

"I think he still loves you too."

"Why do you think that?" She fiddled with the balls of fuzz beading on her bedspread.

Max shrugged. "He asked me all kinds of questions about you."

She couldn't help the way that news made her chest burn and her heart gallop. "Like what?"

"He wanted to know if you still lived here and if you had a boyfriend."

She plucked off a couple of fuzz balls and pushed them into a tiny pile. "Just because people have feelings for each other, Max, maybe even love each other, doesn't mean they should be together."

Max nodded as if he understood. "Dad said he made a dumb-ass move, and you were smart to dump him even if Uncle Dan's his best friend."

Emily stifled a laugh and forced an authoritative tone. "Max. I don't want to hear you say that word again."

"Ass isn't a bad word. It's a donkey."

"Not in that context, it's not."

His eyes grew wide again, and he jumped off the bed. "I almost forgot. He gave me something for you." He ran upstairs, his little feet pounding every step of the way.

Emily stretched her legs. So, Dan was asking about her. Did he still care? And had he finally come to terms with his past?

Muffled but still audible, Max's voice came from upstairs. "Five minutes, Mom, please?"

Robert had replaced the ancient radiators with baseboard heat but failed to plug the holes from the pipes. On the rare occasions the house was otherwise quiet, she could hear everything going on in the kitchen from her basement bedroom.

Elizabeth's voice, too distant to make out, came from another room, followed by Max's plea. "I have to give Aunt Em something. It's really, really, really super important."

The basement door slammed, and Max ran downstairs so fast he tripped on his own feet, falling down the last three steps.

"Ouch!"

Emily rushed over and helped him off the floor. "You okay, buddy?"

"Ow, ow. Yeah. Ow." He held his fist out to her. "Here."

She opened her hand, and Max dropped a small, wrinkled piece of paper into her palm. She unfolded it and read. It was an old Walmart receipt. The ink was smudged on the left side, but she could read the items purchased: diapers, hand cream, cheddar goldfish snacks, and a pregnancy test. Likely one of Elizabeth's receipts. She hoped.

"Other side, silly." Max turned the receipt over and tried to flatten it in her palm. "He wrote in cursive." Clearly, Dan's clever use of cursive left Max disgruntled.

Emily examined the crinkly receipt and the familiar strokes of Dan's handwriting. He traced over his letters in several spots where the blue ink failed to adhere to the slippery paper.

2 Truths and
No More Lies
I love you.
I miss you.

Then at the very bottom, smaller than the rest, written almost as an afterthought:

Can I call you?

Her heart had an immediate answer, but her brain was slow on the draw. She grabbed a pen from the tin can holder on the shelf beneath the steps and set the receipt on top of a *Car and Driver* magazine. She wrote her one-word answer and handed the receipt back to Max. "Do you know if you'll be seeing Uncle Dan any time soon?"

"Yeah. He's coming with me and Dad to the batting cages on Wednesday."

"Can you remember to give him his note back?"

"Sure. For a quarter." He held out his hand.

She blew out a breath and grabbed her change purse from the dresser. "Here." She handed Max a coin. "Make sure he gets it, okay? You won't forget, will you?"

"Nope. Uncle Dan'll probably ask anyway. He made me swear on all of my LEGO mini-figures that I would give you that and bring back an answer."

Emily grinned. Dan still loved her.

He wanted to see her.

She hoped she wouldn't regret her answer.

37

Le langue de l'amour
(Love language)

Emily gathered the papers in front of her, tapped them together, and slid them into a manila file folder. Loose paper clips, a pen, pencil, and small stapler lay in disarray on her desktop. She cupped her hand and pushed the debris to the side of the desk calendar, her gaze snagging on the picture in the corner. She and Dan on a bench outside the ice rink, her arms wrapped around him, practically sitting in his lap. Her tummy tingled, and she took a slow, deep breath to calm her nerves.

Twenty bare desks sat in four even rows in her empty classroom. Long, low shelves filled with textbooks, dictionaries, and other reference books lined the exterior wall beneath the window. A large map of Europe and the French flag hung on the opposite wall. She glanced at the wall clock—the one set to Eastern Daylight Time, not Central European Time. Dan would be here to pick her up for their date in less than an hour. Only one student to tutor. As long as the boy arrived soon, they should finish on time.

Emily opened the file drawer, trying to focus on her lesson. Jamie had switched from Spanish to French at the beginning of the term. He struggled with verb conjugation and vocabulary. Somewhere in one of her files were some flashcards and worksheets she'd brought back from France. They were geared for younger kids, but they might help a high-school senior new to the language.

She grabbed a fistful of papers from the rear of the last folder and plopped them on her desk, thumbing through until she found the right ones. A piece of ivory stationery lay sandwiched between two sample quizzes. Where had that come from?

She peeled back the piece of paper, revealing a handwritten letter from Dan's grandmother. Her chest tightened, and she bit her lips together. Grandma couldn't master the technology necessary to text or chat while Emily was overseas, but she faithfully handwrote a letter each week. Emily scanned the page, trying to recall the subject of this particular letter.

Her heart ached as she slid her fingers over the fragile indents, Grandma's writing steady and strong in some parts, weak in others. Smooth strokes contrasted with jerky ones. This letter addressed the frustration Emily had expressed in disciplining the oldest boy in her charge.

A bright, articulate boy, Pascal was quick to lose patience with himself. His tendency toward perfectionism dogged his diligent efforts. In seconds, he'd go from confident to discouraged, claiming he was a failure. Grandma's advice, gleaned from years of living with and loving her own children and grandchildren, was pointed and insightful.

Don't let him get away with it. Everyone needs at least one person to believe in him. Build him up. I've had that kind of faith in my Daniel. I'm not sure who will take over when I'm gone.

Emily smiled and brushed a tear from her eye. *Subtle, Grandma.*

A knock sounded on the open door. Jamie stood in the entrance, his posture nonchalant as he leaned into the weight of the backpack on his left shoulder. A denim button-front shirt hung over loose-fitting, gray cargo pants.

"C'mon in and have a seat." She pressed out the letter from Grandma, slid it beneath the desk calendar, and gathered the grammar cards.

Jamie slid into the desk directly in front of hers and let his backpack fall to the floor. He pushed a lock of dirty blonde hair from his right eye with the back of his hand. Slouching into his seat, he crossed his long legs at the ankles, revealing unlaced hi-top tennis shoes.

From what Emily had observed in the first weeks of school, Jamie exhibited intelligence, but she'd bet a perusal of his prior report cards would reveal the classic "fails to work to his potential" in the comments. He demonstrated no interest in foreign language or culture; his presence in class fulfilled a graduation requirement.

"Okay." She gave him a confident smile. "So, we've got to bring you up to speed with your vocab and your verb conjugations. Do you mind telling me why you made the switch from Spanish to French?"

The left side of his lips twitched, and he scooted back in his seat. He let out a muffled sort of grunt then said, "It's the language of love, right?"

Emily narrowed an eye at him. "So, this is about a girl?"

He cleared his throat. "A woman."

She straightened the perfectly-positioned papers on her desk and sighed. "I see. Does this woman speak French?"

"Oh, yeah. She knows it well enough to teach it."

Her hands stilled on the papers. A frisson of uneasiness crept up her spine. She swallowed and pursed her lips together. "Well, maybe she could help you then?"

His lips tilted in a full-out smile. "Hey. Now there's an idea."

Her cheeks warmed. He couldn't be referring to her, could he? High school boys had no interest in her when she was in high school. Why would they start now?

Jamie was a good-looking boy. Blonde hair, blue eyes, and a slim but sturdy build. Surely he'd have no problem finding a girlfriend his age. As long as he wasn't a total jerk, and maybe even if he was, he shouldn't have any trouble with girls.

She shuffled the papers in front of her again. "I – I have some flash cards here. Grab a chair from the corner and take a seat next to me. It'll be easier."

"Yes, Miss Kowalski." Jamie grinned and jumped from the seat, grabbed the chair, and slid it in alongside her, its metal feet dragging over the tiled floor. He sat and rested his elbows on his knees, perusing the room from her vantage point and scouring the contents of her desktop.

"We'll start with definitions to get a benchmark. I'll read the word, and you tell me what it means." She pulled a card from the deck. "*Escaliers.*"

He didn't immediately respond, so she shifted her gaze from the card to his face. He stared intently at something on her desk.

His gaze darted to her. He scrutinized her, as if studying her features. Something in his mood shifted. "That your boyfriend?" He gestured, indicating the picture of her and Dan.

"Uh . . ." Not used to fielding questions about her personal life with students, she chose her words with care. "He's a very close friend I haven't seen in a long time."

His brows arched. "Is that a *no*?"

She glanced at the clock, recalculating how long it would be until Dan arrived. She bit her lower lip but couldn't suppress the smile spreading across her face. "No, it's not a no. It's complicated." Then, stifling her urge to giggle like a schoolgirl, she flipped to the next flash card. "And not what you're here to learn . . . *droit.*"

Jamie twisted the lock of hair hanging over his brow and bounced his knee. "You forgot *escaliers.* They're steps. And *droit* means right."

"Good." She glanced up. Jamie's cold stare made her tense. "Is something wrong, Jamie?"

He dropped his gaze to his feet and shook his head. "I think a beautiful woman like you . . ." He looked up. No trace of embarrassment crossed his face, as if it was nothing to say such a thing to a woman almost ten years his senior, his teacher. "You deserve a man who's going to treat you right. Not lead you on."

Emily let out a breath and tried to formulate an appropriate response. This wasn't the kind of remark she'd ever encountered with her fifth graders. And though his assessment flattered her, the rest of it seemed an odd statement from someone who knew neither her nor Dan.

"Being less than honest is detrimental in any relationship," she said.

He peered at her from beneath half-lowered lids, staring.

"I assure you my eyes are wide open where this man is concerned." She laid the cards on the desk and eased back in her chair. "That's all I'm going to say. We're not here to discuss my personal life."

Jamie nodded and averted his eyes.

Forty minutes later she dismissed him, having exhausted her supply of flash cards. He missed only one word. She'd meet with him once more about the verbs, but if he knew those half as well as the vocabulary, tutoring wasn't necessary.

She opened her desk drawer and pulled out a compact mirror and lip gloss. Lips parted, she applied a fresh coat and rubbed her fingertip under her eyes to remove any mascara smudges. She glanced at the clock. Dan would be here any minute. Her tummy tingled again. With unsteady fingers, she tugged the hair on either side of her face, pulling it into place.

Emily slid the drawer closed and used her iPad to glance over her lesson plan for the next week. She propped her elbows on the desk while she scrolled through the document.

If Jamie wasn't struggling with the transition from Spanish to French, why ask for help? And what kind of answer was 'the language of love'? Maybe he had a crush on one of the girls in her classes. A few were fairly fluent. She recalled the girls in Jamie's class, trying to think if she'd noticed anything going on between him and any of them.

"I think I caught the teacher daydreaming."

Emily startled at the sound of his voice.

Dan stood in the doorway, leaning a shoulder against the jamb. He clutched a bouquet of lavender tied with a white lace ribbon. He wore a French blue long-sleeved dress shirt, navy tie, and khaki dress pants.

The butterflies in her stomach rushed for her throat. She swallowed and stood. "How long have you been standing there?"

He grinned. "Long enough to know your mind was a million miles away, but not long enough to make up for the time we've been apart." He pushed away from the doorframe and held the bouquet out to her.

Heat crept up her cheeks. She took the bouquet, held it to her nose, and inhaled the soothing, familiar fragrance. "Mmmm. Thank you."

"You're welcome."

"I'm ready. Let me grab my stuff." She pushed in the chair and shouldered her bag. "Where are we going?"

"I heard about this great little French café." He stepped into the hall and retrieved a large wicker picnic basket. He ambled in, his gaze searching the classroom and landing on the far wall. It had been painted, long before Emily's arrival, to look like the front of a French café, complete with a striped awning and a potted tree. How did he know? *Elizabeth.* It had to be.

"Can I move them?" He gestured toward the desks as the back of the room.

"Oh. Sure."

The desk legs screeched as he pushed two desks together. He squatted and opened his basket, removing a fabric tablecloth with a flowered, beribboned print. He unfolded it, shook it free, and fanned it over the desks. It billowed and fell into place. A stream of items came from the basket: a candle in a small votive cup, plates, utensils, several containers of food, and, finally, two wine glasses and a bottle of French wine.

Wine? A glass of Pinot Noir sounded wonderful but—

"Is this okay? I couldn't forego the French wine, but I found this no-alcohol kind." He held the bottle out for her to see. The label read "*sans alcool.*" "I didn't know if the school had some kind of policy against it. This won't get you in trouble, will it?"

"Uh, no. It's okay, I think." His thoughtfulness warmed her heart. "Let me close the door." She walked to the front of the classroom. As she approached the doorway, a shadowy figure slipped down the hall.

Emily peered down the hall in either direction. No one. No light emanated from the other classrooms. At this hour on a Friday, only the janitorial staff would be around and maybe one or two people in the administrative office.

With her foot, she nudged the rubber doorstop and let the door swing shut. She returned to find Dan lighting the candle then opening the bottle of wine.

Her heart pounded in her chest.

He had gone all out. Dan was a jeans and tee shirt kind of guy. Liked to ride around in his pickup truck. Not afraid to work hard and get dirty. The only time she'd seen him in anything more formal than the cotton pants he occasionally wore to Sunday Mass was at Grandma's funeral.

A picnic in her classroom with French wine, food, and pastries? He wasn't indulging his own interests. He was catering to her. Her heart swelled with affection for him.

She glanced down at her outfit, the ankle-length burnt orange maxi dress she'd chosen in a hurry this morning. She'd worried it might be too dressy for whatever he had in mind, but it was just right.

He fussed with his iPhone for a minute then set it on a desk. French café music filled the room. She smiled at the lilt of the traditional accordion music.

He slid a desk chair into place, holding it for her. "I think everything's ready. Want to sit?"

"Sure. Where did you find all this?"

"French deli and bakery. Great thing about Pittsburgh. Every ethnicity represented." He smiled and winked at her as if eating a fancy meal with her in an institutional-looking classroom was as good as it gets.

He pulled Styrofoam food containers from his basket and laid them on a nearby desk. "*Soup du jour, salade*, baked *brie*, and, for dessert . . ." He smacked his lips together. "Éclairs."

She giggled at his enthusiasm as much as his Americanized pronunciations. As if on cue, her stomach rumbled, and she hugged her arm to her waist. She hadn't had authentic French food since she'd left France. The closest she'd come was French fries, so, not close at all.

"Would you like to learn a little French? I could teach you."

"Hmmm? Sure. I had a couple years of Latin in high school, but I've forgotten most of it." He shrugged.

"Let's start with Grace." She recited the traditional Catholic Grace Before Meals in French, ending in "*Ainsi soit-il.*"

"Amen," Dan added.

He ladled soup into small bowls and handed her a spoon. "Baguette?"

The soup smelled of cinnamon and nutmeg. A crusty piece of bread would go great with it. "Yes, please."

She tasted the still-warm bread. The inside nearly melted in her mouth. "Mmm. This is so good."

A smile lit his face. He seemed pleased that she enjoyed the food. "So, how's the teaching gig? I imagine the switch from grade school to high school takes a bit of an adjustment."

She nodded as the savory pumpkin soup slid over her tongue. "Yes. I love it though. The kids are bright, and for the most part they want to learn."

He sipped his wine, his gaze never wavering from hers. His attentiveness was so earnest, so genuine, it disarmed her.

Not that he hadn't paid attention to her in the past, but it seemed like now he soaked in every detail, memorized every word and nuance. Everything about his attention, his demeanor, struck her as selfless, as if she were everything to him.

"And you do some tutoring after school too?"

She had mentioned her appointment with Jamie when they'd scheduled the date by phone last week. "I can, and I will, if necessary, but today's session was the only one so far. It was . . . interesting."

Dan set a plate of salad in front of her and offered her a small container of salad dressing. "How so?"

"Well, the boy is a senior. He recently switched from Spanish to French. He needs to complete the course as a graduation requirement. He said he needed help with vocabulary, but he knew virtually everything I quizzed him on."

Dan dipped a forkful of greens into his dressing. "That is odd."

"Yeah. And when I asked 'why French,' he gave me this cryptic answer."

"What?"

"Something like, 'it's the language of love, isn't it?' Oh, and he took an interest in you."

Dan's fork froze where he had stabbed it into a cherry tomato. "Me?"

Her cheeks warmed, and she looked at her salad. "I, uh, keep a little picture of us on my desk. From the time we went ice skating." She glanced up as a smile spread across his face.

"You do?"

She adjusted the napkin in her lap. "Yeah. A little one. But he wanted to know if you were my boyfriend—and here's the weirdest part—he said a beautiful girl like me should be careful you didn't lead me on."

Dan chuckled. "Em, he has a crush on you." He popped an olive into his mouth.

The heat crept from her cheeks to her ears and neck, and she couldn't blame the non-alcoholic wine. "Well, it seems unlikely, but I considered that."

"Pretty, young teacher. Teenage boy. Seems like par for the course to me."

She twisted her lips. "I don't know. I hope I handled it all right though. I was polite but firm that my personal life was off limits."

He gathered their empty bowls and spoons and set the cheese plate between them. "Well, my experience with that kind of thing is nil, but it sounds like you handled it right to me."

She took another drink of wine and wiped her mouth with her napkin. "How did your job at the zoo go?"

Another big smile. "Fantastic. And I'm not done yet. Best thing that ever happened to me." His eyes flickered, his expression growing more intimate. "At least business-wise. Not only is the work consistent, but I get paid well too. Plus, I got to know some contractors that have called me to sub for them. And the leads have been great. I'd never have guessed I'd get so many calls from sticking a little sign next to my work. It's been a real blessing."

She laid her hand over his wrist. "I'm so happy for you. Robert mentioned it was going well, but I had no idea. You do great work, Dan. You deserve it."

His Adam's apple bobbed as he swallowed, and it took a second before he answered. "It means a lot to me to hear you say that. Thank you." He repositioned his napkin. "I took possession of the car, the one I paid for. Sold it. So, between that, work, and the rental income, I've paid off all my debts."

Emily nodded. He seemed to have gotten it all together over the last six months.

She drained the last drops of wine from her glass, and as she returned the goblet to the table, her bracelet caught on a fork and knocked it to the floor. She leaned over, picked it up, and busied herself wiping it clean on her napkin.

"I'm so freakin' crazy in love with you I can barely stand it." His words were calm, sure, and completely out of the blue.

She set the fork on the table, blinking absently. She never expected to hear words like that, except maybe in a quiet moment under cover of darkness or in the throes of passion when a man's emotions might be amplified by the desire coursing through his body.

Dan had said them fully-clothed, straight-faced, and stone-sober in a classroom lit by harsh fluorescent bulbs. Metal desks surrounded them, and the faint scent of Simple Green still wafted in from the hall where a freshman had vomited yesterday morning. Despite all Dan's amazing efforts, as romantic settings went, it left something to be desired.

She stared, dumbfounded.

He didn't flinch, laugh, or avert his gaze. He didn't seem to blink or even breathe.

She didn't know whether to laugh, cry, or hide under the desk.

His confidence was new, disarming, and very, very attractive. Dan had changed. It showed in his face. His expressions were less guarded, and anxiety didn't tinge his words. His mood, his attitude, his comportment, everything about him was light years above and beyond the last weekend they had spent together.

"Dan, I—"

He held a hand up. "You don't need to say anything, Em." He smiled and folded his napkin in his lap. "After dinner, I have something else planned. I thought you might like to go to the art museum. I hear there's some French artwork there."

The change of topic filled her with relief. She giggled. "Heard that on the street, huh?"

"Something like that."

Apparently, "French" described the night's theme. She couldn't help thinking ahead to the goodnight kiss.

38

Aimer est divin
(To love is divine)

Emily clutched Dan's hand as they climbed the large stone steps to the museum entrance. The four giant Romanesque concrete columns appeared cool despite the day's heat. As Dan held the door for her, she breathed in the scent that took her back to childhood field trips and family visits. Like the smell of textbooks and fresh pencils that harkened back to the start of a new school year, the deliciously antique smell of the museum resurrected memories of her navy Mary Jane shoes sliding over the hard floors and dizzying gazes at the shimmering chandeliers suspended from the vaulted ceilings.

They moved from room to room, spending a few moments in front of select pieces that interested them. Dan either intertwined his fingers with hers, or when they found something that captivated one or the other, he moved behind her, circling her waist with his arms. He tilted his head around hers, murmuring comments in her ear, some insightful, some silly.

Muted shades of brown blotched and streaked a large, frameless, rectangular piece. "Looks like someone smeared paint on a dog's rear and let him drag it over the canvas," Dan said in front of the modern piece.

She burst into laughter, attracting the attention of a balding, older gentleman with elbow patches on his tweed sports coat.

When they'd stood transfixed before a landscape of a pond teeming with lush lily pads for more than a minute, Dan's warm sigh melted in her ear. "What do they call these paintings with all the little dots again?"

"Pointillism?" She loved all things French but would never be considered an art expert.

"Yeah, that's it. I like it."

Dan took her hand and pulled her toward a romantic painting depicting a woman clad in white robes holding a lamb in one arm and an infant in the other. The woman's porcelain skin glowed as her gaze caressed the child, so contented he appeared to sleep in her arms. The peaceful white lamb stared out from the painting, its eyes dark and focused.

Dan sunk his hands into his pockets. "I've seen this one before."

Emily read the title and artist: "*L'Innocence* by William Adolphe Bouguereau . . . I could stare at it all day."

In her peripheral vision, Dan nodded. He moved behind her, wrapping his arms around her again and gazing at the painting over her shoulder. The warmth from his body, the musky scent of his cologne, and his minty breath in her ear combined to create an almost dizzy, heady sensation. But then she hadn't been near him or any other man in six months.

"Why do you think her feet are bare?" His chin rested on her shoulder.

"Uh . . ." She struggled to gather her thoughts. "It's aesthetically more pleasing. She's outdoors . . . nature's untainted."

"Hmmm, makes sense. Is it supposed to be Mary and baby Jesus?"

She scanned the small plaque on the wall to see if it explained anything pertaining to the subjects. "I don't know. There aren't any halos or anything."

Dan stood silent for a moment before she felt his jaw moving against her temple. "It comes from Latin—innocent. I do remember a little. The verb is *nocere*, to harm. So, unharmed." He lifted his chin and tucked a strand of hair behind her ear. "Do you think it's a good thing? To be innocent, I mean."

She turned her head toward him. "Of course. Who doesn't miss the innocence of childhood?"

He shifted behind her and sighed. "I don't know. When it comes to kids, my own kids, yeah, I want them to be innocent as long as they can, but grown-ups? I don't think we should be."

"Why not?"

He squeezed tighter around her waist, and his warmth spread through her body. A prim, silver-haired woman crossed in front of them, and Emily cleared her throat.

"Well, Jesus goes willingly to the cross. He's not unharmed. And Mary watches. The lamb there, all fuzzy and cute, he goes to the slaughter. We can't escape the loss of innocence. This painting is a fiction. An ideal meant to be sacrificed.

"And why should we be innocent forever? Doesn't pain make us more understanding and empathetic? Doesn't it enrich us, make us appreciate our blessings? It sends us back to the arms of our Father."

Her eyes closed as she pondered what he'd said. Where had such introspection come from? Dan had a college degree; she didn't know in what. His intelligence and diligence were obvious in his work, but she'd never expected to hear such profound analysis from his lips. "Who are you, Dan Malone?"

A beat of silence, then in a voice so low she strained to hear: "I'm the man who loves you. I was made to love you, Em."

He bumped the back of her knee with his. "C'mon, let's move."

They stopped before an alabaster sculpture of two nude figures—male and female—embracing. The man's muscular limbs contrasted with the woman's slim legs. Dan stood behind her again, and she considered telling him she needed some space. The museum's air conditioning couldn't compete with the heat he generated.

His presence was so masculine, so comforting, that she kept quiet. His lips tickled her ear, his breath warm. "Teach me to say something in French that'll turn you on."

He didn't need French for that. He could read from the phone book into her ear like that, and it would do the job, no question. A warm, tingly sensation spread from her ear southward. "Uh. . ." Did her voice really sound all breathy like that? She cleared her throat. "In high school we thought it was funny to say, *'Voulez-vous coucher avec moi?'*"

"What does that mean?" His question sent another shot of warm ripples through her.

"Would you like to sleep with me?" It came out as smooth and rich as honey.

His arms squeezed her waist and pulled her closer despite the fact their bodies were already touching. His voice came louder this time and not right in her ear. "You went around asking horny high school boys that question?"

She tittered like a schoolgirl. "Well, not me personally. But I can't imagine any of them would've had any interest in me anyway. It's not like guys were lining up at my door, Dan."

He stepped back and gently turned her with a hand to each arm. His eyes narrowed, and his forehead wrinkled. "Where does that come from?"

"What?"

"That self-deprecating stuff."

She shrugged. "The truth? Guys have never gone for me."

"Well, I didn't know you in high school, but if you believe that now, then you are oblivious, Emily Kowalski."

"What do you mean?"

"I mean, if I catch one more guy here looking at your breasts or your behind or any other part of you with anything but detached indifference, I'm going to haul off and hit him."

She turned her head from side to side, looking for these supposed men that had been ogling her. No one. No man or boy in sight. "You're delusional."

Their playful disagreement didn't amount to much, but it would serve as an excuse for putting a little distance between them before she overheated. She slipped free from his grasp, turned, and took a half step before he pulled her back. She put a hand against his chest, preventing a full-body slam, which wouldn't do much for the heat factor.

His tone matched the intense look in his eyes. "I'm observant and a wee bit possessive. And I didn't answer your question. Let's see how much French I know." He winked, a smile playing on his lips. "You welshed on my language lesson, you know." He took her hand from the center of his chest and slid it over his heart. "*Oui, mademoiselle. Très, très mucho.*"

A laugh ending in a snort escaped Emily's nose and throat. "*Très beaucoup.* Very much is *très beaucoup.*" She reigned in her amusement and recalled her question. And his reply. Did he say *oui*, as in yes, he wanted to sleep with her? Wanted to, as in, wanted to but wouldn't or wanted to, so let's get out of here and go someplace private? She'd expected he'd changed over the last months, but not in that way.

Apparently neither one of them knew how to follow his statement, and silence settled between them for several seconds.

Dan moved away first. "You ready for our next stop?"

"There's more?"

"You bet your cute little derriere, there is."

If he slapped her behind, she'd bop him in the head. He didn't though. He slipped his hand around her waist and turned her toward the exit.

***

A neighborhood of row homes and duplexes slid by Emily's window. The potholes grew fewer and farther between as they rumbled and bumped up a steep cobblestone street lined by postwar Cape Cods and box-like ranch homes. They'd passed two Catholic churches already, but Dan had stopped at the third one. One she'd never been in, and from its location, one she doubted he frequented. He put the truck into park and killed the engine.

"We're going to church?"

"Yeah. C'mon." His eyes sparkled with mischief as he grabbed the door handle and pushed.

He came around to her side, opened the door, and held her hand as she stepped onto the uneven brick sidewalk. The sun slid below the horizon, and the cool air chilled her shoulders. She rubbed a hand over her bare arm.

"Chilly?"

She nodded. "A little."

Dan reached into the truck and pulled out a dull-green, thermal, hooded sweatshirt. "It doesn't go with your dress, but, if you're cold . . ."

"Thanks." She draped the jacket over her shoulders. It smelled earthy, like he'd worn it as he turned soil or laid stone.

They climbed the steps to the entrance. Dan pulled open the heavy wooden door, the hinges grinding, and ushered her into the dark narthex.

Emily halted in the dim space, waiting for her eyes to adjust.

Dan opened a set of glass doors, pressed her forward, and followed her into the main church.

Evening sunlight streamed in through the stained glass windows, casting a reddish glow over the pews. Dust motes danced and floated in the warm rays. It smelled faintly of incense and Murphy's Oil Soap.

Dan proceeded toward the altar. The sanctuary lamp glowed behind red glass next to the tabernacle, a square gold one adorned with images of lambs and wheat. He stopped when they reached the foot of the altar, the place where an altar rail had likely stood fifty years earlier.

"Pray with me?" His brows lifted in supplication.

She nodded and knelt alongside him. Everything about the evening had been unexpected. She couldn't imagine why he'd brought her to church, but she wasn't disappointed. The dim, quiet church and the presence of God flooded her soul with peace.

"So," he said, kneeling but looking in her direction. "In keeping with the French motif tonight, this is St. Catherine Labouré Church."

"I noticed." She didn't know a whole lot about the French saint beyond that her body lay encased in glass in Paris, intact and incorrupt, as if she were sleeping. Emily regretted not visiting the French church to see it.

Dan fished something out of his pocket. He opened his palm in front of her, revealing a silver medal. "You know what this is, right?"

Her gaze drifted over the shiny oval depicting the Blessed Mother with rays of light shooting from her fingertips. "A Miraculous Medal?" Emily had one herself somewhere. She received one on a chain as part of a Confirmation gift from her godmother. Emily had chosen St. Catherine of Siena as her patron, but her godmother had confused the two saints. The chain sat in her jewelry box, seldom worn.

"Yeah. This one was Grandma's." His gaze met hers. Such affection, respect, and now sadness shone in his eyes when he spoke about her. "She was a simple woman. And I mean that as a compliment. I'd be a lot better, lot holier man if I had half her simplicity." He sighed. "Anyway, this was hers. She used to wear it pinned to the inside of her bra."

Emily cocked an eyebrow at him.

"Don't ask. Just trust that it's true." A grin slipped. "I considered having it buried with her, pinned to the inside of her dress, but my mom convinced me to keep it. She said . . ." His voice resonated thick with emotion, and he cleared his throat. "She said that the prayer, the Miraculous Medal prayer, was a powerful thing. And that Grandma prayed it every day for me, multiple times a day in the months after my breakup with Kristen."

He fingered the medal where the words to the short prayer were inscribed around the edge.

"So, while I was getting drunk and high or pigging out or lying around wasting my life feeling sorry for myself, Grandma repeated this little prayer for me over and over. The day I came to Grandma's to take her shopping—cause I kept doing that even when I had a hangover or whatever—and told her I was going to change, big time, and get my act together, she burst into tears."

Emily slid her hand along his arm then took the silver medal he held between his fingers. "Why did she cry?"

"Because it was July 27, the day St. Catherine Labouré was canonized."

Emily smiled through the tears clouding her vision.

Dan took the medal back. "I had this little medal tucked in my wallet. And after you kicked me out of your brother's place and out of your life—and rightly so, I prayed. I've prayed that same little prayer every morning and every evening, and whenever I'd think of it during the day for the last six months. And today, I've got my miracle . . . Because you're here with me."

Tears welled in her eyes, and her throat thickened. Could he mean that? She remembered his note to her—"no more lies." *He meant it.*

"So, I want to thank St. Catherine Labouré for interceding, but mostly I want to thank God. For you, Emily."

Tears slid from her eyes, and she wiped them away with the back of her hand.

He turned toward the altar again, folded his hands, bowed his head, and did something she'd never heard him do—pray spontaneously. "Lord, thank you for this beautiful, virtuous woman next to me. I don't deserve her forgiveness or her love any more than I deserve Yours. But I understand grace is a gift, and I'm gonna stop being self-centered and wringing my hands about how unworthy I am and just accept it. So, if it's Your will that she and I be together, then I ask you to bless us and help us, me especially, not to screw this up again. Amen."

He withdrew a delicate silver chain from his pocket, slid the medal on, and put it around her neck. His hands brushed her bare skin beneath her hair as he fastened the clasp. A chill shook her shoulders despite the extra warmth from Dan's jacket.

"Grandma said this medal kept her safe. I don't think it was the medal. It's not worth much." He shrugged. "But the faith behind it. I want you to have this. I want to keep you safe." His hazel eyes shone with affection and glistened with tears.

Despite her efforts to hold them back, tears soaked her lashes and rolled down her cheeks. "Thank you," she murmured.

He reached a hand behind her head, tilting it downward, and kissed her hair. "You're welcome. I want you with me for a long, long time, Em."

39

Scellé avec un baiser
(Sealed with a kiss)

Dan jogged around his truck, reaching Emily's car door as she exited and stepped onto the curb. He wished she'd waited for him.

"You didn't need to follow me home, you know." His jacket still draped her breezy summer dress, the frayed cuffs hanging beyond the tips of her fingers.

"I wanted to. This is a date." He grasped her fingertips then laced his fingers with hers and swung their hands between them. "I'm supposed to see you home safely." True, but he'd also extend this perfect night with her any way he could.

A lone, dim light emanated from the recesses of Robert and Elizabeth's house. Probably the light above the kitchen sink. Moonlight and a flickering streetlamp lit the front yard.

Dan snaked his arm around Emily's waist as they ascended the steps. "I thought maybe you were trying to lose me back there."

She glanced his way and smiled. "I believe I've lost you enough to last me a lifetime."

"I hope so." Dan smirked and slowed as they reached the top step. "You have kind of a lead foot."

"I do not." She shoved his arm, but her twinkling eyes belied her denial. "What's the matter? Can't keep up?"

Her batting lashes and crooked grin brought a smile to his face. "I'm here, ain't I?"

She stopped at the door but made no move to open it.

Dan clenched his sweaty palms. Why the sudden attack of nerves? They'd been side by side all evening, and it felt like no time had passed since they were last together. The comfort, the ease, the attraction—all still there.

Emily gazed at him with expectant eyes, twisting her hands where they peeked out of the overlong sleeves.

He'd thought this through umpteen times in the week that had passed since he'd called to arrange their date. He would not kiss her. Tonight they'd re-established their friendship, their connection, their love. He'd walk away and leave her with a clear head to decide once and for all if this was what she wanted, if he—despite all his flaws and weaknesses—was her heart's desire.

He swallowed hard and inched closer, enveloping her in his arms, hugging her.

She looped her arms around his waist and rubbed his back. After a moment, she sighed and leaned farther into his embrace.

Dan squeezed her tightly and rested his chin alongside her head. Her hair lay soft and silky against his skin, and a sweet herbal scent teased his nostrils.

Several bats chittered as they swooped between the houses. A car passed on the street behind them, and the booming bass of a rap song reverberated.

She spoke softly into his chest. "Thank you. I had a wonderful evening. The best ever."

He smiled and loosened his arm to stroke hers. "You're welcome. Tonight was good." His pulse thundered in his ears. He had to ask. "I . . . I hope we can do this again."

She didn't answer. She pulled back.

His gut tightened.

She lifted her head, eyes gleaming. "You can count on it."

Dan exhaled. "I hoped you'd say that." His heartbeat thrummed in his ear. "I'll let you go." He stepped backward. "My, uh . . . my jacket?"

"Oh." She shrugged out of it and pressed it into his arms. "Thanks." She peered at him, hope and expectation shimmering in her eyes.

Not gonna kiss her. Not tonight. "I want to be sure you get in okay, so . . ."

She blinked, but he didn't miss the disappointment there.

"Let me find my keys." She rummaged through her purse, produced a couple of keys attached to a ring holding about a thousand retail rewards cards and a plastic-covered picture of some kids and the Easter bunny, and unlocked the door. "Good night." Then she slipped inside the door and stared through the screen at him. "Thanks again."

"My pleasure." He dipped his hands in his pockets, and after a little bounce that afforded him another second or two on her stoop, he turned and padded down the steps.

He made it to the sidewalk in front of his truck before the regret nagged him.

She'd felt so good against him. She'd wanted him to kiss her, no doubt about it. What was the point of not kissing her tonight? She'd already said she wanted to see him again.

He leaned his outstretched arms against the hood of his truck and tapped his foot on the sidewalk, waffling back and worth. Get in the truck and hightail it home or turn back and kiss the living daylights out of her?

He glanced at the house in time to see her face slip behind the living room curtain. *She'd been watching.* That cinched it for him.

He jogged up the steps and rapped on the door, ignoring the lit doorbell. He waited a few seconds and lifted his fist to knock again when the door swung open.

Emily cracked the storm door, allowing him entry.

"Did you forget something?" Her eyes widened in curiosity, her long, dark lashes batting her luminous skin.

He stepped toward her, his breaths rapid and shallow. "Not exactly," he mumbled before he slid his palms over her cheeks. His fingertips slid into her hair while the pads of his thumbs stroked her silky skin, which turned an attractive shade of pink beneath his touch.

"Then why'd you come back?"

He could do this one of two ways—gentle, tender, and saturated with the love radiating from his heart. A simple graze of his lips over hers that couldn't possibly sully their reunion. A fleeting, gentle kiss that respected how precious she was to him.

Or he could crush his lips to hers with the weight of six months' pent-up attraction.

Her tongue slipped between her lips then retreated, and she bit her lip.

No contest.

His lips met hers in an action more akin to devouring than tasting.

A little squeak came from somewhere in the back of her throat, and then she relented, matching his ardor with passion of her own. Her hands gripped his biceps, squeezing his muscles, pulling him closer.

Only he couldn't get any closer short of . . . *Best not to go there. Not even mentally.*

He kissed her a minute or two then pulled away. He groaned and blew out a breath, clenching and releasing his hands, hoping to rein his galloping heart to a slow trot. He bit the inside of his cheek, still tasting her sweetness, her unguarded affection. "Damn. That was a long time coming."

She burst into laughter and slapped a hand over her mouth. "I couldn't believe you were going to leave without a goodnight kiss. I thought maybe I needed a breath mint."

Emily reached for him, pure joy radiating from her eyes and face as she threw her arms around his neck. Her lips pressed his cheek, his temple, and his ear, although she had obvious difficulty getting her lips to cooperate because of her mile-wide smile. "Please don't go that long between kisses." She loosened her grip and tilted her head so he could see her face. Every trace of levity disappeared. "Ever again."

He sucked his lips in, trying to keep his emotions in check. His voice came out hoarse and filled with feeling. "If I had my way, a day wouldn't go by without kissing you."

***

A large, golden harvest moon hung above the treetops, flanked by wispy clouds. Nearly all the leaves on the fringes of the plowed cornfield had turned brilliant shades of red and yellow, but most still clung to the branches. While Emily's relationship with Dan had gone from desolate winter to full-blown summer heat over the past six weeks, Pennsylvania had slipped from late summer heat to autumn chill. She zipped her jacket to her chin and hugged her arms close to her body.

She peered around a group of teens, trying to glimpse the front of the line and the entrance to the haunted house. Still a good twenty-minute wait.

Dan would have plenty of time to return from the port-a-potty. Poor guy. But he did down two large cups of hot chocolate.

A warm aroma drifted from a gigantic pot of kettle corn roasting beneath a lean-to. With every stir, the sweet and salty scent tickled her nose and made her mouth water. Maybe she could talk Dan into buying them a bag after they—

Something slammed Emily's back, forcing her forward. Her hands shot out, landing on the girl in front of her. Emily and the girl stumbled out of line. "Ummph."

A strong hand gripped Emily's arm. "Oh, man. I'm sorry."

Emily straightened and pushed her loose hair behind her ear. "It's, uh, I'm okay." She regained her footing then lifted her gaze to the careless oaf who had nearly bulldozed her. A shock of blonde hair hung over cerulean eyes. "Jamie?"

He dropped his hand and blinked rapidly, his blue eyes glassy and dilated. "Miss Kowalski? I'm so sorry. My buddy shoved me, and I . . ." He glanced over his shoulder, but no one was in sight. "This won't affect my grade will it?" He cracked a lazy smile.

She breathed a little laugh. "No, of course not." She smoothed out her gray fleece jacket where it had bunched.

"You here with your boyfriend?"

She tilted her head. What was this boy's interest in her love life? Did he have a crush on her like Dan thought? "He's using the facilities." She gestured to the line of port-a-potties.

Jamie nodded. His eyes sharpened, and his lips tightened. "Well, I gotta catch up with my buddy." He jerked his thumb in the direction of the cornfield. "Save a dance for me tomorrow night? Danny Boy doesn't have to know."

Emily's mouth gaped. A dance? And how did he know Dan's name?

He trotted off beyond the kettle corn, where a line had formed. Her gaze followed him to see if he'd met up with his friend, but she lost him in the crowd.

Hands jabbed into her waist from behind, and she jumped and spun around.

Dan dug his hands into his jean pockets, laughing. "Gotcha."

She laid a hand over her heart. "Geez, Dan. Scare me to death before we get inside, why don't you?"

He grinned and rubbed his gloved hands together. "This is going to be fun. If you're this jumpy outside, you're going to be screaming bloody murder and jumping into my arms once we get inside."

She swatted him in the chest. "You'd like that, wouldn't you?"

He waggled his eyebrows. "You miss me?"

"No time to miss you. I had company."

He arched a brow and glanced around. "Who?"

"One of my students. Actually, the boy I tutored. Jamie. He ran into me. Literally."

He nodded. "I had an interesting trip to the john too."

"What do you mean?"

"I wait in line forever, and I'm in there all of two minutes, and someone's banging and pushing on the back like they're trying to tip it."

"For real?"

"Yeah. I came out and searched all around, but I couldn't spot anyone." He shrugged. "Some jag-offs playing tricks, I guess."

"I guess." Inexplicable unease snaked through her veins. It was probably nothing. Jamie's sudden impact had unsettled her. And his odd remark. That was all.

The wind picked up, rustling the dried, brown corn stalks. Emily shivered.

"Cold?" Dan rubbed her shoulders.

She hugged her arms tight to her body. "A little."

"I have something that'll warm you up." He unzipped his old, brown leather jacket three-quarters of the way down, reached into an interior pocket, and withdrew a vintage-looking tin flask.

Her eyes widened. "You brought alcohol?"

He smiled. "Apple pie moonshine. A couple of shots."

She shook her head but grinned. "You're bad."

"Don't look so shocked. I didn't distill it in my basement; I bought it at the liquor store. And this . . ." He held the flask where light from the kettle corn stand shone. "This was my grand pap's. Had it stashed with all his World War II stuff. I found it with Grandma's things." He turned it in the light, admiring both sides. "Every week I find another treasure she left behind. A bag of cookies crammed in the back of the freezer, a collection of Mother's Day cards from her kids and grandkids, a shoebox filled with Pap's stuff. It's like she's still there, still looking out for me."

His enduring love for Grandma made her heart as gooey as a caramel apple. She'd known from the first time he'd mentioned her on their muddy excursion to the farm that Grandma held a special place in Dan's heart. "She is, I'm sure."

Dan took a swig. "Mmm. Warm you right up. I promise." His eyes sparkled with mischief.

Emily shuffled ahead as the line moved. "Did you save me any?"

"Maybe. Want a taste?"

She narrowed an eye at him and considered whether he was up to something with this little game. She sighed. "Oh, what the heck. Sure."

Dan moved closer and dropped his free hand to her hip. "Kiss me."

She jerked her head back. "What?"

His grin grew. "You heard me. Kiss me."

So that's what he was up to. "Like you have to extort kisses from me." She rose onto tiptoes and planted a gentle kiss to his lips. They were warm, soft, and tasted like sweet apples and cinnamon. "Mmm. I'd like some more."

He dropped his head to kiss her again, but when his lips were a fraction of an inch from hers she wedged her hand between them and pushed his chest.

"More moonshine. Not kisses."

Dan reeled back and clutched at his heart. "You wound me."

They inched forward in line.

Emily laughed and snatched the flask from his hand, raised it to her mouth, and drained it. The moonshine burned a liquid trail down her throat and through her chest. "That's good." She cleared her throat, letting the warmth subside. "Really good."

They approached the front of the line, and Emily handed the flask back to Dan. The door creaked open, and a long-faced ghoul dressed in a black cape and Nike Airs ushered them into the house. A series of high-pitched screams emanated from deep within the house, and the burnt, sweet smell of a fog machine wafted out along with a white puff.

"Ladies first," Dan murmured in her ear, ushering her forward with a hand to her back.

40

Le chambre interdite
(Bedroom restricted)

"I did *not* scream like a girl." Dan glanced at Emily in the passenger seat.

The smirk pasted to her face amused more than irritated him.

"You're right." She patted his thigh. "It was more like a frightened toddler. Baby Ben does the same thing every time I bring out that creepy Gollum puppet."

He shook his head. "I wasn't expecting that dude with the scythe to move, that's all."

She laughed. "Obviously."

The conversation lulled, and he tapped his fingers on the steering wheel in time with the beat of the One Republic track on the car stereo. He focused on the road, calculating the remaining distance.

He'd almost completed the remodeling projects on Grandma's house—make that *his* house. His tenants had left after six months, giving him unrestricted access to the house the last couple of months. It was time to show Emily what he'd done. Up until now, he'd managed to keep her away by meeting her at Robert and Elizabeth's house or at school. As they left the Halloween attraction, he'd asked her if she'd like to see his progress, and she'd agreed. More than agreed. Her eyes lit, and she'd bubbled with excitement. He hoped his work didn't disappoint. Or scare her off.

He opened the truck door, and she stepped onto the sidewalk, wrapped her arms around his waist, and squeezed tight.

"Thanks for bringing me on the grand tour. I love this house. I can't wait to see what you've done with it." She released him and took his hand but waited for him to lead.

He took a deep breath, squeezed her hand, and started for the house. When they reached the door, he fished the key from his pocket. He turned the deadbolt, then the lock. His hand stilled on the knob for a second. *Please, God, let her like it.* All of sudden this seemed like a bad idea. What had he been thinking? Maybe he could do an abbreviated version of the grand tour and skip the master bedroom.

The knob turned with a click, and the door opened. The faint smell of cinnamon filled the entryway. It more often smelled like spackle or new carpet these days, but he'd planned ahead and burnt a pillar candle in the kitchen before he'd gone to pick up Emily.

She lifted her nose and sniffed. "Mmm. Smells so nice. All warm and homey." Her smile sagged, and her eyes dimmed.

"What's the matter?" He glanced around the room. She hadn't even gotten a look at the place yet. What had wiped away that smile?

She shook her head. "Just missing Grandma. Always smelled like freshly-baked chocolate chip cookies when I came over. I can still see her standing at the counter—" Her eyes darted to the kitchen. The small bay window above the sink was unchanged, but that's the only thing that she would recognize.

"Oh, Dan." She scraped her feet over the doormat a couple of times then strode to the kitchen. The galley-style kitchen no longer resembled the narrow room filled with dark walnut cupboards, white and gold Formica countertops, and olive-colored appliances.

The eggshell cabinetry, granite countertop, and tiled floor opened the room up, making it contemporary and inviting. She ran her hand along the side of the stainless steel refrigerator and the matching brand-new gas stove. A large vase filled with sunflowers and orange chrysanthemums sat on a wheeled, wooden microwave cart at the end of the room.

"This is beautiful." She turned around in the room, taking in the details.

"See the backsplash?" He pointed to the broken, colored tiles above the sink. "That's from the old tile that was in here and even some of Grandma's old dishes."

She turned her gaze back to him, her eyes watery. "I love it."

His heart swelled. Maybe he could show her the master bedroom. Maybe she'd be okay with it. "Let me show you the rest."

He'd refinished the hardwood floors downstairs and repainted the walls in fresh, subtle shades—beige in the dining room, pale green-gray in the living room. An oriental rug covered the center of the living area. White wainscoting lined the lower half of the dining room walls, and a new chandelier and ceiling fan hung above the oval, mahogany, double-clawfoot dining table. The most notable difference in the rooms was the lack of Grandma's ever-present knickknacks and houseplants, which had covered every bare horizontal surface.

He followed Emily to the base of the stairs where he opened the door to the powder room.

"Aw, you didn't keep the pink tile and wallpaper." Her voice dripped with false disappointment. "Or those fluorescent lights flanking the mirror." She shuddered. "They always made me look like an extra on *The Walking Dead*."

Dan grinned. The bathroom *was* a huge improvement. Pale blue paint, recessed lights, a white pedestal sink, tile flooring, and a more efficient commode.

He waited as she admired the little room then flipped the light switch and climbed the stairs. He'd had a heck of a time getting the carpet off before he could paint the risers.

The full bathroom upstairs had undergone a transformation similar to the powder room downstairs. One major change would stand out. He bit his lower lip and waited for her reaction.

One look and her hand flew to her chest. "Oh, Dan, it's beautiful." Her hand slid along the rim of the clawfoot tub he'd found and restored. It was remarkably similar to the one he remembered from years ago, before Grandma's age necessitated a change in tubs.

He led her through the two small bedrooms, which he'd painted pale yellow, suitable for a nursery or children's room. Except for a few boxes in the corner of each, they remained empty. But he hoped not for too many years.

When she'd stepped out of the smaller of the two rooms, he showed her the linen closet, redesigned to make maximum use of the small space.

They neared the master bedroom, and a surge of anxiety made his stomach clench and his throat constrict. He tried herding her toward the staircase.

She laid a hand to his arm. "What about the other bedroom?"

"Hmm?" Could he play it off as if he didn't know what she meant? No. He could lie, tell her he hadn't gotten to that room yet. But he had.

No more lies.

He sighed. "Truth is, I'm not sure you'll like what I did with it."

She scrunched up her face. "I love what you did with the rest of the house. I can't imagine not loving this room too." Her gaze searched his face. "You're nervous. You don't want me to see it, do you?"

Without giving him a chance to respond, she stepped into the room and flicked on the light. Her gaze traveled to the largest object in her line of sight: the dresser with attached mirror. Nothing unusual there. She stepped in further, taking in the details of the furniture and décor.

The bed, dresser, and nightstands were made of oak, darkened with a walnut stain. A quilt made of hunter green and burgundy squares covered the bed. A single, cream-colored, oval throw pillow with lace trim lay atop the standard-sized pillows piled beneath the headboard. Above the bed hung a wooden cross with a pewter corpus.

She turned, taking in the remaining items in the room—a small table lamp on the nightstand and a rocking chair with one of Grandma's handmade afghans, a beige one with green woven throughout.

The decorations on the remaining wall, best viewed from the bed, caused her to wheel around and face him. Her eyes were wide and her voice tentative. "This is our bedroom, isn't it?"

Heat crept up his neck, and he tried hiding his blush by rubbing at the tensed muscles. He'd taken care to decorate the room with both masculine tones and feminine touches, as much as he knew how, anyway. Wooden letters painted in muted shades spelled "Malone." A sleek black frame encased a vertical print of the Eiffel Tower. A print of William Bouguereau's *L'Innocence*, the piece they had admired at the art museum, was mounted on a green matte with a wooden burgundy frame.

"Dan?"

His nervous reply rushed and roared over his lips like white caps heading toward the falls. "It'll be mine. I mean, it is mine, but now I'll live here. My lease is up at the end of the month. I'm going to move in while I finish the basement. And there's still the mudroom. "

She reached for his face and caressed his cheek. "Slow down." Her lips twitched as if she held back a grin.

He nodded, took a deep breath, and continued. "I had you in mind when I did this." He glanced at the Bouguereau painting, the shades of luminescent white grabbing and holding his attention as they always did. His gaze slid back to hers. "Obviously, I guess . . . It doesn't freak you out, does it? I mean . . ." He stuffed his hands into his jeans pockets. "I didn't presume. Even if you forgave me, I didn't presume you'd want to . . . to try again with me. I just . . . doing all this was good therapy for me this summer. For real. The counselor said it would be a good use of my time. Kinda working through things. Y'know, working with my hands. Fixing things. Making them like new again. A lot of that had to do with you. With us."

She hadn't spoken, and he wished he had some indication what was going through her mind. When he got through his convoluted explanation, would she embrace him or recoil from him?

"I know what you're thinking, but I like it for me. It's the first place that feels like home since I was a kid. Before my dad died."

She still didn't speak, but her eyes held a tender look.

"I hoped you'd like it though in case . . . I know I haven't asked you to . . . y-you know how much I love you, don't you?"

Emily brushed her fingertips below her eye. A tear? That could be good or bad.

She tugged on her lower lip with her teeth. "Show me."

He wrinkled his brow. "Show you . . .?"

"Show me how much you love me." The doe-eyed look she gave him almost buckled his knees.

When his addled brain finally got the message—and her demand—his lips stretched in a smile. He breathed deeply, in and out. "That's a dangerous request, Em, and you know it."

Her brown eyes twinkled. "A little danger can be fun, don't you think?"

His eyes flicked to the bed. If she had even an inkling how that tempted him, she wouldn't tease him like that. He stepped closer, close enough to let his fingers glide over a thick strand of auburn hair falling over her shoulder and onto her chest. "Depends what kind of danger you're talking about, I guess. If it endangers your heart or soul, even the slightest bit, I don't want anything to do with it, but I want to spend my life showing you my love a dozen different ways every day."

If the dazed look on her face were any indication, he'd stunned her into silence.

He pursed his lips and lifted his brows. "So, you haven't said . . . *do* you like it? The bedroom?"

She found his hands and held them, letting their arms hang between them. "I love it."

"And I haven't creeped you out? I promise there's not an Emily shrine hidden in the closet or anything weird."

She giggled. "No pictures or newspaper clippings tacked to the wall in the attic?"

He shook his head. "I keep a picture in my wallet and on my phone. That's it. I swear."

She squeezed his palms. "It's okay, Dan. It's not like I'm the chick down the street you've been stalking with a pair of binoculars. We're close. And, I love you too."

She dropped his hands and slid her arms around his neck, pulling his face towards her. "I love you so much."

His chest burned, and he closed the small distance between them, pressing his lips to hers. The fact that his bed—maybe someday their bed—sat a couple of steps behind them teased his senses. It would be so easy . . .

He pulled away. "I-I should take you home."

She twisted a lock of hair at his nape. "It's not that late. We haven't been alone like this in forever. And, there's still your boundaries, right?" She smiled, as if his rules were a quaint idea meant to appease their parents, not the only thing keeping him from doing something he desperately wanted at the moment but would regret later.

"My boundaries are crumbling, Em."

Her gaze penetrated him, as if she just recognized his seriousness.

"I need to get a ring on your finger before you change your mind about me or before I do something I swore I wouldn't do again with anyone but my wife."

Her breath hitched, she blinked, and a completely unguarded expression passed over her face. *Innocence.*

"I want to be your first, your last, and about a million times in between." Crumbling boundaries was a gross understatement. His will cracked like an imploding demolition. One second it was there, the next it collapsed on itself, thundering to the ground.

With a rough jab, his hand threaded through her hair and behind her head as he crushed her lips. He pressed forward, backing her into the bed.

The backs of her knees hit the mattress, and she fell back, immediately scooting farther onto the bed into a more comfortable position. He climbed onto the bed, knelt, then stretched his arms out on the mattress above her shoulders, suspending himself above her. His pulse throbbed in his neck, and his heart pounded in his chest.

Not like this. Wait.

The thought came to him from out of nowhere.

Not nowhere. Somewhere. From his conscience, God, his brain—if *that* was still functioning. He planted one foot and then the other back on the floor then extended a hand to Emily.

Bewildered was the only way to describe the look on her face as she propped herself onto her elbows. She hadn't protested one bit, but if pressed much further, she would've. Maybe she could make out with him on the bed and still have the will to stop, but he couldn't, and he knew it.

"Sorry, Em. I can't. Let me take you home."

She took his hand, and he tugged her into an upright position.

Her light kiss pressed against his cheek. "Sure. I didn't mean to—"

He shook his head. "It's okay. I just . . . I'll do this right with you. I promise."

***

Emily turned the knob and leaned into the door with her shoulder. The door gave way, and she fell forward, landing in Robert's arms.

Dan's hand steadied her elbow from behind.

"I'm glad to see you too, sis." Robert squeezed her in a bear hug then tousled her hair.

"Stop it." She wrenched herself out of his arms with a low growl. "You spying on us or something?"

Dan slipped in behind her, the grin on his face mocking her irritation.

"Lighten up, will you?" Robert closed the door but left it unlocked. "I was heading to bed when the truck pulled up. Thought I'd save you the trouble and open the door for you."

"Oh. Sorry." Maybe she was a bit touchy. Robert and Elizabeth had graciously opened their home to her—again—when she'd needed it. She should show more gratitude. Lately she'd longed to be back on her own again though, where little kids didn't dog her every step and her brother wasn't privy to every move she made.

"Yeah, well. Last time I try to be nice." He turned his attention to Dan and extended his hand. "What's up, buddy? How's the house coming?"

Dan grasped his hand and shook it. "Good. I showed Emily what I've done." He glanced at her.

She recalled the room decorated to suit her, and Dan forcing her back onto the bed. Her cheeks warmed, and she averted her gaze.

"Let me know when you're ready to install that dropped ceiling in the basement. I'll give you a hand."

"Thanks. I will." He turned back to Emily. "I'm gonna head out. When will I see you tomorrow?"

"Early or late I guess, because of the dance."

"The dance?" Dan's brow furrowed, and his eyes narrowed.

Hadn't she told him?

"Yeah," Robert said. "She has chaperone duty tomorrow night. School Halloween dance."

"Did I forget to mention it? I was going crazy trying to come up with a costume."

"You mentioned the costume, but I thought it was for school."

Robert shook his head. "I tried to help, but she didn't like any of my suggestions."

"Yeah. You're a big help." She glared at Robert, and her tone rang flat. "Bearded lady, old crone, fat opera singer."

He shrugged. "I'm doin' him a favor." He winked at Dan. "A guy likes his girl to wear those skimpy French maid costumes and sexy cat outfits for him, not for a bunch of boys who already spend forty minutes every school day eyeing her up."

She rolled her eyes. "First of all, you both know I don't wear that stuff. Second of all, I'm sure there will be an abundance of inappropriately-dressed girls their own age there. No one will give me a second look." She recalled Jamie's remark—*Save me a dance.* Did he really have a crush on her? Could he not see how out of line his remarks were—especially about Dan?

Robert punched Dan lightly in the arm. "Unless she wears a Princess Leia slave getup."

Emily groaned. "What is it with guys and that slave outfit?"

Dan laughed. "Let me buy you one, and you can find out."

She crossed her arms over her chest. "The language teachers finally decided we'd wear Day of the Dead costumes. Of the not-sexy and not-too-creepy variety. You wouldn't believe how hard that is to come by." She let out an exasperated sigh as she thought of the dozens of ghoulish masks and skimpy skull-adorned corsets she'd scrolled past on the Internet.

"How about lunch, then? I'll pick you up at noon." Dan gave her a quick kiss. "Love you," he whispered.

For some reason, the fact that he'd said that he loved her, however softly, in front of Robert, thrilled her. Dan was all in this time. No backpedaling or pussyfooting.

She smiled. "And if the dance doesn't go long, I'll treat you to ice cream afterwards."

"Sounds good." Dan glanced at Robert as he stepped outside. "Catch you later, man."

Robert nodded. "Yep. Goodnight." With a soft click, he shut the door behind Dan and twisted the deadbolt.

He draped his arm over Emily's shoulder and squeezed. "I think it's gonna take this time. He's in a good place. And he's crazy about you."

She slid her arm around his waist, not bothering to hide her smile. "It's mutual."

"Good," he muttered. "It's about time you get out of my basement, little girl."

41

Déguisé

(In disguise)

"I got it covered. Go." Emily motioned her fellow language teacher Karyn toward the restrooms. A Cee Lo Green song pumped through the speakers at a volume requiring her to shout to be heard. "Take your time."

The music came to an abrupt end and the DJ chattered.

"Thanks." Karyn's long, green, peasant-style skirt swished as she walked past. A cellophane wrapper filled with saltine crackers crinkled as she gripped it in her fist. White face paint covered her face, and intricate green and purple designs highlighted the skeletal structure of her eyes and nose. Through all the makeup, it was impossible to determine her skin color, but Emily guessed it was a pale green.

Karyn had confided her eight-week pregnancy to Emily, although she hadn't yet informed the principal or her Spanish students. Thirty minutes into the dance, she'd made more trips to the bathroom than potty-training Tessa, who'd upped her Hershey kiss rewards by guzzling from a quart-sized water bottle.

Emily surveyed the rollicking scene. Students huddled in clusters beneath dangling plastic spiders and neon green webs. A few leaned against the wall where corn shocks were propped alongside straw bales. Except for a handful of creative getups, most of the costumes failed to impress. With only half the fluorescent lights on the perimeter of the cafeteria lit, she spotted five hippies, eight sexy witches, half a dozen vampires, and too many zombies to count. A small pack of boys in black morph suits wove in and out of the dancers.

Her own costume had turned out better than she'd expected. As they'd planned, she and Karyn wore identical skirts, white blouses adorned with a red and turquoise Aztec design, giant gold hoop earrings, and ribbons woven into the long braids in their hair. The makeup highlighted skeletal features yet somehow remained more pretty than creepy.

"Miss Kowalski, Miss Kowalski! We need your help." A high-pitched plea rose above the throbbing bass of dance music.

Molly and Lourdes, two of her best sophomore students, bounded up alongside her. Molly's disguise consisted of a transparent umbrella with strips of bubble wrap hanging from the inside. She wore a white turtleneck with white yoga pants as part of her jellyfish disguise. Lourdes, with one arm pressed against her waist, wore knee-high black boots, a wispy red skirt, and a black corset over a flouncy white blouse. A feathered tricorn hat and a foam sword rounded out her sexy pirate outfit.

"Bonjour, girls. *Comment allez-vous?*"

"The hooks on Lourdes's corset are popping open, and I don't know how to close them." Molly pleaded with hands folded around her umbrella handle. "Can you fix them?"

"Please, Miss Kowalski." Lourdes's voice rose to a high-pitched whine. "I'm on the verge of a major wardrobe malfunction." She twisted her torso, revealing the torn garment.

Several cheap-looking gold hooks had ripped from the seam, exposing freckled skin on her back. Emily ran her hand along the seam, assessing the fabric while she tried to formulate a quick fix to ensure the costume continued to cover what it should.

"I have a few safety pins in my purse. We could try those, but I have to wait until Mrs. Mancini gets back from the restroom."

Molly stood behind Lourdes, trying to hide her ripped costume.

In a couple of minutes, Karyn returned, her fist pressed against her lips. She managed a smile for a passing student.

Emily touched her arm. "You okay?"

She nodded and nibbled a cracker. "My energy is totally sapped, and I can't keep anything down."

"Hang on." Emily grabbed a folding chair from the stack in the corner of the cafeteria. She plunked it in front of Karyn. "Here. Sit down."

Karyn eased into the seat and pressed her hands against her belly. "Thanks."

"Are you okay for a few minutes?" She motioned to Molly and Lourdes, who still waited for her help. "I'm going to help one of the girls with her costume."

Karyn waved her off with a saltine. "Sure, go. I'll be here munching my crackers."

"C'mon girls." Emily led the jellyfish and the pirate toward the ladies room. She ushered the girls through the steel door. Coming from the shadowy cafeteria, the fluorescent lights blinded her for a second until her eyes adjusted. Two girls dressed as bunnies emerged from the last stall, giggling. The scent of watermelon lip gloss trailed behind them as they squeezed past and out the door.

"Okay. Let me see what I can do." Emily dug through her purse until she found the tiny resealable bag holding half a dozen small safety pins. "Turn around, Lourdes."

Emily bit one pin between her teeth and popped another open. She grasped the sides of the corset, tugged, and threaded the pin through both pieces of fabric, clasping it shut. She took the second pin from her mouth and did the same, only it wouldn't close. It appeared, in an effort to find the most form-fitting bodice possible, Lourdes bought a size too small. "Take a deep breath and hold it."

Lourdes inhaled, sucking in her already-flat stomach, and Emily fastened the pin.

"There. Good as new." Emily surveyed her handiwork and shrugged. "Almost."

"Oh, thank you, Miss Kowalski." Lourdes threw her arms around her. "You're a lifesaver."

"You're welcome." Emily wrenched her face to the side so her makeup wouldn't smear. "Don't make any sudden moves though. I'm not sure how long that'll hold."

Molly tugged open the door for her friend. "Thank you, Miss Kowalksi." She leaned toward Lourdes and spoke in an eager voice. "Let's go. I think Mike's here now." Her face split in a huge grin.

"Have fun!" On Emily's last word, the entire place went dark. Dim reddish light filtered in from the cafeteria, likely from the battery-powered exit sign. A pop sounded, as if from a speaker, and the music died, leaving an eerie silence in its wake.

A blast sounded.

Once, twice, and then a third burst.

Dozens of simultaneous high-pitched shrieks followed.

Emily's heart pounded. What made the sound? Firecrackers? A gunshot? She didn't know which. "Molly, Lourdes."

The girls stood frozen in the open doorway, Lourdes's silhouette enlarged due to her feathered hat. Molly's jellyfish took on a russet hue.

Emily tugged them back. She strained to keep her voice calm but urgent. "Close the door."

It swished shut, and they stood in pitch blackness. Emily reached a hand out and stepped forward until her fingers tangled in Molly's bubble wrap. "I want you two to go into the rear stall, lock the door behind you and wait. Do not come out until a teacher or some authority comes to get you. Do you understand?"

Soft sobs and a hiccup came from the direction of the girls. They may have nodded, but she couldn't see.

"Girls, I asked if you understand. Keep quiet and do not leave that stall."

"Y-yes, Miss Kowalski," Molly whispered.

"We'll wait in the stall." Lourdes' voice came out low but uneven.

Their costumes rustled as they shuffled along. They'd have to feel their way to the back. Molly mumbled something, and then in a soft wail, Lourdes's voice carried over the slam of the stall door. "I don't want to die a virgin."

Emily rolled her eyes and raised a hand to rub her forehead. She remembered her makeup and let her hand fall to her side. The whole thing may be a minor electrical problem, but that didn't stop the girls from engaging in high drama. Some bumping and jostling came from the rear stall, probably Molly's umbrella.

"I'm going out to check on things. Stay put." Neither girl responded, but Emily staggered ahead. If it were a true emergency, she had easy access to an alternate exit to get help. First, she'd find out what was going on.

It had gone quiet since the initial series of shrieks and cries. Now, as she opened the door, she glimpsed the pandemonium. Teens gathered in clusters, some crying and hugging, a few boys snickering. Costume accessories lay abandoned on the floor amidst pieces of straw and corn stalks. The faint odor of sulfur wrinkled her nose.

"He has a gun!" someone yelled from the middle of the low-ceilinged room. More screeches followed, then a booming voice she recognized.

"Everyone move carefully and quietly to the inside wall. Take a seat in front of the vending machines." Mr. Brewster, the American history teacher, commanded respect with his voice, his size, and his excellence. The students quieted and silhouettes moved in the direction of the darkened machines.

Emily scanned the room, trying to discern whether any threat existed. Yes, someone had said they'd seen a gun, but in a dimly-lit room filled with high-strung teens in costumes, some bordering on emotional cataclysm on a *good* day, it may not have been a reliable assessment.

Figures in strange hats, carrying odd-shaped objects moved to the side. Toward the center of the room, an empty folding chair sat next to what appeared to be a pile of coats or discarded costume pieces. She took a few steps forward. The heap wore shoes. And it . . . it moved. Could it be Karyn? Had she fallen or been hurt?

Emily hurried toward her, afraid to go any faster than a light jog with all the debris scattered across the floor. As she neared the chair, she could make out the green skirt that matched her own. "Karyn," she called, as her foot slid out from underneath her.

Her hands went out to her sides, ready to brace for the fall against the hard floor. Her other foot snagged on something, twisting behind her.

She came down hard on her tailbone. The side of her head and ear scraped against something sharp. A searing pain shot from her scalp to her ear as she slid forward, and the back of her head slammed into the floor with a thud.

The ceiling tile squares blurred and crossed, and stars twinkled and faded in her peripheral vision. Everything went black.

***

Dan bowed his head and tousled his hair. White powder cascaded to the floor. He'd never get all the drywall dust out. He shook his head a final time and assessed what he'd accomplished so far. A few sheets of drywall measured and cut. One wall framed. Not much.

Robert had offered his help with the basement, and then he'd left for an overnight scout trip with Max.

What time was it? He glanced at the glass block windows. No light penetrated. He guessed the time was somewhere between eight and nine o'clock. In another hour or so, he'd see Emily. He'd bet she looked cute in her Mexican outfit.

Sheets of cut drywall lay piled against the poured concrete wall. He couldn't do any more by himself. The rest would have to wait until he had help. At least that's what he

318

told himself. His cell phone ringtone sounded from upstairs. Dan wiped his hands on a rag and took the stairs two at a time. Maybe it was Emily, done early with the dance. He could shower and meet her in a half hour.

Robert and Elizabeth's phone number displayed on the caller ID. It couldn't be Robert, but why would Elizabeth call him?

"Hey, Dan, it's Elizabeth." A child cried in the background. Girl or boy, he couldn't tell. They all sounded the same. "Have you heard from Emily tonight?" Elizabeth's voice sounded tight, tense. Could be from the background commotion. She'd be on her own with the kids tonight.

"No, I thought it might be her calling, but the dance isn't over until . . ." He glanced at the time on his phone. "Uh, ten o'clock, so, it's probably too soon. What's up?"

"I'm kind of worried. I heard something on the radio." A screech pierced the air but didn't distract her. "You know, we're running a little late here with baths and bedtime tonight, and all the dishes . . . Then they said on the radio—I turned it on while I loaded the dishwasher—"

"What'd they say? What happened?"

The urgency in her voice, the inability to finish a thought put Dan on edge. Something was wrong. "Is Emily okay?"

"There was a shooting at her school. At the dance."

Dan froze, not breathing for a couple of seconds. "Is anyone hurt? What else did they say?" His heart pounded, loud and insistent, piercing him like the nails he'd driven into the walls he'd been framing.

"Nothing. Just that emergency crews are on the scene. The school's locked down."

Dan glanced around the room, looking for what, he didn't know. "Okay. I'm on my way there. Call me if you hear anything, okay? And I'll do the same."

"Will do. And, Dan . . ." Her voice wavered, and more cries emanated from the background. Her last words came out so soft they were barely audible. "Pray hard."

Dan nodded then remembered Elizabeth couldn't see him. "Yeah. I will." He ended the call and tried punching in Emily's number. He scooped his keys and wallet off of the counter and sprinted for his truck.

42

L'appréhension

(Apprehension)

Flashing red and blue emergency lights leant a purplish-brown cast to the night sky. The high school appeared dark save for the large inverted horseshoe-shaped building that housed the gymnasium and, beneath it, the cafeteria. A growing crowd of onlookers gathered on every sidewalk leading away from the complex, wooden blockades separating them from the police and emergency medical personnel.

Dan parked his truck as close as he could, more than a block away, and ran toward the school. A cold breeze sent shivers through his arms and chest. He fumbled with the zipper on the lightweight jacket he found in his truck, the one he'd let Emily wear after the museum visit, knowing it wouldn't keep out the cold for long.

Why so many first responders? Did they anticipate casualties or were they here out of an overabundance of caution?

His feet dragged to a stop as he reached a group of ten or so people gathered at the edge of the sidewalk. The walk ran perpendicular to a short driveway connected to a service entrance, probably where the cafeteria received deliveries.

In front of him, parents and teens milled about in groups of two or three talking rapid-fire into their cell phones or hugging one another. The EMTs stood at the rear of their vehicles without any patients to attend. The police stood alongside open car doors, talking to each other and occasionally ducking into a car.

Dan tapped the shoulder of the woman in front of him. Someone had to know something. She turned immediately, her eyes anticipating a question.

"Is there any news?" He gestured toward the building. "Has anyone come out?"

The woman, round-faced with blonde highlights and glasses, looked to be in her mid-50s. She shook her head then hugged her arms to her chest, squeezing the air out of her stadium jacket. "Nothing new." Her sad eyes and downturned lips evoked sympathy.

"Anything old? I only heard there was a shooting." *Please tell me I'm wrong.*

She nodded. "My daughter is inside. She texted her brother forty minutes ago. Said her phone was almost dead. As usual." She glanced at a lanky, tow-headed kid with glasses who Dan assumed was her son. "She said they heard something like gunfire, and one of the teachers fell and twisted an ankle."

His chest tightened. "Was anyone shot?"

"She wasn't sure, but she didn't think so."

Dan exhaled. His repeated calls to Emily had rolled to voicemail. He feared the worst when the woman said a teacher was hurt. "And nothing from the police?"

"Only that they think the perpetrator is still in the building. That's why it's all locked down." She gestured toward the building. "They sent in a couple of EMTs though, to treat the injuries."

"Thanks." Dan nodded and rubbed his cold hands together.

"Sure." She faced the school and draped an arm around her son.

Seconds later, she swiveled back. "If you don't mind me saying, you look too young to be a parent. Do you have a brother or sister inside?"

He shook his head. "No. My girlfriend's a teacher."

The woman's face brightened. "What does she teach?"

"French. She started at the beginning of the school year."

She laid a hand on his arm. "Is your girlfriend Miss Kowalski?"

Dan smiled. Just hearing her name brought a small measure of comfort. "Yes."

Suddenly "girlfriend" seemed a woefully-inadequate description of Emily. She meant so much more than that childish moniker conveyed. She was his salvation.

He remembered Grandma's admonition to "take Emily off the pedestal." Okay, technically Jesus was his salvation. It sure felt like Emily had saved him from himself though—more than once.

"My daughter and her best friend love her." A genuine smile spread across her face despite the worry lines creasing her forehead. "They go on about how pretty she is and how she makes class fun."

He couldn't dispute the "pretty" remark, and though he hadn't seen her in a classroom of students, he'd seen her with people of all ages and knew instinctively she excelled at what she did. Not because she was technically the most proficient, but because she cared. Deeply.

The woman dipped her head and flashed a coy look. "Molly's friend also said Miss Kowalski had a hot boyfriend." She shrugged. "Saw his picture on the teacher's desk."

He lifted his chin in acknowledgment, but averted his gaze. What could he say to that?

The woman laughed. "I'm sorry. I didn't mean to embarrass you. At their age, scoping out good-looking guys is top priority." She opened her mouth to say something more, then apparently thought better of it and sealed her lips.

The distorted sound of words called through a megaphone caused everyone to whirl around, intent and alert. From where Dan stood, it was impossible to make out what was said.

The EMTs came to attention, making sure their supplies and equipment were at the ready. Two police officers stepped away from their vehicles and moved a couple of the barricades to the side.

Seconds later, a stream of students exited the service entrance. They started out as if assembled in a parade formation, but halfway up the drive, as they spotted their friends and families at various points along the perimeter of the school grounds, they took off in a run.

A girl with long, brown curls dressed all in white sprinted toward them. She clutched a busted umbrella trailing large swaths of plastic behind it.

The woman he'd spoken to bounced lightly on her heels. "Molly!" she called.

The girl ran faster, circled the barrier and launched herself at her mother and brother. Loud sobs quickly muffled in her mother's coat. Her brother slowly extricated himself from the hug and stepped back. His eyes glistened with unshed tears.

Dan's muscles tensed. It was an awfully emotional scene for a situation that he'd lulled himself into thinking wasn't too serious. Or could it just be teen melodrama?

When they'd pulled apart, the girl wiped her makeup with her sleeve, leaving a big, black smudge on her cuff. She glanced up at Dan. Her eyes widened as if she recognized him, but he'd never met any of Emily's students.

The girl's mother caught the look and turned to Dan. "This is Molly."

She placed a hand on each of Molly's shoulders. "Molly, this is Miss Kowalski's boyfriend." Her gaze lifted to Dan. "I'm sorry. I didn't get your name."

"Dan. Dan Malone."

"Dan." She turned again to her daughter. "Did you see Miss Kowalski tonight? Do you know if she's okay?"

Molly's sleeve jerked to her mouth, and a fresh round of tears sprung from her eyes.

Dan wanted to grab the girl and give her a firm shake. What had happened to Emily? "Do you know something? Did . . . did something happen to Em—I mean, Miss Kowalski?"

Molly hiccoughed a couple times. Her mom squeezed her shoulders, and she calmed.

"Lourdes and I—that's my friend—we, uh, Lourdes's costume ripped. Miss Kowalski took us to the restroom to fix it. She pinned it together, and then all the lights went out, and we heard gunshots." Her hands trembled and she clutched them together. "Miss Kowalski told us to hide in the back stall and not come out. So we did."

Dan's heart raced. They hid. What did Emily do? "Did she stay with you?"

She shook her head. "No. She went out to see what was going on."

Emily went out there? What had she been thinking? She had a safe place to hide. Like always, she hadn't thought of herself. She'd thought of others—her students. "Did you see her when you came out of the bathroom?"

She bit her lower lip. "I'm not a hundred percent sure."

Dan's gaze locked on hers, unblinking. "What did you see?"

"It might not have been her, but I thought I saw . . . I think she was on a stretcher."

"She was hurt?" A surge of adrenaline burned through his veins. Emily had been injured. His gaze flicked to the emergency vehicles and then the blocked entrances. He had to get to her. Had to see if she was okay. He pressed his fingers to his temple.

A siren wailed.

Everyone's attention darted to the emergency vehicles. Within seconds, a group of six officers in full riot gear emerged from the service entrance. Sandwiched between the first two, a tall, lean figure encased in a black morph suit loped along, his head drooping. His hands—the height and build suggested a male—were bound behind him.

The students had come out and now the kid he presumed was the perpetrator. Why hadn't Emily been released?

He pressed a hand to Molly's shoulder, getting her attention as well as her mom's. "Thanks. I've gotta go see what I can find out."

Dan squeezed between the onlookers, tapping arms and making excuses as he went. He finally hit empty sidewalk and jogged toward the emergency personnel. He slowed as he reached the point where the sidewalk met the drive. More wooden barricades blocked access to the school.

He spotted an EMT in the grassy area. The man, twenty-something with short dark hair and dark skin, bent and retied his bootlace.

"Hey!" Dan called to him.

The man turned in either direction.

Dan waved.

The man again looked in either direction then approached. He stopped on the opposite side of the barricade. "No one past this point. Sorry, man."

"I need to know what happened to my girlfriend. She's a teacher. It looks like all the kids came out and now this guy." He pointed to where the guy in the morph suit stood next to a patrol car, flanked on either side by officers. "I'm worried sick about her, and one of the girls that came out thought she saw her on a stretcher."

The man's expression didn't change. He stared at Dan, seeming to assess his trustworthiness. "Okay."

He reached for the two-way radio holstered to his hip. He pressed a button, and it clicked to life. "What's her name?"

"Emily Kowalski. She had on some kind of Day of the Dead costume. I-I didn't even see it."

The man nodded and turned his back, speaking into the walkie-talkie.

Dan paced a few steps in either direction and hugged his arms to his chest. The cold air penetrated his thin jacket. White dust still covered his boots.

"Okay. Here's what I got."

Dan stopped pacing and darted toward the barricade. "What?"

"I think they're bringing her out now."

"Is she hurt, was she—?"

"No one was severely injured. Mostly bumps and bruises from panicking in the dark."

Dan nodded. "Where will they bring her out?"

As the man glanced back, the doors opened again. One gurney, then another wheeled out through the doors.

"C'mon." The EMT motioned for Dan to walk around the barrier then led him toward the ambulances, presumably where those gurneys were headed.

As the first one out rolled to a stop, Dan tried to determine whether it held Emily or not. A piece of green fabric hung over the side. Her skirt?

He raced toward the woman. White makeup covered her face except for a red streak along her temple. Blood?

He reached the gurney and leaned forward to get a better look. "Emily?

She opened her eyes. Rich brown eyes. The ones he wanted to stare into for the rest of his life. His heart lurched.

"Dan." She choked on the word, yet relief sounded in her voice. "I feel so stupid."

He jerked forward ready to fall over the gurney in a less-than-manly display of blubbering at the mere sight of her, and *she* felt stupid? "Em, you're okay. I was so afraid . . . why would you feel stupid?"

She smiled, and the drying makeup around her face crinkled. "The only reason I didn't walk out of there like everyone else is because I'm a klutz. I saw someone down, my friend Karyn, I thought. I raced to her in the dark, slipped on something, scraped up my head . . ." She touched her fingertips to the side of her head where she'd been bleeding. ". . . and conked my head on the floor. They say I was out cold for a little bit."

"There's nothing stupid about that." He reached to touch her temple then stopped, afraid he might hurt her. "And isn't your friend Karyn the one who's pregnant?"

She put her finger to her lips. "Shh. That's a secret. But, yeah. I saw her on the ground."

"What happened?"

"She must've been right there where it happened. The explosion or whatever. I don't think there was a gun. She wasn't hurt though, just passed out. Dehydrated. She'd spent practically the whole evening vomiting in the bathroom. She has terrible morning sickness."

"Where is she?" He ran a hand down her arm, the fabric cool to his touch.

"Still inside maybe? They were going to give her some fluids."

A stocky female EMT approached Emily from the opposite side. "We're going to take her to the hospital, have her checked out. Mercy Hospital, if you want to follow us."

"Yeah, I do." He leaned over and kissed Emily's temple. Her familiar fragrance had all but vanished, replaced with a stringent scent. The makeup or something else? "I'll see you there. I love you."

"Love you too."

He stepped back as they lifted her into the ambulance. Once they'd closed the doors he loped toward his truck, texting Elizabeth as he went.

43

À la suite de . . .
(Aftermath)

Dan tugged the end of the green silk ribbon and released the bow at the end of Emily's braid. He pushed his index finger, which suddenly seemed large and cumbersome, through the space between the overlapping sections of hair, loosening the plait. As he separated the strands, red and brown wisps co-mingled, curling and springing back into their twisted formation. He combed his fingers through them, then repeated the process on the other side. Each lock of hair slid through his fingers like strips of satin. The softness, her nearness—and above all her safety—finally calmed his spirit. "There. Better?"

"Yes, much." She dragged her fingers through her hair and sighed. Tiny red lines streaked her eyes, but they still brought life and warmth to the sterile hospital environment. "They were so tight. Not helping with my killer headache."

As he smoothed the last pieces down, he spotted white blotches beneath her chin and on her neck. "Hang on. They didn't quite get all the makeup off."

He stepped into the bathroom and re-emerged with a moistened paper towel. "Lift your chin."

Emily obeyed, and he wiped away the remnants of her makeup. He had been relieved to see it gone. The fear of losing her and then seeing her looking like a painted skeleton disturbed him.

Traces of runny white trailed down her neck. He set the paper towel aside and reached for the top of her blouse. "May I?"

She grinned. "Two buttons. You don't get three unless you wine and dine me with filet mignon first."

He smiled, glad to see she'd retained her sense of humor. The buttons slid easily through their holes, and he spread the collar open. He retrieved the damp paper towel, held it over her collarbone, and froze.

A sterling silver chain hung around her neck. He plucked it between his thumb and forefinger and slid the pads of his fingers along the smooth chain until they reached its apex. He fingered the Miraculous Medal he'd given her.

Tears stung his eyes. Blinking them back, he bent and kissed the medal. "Thank you," he murmured.

Emily's hand rested on the back of his head. Her fingernails traced four parallel trails, creating a tingling sensation along his scalp. "What's the white stuff in your hair?"

Dan sniffed, composed himself, and straightened. "Dry wall. I was working in the basement when Elizabeth called."

She nodded. "Oh."

He'd never seen her look more fragile or beautiful. The fact that she needed him here—at least wanted him here—threw his protective instincts into overdrive. "How about if I find out when I can take you home?"

"Okay. Sooner the better as far as I'm concerned."

"Be right back." He kissed her and pushed open the heavy door then headed down the bright hallway toward the nurses' station. The scent of burnt microwave popcorn intensified as he approached the desk.

A baby-faced man in green scrubs leaned against the counter. He didn't look old enough to shave, let alone have a nursing degree.

"Excuse me. My girlfriend's in Room 417. Emily Kowalski. The doctor discharged her, but we were wondering when someone could swing by with the paperwork and stuff."

"I'll be right down," Baby Face said.

Dan glanced at his name tag. "Thanks, Pete. She's anxious to get home."

"Give me ten minutes. I've got one stop to make first."

"Thanks." Dan started back when his phone vibrated in his pocket. He stopped, pulled it out, and read a message from Elizabeth.

They ID'd the guy in the morph suit. A senior. James Handerhan.

Jim?

No way. No *freakin'* way.

Dan jabbed at the link she'd sent. The local CBS-affiliate's website opened. He tapped the triangle in the center of the screen and watched as the guy in the morph suit was led away from the school by the police. He'd seen that, but from a different angle. The video cut to another scene outside a patrol car. An officer lifted the top of the morph suit over the guy's head, revealing a shock of blond hair.

Dan staggered back a step. Jim. Kristen's brother.

The reporter ended the piece by noting that contrary to what had been reported earlier, there were no weapons involved. Small explosives—firecrackers—were responsible for the disturbance. Jim's motive remained unknown.

Dan breathed deeply, the revelation rocking his equilibrium. He sent Elizabeth a quick reply. *Bringing Em home. Should be there within the hour.*

***

Emily slipped off her shoes, kicked them to the corner, and sat on her bed. "I need a shower." She couldn't roll off her pantyhose with Dan standing there.

"Yeah. Go ahead." He unzipped his thin jacket and tossed it over the back of her chair. His gaze ran up and down her costume. "It turned out great. Your outfit, I mean."

"Thanks." She stood and, with a shaky hand, picked at a loose thread on her blouse. Since he made no move to leave, she shuffled toward the bathroom. Not that she wanted him to *leave* leave, just give her a few minutes. Nothing bad had happened to her, but she couldn't shake the anxiety plaguing her. She had to visit the police station in the morning, and she was completely out of sorts. She didn't want Dan to go.

331

Emily closed the bathroom door and leant against it, breathing deeply. *Get it together, Emily. Just a little scare.*

She pushed off the door and grabbed her toothbrush from the holder and the toothpaste from the vanity drawer.

Dan's feet thudded up the steps.

She could hear everything going on in the kitchen, starting with his footfalls.

"How's she doing?" Elizabeth's voice. From the sound of it, she stood at the far side of the room, at the end of the kitchen counter where she often sipped coffee, wine, or herbal tea.

"Okay, I think." A short pause. "I don't think she should be alone. She seems . . . anxious."

Got that right. She was as edgy as a hippo on a high wire. Teetering on the brink of full-blown meltdown.

"I hate to move the kids when they're asleep. And I can't sleep downstairs with her. Ben still wakes at night and crawls into our bed. Since Robert's gone, she could sleep with me, but Ben kind of thrashes around. Don't know how conducive to rest that is for her. We're used to it, but . . ." Her voice trailed off.

"I was hesitant to suggest it because of the kids, but I could stay. I'd like to, but I understand if—"

"This is an extraordinary circumstance. It's fine, Dan."

Emily spit in the sink, rinsed, and gripped the Corian top, sighing deeply. Her tension eased knowing she wouldn't be alone tonight.

"I'll grab the air mattress and some bedding for you." Lighter footsteps moved down the hall.

Emily turned on the shower, running her finger under the stream of water a few times until it warmed. She shed her clothes, stepped into the stall, and pulled the curtain shut. The hot water ran through her hair, loosening the kinks created by the braids. The soothing warmth eased the tension in her head and neck.

Ten minutes later, she emerged from the bathroom in a long, blue terrycloth robe, a towel wrapped around her hair.

Dan knelt on the floor tightening the air seal on the mattress. "I'm staying. If you want me to, that is."

She smiled and hugged her arms to her chest. "I'd appreciate the company."

He returned the smile and set about stretching sheets and a blanket over his bed.

She grabbed her Pink Panther sleep pants and a black tank top from her dresser and returned to the bathroom to dress and towel dry her hair. By the time she'd come out, Dan's bed was made up. He grabbed Robert's sleep pants and an undershirt Elizabeth had probably given him and headed for the shower, kissing her cheek as he passed.

Emily turned down her covers and climbed into bed, propping herself in a seated position.

In only about five minutes, Dan returned, her brother's clothes hanging loosely on him. He grasped the sleep pants around the waist and tugged them up as he walked.

She smirked.

"What's the smile for?" A grin broke free.

"You in Robert's stuff. He's got a few pounds on you I guess."

Dan sat on the edge of her bed and took her hand in his. "Want to pray with me?"

"Sure." His hand warmed hers, making her feel safe and cared for.

Dan recited a familiar Act of Contrition. He squeezed her hand and continued. "God, thank you for keeping Emily safe and everyone else too. Bless all the police and EMTs and everyone that came to help."

She couldn't help watching him, her heart turning to mush. His stiff posture and stilted speech made her think he wasn't used to praying with anyone. At least not prayers off the top of his head, the personal kind.

He glanced up.

"Oh. My turn?" She closed her eyes. "Thank you, God, for keeping me safe. And Karyn and her unborn baby. And for Dan being here with me." She opened her eyes, glimpsing Dan's soft smile.

"Get some sleep," he murmured and placed a warm, tender kiss on her lips. He probably meant it to reassure and comfort her, which it did, but it also started her heart to pounding. They were alone . . . on her bed . . . not wearing a whole lot.

Dan feathered his fingers through her damp hair, released her, and tucked her under the covers like the kids upstairs.

She didn't protest.

The air mattress squeaked as he rolled onto it.

She closed her eyes and fell asleep.

***

Dan's eyes flicked open and focused on the ceiling tiles suspended above him. A thud, then the patter of footsteps. A squeak, a shriek, some crying, and then silence. He turned onto his side, his shoulder and hip aching where they pressed into the hard floor. With a jerk, he tossed his covers off and examined the air mattress. A flat layer of wrinkled plastic lay between him and the thin carpet. Apparently, his bed had sprung a leak.

Emily's bed creaked as she turned. Some part of her smacked against the headboard.

"Em, you awake?"

"Yeah. You too?"

"My mattress deflated."

She flicked on the bedside lamp and leaned over the side of the bed, eyeing his predicament. A grin lifted one corner of her mouth, a contrast to her red, swollen eyes.

His heart sunk. "You've been crying."

She sniffed and rolled onto her back. "I'm sorry. It's silly."

He pushed the remainder of his covers off and stood. "Don't be sorry." He glanced at her twin bed. Not nearly enough room for both of them, but he'd try. "Scoot."

She blinked at him, then scooted over, allowing him to climb in.

He switched off the lamp and lay on his back on the edge of the mattress. The narrow bed barely held them. He lifted his arm so Emily could snuggle against him.

She burrowed alongside him, resting her head on his chest and her arm across his waist.

He tightened his arm around her shoulder. "Crying's not silly. Not after the night you had."

She shuddered against him.

"You want to talk about it?"

Her hair brushed from side to side against his chest.

A weight heavier than her head settled on his heart. He needed to tell her about Jim. Before she went to the police station.

"I've got to tell you something."

"Hmm?" Her voice was soft, sleepy.

"I saw a video of the kid responsible for last night. The police lifted the hood off his morph suit."

She raised her head, and her eyes, ebony in the near dark, stared into his. "Who is it? Is he a student?"

He propped an elbow underneath him so he could see her better. "Yeah. A senior."

"What's his name?"

"I know him, Em." Did *she* know him? Was he a student of hers? Kristen's mother and brother had moved after Kristen's dad left them. Dan had never given the school district a thought. "It's Kristen's brother."

She bolted upright. "What? Kristen? I don't understand."

"Jim's her younger brother. Always quiet. Never much liked me." And based on their last encounter, it seemed Kristen had fed him some garbage about how Dan had taken advantage of her then dumped her.

335

"I can't think of any Jims. Maybe I don't know him. What's his last name?"

"Handerhan. James Handerhan."

She clapped a hand over her mouth. "Oh, my gosh."

"What?" She knew Jim? Was she his teacher?

"He . . . he goes by Jamie at school. I-I tutored him."

Dan sat upright too. "Jim's the kid you tutored? The one I said had a crush on you?"

She nodded, her eyes wide.

He shook his head and cursed. "Em, this ain't right."

"Do you think he . . . he connected us?"

Dan lay back on the pillow again, and Emily fell against him. He squeezed her tight, remembering the scene when Kristen faked everyone out at the hospital: Jim's eyes raking up and down Emily in the waiting room. "Yeah. He connected us all right."

No way was it coincidence. Jim had seen Dan with Emily—though *she* hadn't gotten a good look at *him*—transferred to her class, set himself up for one-on-one tutoring. Then last night . . .

"Were you and the other teacher—Karyn, right?—you were dressed identically, weren't you?"

"Yeah." Her hand rubbed circles over his thin tee shirt.

"And the explosion, the firecrackers or whatever, she was right there?"

"Uh-huh. You think Jamie mistook . . . you think this was about me?"

"You? Me? Us?" He blew out a breath. "I think I should go to the police station with you in the morning."

They lay in silence for a long time, Dan's brain ticking through the possibilities, remembering all he could about Jim and his character.

Emily's hand drifted south from his chest, over his waist, and rested atop his sleep pants just below the elastic band.

He froze and sucked in a breath.

"Daniel . . ." Just the breathy sound of his name on her lips, her nearness. His heart pounded, and he became hyperconscious of her warm, soft body tangled up with his. For God's sake, why had she slid her hand there?

He pressed his hand over hers and inched it back to his waist.

"I think I understand now." She spoke softly into his shirt—no, her brother's shirt. "About sex and comfort."

He inhaled deeply and exhaled slowly. *Lord, give me the strength to resist. Help me do what's right here.*

"We'll get there, Em." He squeezed her shoulder. "This is gonna have to do for now."

She nodded against his chest.

It didn't feel like enough. She needed reassurance. Love. Protection. To belong to him for real. He released a ragged sigh. God would have to fill in the empty cracks.

She nuzzled against him. "I guess this isn't quite what you had in mind when you said you wanted to sleep with me."

Relieved to hear the humor in her voice, he smiled and pressed a kiss into her hair. "I promise, Em, next time we share a bed, it will be more fun."

"You'd better deliver on that promise." Her wistful voice warmed him.

"Count on it."

44

Pour ceux-ci nous sommes reconnaissants
(For these we are grateful)

The scent of freshly-brewed coffee overpowered the lingering aromas of tomato sauce and oregano. Dishes clattered, adults laughed, kids yelled and scampered through the room. Emily should've been intimidated by her first big family gatherings with Dan's mom and sisters. Instead she felt content, maybe elated.

His mom had hosted Thanksgiving dinner for sixteen without problem the day before. Tonight's dinner had been simpler: giant pans of lasagna, a huge bowl of salad, and several loaves of Italian bread for thirteen hungry mouths.

Emily stood with her back to the counter, sandwiched in the corner between the sink and the refrigerator. The other women in the room moved about with ease, familiarity, and purpose.

Colleen closed the refrigerator and stood next to Emily. "So, are you begging Dan to take you home yet?"

Emily pushed off the counter. "No. Not at all."

"We're not driving you nuts?" Her head tilted toward the living room where three of Dan's teenage nephews wrestled on the living room floor. A thud, a clatter, and a crash sounded, and Maureen and Tish ordered their boys to opposite ends of the couch.

"No, my brother and sister-in-law have five kids. I'm used to the ruckus. I feel so useless though. Is there something I can do to help?"

Colleen glanced around the room. "This'll be cleaned up in five or ten minutes. How about you help dish out the dessert?"

"Yay, a job. I'm on it."

Dan, with a green and white dishtowel draped over his shoulder and the sleeves of his gray Henley shirt pushed up to his elbows, sauntered into the room. He came from his mom's tiny laundry room where he'd been scouring a large pan in the deep sink. He squeezed between Trish and his niece and handed the pan to Colleen. "Spic and span. I don't know where this goes."

Colleen inspected it, running her fingernail in the corner. It must've passed muster because she accepted the pan and walked off to return it to its home.

Dan flashed a smile. "Still doin' okay?"

"Yep," Emily said. "I'm waiting for everyone to finish up so I can plate the dessert."

He whipped the dishtowel off his shoulder and snapped it at her thigh.

"Ouch!"

He grinned, and a devilish spark glimmered in his eyes. "Come here. I'll give you something to do." He grabbed her hand and yanked her from the corner, making excuses as they squeezed out between the crowd at the sink and the kitchen island.

Nudging the door to the utility room open with his shoe, he tugged her inside and closed the door behind them. The only light came from beneath the door and the small, high window at the opposite end of the room. With his hands on her hips, he directed her back against the narrow wall opposite an ironing board, a broom, and a stack of buckets.

"I bring you here thinking I get to spend three uninterrupted days with you, and we never get a friggin' minute alone." He stepped closer with one foot and then the other until he stood flush against her.

Tension coiled in her stomach and warmth spread through her entire body. She wrapped her arms around his neck, crossing them at the wrist. "I thought you brought me here to spend quality time with your family."

"That too. I think we've had enough of them to last until Christmastime, don't you?" He lowered his lips to hers.

She mumbled, "Maybe," as his lips captured hers. After no more than a quick kiss here and there over the last three days, his soft, tender kisses affected her more than usual. One of his hands slid up her back, and she groaned and pulled away. "They're going to wonder where we are."

He moved to press a string of kisses along her ear, neck, and down to the sensitive spot along her collarbone. "Let 'em wonder."

She pressed her hands into his shoulders and wriggled away. "I'm supposed to—

He kissed her again on the lips, dissolving all her thoughts.

" . . . the dessert?"

"What?" he murmured as he nuzzled her ear. "This isn't better than that pretzel Jell-O thing Kerry made?"

"Mmm. You know it is." Her breaths were shallow and desperate longing swelled and crested inside her. *Heck with it. His family. His mother's house. If he doesn't care, why should I?* Because at that moment, there wasn't a thing she cared more about than the handsome man whose strong body pressed against hers. The man she loved with her whole heart. The one she wanted to spend the rest of her life loving. She hoped a marriage proposal was coming soon, because she could only take so much more of this before her resolve cracked.

A rattling knob, a scraping door, and a flood of light caused her to jerk away from Dan.

His hands held tight to her hip and back, keeping her close.

"Daniel Joseph!" Dan's mom's petite frame filled the doorway. She spun on her heel and took a half step out of the door, leaving one hand on the knob. Presumably affording them a moment's privacy to get themselves together. Or apart as the case may be.

Warm light streamed in from the kitchen, revealing Dan's dancing eyes. That and his swollen lips. "Sorry, Mom. We haven't had a moment alone since we got here Wednesday night."

Emily's flushed cheeks now burned as if someone had lit a fire beneath her collar.

His mom glanced back. "Based on what I'm seeing, maybe that's a good thing." Her voice was stern but her growing smile gave her away. She swatted Dan's arm with a limp hand. "I can't even remember what I came in here for. Dessert's ready."

"We'll be right there." Dan, still grinning, closed the door behind her. "Sorry for the interruption." He leaned in for a quick kiss and, reaching behind Emily, pinched her butt.

She smothered a squeal in his shirt.

He winked. "I'll never look at this room the same way again." His hand grazed her back.

"Yeah, well." She smacked away Dan's hand before he pinched her again. "Probably a good thing your mom came in when she did."

Dan's grin widened. "Are you saying I'm getting to you, Miss Kowalski?"

She let out a sharp laugh. "You might say that. You might also say it's high time we came up with a remedy."

"Already on it, sweetheart." He bopped her nose lightly with his index finger. "Let's go have dessert."

***

Dan stretched his legs under the dining room table and swung his arm around Emily's seat. Steaming cups of coffee sat in front of his sisters, his mom, and Emily. The tea he sipped, courtesy of Trish, tasted like boiled weeds.

The teens and kids had taken over the TV in the living room while his brothers-in-law retreated to the basement to watch a football game. Dan stayed with the women because he neither cared for animated Christmas specials featuring characters he didn't know nor college football, but mostly

341

because he cared about Emily. His family had readily welcomed and accepted her, and he was grateful.

She'd been quiet when they arrived Wednesday night, but now she participated in the conversations, laughed at the family jokes, and smirked at the swipes his sisters took at him.

Colleen sat across from them, stirring a heaping spoonful of sugar into her coffee. "So, what ever happened with Kristen's brother and the fracas at the Halloween dance?"

Dan's arm tensed around the seat. Why did she have to bring that up? The two most uncomfortable subjects for Emily: Kristen and that blasted Halloween dance. He'd insisted she call him, no matter the hour, when nightmares troubled her. She'd called him at least a half dozen nights since the dance.

Emily's gaze darted to him, her hand landed on his thigh, and her cheeks paled.

He took her hand in his. "Well, Jim's eighteen, so he's being tried as an adult. Last I heard, he had a string of charges stemming from his stupid stunt."

Colleen sipped her coffee. "So, why did he do it?"

Emily squeezed his hand. Her voice was meek. "He, uh . . . he's not exactly mentally stable. Not according to the psych evaluation they did."

Dan surveyed his family's reactions. Colleen set her spoon on the table and dropped her hands to her lap. They all stared silently, waiting for further explanation.

"No one's sure why. He never liked me to begin with, but he was under the impression I broke things off with Kristen and caused all her financial troubles." He slid his arm from Emily's chair to her shoulder. "He knew the surest way to get me was through Emily, but I think he developed a crush on her."

Emily's chin lowered, her eyes fixed on the tablecloth.

"I don't think he wanted to hurt her. Just scare her." He rubbed her shoulder in a soothing motion.

342

She lifted her head. "Except another teacher and I wore identical costumes, and he got us mixed up. So, the firecrackers went off next to my friend while I was helping a girl with her costume in the bathroom."

Emily deferred to him as his sisters and then his mom asked more questions. Her fingers grew cold, even clasped between his, and she'd subtly shifted closer to him.

"Can we talk about something else?" He and Emily had satisfied his family's curiosity. No reason to ruin the whole evening. "This is still a sore subject for us."

Colleen apologized, and the conversation moved on to the weird caveman diet Kerry adopted.

It grew quiet, and Dan nuzzled Emily's neck, placed a kiss there and whispered, "I love you." He smiled as her cheeks bloomed like the pink poinsettia in the center of the table. He straightened, caught in his mother's gaze.

She didn't miss a thing.

He lifted his arm from Emily's seat, pushed his chair back, and took his mug to the sink, eager to pour the wretched liquid down the drain. A grass-like aroma rose from the green fluid as it swirled down the drain, and he grimaced.

His mom brushed against him, slipping an arm around his waist. "Emily's beautiful."

He turned his gaze to Emily.

She remained at the table, laughing at something Colleen had said. She caught him staring and gave a little wave. The thick hair around her face was pulled back with a clip, making it look fuller and longer. Soft makeup drew attention to her eyes, cheeks, and lips. She wore a red shirt beneath her tan cardigan sweater with blue jeans and boots.

His mom relaxed her arm around him and elbowed him in the side. "I meant on the inside."

"I know."

"I couldn't always say that about the last girl you dated." Hurt and disappointment laced her words. God only knew how many prayers his mother had offered for his sake while he dated Kristen. Especially at the end.

She turned toward him alongside the sink. "I hope you haven't made the same mistakes with Emily that you—"

He laughed. "Nope. Made all new ones with Emily. And amazingly she loves me despite them."

The lines around his mother's eyes still wrinkled with worry. Her concern lay with a specific mistake.

He leaned down and whispered in her ear. "We're not sleeping together."

His mother smiled. "I hoped not. Grandma Malone spoke so highly of her." She patted Dan's arm, and her eyes welled with tears. "I haven't seen you this happy in years."

Dan forced a smile. Why did that innocuous comment feel like the kiss of death? Was it possible to sustain happiness for any length of time? If not happiness, maybe joy? He supposed he'd find out.

45

Superficiel

(Skin deep)

Emily stepped inside and tugged on the door of Dan's tree lot shack. It didn't budge. She pulled again, and again, and it closed, sealing off most of the cold air and swirling snow. The rickety shack hadn't improved since she'd first set foot in it two years ago. Its owner, on the other hand, had. She recalled Dan with his scruffy beard and mustache, closed off and gruff. A veritable Scrooge.

She set the canister of ice melt in the corner and tapped on the lid with the heel of her hand. The scent of hot chocolate drifted from Dan's tiny table. Two steaming mugs sat side by side, miniature marshmallows heaped above the rim.

"I threw some salt out on the walk again. That little bit of snow melted this afternoon and refroze." She loosened the rainbow scarf around her neck and pulled off her gloves.

"Thanks. Come sit with me." Dan scooted back his chair and patted his lap.

Emily sat crossways on his lap, her arm around his shoulder.

Once she'd gotten positioned, he handed her a mug of hot chocolate then took the other for himself.

She blew across the top of the mug and took a tentative sip, getting more marshmallows than cocoa. "Mmm. Thank you."

Since they'd arrived home from their Thanksgiving visit with Dan's family, he'd spent every weeknight and weekend in the little booth. Most days, Emily joined him. When someone picked out a tree, Dan took care of the wrapping while she handled the payment and general Christmas niceties, sometimes offering a sample from a plate of Christmas cookies she'd baked.

Downtime exceeded work time, so they often worked on a jigsaw puzzle or played games on their phones, but mostly they talked. She'd been surprised when Dan informed her he wanted to sell trees again this year, but he'd said he was saving for something special, and she couldn't wheedle any more out of him.

"So, who buys the night before Christmas Eve?" She drank slowly, letting the hot mug warm her hands. "Stressed-out procrastinators, cheapskates, Eastern-Rite Christians?"

"Mixed bag. Bratty little sisters who enlist their stubborn brothers for help?"

Her lips curved in a wry grin. "Zing."

He laughed, hearty and full. A sound she heard little of early in their relationship, but one that she had come to love.

Movement at the edge of the lot caught her eye. A couple walked arm-in-arm along the main aisle, barely looking at the trees. They stopped and the woman pulled the man's head down and kissed him.

"Man, they're worse than us." Dan tapped her behind.

She set her mug down, grabbed her gloves, and smacked him on the head. "Let's go see what they want before they get too amorous."

She stood, and Dan followed her out of the shack, the sound of wood scraping against wood confirmation that he'd closed the door behind them. She waited until Dan caught up, tugging on his gloves and adjusting his hat.

Dan stopped. His eyes widened, and his cheeks paled despite the icy wind beating against them. "Can you get this one, Em?" He nodded toward the couple. "The guy should be able to load it on his vehicle. Give 'em five bucks off or something. Give it to them for free. I don't care."

She tilted her head and wrinkled her brow. "Wait. Why?"

But he'd already hightailed it for the shack. Was he sick? He'd seemed fine a minute ago.

The man tried to get her attention, waving with one arm while the other arm hugged tight to the woman.

Emily glanced at Dan's retreating form and sighed. She'd have to handle this one herself and then find out what was the matter. She stretched her hands out, pulling her gloves tighter over her fingers and headed toward the couple. Thick, wet snowflakes fell from the sky, catching her in the eyes. She brushed them away and strode toward the lovebirds.

They looked like something out of a toothpaste commercial. Snappy scarves, fashionable hats, and expensive boots. Tall, dark, and handsome matched to perfection with petite, blonde, and drop-dead gorgeous. Emily risked being blinded on approach by their sparkling eyes and white teeth reflected off the fallen snow. They engaged in another lip lock.

Emily waited, clapping her gloved hands together a couple of times in an effort to get their attention.

The woman protested as the man pulled away, and she clung to his neck as he faced Emily.

"Can I help you find a tree? We're a little picked over, but I'm sure we can find something here that you'll like." Emily gestured toward the remaining full row of trees, still a good mixture of varieties and heights.

"Already know the one we want," the man said. He walked to the row—female companion still attached—and grabbed a seven-foot Frasier Fir by the trunk. "How much?"

"Normally, that would be a sixty-dollar tree, but I can give it to you for fifty tonight considering you'll have to get it onto your car."

He glanced at the beautiful blonde, whose head bobbed up and down with glee. "It's perfect. Let's get it."

"We'll take it for fifty, but I'm not sure I can manage loading it myself."

"I'll help. It should be no problem for the three of us." She hoped that was true. Dan made it a one-person job, but she'd merely watched. She hadn't had to load and strap one on herself.

She turned and searched the shack for signs of him. *Where the heck is Dan, and why can't he help?*

He peered out the window until he caught her gaze then disappeared behind the door.

"I'd love to help, but Rich won't let me." The woman gazed at her companion with adoring eyes. "I'm four months pregnant. You'd think it was a disability the way he acts. And he's a doctor." She rolled her eyes for effect and feigned irritation.

Emily stifled an eye roll of her own. It was sweet, though. She imagined she'd be giddy if Dan treated her with such kid gloves when she carried their baby. "Well, my boyfriend usually manages by himself, so I'm sure two of us can swing it somehow."

Rich slipped his wallet from a back pocket and unfolded several bills. "Here you go."

Emily took the money and shoved it into her jacket. "Thanks. Let me get some more twine."

She grabbed a bunch of twine where it lay on the ground at the end of the row.

Rich grunted and wobbled a bit as he hoisted the tree, half carrying, half dragging it toward his vehicle. He stopped in front of a late model BMW. No roof rack.

He huffed and brushed the needles from his jacket as Emily struggled to make a loop knot. After fiddling for a few minutes, she came up with something that approximated a knot. She and Rich shoved the tree on top of the car while she silently prayed it wouldn't scratch the roof of the expensive vehicle. His wife or girlfriend giggled with delight.

"Would you open the passenger side door please?" All Emily had to do was tie it down in a couple of places, and they'd be good to go.

Rich popped open the locks and held open the door.

Emily tried to toss the rope over the tree so the opposite end reached the driver's side door. It fell short, so she reined it in and tried again. She glanced over her shoulder at the shack. No movement. Her third effort succeeded. "Okay. If you can feed that back through to me . . ."

Rich rounded the card and jerked open his door, started the car, and opened his window. He shut the door and thrust the rope toward her on the passenger side. "Here," he snapped.

She bit her lip and forced the snark out of her tone. "Um, unless you plan to crawl in through your window, we should tie it on with the door open."

Silence. Then, "Oh." The rope slithered back through the plush interior and out the window. Rich opened the door and fed the rope through again.

Emily grasped it and secured it to her end with another knot. Grabbing another length of rope, Emily worked on another loop knot. She struggled again, her exasperation bringing her near to tears. Where was Dan?

As if in answer, warmth seeped over her back and shoulder. She inhaled the scent of Dan's musky cologne and sighed.

"Need a hand?"

"Yes." She shoved the twine into his hands. "I was ready to cry. I can't get this knot." She glanced at him, trying to gauge what the problem had been and whether everything was okay now.

He kept his head bent, his eyes down, and his back to their customers.

She laid a hand on his arm. "Okay?"

He nodded and held out the knotted rope. "Got it." An awfully gruff retort if everything was A-okay. He slung it over the lower end of the tree in one deft movement, and the end dangled over the rear driver's side door.

Rich fed it through the door without any prompting while the woman sauntered around the car.

Dan secured it. He tightened the front rope for good measure then stepped back from the car and turned toward the lot—

The woman snagged his elbow.

Her eyes grew big as saucers, and her red lips parted, showcasing those pearly whites. "Dan?"

He stilled but didn't turn or respond.

A sense of unease slithered up Emily's spine. "You know each other?" She tried for pleasant and light, but it came out strained and shrill.

The woman smiled seductively, looking confident and cognizant of every one of her charms. In a voice too low for Rich to hear, she said, "Honey, there isn't a part of me Dan Malone wouldn't recognize."

Like a rabbit sensing danger, Emily went still as a statue, but the threat remained. And she had nowhere to run. She was face to face with Kristen.

Dan scowled and cupped his hand around Emily's elbow, exerting gentle pressure, obviously trying to extricate them from this mess.

For some reason Emily couldn't move. Didn't want to budge. Maybe if they finished this now, they could all put it behind them forever.

"You must be Jim's teacher. I know it's a funny-sounding Polish last name. Miss . . . Miss . . ."

Emily tried for strong and confident, but it came out weak and pathetic. "Kowalski. Emily Kowalski."

"Em," Dan's voice rumbled in her ear. "We don't have to do this."

"It's okay, Dan. I don't want to interfere with your little love affair." Kristen glanced at Rich, who stood with one foot in the car, tugging on the twine. "I have my fiancé, Rich. And the baby." She rubbed her gloved hand over her abdomen.

Dan's eyes darted to Kristen, pain and anger festering there.

"He starts his residency in North Carolina next month. So, we're starting a whole new life." She gave a happy little shrug, seemingly unable to contain her glee.

Emily should've followed Dan's lead. The sooner these people were gone, the better. She turned to leave, but Kristen grabbed her upper arm.

"Hey. I'm sorry about what Jim did." For a couple of seconds her tone was deferential, and her words sounded sincere. "For what it's worth, he didn't know the whole story." She glanced at Dan. "And he did like you, Emily. Now maybe he can get the psychiatric help he needs."

Emily nodded, biting her tongue. "Maybe you can get two-for-one with the shrink," didn't seem like the wisest or kindest remark.

Kristen dropped her arm as Rich returned. Oblivious to the tension in the air, he encircled Kristen in his arms and kissed her temple.

"We're good. Thanks for the tree." He directed his words to Emily, then nodded to Dan and folded Kristen under his arm.

His gazed lingered. Did he recognize Dan? Had they met?

Kristen's cheeks pinked, and her eyes danced. "Merry Christmas."

Emily's stomach pitched. She gritted her teeth and smiled. "Same to you." *Salope.* The disparagement seemed less offensive *en Français.*

Dan's voice rumbled behind her, but she couldn't make out what he said.

Rich opened the car door for Kristen, kissed her, then settled her in the front seat before jogging to his side of the car. They sped away, tires skidding on the refrozen slush.

Emily buried her face in her hands. Hot tears stung her eyes.

Dan's arms closed around her. "It's okay, Em." He helped her straighten and turned her toward the warm shack.

"You never told me she was so beautiful." If she were taller, she could model, and despite being pregnant and bundled for the cold, Emily could tell what kind of body hid beneath.

He shrugged and looped his arm around her. "I guess it never came up. I don't see how it's relevant."

Was he serious? All she could think of was Dan kissing Kristen, touching her, the two of them together. And then her own plain, average looks. Her stomach ached.

Dan shoved open the shack door, closed it behind them, and held out the open chair for her until she sat. Then he crouched in front of her, one knee resting on the floor, and slid the gloves from her hands.

He took her hands in his and kissed the backs of them. "Em, she's like a sarcophagus. Lustrous and alluring on the outside, rotten and putrid on the inside. I think she's got a world full of hurt eating her up."

He clasped her hands. "I've forgiven her—and you should too—but I didn't expect this, obviously." His thumbs stroked her hands. "You know the pain she caused me. I don't care what she looks like. And for the record, she's nowhere near as attractive to me as you are."

She wanted to call him a liar, but when she looked in his eyes, she believed him. Crazy as it was, he believed what he said. He found her more appealing.

Her gaze dropped to her lap, and she twisted one of her hands free from his and brushed a tear from her cheek.

"Hey."

She didn't move. All she wanted was to be left alone to— she didn't know what. Feel sorry for herself?

He caressed the soft skin beneath her chin, lifting her face, drawing her eyes open.

"I want *you*. Kind, generous, smart as a whip, great sense of humor . . . Beautiful. The soul-deep kind of beauty you can't fake." He stroked her cheek, and his gaze roamed her face, the love evident in his eyes. "You know that."

She did. Despite every rocky start and restart they'd had, she knew. She loved him too. Any idealized notions of a perfect life together, she'd dismissed long ago. He could be stubborn and moody. She struggled with self-doubt and envy. But by the grace of God, they could make it. She knew they could. They'd both changed and grown.

Dan waited for her acknowledgment. "You do know that, right? You're all I ever want, Em."

She finally sniffed and nodded, then wrapped her arms around his neck, pulling him toward her so that he had to steady himself with a hand to the seat of her chair.

After a few moments, she released him, feeling silly for making such a fuss. So his ex was gorgeous. So what? They both knew enough, suffered enough, to know the things that mattered, that endured. Looks weren't one of them.

Dan checked his watch. "Hey, let's call it a night. And a season. Anyone wants a last minute tree, they can help themselves." He gave her a hand up, unplugged the heater, switched off the light, and led her into the cold again.

He wrapped his arm around Emily, tugging her close. "Besides, Kristen moving hundreds of miles away to find her happily ever after is the second best Christmas present I could get this year."

She cocked a brow at him. "Second best?"

"Yep. And that's all I'm saying."

46

Joyeux Noel

(Merry Christmas)

The door to the nave swung open, and Dan held it as Emily slipped in ahead of him. A musky vanilla scent lingered in her wake. He stepped in behind her, dipped his fingers in the holy water font, and blessed himself.

Dim overhead lights and heavy silence created a solemn atmosphere despite the dozens of people already filling the pews for Midnight Mass. Yellow lights intertwined with garland twinkled beneath the stained-glass windows lining the exterior walls. Pillar candles in large, glass hurricane vases encircled by red poinsettias lit the ledges. A mixture of red, white, and pink poinsettias surrounded the altar and the tabernacle. Beaming with multi-colored lights, evergreen trees of various sizes stood in groups of two and three in every corner of the sanctuary.

At a side altar, straw spilled over the edges of the platform displaying the nativity scene. An angel hung suspended above the scene, directly above the infant Jesus in the manger. Mary and Joseph flanked the Christ-child, their adoring eyes gazing at the newborn King.

Inside the door, Emily waited for Dan to lead them to a pew. She stuffed her gloves in her pockets and unbuttoned her navy pea coat. Running a hand beneath her hair, she freed it from her collar. Her eyes flicked to Dan, appraising him from head to toe.

A jolt of nervousness shot through him as he removed his overcoat, laid it over his arm, and patted the interior pocket of his suit coat. *Still there.*

He chose a row near the front, allowing Emily to genuflect and enter before him. Grabbing her sleeve, he helped her remove her coat, laying it on the pew beside him.

She wore a red sweater that dipped in the front where her Miraculous Medal lay against her chest. Small silver balls dangled from her ears, peeking through her hair, a perfect match to the silver necklace. A long black skirt, slit up to the knee, rounded out her outfit.

Dan lowered the kneeler. He dropped onto the padded surface and bowed his head over his folded hands. A dozen different thoughts skittered across his mind, and he couldn't focus on a single one. He had so much to be grateful for, so many reasons to love and praise God's goodness, and so many desperate pleas for the future, but not one would formulate into a coherent thought. He breathed and tried to concentrate on God's presence. For now, that would have to be enough. After a few minutes, he glanced at Emily.

She caught him staring and brushed her hand across his back, then intertwined her arm with his.

An introduction to "It Came Upon A Midnight Clear" rang from the pipe organ, and they sat back in the pew, lifting the kneeler out of the way. A chorus of children sung, their soprano voices descending from the choir loft like snowflakes on the breeze.

Emily scooted against him, resting a hand on his leg, the other remaining in her lap.

He lifted the hand from her lap, holding it in his, letting his fingers gently caress hers, taking extra time with her bare ring finger.

The music continued for a half hour before the liturgy began. Dan repeatedly reined in his wandering mind throughout the Mass, and in spite of his distraction, the joy of Christmas permeated his heart in a way it never had before.

The deacon gave the final blessing, and Dan wrapped his arm around Emily and leaned against her as she moved her hymnal in his direction. The congregation—an overflow crowd typical for Midnight Mass—joined in singing "Joy to the World." They sang the closing stanza of the third verse, and another wave of nervousness crashed over Dan.

Again he patted his pocket. *Got it.*

People spilled out of either end of their pew. Robert and Elizabeth and their kids said they'd be at this Mass, but Dan hadn't spotted them yet.

"You want to take a look at the nativity scene?" He gathered up their coats and draped them across his arm.

"Sure." She grabbed her small black purse and took the hand Dan offered.

He led them into the aisle, then to the front of the church where families gathered around the nativity. Dan's parents had made a practice of having the kids visit the manger after Christmas Mass, but at this time of night, few young children were present. He stepped closer as people said their prayers before the crèche and moved on.

"You okay?" Emily's brow wrinkled and her eyes narrowed, but it only heightened the chocolate brown of her irises, so prominent tonight. Probably because of the eye makeup she didn't ordinarily wear.

"Um . . . fine, yeah. Why?"

Her fingers wiggled against his. "Cause your ice-cold hand has got mine in a death grip and you're so antsy." She looked him over, her gaze lingering at his foot tapping at a rapid clip.

"I am? Anxious for Santa to come I guess."

She grinned. "Right."

A group of eight or ten people moved off to the other side of the nativity, leaving only one family in front of them. Dan nodded to the fabric-covered bench in front of the first pew. He presumed its purpose was for people accompanying someone in a wheelchair. "Go ahead and sit down."

She gave him a queer look. "Okay." She drew out the syllables, clearly not understanding why she should sit.

The last family moved on, and the church reclaimed some of the peace he'd felt before Mass. The organist continued to play a Christmas postlude as people gathered in the back of the church or straggled towards the doors.

Dan laid their coats on the bench next to Emily and dropped onto one knee in front of her. "Merry Christmas, Em." He lifted her hand and kissed it.

A stunned look flashed on her face, then joy lit up her eyes. She knew now why he'd been so anxious.

"I'm not the kind of man who can write poetry or make a fancy speech. I can't even talk about my feelings much."

Her eyes glistened. He had her rapt attention.

"But I am the kind of man who can love you and protect you and work hard for you, and our family." His voice cracked on the last words, and he cleared his throat.

He slipped his hand into his suit coat pocket and pulled out a black ring box. He opened his mouth to continue, to ask the most important question of his life—

Something jutted into his foot.

A shriek that could shatter glass came from behind him.

Turning around, he found a blonde-headed boy, maybe two or three years old, his eyes squeezed shut, howling on the floor as blood dripped from his lower lip.

A woman—the boy's mom?—rushed over with a tissue in hand. She blotted the boy's lip. "Shh. It's okay, honey."

"Is he all right?" Dan asked, unsure if he should get off his knee or if that would disrupt things more. He leaned back, resting his weight on his foot.

The woman glanced at Emily, then him. "He'll be fine. He tripped on your foot, and he must've bit his lip."

Dan had thought he'd left enough room behind him for people to pass. "I'm sorry—"

"Totally not your fault. He doesn't look where he's going. Happens ten times a day. Doesn't help that he's half asleep." Her gaze darted from Emily to Dan. "I'm sorry he . . ." She held the tissue against the boy's lip. At least his tears and wails had turned to whines and sniffles.

She looked again at Dan, her eyes moving from his face to his bent knee to his hand where he still held the ring box. Her free hand went to her mouth. "Oh. I'm so sorry. Oh, my gosh. Let me get out of your way."

"No, it's okay," Dan said with little conviction. He wanted to reassure the flustered lady, but he didn't know if it was okay or not. Had he screwed things up yet again? His proposal to Kristen had been perfect. Wine, romantic music, roses. He'd delivered it flawlessly. It had merely served to increase the shock when her eyes turned to ice, her expression hardened, and she said "no."

The woman and her son slunk off, and Dan turned his attention to Emily. He pushed forward from his foot so that he kneeled upright again. "I'm sorry I messed this up." He let his head drop into her lap.

She ran her fingers through his hair, leaving a trail of warmth along his scalp. "No. It's fine. Really."

He lifted his head. He'd botched what should've been one of the most special moments in her life, and she didn't mind.

She smiled, tears brimming in her eyes. "It's okay, Dan. Continue, please."

The litany of mistakes she'd forgiven him grew longer. And the whole kid-crying-in-the-middle-of-her-proposal thing didn't seem to faze her.

He saw the babe in the manger in his peripheral vision, then flicked a glance at the wooden crucifix in the Station of the Cross hanging on the wall behind her. "I would lay down my life for you, Emily." One last breath to summon his courage. "Will you marry me?"

"Yes." Not a moment's hesitation. Joy radiated from her eyes, her face, and in her voice. "Yes, I'll marry you."

He sighed, the anxiousness melting away in an instant. The organ music reached a crescendo, and his gaze roamed to the choir loft. "Is that 'The Hallelujah Chorus'?"

Emily inclined her ear in the direction of the pipe organ and giggled. "Yep. Who says God doesn't have a sense of humor?"

With a snap, he flipped open the ring box and carefully pinched the ring encased in a velvety grip. Holding it out to her, he waited for a reaction.

She looked from the ring to him and back to the ring again. "Is that what I think it is?"

Nodding, he reached for her left hand and slid the ring down her finger. He withdrew his hand, and his heart filled to capacity with love and satisfaction.

Her eyes lit in recognition. "It's Grandma's, isn't it?" The large blue sapphire in the antique setting caught the light as she tilted her hand, admiring the ring.

"It was Grandma's. She gave it to me. And I'm giving it to you. Like she always wanted."

A tear trailed from one eye, then the other, and she wiped them away. "I can't tell you what this means to me, Dan. It feels like she's right here with us."

"She is, Em. And she gave our relationship her blessing a long time ago. I wish she were still here to see us marry."

"Me too." She wiped the back of her hand across her eyes then leaned forward, pulling him up onto the bench beside her, hugging him tightly.

He buried his face in her hair, breathing deeply of perfume, her shampoo, everything that was Emily.

When she loosened her hold and separated from him, he lifted a hand to her cheek, rubbing it gently with his thumb. "Seal it with a kiss?"

She leaned forward, her eyes shuttered close, and she pressed her lips to his. The only lips he hoped to kiss for the rest of his days.

47

Merci

(Thank you)

Dan scooped their coats from the bench and stepped aside to let Emily precede him up the aisle and toward her family. Before she could get a foot in the aisle, an elderly couple crowded in from the side. The silver-haired man hobbled with his cane, supporting the elbow of the white-haired woman hunched over and clutching the rail in front of the pew for all she was worth. He and Emily would have to give them some space.

The well-worn, beige, cardigan sweater with tiny, golden baby feet pinned to the shoulder caught his eye. *Wait, is that . . . ?* Dan started toward the hunched-over woman and spoke loudly. "Mrs. McIntyre, how are you?" He hadn't seen Grandma's friend Alice in months.

She stopped shuffling and glanced up with a peaceful expression. "Daniel, I thought that was you. I hoped you'd be here. You brought your grandmother to Midnight Mass faithfully for so many years." Her eyes clouded. "I miss dear Mary Eileen."

Dan's chest ached. He missed her too. So much. Especially now, when he had such happy news to share with her. "Mrs. McIntyre, this is my . . ." He cast a quick glance at Emily.

She grinned and squeezed his hand.

"This is my fiancée, Emily."

Alice's entire face lit up, her eyes alert and wide. It shaved off at least a dozen years. "Did you say your fiancée?"

"Yes, ma'am." He'd never heard his voice so chipper in the wee hours of the morning.

"Well, I'll be darned. Congratulations."

"Thank you." Acknowledging it out loud was surreal. Emily had accepted. He was getting married.

"I knew God wanted me at this late Mass for a reason. I was so busy this afternoon, baking macaroons, you see." She made a cookie shape with her hand then returned it to the pew for support. "I use maraschino cherries."

Emily giggled, her eyes on Alice but her mind apparently elsewhere. He'd never seen her so radiant. He couldn't wait to share the news with Robert and Elizabeth. She said *yes!*

"Ankles and knees aren't what they used to be, " Alice continued. Was she on the same subject? What happened to the cookies? "So, I told Henry . . ."

Henry had been gazing at his shoes, but glanced up at his name, a blank stare on his face.

"Isn't that right, dear?" She nudged Henry in the side.

"Hmm? Yep, that sounds about right."

Dan stifled a grin. The man had no idea what she was talking about.

"That chair Anne gave me—she's my niece Rita's mother-in-law—well, she's passed on, but the chair . . ."

Dan glanced at the pews behind them, the happy news ready to burst from every seam. Robert and Elizabeth had wrangled their children into their coats. At least the kids who remained awake. The two youngest lay slumped over in the pew. Elizabeth, anticipating Emily's answer, had planned a celebration for them. He didn't want to seem rude to Alice, but he and Emily needed to go. By the sound of the bubbly laugh coming from Emily's lips, she was ready too.

"So I woke, and I said to Henry, 'Henry, I hope that handsome, young grandson of Mary Eileen's is at Mass tonight, because I just have to tell him. Maybe he can make sense of what my dear friend said.'"

Dan's rambling thoughts straightened, and his attention snapped to Alice. She'd dreamed of his grandmother? And Grandma had a message? As much as Dan wanted to dream of Grandma, he hadn't. Not once.

"What was your dream about, Mrs. McIntyre?"

"Well, your grandmother didn't speak, mind you. She was dressed in her Sunday best, like I remember her when we were girls. Maybe sixteen or seventeen. She had a beautiful muff that I just—oh, I envied her with that muff. Her lips seemed to move, but I couldn't hear her. So I says to her, "Mary Eileen, I can't hear you.""

Dan's gaze flicked to Robert's family, still waiting on them. He held up a finger then turned to Alice and nodded, urging her to continue.

"She opened up a card, and there on the top it said. 'Mercy's gift is peace.' Now, I haven't the faintest clue what that means."

Dan didn't either.

"Your grandmother had the most beautiful handwriting. All neat and even. Fancy curlicues on her letters. Never once got her hands smacked with a ruler in grammar school." She shook her head. "Anyways, it looked beautiful, but she misspelled 'mercy.' She spelled it M-E-R-C-I."

Dan's heart stilled. He squeezed Emily's hand in his. "Did it say . . . did it say anything else, Mrs. McIntyre?"

"Oh, yes. It read, 'She's in good hands.'"

Dan's throat tightened. "She?" he croaked.

"Yes. Does that make any sense to you?"

"Yes, yes, it does." His throat constricted, and tears stung his eyes. His heart pounded against his ribcage. "Thank you so much, Mrs. McIntyre. You and Mr. McIntyre have a blessed Christmas. Emily and I need to meet up with her family." He gestured behind him.

"Oh, my. I didn't mean to hold you young people up."

"Not at all. Merry Christmas." He touched her shoulder and kissed her cheek.

She smiled, then turned to Henry and nudged him along.

Dan dropped Emily's hand and turned away from her and the few remaining people mingling in front of the nativity scene. He stepped forward, gripped the pew rail, and pinched his eyes shut with his fingers. *Not going to cry.* His gut ached as if he'd had the wind knocked out of him.

Emily ran her hand up and down his back. She leaned forward, her hair spilling over her shoulder and into his line of vision.

"Dan, are you all right?" The corner of her eyes creased with worry. "Was it something about the dream? I've been missing Grandma a lot lately too."

"It's more than missing her, Em. The message in the dream. It was for me." He looked up, meeting her gaze.

She removed her hand from his back and pried his hands from the pew, clasping them to hers. "What is it?"

"It said, 'Merci's gift is peace.'" His throat felt thick, making it hard to swallow. "Em, that's what I named the baby. Merci. I couldn't get a feeling for whether the baby was a boy or a girl, so I went with something that could fit either, I guess. Then I changed the y to an i because, well, because it's French, and you . . ."

She nodded.

"And St. Paul says to be grateful, right? In all things, no matter what. So, I was grateful for the baby's life, even though it was too short. So, *merci* . . . thank you. It fit."

Emily's eyes filled with tears. "Oh, my gosh, Dan. She gave you a message from Grandma. About your unborn baby."

In the months after his breakup with Emily, as he'd grieved the loss of his child, Dan had found solace in one thing—an image he'd conjured of Grandma rocking the baby in her antique chair. A smile lit her face as she held the infant bundled in a white, crocheted blanket.

He bit his lower lip and nodded. "It's a girl, Emily. I entrusted her to Grandma's care. And she's with . . ." He swallowed hard, trying his best to hold himself together. "She's with Grandma."

Emily pulled him into a hug, holding him close.

He squeezed his eyes shut, absorbing her warmth and love.

The organ postlude ended, and a child's whine filled the otherwise quiet church. One of Robert and Elizabeth's kids. How hard had it been for them to get their kids through a long Mass in the middle of the night? He let go of Emily. "Your family's waiting. Let's go tell them the good news."

Dan held her coat open for her, slid the sleeves over her arms, then slipped it over her shoulders. He shrugged into his own coat and followed Emily to her brother and his brood.

Elizabeth sat with Ben curled in her lap open-mouthed and sound asleep. Despite her pale complexion and tired eyes, she gave them a hundred megawatt smile. "Well? Anything you want to share?"

Emily's rosy cheeks ballooned as she beamed and held up her hand, showing off her ring.

"She said yes." Was that his voice? He sounded like a giddy high school kid who had just secured a date for the prom.

Elizabeth fidgeted in her seat, obviously joyous but frustrated she couldn't get up and congratulate them properly.

Robert thrust a hand out. He gave Dan's hand a hearty shake then pulled him into a sort of hug, thudding his back with his free hand. "It's about time, brother."

The older kids crowded around, hugging Dan's legs and throwing their arms around Emily.

"Hey, sooner we get home and go to bed, the sooner Santa can come." Robert ushered the kids into the aisle. "Let's go."

Dan and Emily helped get the kids into their coats and haul them to the minivan.

"Okay, everybody's in." Dan stepped back and allowed the experts to fasten the harnesses and belts. A cold breeze blew, and he closed the top button on his overcoat. "We'll see you at your place."

"Thanks," Elizabeth called from the opposite side where she tightened Tessa's seat belt over her puffy coat. "Champagne and Christmas cookies await. Well, for you anyway."

Emily scrunched her brow. "You're not toasting us?"

Elizabeth fired a glance across the van at Robert and grinned. "Uh, I'll be abstaining . . . for the next seven months."

Emily gasped. "You're—?"

"She's pregnant. Again." Robert's smile belied the put-upon tone.

Dan's gaze lifted to the sky where the clouds drifted apart revealing a bright crescent moon. His heart swelled with joy and peace. He'd never had so many reasons to praise God's goodness and mercy.

The sidewalks glistened with frost and patches of ice remained here and there. Dan took Emily's arm in case she slid in her high-heels.

He glanced at the snowflakes drifting in the lights of the parking lot. "I'm glad you dragged Robert out to get that tree. Can't believe it was two years ago." He kept his eyes on the walk in front of them to be sure they wouldn't slip.

Emily laughed. "Yeah. Me too. Seems like a lifetime ago."

"Sure does." They walked in silence to his truck. As they reached the passenger side door, small, icy snowflakes began to fall. One here, one there, one right on Emily's nose.

Dan brushed the flake away with his thumb then caught a strand of her hair between his thumb and forefinger. A snowflake landed there and quickly melted.

She inched closer to him, backing him against his truck, a simple action wholly unlike her. She ran her hands up his lapels, twisting and toying with them. She leaned into him, seductively pressing him into the door. Biting her lower lip, she peered beneath long, dark lashes.

"Two Truths and a Lie." Her voice was coy, flirty.

She tilted her head and stared. "I've never in my life been as happy as I am right now." Sincerity shone in her eyes.

She caressed his stubbly cheek. "I will be incredibly proud to call you my husband."

His heart thudded in his chest. After Kristen, he'd never expected to hear those words.

Leaning her full body weight against him so that he could feel her, even with their bulky coats, she nuzzled his neck and whispered. "We should take our time with the wedding thing. I mean, what's the hurry?"

One side of his mouth quirked in a grin. He breathed deeply of her warm, spicy fragrance, her essence, wanting more than anything to marry her that moment. "Liar," he murmured in her ear.

She giggled and continued to drive him crazy by kissing his neck and his ear, her breath warming his cold skin.

"How about we pick a date right now?" He reached for the phone in his pocket.

She smirked. "I think it can wait until morning but no longer." She pulled back, slipping her hands over the lapels again. "So, no one's here to record it for the ViewTube. Are you gonna kiss me or not?"

He grinned. "I'll never make that mistake again. From here on out the answer to that question is always yes, got it?"

"I got it, but I still didn't get my kiss." She pouted as if she were a child denied her Christmas candy.

He pressed his cold hands to her cheeks. She squeaked and tried to jerk backwards.

He held tight then brushed her neck and wove his fingers though her hair. Another stray, icy snowflake danced and landed on her cheek. He marveled at its delicate intricacy, its purity, uniqueness, and fleeting beauty. His lips lowered, a hair's breadth from hers. "Merry Christmas, Em."

Acknowledgments

Thank you to my husband, Michael, and my children Michael, Felicity, Miriam, and Jacob for their patience and encouragement.

Thank you to Michelle Buckman for her generosity and editing skill.

Lora Owings, thanks for checking my very rusty French. If any errors remain, it's because I failed to convey the English context properly.

Thanks to all those who read my manuscript and offered suggestions: Olivia Folmar Ard, Ann Frailey, Therese Heckenkamp, Don Mulcare, Susan Peek, Barb Szyszkiewicz, and especially Theresa Linden, who served as critique partner, beta reader, prayer partner, adviser, and cheerleader. It sounds trite, but it's true – I couldn't have done this without your support and encouragement.

About the Author

Carolyn Astfalk resides with her husband and four children in Hershey, Pennsylvania. For ten years, she served as communications director for the Pennsylvania Catholic Conference (PCC), the public affairs agency of Pennsylvania's Catholic bishops. The PCC advocates for religious liberty, pro-life, pro-family, Catholic healthcare, and Catholic education issues before state government.

Carolyn's column on state and national news related to the PCC's interests appeared regularly in Pennsylvania's diocesan newspapers. She also appeared on the statewide television program PCN Live and was a guest on then-Bishop Donald Wuerl's television program, "The Teaching of Christ." In 2005, she resigned from the PCC to be home full-time with her children.

Carolyn is volunteer chairperson of Real Alternatives, Inc., a non-profit, charitable organization that administers alternative-to-abortion funding in Pennsylvania, Indiana, and Michigan. She is a member of the Catholic Writers Guild, Pennwriters, and the Pennsylvania Public Relations Society. Her writing has appeared in *New Covenant* and *Lay Witness* magazines.

Visit Carolyn's blog, My Scribbler's Heart, and sign up for her author newsletter at www.carolynastfalk.com.

Also from Carolyn Astfalk:
Stay With Me
Full Quiver Publishing
2015

Made in the USA
Middletown, DE
28 April 2019